THE
HANDS
OF THE
CHILDREN

JOSE OSBORN

NEWMAN SPRINGS PUBLISHING
320 Broad Street
Red Bank, NJ 07701

First originally published by Newman Springs Publishing 2020

ISBN 978-1-64801-799-5 (Paperback)
ISBN 978-1-64801-800-8 (Digital)

Printed in the United States of America

1

22nd of Opacus; Mortal Year 523

Kenjo

Kenjo felt the crisp morning air against his bruised fingers as he slid on his black leather gloves. He cursed at himself as he winced in pain, the events of last night flashing through his mind, full of regret from not wearing them before he could hear a gentle "I told you so" in the back of his mind.

Pulling up his hood just enough to cover his ears from the cold hands of a gentle breeze, he walked off the porch and across the yard, fresh morning dew still hanging on blades of grass. Passing through his gate and down the worn stone steps that zigzagged their way down from the top of the hill where his house sat to the town of Saussion below. Dark brown and messy hair stuck out from his head, a right eye of gold, a left of red darting from side to side as he traversed the cobblestone streets.

Saussion was relatively quiet in the early morning hours, save for two sets of individuals: The shop owners who began their days by flipping their signs from closed to open before meticulously cleaning off the entrance to their shops. Some even scrubbed the entire front wall just to make it more presentable.

Kenjo thought it was a little much seeing as it would just get dirty again before the day was over. But nonetheless, he was impressed by how dedicated they were to their business.

The other individuals that were up before the sun had risen were two guards on patrol. They took up the very center of the street, and people always gave them plenty of room. Adorned in armor of freshly polished steel, pieces gleaming as they caught the sun's rays as it began to rise above the horizon, on one hip, a broadsword sat sheathed, on one forearm a medium shield. From the looks of it, it seemed able to cover from their neck down to their waists.

The shields bore the crest of Samil: A human head, one part with flesh, the other half the skull—a symbol of everlasting might in life and death—adorned with a golden crown with three points replaced by weapons: A sword, an axe, and a lance. There were two rumors behind that design, one being that those were the weapons wielded by the first three kings of Samil; the second and more recent rumor, however, was that they were the weapons wielded by the three strongest knights of Samil. Kenjo tended to believe the latter as he found plenty of Samil's history skewed as it was.

Had one guard not been two heads shorter than the other, they would have looked like perfect copies with their faces concealed under their helmets. At one point, they looked at Kenjo. He felt their suspecting gaze for a moment before they continued down the street without a word. The rest of the town was still asleep. That was the way of those who called Saussion home. They would not begin their day until the sun was high enough. Even the laborers started their days late.

Much like the business owners, most travelers were up before the town was. And it was that very reason Kenjo was walking the streets now. He had a traveling merchant to meet, selling an item from the north. And with how dead the streets were, Kenjo knew there was no need to rush.

"Why do you always make us go into town at such awful hours?" asked a gentle feminine voice as he walked. "Not only are the streets boring with no one to look at, it's chilly, and the academy isn't even open today."

"You know you could have stayed home next to the fire," he replied. "Or you could walk next to me instead, Vallarya."

"First off, no, I cannot leave you alone in this town for a moment. Secondly, are you crazy? I don't want to be any colder than I already am. I am quite content right here, feeling what you do. Though, would it kill you to pull up your hood some more? Our ears are getting colder."

Kenjo reluctantly pulled his hood up, causing it to cast a shadow over his face. "Better?"

"Yes," she giggled. "Thank you."

"Oh, to answer your question, the only reason we're out so early is because that merchant leaves today remember? He had that silk my mom wanted. And according to her, that northern silk hardly ever makes its way to Saussion."

A shop owner looked at him as he passed by. His eyes alone carried judgment and concern for the boy who appeared to be talking to himself. But he said nothing as his pace increased, trying to make some distance between them.

"And that right there is why I prefer it when you walk by me," he sighed, glancing back over his shoulder. "They already think I'm strange."

She laughed. "Can you blame them?" Her laughter echoing throughout his head. When he finally arrived at the center of town, he instantly spotted the familiar white wagon of the merchant. A white canopy stretched out over the back of the wagon to a stand where he was laying out his goods for display. Many were inlaid with gems, sparkling in the morning sun.

"Hey, do you still have that silk from Yoketsu?" asked Kenjo as he stopped in front of the stand.

A short man looked up at him. Glasses resting on the tip of his nose, a long black beard stretched down to his chest. "Oh, if it isn't the boy from the other day," he said, pushing his glasses closer to his face. "Can never forget those eyes of yours. The Zishagale silk? I sure do, which is surprising seeing as it has caught the eyes of every customer. Yet, you remained the only one who had any desire to actually buy it."

"Twenty gold, right?" asked Kenjo as he pulled a small brown bag from the folds in his cloak.

"Lemme just count it before you," said the merchant, taking the bag. He pulled the knotted string, holding it closed, and emptied its contents on the stand. Satisfied with the twenty pieces of gold, he bagged them back up before climbing into the back of his wagon, returning seconds later with a large spool of shiny red thread. "Here we are. All yours."

As the spool sat there, catching the sunlight, the silk began to shimmer. Then the entire spool started to change colors from red to blue to green to yellow to white to purple to black, and then back to red. Kenjo picked it up in one hand and nearly dropped it back to the table. It was far heavier than he expected it to be.

"Careful now," said the merchant, watching as he took the spool in both hands. "That's the same type of silk they use for their lighter armors up there. A spool like that has some weight to it."

"I see that now," said Kenjo, turning to leave. He wanted to make it back home before his parents woke. "Thanks again."

"*Oh!* Wait, boy," the merchant called after him stopping him in his tracks. "Would you happen to know where other tailors are in the south here? I traveled down from the capital. Everything else sells but my thread."

"Tell him to try Lanercost to the east," said Vallarya. "I know there is a lot of them there due to the cotton fields nearby. Of course, I am sure he could find someone even further south, but I don't think he's prepared for that kind of travel."

"Lanercost," said Kenjo. "It's roughly a week from here by horse."

"Thank you, thank you. I hope that silk serves you well."

Kenjo nodded and headed back home just as the town was starting to fill with life. Lumberjacks were headed toward the mill. Fishers walked down the street, pole and tackle in hand, destined for the large lake on the western side of town. It's bounty of fish eagerly awaited them. As he continued, the smell of baking bread filled the air. The chefs at the tavern were preparing for the day's meals.

Walking back up the stone stairs to the top of the hill, he unlatched the gate and walked inside. His father was sitting on the porch, rocking in his chair, sipping a cup of coffee. Brown eyes followed each step he took as if awaiting him to do something.

"You got the thread, I see," he muttered, taking another sip. "Is that your attempt at making amends for what you did last night?"

Kenjo's foot hovered above the porch as his words reached him. Thinking carefully about what to say, he replied, "Don't know what you are talking about. Only got this because Mom wanted it. And it saved you from getting it for her."

"Mm-hmm." He took another sip. "And where is Vallarya?"

"Right here, sir," she said, her voice no longer locked in Kenjo's mind.

Black particles quickly drifted out of Kenjo, coming together next to him. They were rearranged by unseen hands, first into a humanlike body before her fair skin and clothing manifested. Her long black hair reached down to her waist, ending in curled white tips. Her eyes were the same as Kenjo's, a right of gold, a left of red. She grasped her arms and shivered as a gust came through.

"What were you two doing last night?" asked his father, his eyes focused entirely on her.

"Whatever do you mean? We were here, studying late into the night. There is a big exam coming up, and it includes far more than we initially thought. I do apologize for both of us if we were too loud."

He began to sip his coffee loudly. "Mm-hmm." He pulled the cup away, swished the brown liquid around in his cup, and looked back to Kenjo. "Kenjo, meet me in the backyard after you give your mother the silk."

Kenjo's heart sank to his stomach. Vallarya looked to him with worry. He only shook his head at her before proceeding in the house. She followed close behind. His father returned to drinking his coffee, eyes focused past the front gate to the tops of the town buildings below.

The front door opened to a large living room. In the center sat two brown leather couches flanking an oak table. On the left side of the room burned a small fire in the fireplace, muffled pops filling the quiet room. On the right side, a staircase led to the second floor where the bedrooms were. Kenjo walked through the living room to the kitchen. His mother was humming away behind a marble counter as she watered various plants scattered about.

She looked at them with a motherly smile, her humming coming to a stop as Kenjo placed the spool in an empty spot on the counter. The sunlight came through the window and hit the shiny red silk, causing it to start alternating colors again.

"Oh, Kenjo, Vallarya, thank you!" she said, putting down her watering can and getting closer to examine the silk. She grabbed one end and pulled a strand out just enough for her to thumb it. "Genuine aurora silk of the Zishagale! I never thought I would get the chance to work with it again. How much do I owe you two?"

Kenjo didn't reply, instead walking away and out the back door at the end of the kitchen. His head hung low, eyes fixed on his feet. His mother's eyes followed him until he disappeared behind the door.

"Don't worry about it, Lady Alexander," said Vallarya. Pulling a book from the bookshelf below the kitchen counter, she lay down on one of the couches and began to study its contents. "He's...well, we are in trouble."

"Vallarya, please call me McKenzie. We've known each other for too long for you to keep addressing me like that." She let out a long sigh before crossing her arms in front of her. "How many times is that now?"

"Twenty something, I think," she replied, her mind focused on the book in her hands. "But last night was a pretty big one. Edwards is dealt with. Got him in chains and already on the way to the capital."

"Ah, so that's where you two were."

Vallarya shot up instantly at the sound of his father's voice. The book fell from her hands and hit the wooden floor, her heart nearly escaping from her chest. "Nope."

His face was flushed with anger. Massaging his brow between his thumb and index finger, he looked to the ground, then back to her. "When will you stop lying for him?"

"Honestly, I don't know... When did you two stop lying for each other?"

"You got a sharp tongue," he replied, heading for the back door. He sat his cup down on the counter and grabbed the knob.

"Be easy on him, Ryan," said McKenzie walking up to him.

"If what she said is true, then they may have caught some unwanted attention. He needs to learn." Ryan glanced back at Vallarya. "They both do."

The door slammed loudly behind him as he stepped out into the cool morning. McKenzie grabbed the silk and stood over the couch behind Vallarya. "Is Kenjo's and your armor still upstairs?"

"Yes, ma'am."

"Good. Well, while I am working with this, do you mind making breakfast? After all, with your late-night heroics, I doubt you actually need to study."

Vallarya opened her mouth to reply, but no words came out as McKenzie was already halfway up the stairs. Closing the book, she threw it on the table, got up, and headed into the kitchen. She could tell it was going to be a very long day.

Kenjo and Ryan stood in the backyard, their arms up, hands in fists, both waiting for the other's strike. Weight had shifted to the balls of their feet, swaying from left to right, ready to push off. Kenjo struck first, a slight jab. Ryan swayed out of reach and jabbed back. Kenjo pulled his arm back quickly to close the opening.

Kenjo swung again. Ryan ducked low and connected his fist to his exposed side. Blow after blow followed until Kenjo finally got out of his reach. Ryan didn't let him go for long, closing the gap in seconds. Kenjo raised his arms to block, plates of black stained glass formed along his forearms, nullifying the impact. Ryan was caught in surprise, allowing Kenjo a chance to strike back.

He feinted right, brought his fist to his distracted father's left jaw. As he staggered back, he leapt after him. Ryan dodged the first few, falling for another feint. He left the other side of his face open. Kenjo struck. Black stained glass met crimson as plates manifested along Ryan's jaw. A small chuckle came from both as smiles took over their faces and their fight continued, plates manifesting over different parts of their body to prevent themselves from being struck.

This had been the daily ritual since Kenjo was little. Though, back then, it involved a lot more training; nowadays, with him being older, his father preferred to just spar with him to keep them both from getting rusty. Ever since he joined the academy, they had sparred less, but that had not stopped Ryan from turning this spar into a lesson. In mere seconds, the fight became one-sided, and he beat Kenjo down to the ground.

Kenjo lay there, looking at up the sky, breathing heavily. Just that alone was enough to cause him pain. And it felt like the left side of his face was beginning to swell. Ryan stood over him. The plates around his arms vanished. Kenjo smiled at the sight, Ryan's face was swollen too. It was a victory to him.

"Hey, you two!" yelled Vallarya.

Kenjo raised his head just enough, wincing in pain all the while to look at her. She was standing on the back porch, waving her upper arms frantically in the air. From her elbow down was gone, a black mist forming a ring around the stub. Kenjo looked down and noticed he still had the black plates on his arms.

With a thought, they disappeared, causing Vallarya's forearms to reappear, the black mist fading away. She wiggled her fingers before opening the door.

"Sorry!" yelled Kenjo. Her reply was a slamming door as she went back inside.

Ryan took a seat next to him. "You know why I hate you going out at night like you do, right?"

"Because you think it's wrong?" replied Kenjo, lying back down and gazing at the sky.

"Yes... No... No, it's not wrong," Ryan let out a long sigh. "It's just not safe to do, Kenjo. In another time, yes, but now... Every day you do something like this, it only draws more eyes to you. I am looking out not only for you but—"

"You don't need to," interrupted Kenjo. "You mention it every single time we do this. And I can't help but read something about it at the academy. Something like, 'The Age of Heroes is over, blah,

blah, blah. Hail King Victor, the righteous king of Samil.' That's how anything on the subject ends, by the way."

Ryan's face tightened, biting his tongue as an old memory flashed through his mind. "Aside from being a Kryzen, You and Vallarya wield the Hands of the Children. Do I really need to remind you about why we ended up in Saussion in the first place? But I will say it again and again until you get it out of your head. Times have changed."

"No, you don't." *The oath of the hands,* thought Kenjo as he closed his eyes. "In the absence of the gods whom seldom answer, to whom we pray, do we take the Hands of the Children as our own. To guide the world as they cannot until the dawn of a world without Nothingness."

Ryan laughed. "Yeah, that's pretty close. Maybe one day we can go back to where you two grew up, and you can remember the oath you took. I'm sure there's still a record of it there, whether it be a scrap of paper or one of the tablets. Though, no matter how many times you look at it, it's hard to live by that oath anymore." Silence passed between them before Ryan spoke again. "You have a good *Other.*"

"I do, though I still think she would be better off with another *Anchor.*"

"Probably. But you don't want her to leave, do you?"

Kenjo's face turned red as he understood what his father meant.

"Promise me you won't do this anymore. Promise me you'll just focus on your studies with her and leave this dream behind."

It was Kenjo's turn to laugh. "I did not realize you wanted to teach me how to be a liar and hypocrite at the same time."

Ryan slugged his bruised side before getting up. "That girl's tongue is wearing off on you. Keep her safe like she does you. She has a bright future ahead of her, probably even brighter than yours."

Kenjo did not reply as his father walked away. Minutes passed by, and the sky above was replaced by Vallarya's face. Hands on her thighs, she was bent over, looking at him. She cocked her head to the side, curiously.

"You going to get up?" she asked. "Aren't you used to this by now? How much pain can you really be in?"

"You're not the one who had to fight him," groaned Kenjo as he sat up.

She helped him to his feet and supported him as they walked to the house. "And you're not the one who's arm disappeared, dropping a knife from your hand. Nor did you nearly fall carrying hot plates as your leg was taken from you."

"I said I was sorry."

"Yeah, yeah. After breakfast, we will get your bruises looked at."

*****

A week later, Kenjo and Vallarya walked down the main street of Saussion. With Edwards no longer working there, the nights had been rather peaceful for the past week. No longer were his men mugging people in the alleyways. Nor were they stealing from the merchant's and shops. It should have happened a long time ago, but Edwards connections ran deep, allowing him and his men to bribe the guards, anyone who got locked up in the town jail was almost immediately released. The whole thing left a bad taste in both of their mouths, but right now, they couldn't fight their smiles.

Vallarya held a small cup in her hand filled with a brand-new ice cream. The moment it touched her tongue, a sweet taste lit up every single taste bud. Overwhelming sweet was replaced by a delicious strawberry flavor with a lasting aftertaste. She licked her lips after another spoonful and found them coated in the same sweet taste. Small talk about the academy passed between them. Vallarya had aced her exam. Kenjo had the sixth highest score of two hundred students.

A scream cut through their chatter, stopping them in their tracks and pulling their gaze away from one another. They were looking toward a dark alley; no guards were in sight, and that was all it took to provoke a response. Kenjo's body had already started moving toward it, stopping as Vallarya grabbed his wrist.

"Kenjo, at least pull up your mask if not your hood," she said.

Kenjo did so as she let go, body turning into black particles before merging with him and vanishing from sight. Peeking around the corner, the two of them could barely make out someone on the ground being kicked repeatedly by two men.

Kenjo's feet made no noise as he walked in the darkness of the alley. He grabbed one by the arm and tossed him away. Before the other could react, he punched him twice in the stomach before sweeping his legs out from under him. Leaning down, he offered his hand to the man on the floor. He took it gratefully.

"T-Thank you," he said shakily. A weak cough followed; they could make out the blood that was now on his hand.

From their touch, Kenjo began to read his memories to see exactly what was going on, and both his and Vallarya's hearts began to beat faster and faster as the tapestry flashed before them. All three of them were guards, and this was nothing but a trap just for them.

"I assume you were the same one who got Edwards," said another voice. A dagger of blue light flew across the alley and struck Kenjo's arm. Letting go of the guard's hand, he pulled the dagger free and dropped it, clutching his arm as he lowered himself to the ground.

The owner of the dagger wore a blue trench coat that reached down to his shins. Blonde hair stuck out the top and sides of his head, his face hidden behind a faceless blue mask; how he could see out of it was a mystery to them. The dagger on the ground returned to his hand flew through the air and back to his hand as if pulled by an invisible string. Held between his thumb and index finger he flicked his wrist, three more appeared between his fingers. Bringing them close to his head to illuminate his faceless mask, the light illuminating his faceless mask in a frightening aura.

"I wasn't aware there was any Kryzen in this town," he said. readying to throw all four daggers. "I could have sworn they had all been purged in the south or been conscripted. But with your arm remaining intact. I can tell we slipped up somewhere."

Kenjo didn't reply as he felt the blood slide down his fingers. He looked to the end of the alley. He could step away. He could make it home easily with it being night, but the enemy in front of them was unpredictable.

"No answer? Very well. In the name of his majesty, I will pass judgement with my own hands and execute you myself."

Four more guards had entered the alley on either side. blocking off the clear path to their escape. Kenjo rolled out of the way as the daggers flew by him, embedding themselves into the ground behind him. Plates of stained glass formed along his entire body. In seconds, his appearance changed from that of a civilian to a knight in black armor. Wasting no time, he charged at the man in blue.

"You have the *Hands?*" he asked, surprised, backpedaling to avoid Kenjo's swings. When he reached the four guards, he leapt over them, the unfortunate one in the front being sent to the ground as his fist landed.

The remaining three in front came at them with their swords drawn. Kenjo deflected a blow, grabbed his wrist, and twisted the arm, forcing him to release the blade. As he started to scream, his elbow rose, quickly silencing him. Another sword came from the side. A black mist arm reached out and grabbed the blade holding it in place. The guard struggled to yank it free. Kenjo turned and delivered three punches that sent him unconscious to the ground, his armor dented in each spot he hit.

The remaining guard swung wide. forcing him back. A vertical swing followed. Another arm appeared, catching the blade above his head, and Kenjo took the opportunity. Twenty powerful and quick jabs came out, denting the armor inward, breaking the guard's ribs, and sending him to the ground in agony. Another dagger of light flew as he fell, catching Kenjo in his left arm. The plate was thick enough to catch it before it could pierce the skin underneath. He pulled it free and tossed it back.

It stopped in midair before the man's face. He smirked. Touching the tip, it turned around. Three more blades formed in the air next to it, and they launched at him. Kenjo ducked underneath. As they passed overhead, they flipped around and came back. A black mist leg came out of his side and shoved him out of the way as they returned to their owner.

The man had stepped closer, the shadows of the alley surrounding him on all sides, and Kenjo did not hesitate to take advantage of the situation. He stepped off, vanishing from sight and reappearing, standing in the shadow at his side. Striking him in the back of the head, he stepped to the other side as he turned around. Another strike. Again, he turned only to be hit from the other direction.

The man swung where he predicted Kenjo to be next. Kenjo reappeared. slightly out of the way. Grabbing his outreached arm, he lifted him over his shoulder and slammed him back first into the wall. More guards were stepping into the alley. Weapons drawn, they charged. Kenjo looked out the other way and stepped to the shadows in the distance, not stopping until he made it home.

Kenjo came crashing through the door, Vallarya separating from his body. She scrambled to help him to his feet. A loud crash of breaking glass filled the air, and they looked to see McKenzie looking at them in worry, not even so much as a glance at the broken glass at her feet.

"Ryan!" she yelled, assisting Vallarya with getting Kenjo up.

He came rushing down the stairs at the sound of his wife's voice, face flushed with rage as he noticed his wounded son be helped to the couch.

"What did you two do?"

"We helped someone," said Vallarya. "He was being mugged. From the shadows, it looked like he was being beaten to death in that alley. We couldn't just walk away! But then we read his memories. It turned out he was a guard. It was all staged! Then this man in blue came at us with even more guards. We had no choice but to run."

Ryan glanced out the window. Torches were cresting the hill from the steps. "Get him upstairs, bandage him up, then start packing all the essentials you don't want to leave behind."

"We're leaving?" asked Kenjo as he got up, using Vallarya as a support.

"Thanks to two idiots who can't even go a week without playing hero."

McKenzie urged them up the stairs. Grabbing two large bags, she threw one in each of their rooms as Vallarya started bandaging up Kenjo's arm. Ryan's eyes never left the yard, watching the movement of everyone who came up the hill, the man in blue out in front, approaching the door.

"Of all people to meet," he muttered as they started knocking on the door. Ryan opened it with a large smile on his face.

"Well, hello, Arthur, I see you still wear that ridiculous mask. What are you doing in Saussion?"

"R-Ryan?" he asked, astonished. "Are you telling me the most wanted man in Samil was living here in Saussion this whole time? I expected you to be much farther west, maybe even Zell."

"Nah, that ain't me. I spent my time there and never cared to go back. And with how bad the soldiers are these days, not to mention the fingers like you, it was far easier just to hide here." Ryan laughed, wiping a tear from his eye. He could feel the anger rising behind his mask. "But as much as I would like to catch up, I can see you and your fellows are here on business. How can I help you this evening?"

"Eight of my men and myself were assaulted by an unidentified Kryzen. We thought we saw him running up this hill. Have you seen him?"

"Don't have a clue who you are talking about. I was just trying on some new clothing my wife made for me. You remember McKenzie, don't you?"

"I do... How curious, Ryan. Why would you lie to me, of all people?" A dagger formed in Arthur's hands. Pointing it at Ryan, he awaited his response.

"Oh. Shit, you hit him, didn't you?"

"Before they tossed me into a wall. Yes."

"I bet that felt more embarrassing than anything. Fighting him at night has always been a mistake. I only spar with him during the day. Otherwise, he has too much of an advantage. There's no point in playing it off. Come on inside."

Ryan stepped forward, leaving the door behind him wide open. Arthur nodded, the dagger in his hand disappearing as he passed by. Counting the guards behind him, Ryan took stock of their equipment. Their sword hands palmed the hilts of the blade at their waists.

Each one held a torch aloft in their free hand. *Five isn't too bad,* he thought.

As Arthur stepped into the door frame, Ryan struck. Grunts and screams filled the air, followed by the sound of five heavily armored bodies hitting the grass in one unison thud. Arthur turned around and saw Ryan dusting off his hands with a smile.

Beneath his mask, his face became hot; three blades formed between his fingers. He aimed for his arm; they found their mark in crimson plates. Flicking his wrist, he called them back, but they remained firmly held in place.

Ryan wagged his finger in front of him. "Has it really been that long, Arthur?" He glanced over at the blades trying to wiggle free. "Have you really forgotten about my magic in the past thirty years since we last spoke? What a shame. I could have sworn mine was unique and unforgettable."

He sent the blades flying towards Ryan as he stepped off up until he lost sight of him. Something hit against the back of his leg, and he found himself rushing to the ground. A hand palmed the back of his head and brought it rushing to meet the grass. Blades of light erupted from his back, forcing Ryan off him.

Pushing to his knees, he turned a blade at the ready. A crimson gauntlet flashed into his vision and collided with the right side of his mask, breaking it at the point of impact, revealing a light-blue eye and a pale face. Ryan followed with an uppercut, sending him back to the ground.

"I'm sorry, Arthur," Ryan said, stepping over him, his voice turning solemn as he spoke. "But because it's you, I can't let you walk away from here. I really do wish we could have met some other way, caught up like old times, but we both know those days are long gone."

Arthur struggled to get up. His head would not budge as if it were attached to the ground. His right knee where Ryan had hit him earlier remained firmly stuck to the ground as his breathing became desperate. "You would go as far as killing a Royal Finger, Ryan? For what, a Kryzen who refuses to serve the crown? Don't add more to the list, traitor."

"That Kryzen is my son," responded Ryan, his fist tightening at his side. "The crown was the traitor before I was."

Kneeling, Ryan took Arthur's neck in his hands and finished the fight. Arthur struggled back, only to have his remaining limbs pinned to the ground. Soon, the life faded from his eyes, the blades of light stuck in Ryan's arms fading along with it. Standing up, he headed back inside his home to find the three of them waiting, bags slung over their shoulders. Resting against Kenjo's back was a large great sword with a snow-white blade.

Kenjo looked past him and saw the six bodies lying on the ground. He knew Arthur was dead, but as for the guards, he had no clue. He was tempted to ask his father, but upon his angry eyes falling on him, he figured it was best to leave it alone for now. They left their home behind, heading for the stables that stood at the southern gates of Saussion.

Their pace was brisk, not a single pause nor a backward glance, eyes focused only on the street ahead of them. The clanking of metal boots filled the air as they ducked through an alleyway. At least fifteen more guards were headed to their home. Kenjo and Vallarya's hearts were racing. McKenzie placed a hand on their shoulders and ushered them after Ryan as he crossed another street.

Ryan went inside the stables and woke the owner. Handing him a heavy bag of coins, he obtained three horses. With Kenjo's help, he fit their bags onto the horses, and they rode out into the night, Ryan in front, Kenjo and Vallarya sharing a horse in the middle as McKenzie brought up the rear.

Vallarya wrapped her arms around Kenjo, resting her head against his back. She felt her heartbeat begin to calm. Listening to Kenjo's, she could tell he was still afraid, but it was hard to tell if it was because of the guards or because of his father. As the horses picked up speed, the beating of his heart was drowned out in their galloping hooves. The town they had called home for the past thirteen years turned into a speck in the distance.

2

27th of Opacus; Mortal Year 523

Kenjo

*I*t took them five days to finally arrive at the port city of Manfo situated on the western coast of the continent. From Saussion, they passed through the Plains of Zovon, a vast and unsettled land. It was a journey filled with little rest as they traveled the rolling hills. In the past, the kingdom of Samil had tried to settle the plains, even tried to maintain just a road connecting Manfo and Saussion, but nature always reclaimed it at an uncontrollable speed, making the nobility abandoning the notion and instead allowing the herds of wild animals to continue their dominance of it.

During the first four days, Kenjo and Ryan talked very little, Vallarya and McKenzie being the only voices to break up the otherwise awkward silence that followed their stops to give the horses rest. On the fifth day, Kenjo approached Ryan and apologized. Ryan had only grunted at him and shrugged. His mother assured him he had accepted the apology, but Kenjo was not convinced in the slightest.

"How much did you hear the other night?" asked Ryan as Manfo came into view. He brought his horse to a trot as Kenjo and Vallarya pulled up beside him.

"Enough to have questions," replied Kenjo. "The man in blue called you a traitor. Why was that?"

"I walked away from one life and started a new one," he replied, looking back to McKenzie. She nodded with a smile before going back to watching the plains around them. "Me and your mother, we used to be Royal Fingers, under service of the old king."

"*What?*" they both exclaimed. Not once had Ryan or McKenzie mentioned anything of the sort to them. "Wait, wait, all those stories from your mercenary days?" asked Kenjo.

"From when we were fingers. Every last one."

"Unbelievable," muttered Kenjo under his breath, the surprise and amazement gone from his voice, replaced by a sense of anger at being lied to.

"Who was he. Ryan?" asked Vallarya as Kenjo fell silent.

"An old friend." Ryan shook his head. "No, friend is too much. He was more a pain in my ass than anything. His name is Arthur. As a recruit, he was a good man, a good example for any finger to follow. But when he moved up in the ranks, he became cruel, found a sick satisfaction with doing the dirty work of hunting people." Ryan ran a finger along his chin. "Right there was the one and only time he ever struck me. I was fed up with him one day. He lashed out at me before we were both subdued by those around us. Luckily, he only cut me, and the blade didn't remain. Otherwise, we probably would have never been able to leave that life behind…"

"He can track them?" asked Vallarya, fascinated at the thought.

"Yeah, any blade he makes he can track. That's how he followed you idiots."

The smell of the ocean filled their nostrils. It had been well over a year since they had been this close to the ocean. Stone walls surrounded the sides of Manfo, touching the plains. The magic of the plains faded away the closer you drew to the coast, allowing Manfo to be built in the first place.

Passing through the gates, they all eyed the guards adorned in the same armor as those back in Saussion. None stopped them, however, waving them on through the gates as clanking chains widened them for all three horses to pass side by side. Manfo was bustling with life. The entrance was crowded with people waiting to get into one of the three stables that lined the front. Taking a spot in line, the four of them waited patiently to hand off their horses.

Once they paid the fees, the four of them took their bags and headed into the center of town, music growing louder as they approached. Along the street they walked. A small group of horn blowers played a triumphant melody. Kids danced around as parents clapped and cheered them on. They didn't delay, making their way to the docks themselves to find a boat headed to the other side of the known world. Ryan wanted to leave it all behind him.

A line stretched out of a large building that sat in the center of the entrance to the harbor, large wooden fences protruding from each side to wall it in entirely from the public, making sure anyone who wanted to ride the boat went through that building first. Taking their spot at the back of the line, the four of them remained silent, eyes occasionally looking around for any guards in case one was to notice them.

"It seems word hasn't gotten this far," whispered McKenzie into Ryan's ear. "I think we can ease up a little."

"Stay on your toes," Ryan whispered back, his eyes darting to two guards walking past them. Their eyes met for a fleeting moment before they went on their way. "There's no telling when the word will get around. As long as it hasn't reached the capital yet, we should be fine. But even then—"

"Yeah I know," she cut him off. "Ease up, though, Ryan. Not just for the kids but for your sake too. Relax." McKenzie took his hand in hers. "You know I always wanted to go back to Zell."

"Oh, don't you dare," he groaned.

"Hey, there's a bright side to everything." She smiled.

After about an hour of standing in line, they had finally managed to make it inside the building itself. Kenjo and Vallarya were instructed to take a seat in the few empty chairs that lined the walls of the building. Ryan and McKenzie waited in line for the tellers to purchase tickets. Keeping his head down, Kenjo looked over Vallarya's shoulder as she pulled out a book. It was something to do with politics, causing him to quickly lose interest.

A few minutes later, McKenzie sat down with them, handing each of them their ticket. "We are going to have a slight delay, it seems. All the ships already left for Zell. So we are going to take a boat ride north to Gennegnan."

"That's closer to the capital, isn't it?" asked Vallarya. "Is that wise after what happened?"

"Probably not. But it's the only choice we have. It's better than the alternative of staying here for another week or two before a boat sets sail."

"Why are we going to Zell anyways?" asked Kenjo, the thought of leaving everything behind turning into worry.

"Because Kryzen can be free there," muttered Ryan as he came up to them with another bundle of tickets. "So that should you two continue to disobey, at least you won't have stirred an entire nation to come after you."

Thirty minutes passed by in silence. The four of them listened for the attendant to call for boarding. Making their way through the crowds, they boarded the small white boat that would ferry them north. By the time everyone was on, they were standing shoulder to shoulder along the deck, hands grasping the rails so they could hold their ground as more passengers pushed their way onto the ship.

The captain was a smaller man with a large gut hanging over his waist. His cap came down just over his eyes. It was a wonder how he could see. Twisting the ends of his moustache, he whistled, calling his crew to attention. With a few quick hand signals, he split them up, and they disappeared below deck. Seconds later, the engines began to roar, and the ship took off, ramping up speed the further away it got from the port.

Vallarya put her hand on Kenjo's and squeezed. Closing her eyes, she found herself afraid to look at the sea. "I don't like this."

"It's really pretty, Val," he said. "Look at the fish out there."

She slowly opened one eye to peek. Following his finger, she saw it leading out into the blue sparkling ocean. A school of red fish leapt up out of the water, catching the sunlight before diving back to the waves below. As their shiny scales jumped, they broke the sea again. Both of her eyes were wide open in awe.

"You aren't wrong," said Vallarya with a large smile. "It's beautiful."

After an hour and a half of travel, they arrived at Gennegnan. Departing from the ferry, they found themselves standing at the ticket gate, and they felt fear simultaneously enter their bodies. Soldiers of Samil were marching through the city, boarding ships on the far ends of the docks, bannermen waving flags as their battalions disappeared from sight on to the largest ships that Kenjo and Vallarya had ever seen.

"Oh, this ought to be fun," said Ryan as he led them down the dock

*****

Gennegnan was the second largest port city along the western coast of Samil, its sister port to the north, Camvers, dwarfing it in size and populace. Nonetheless, it was larger than Caprae and Saussion combined. Land stretched out past the harbor, a lighthouse standing tall at the tip, while watchtowers of stone stood tall along the land. On a normal day, it provided solace and peace, but right now, they only made them uneasy. With the towers and the army moving throughout, there was little to no escape should anyone notice the four of them passing through.

Ryan led them toward the far end of the docks at a brisk pace, making it difficult for the others to keep up with him. Once or twice, they became separated by a group of civilians trying to get out of the way of a battalion. Back with him, they continued on past the military ships and to the merchant section of the docks.

The moment they had arrived at the merchant's section, the smell of fish filled their nostrils. Stepping closer, Kenjo and Vallarya found themselves covering their nose in order to make it through the strong odor coming from the open barrels. More were being taken off one of the two ships that was moored. In their mind, it wasn't what they had pictured a merchant to be sailing. There was nothing that really made it stand out, save for a single white line that wrapped around the body of the ship.

As for the other ship, it was exactly what they remembered from the academy. Golden stripes lined the upper half of the body. In between each stripe, flowers of red and blue were painted in full bloom. Two large men lifting a crate came down the ramp, reaching from the ship to the dock, followed by a scrawny boy lifting a box of his own, his arms shaking from its weight.

"I want you to wait right here," said Ryan, pointing at a pile of rope next to one of the posts. "Let me talk to him alone first." No one argued with him, and he walked away.

A short man was going over a checklist as he opened the crate delivered by his men. As Ryan got closer to him, they could make out his unkempt white hair and his untrimmed beard. He seemed to care far less for his appearance than most merchants. Even his uniform, a black suit with gold cuffs, looked as if it hadn't been washed in days. The merchant crest, a red and blue rose wrapped around one another with stems of gold coins, was faded on his back.

When Ryan reached the barrels, the man lifted one hand toward him, motioning for him to stop. His eyes, unmoving from his check-list, watched his men open the box in front of him. With a quick peek, he made sure everything was accounted for and motioned them to take it to the end for delivery. Turning his head, he glanced Ryan over before turning his attention back to his task.

"You don't look like a worker," he said, checking off another barrel.

"And you don't really look like a merchant," said Ryan. "Would it kill you to let your wife take care of your uniform. If I remember correctly, she was one of the most renowned tailors, is she not, Baxter? Even gave McKenzie a run for her money back in the day."

"That voice…" The old man looked back to them, his book and pen almost falling from his hands as he realized who it was. "Ryan? What the hell are you doing here?"

"Lower your voice, my friend," Ryan said, walking forward and placing his hand on his shoulder. "Really, though, keep it quiet. The guards, let alone the soldiers, might get to curious hearing a wanted man's name."

"It's been damn near thirty years, and the time I see you again... you're even more wanted than the last time."

"Did my bounty really change?"

"Let's just say I could probably put five generations of five kids through the academy and still live out the rest of my life without a day of work."

"Well, I am guessing by now you got, what, maybe a year left in ya? That doesn't sound like nearly enough of a bounty."

As Ryan laughed, Baxter pushed his hand away and went back to checking the barrels. "Well, we all can't be lucky enough to not age in our prime. What brings you to Gennegnan? To my ship, of all things?"

"The next time you go west, we need to be on the boat."

Baxter spat, "You sure you want to go west? You may be a wanted man, but that hasn't really changed in the thirty years since you committed treason. You could probably stay here just fine. People already kind of forgot, you know. Only ones that still really pay attention are the mercs and the bounty hunters. Yet, even then it seems they haven't had any luck with you."

"I would argue that the wanted posters closer to the capital beg to differ. And it's not just for my sake," he said, looking back to Kenjo and Vallarya who were watching them exchange words. McKenzie smiled at him and Baxter as she started to walk over to them. "Those kids... They need to go over there. Samil isn't good for them. They've made it these past few years by some miracle. But lately, I am starting to realize that if they want to live to see children of their own, they won't be able to do that here."

"You know, normally, I would agree with you, but do you not know the situation in the west?"

"No, but judging by the looks of it around here, I would wager we're preparing for war... Or is there something else I am missing?"

"Samil is just preparing. War hasn't even been declared yet, and look at all of the soldiers and weaponry around here. I'll tell you what. Go to the tavern at the end of the docks. Let them know you're a friend of mine and have them set you guys up with some rooms. I have to finish looking over this next haul. We can finish catching up over beers. Sound good?"

"It does, but you never said if you would take us or not."

"Let's discuss that after you hear what I have to say."

Ryan nodded and let Baxter go back to work. He led the others back down the docks and up a flight of stairs that led to a street that curved into the main drag. To the left of the stairs was the tavern Baxter had mentioned. On the bottom floor was the bar full of countless round tables. Large wooden barrels lined the back wall where the bar and the two bartenders who worked it stood.

Waitresses walked around, carrying trays of drinks to their designated tables. Smiles never seemed to fade from their faces, and anyone they served always had a smile after. Boots and long skirts that reached below their knees were the uniform of choice, shirts with ruffled sleeves covering their upper bodies, each shirt back bearing the merchant's crest. Approaching the bartenders, Ryan mentioned Baxter's name, and they grabbed two room keys from below the counter without question.

"You'll be on the third floor," said one as he pointed to the stairs to the right of the bar. "Take them up and go right to the top. Your rooms will be the first two on the left."

"Thanks," said Ryan as he took the keys. Tossing one to Kenjo, the four of them walked up the steps and found their rooms. Kenjo and Vallarya went to one while Ryan and McKenzie went to the other. They were quite spacious for a tavern room. A large bed took up the middle of the room, a nightstand and lamp on each side. Placing their bags and his sword in the closet, Kenjo sat down on the bed.

Vallarya took a seat next to him and placed her head on his shoulder. It felt good to finally be sitting in an actual room than out on the road, even if it wasn't going to be permanent. Her hand found her way to his, and she clasped it firmly.

"I know the plan is to go west," said Vallarya. "But after that... what did you want to do? I would like to go to the academy. But what about you?"

"I don't know," replied Kenjo. Turning his head toward her, she looked up to him in response. "I'll probably join you at the academy and continue classes. But since heroes and Kryzen are legal over there, I might look into mercenary work a bit more."

"I don't know... I think it is better without having gold attached to it. But being able to do it without having to worry about catching the guards' attention sounds great. Let's try to get in the academy when we get there."

"Yeah," he said with a smile

"Although hero work does sound a bit more thrilling."

"Well, we've got plenty of time to make up our minds. Let's get some food and then get some sleep before tomorrow. I don't know how comfortable those merchant boats are going to be for us."

Vallarya nodded, and Kenjo led her back downstairs to the dining area. Noticing his parents, Kenjo decided to take a table just in ear's reach but out of direct sight of his father. Baxter sat across from him, taking a large drink from his glass. Ordering food, the two decided to pass the time with fake small talk as they waited for the conversation between them to take off.

McKenzie sat, eating her sandwich quietly, eyes darting back and forth between the two of them. Unsure of who would speak first, she took a drink of water. They remained quiet. Unsure if they would even speak, she looked around and noticed two guards get up from a table near them and walk out.

It was in that moment the silence was shattered, and Baxter became a chatterbox. "So you haven't kept up with the news lately. Was your hiding place for the past thirty years a cave with no connection to the outside world?"

"No," replied Ryan. "However, the town didn't have much to say in regards to this. Nor did many soldiers pass through."

"Mm-hmm... Well, the king—or should I say the sovereign as he has proclaimed himself—and his faithful military are pursuing all-out war on two fronts, both against Ivofir and Zell."

Ryan choked slightly as he finished his beer. "Is there something particular they want?" asked Ryan as he waved the barmaid for another round of beers.

"All for the Blades of the Mother. You know those weapons—"

"Yeah, I know them, Baxter. I was a Finger after all. Are you sure that's what they want? Do you know why?"

"They've come asking," Baxter said, finishing his beer, "around at the merchant's guild. If we ran across any recently, you know how us humble merchant's work. Everything has gold tied to it. Information, goods, and so on. For all my years of work, that has never been an issue. Until this—beat and tortured any merchant they could get their hands on. Blood stains the carpet in the grand hall, and they won't let us change them either." Baxter's hand was shaking as he took up the next glass of beer. "I really don't know why relics would be worth beating them."

"They struck a merchant?" Ryan slammed his fist on the table. "An unspoken law that hasn't been broken in how long? That's worse than my treason!"

"Ryan, calm down," said McKenzie, placing her hand on his. She looked around to make sure no one was listening, and that's when she noticed Kenjo and Vallarya. Forming a half smile, she turned from them and focused on the two at her table.

"Yeah, but when you think of the objects in question"—Baxter let out a sigh—"can you really blame them? The western coast is already lined with warships. They're giving them both a chance to hand them over. But regardless of the answer, I am sure war will follow. Do you remember how many they had before you left?"

"I believe it was twenty… There's only forty in record, isn't there?"

"They're at thirty-three now. Hunting for seven more. Rumored that at least two to three are in Zell. The rest north in Ivofir. I can guarantee you a safe arrival. But after that, I don't know."

"I'm sorry," said Ryan, regret clear on his face. "The nation really went to hell after I left, huh?"

"Nay, even had you been there, I doubt Victor would have done things any differently. Don't hold yourself responsible for what the young king did."

Ryan finished his beer as he placed it back on the table. He looked into it as if the empty cup had the answer he wanted. "You're leaving tomorrow?"

"At dawn."

"Have room for us. We'll be there, Baxter. Maybe during our voyage, we can catch up normally instead of all this kind of talk, eh?"

"Sure, old friend," he said, holding out his hand.

Ryan shook it and stood up to leave with McKenzie following. Bowing to Baxter as she left, the two headed back upstairs. McKenzie positioned herself to keep Kenjo and Vallarya out of Ryan's sight. She knew they would have a bunch of questions for them. But that could be saved for another time. Ryan was in no mood for talking anymore.

Kenjo and Vallarya finished their meals and sat in silence. Their minds were racing with questions, but they did not know where to start. Vallarya looked across the table at him. He was there, physically. Mentally, however, Kenjo was off in another place. She reached his hand out and touched his. He jumped in his seat, his eyes darting to hers.

"It's just me Kenjo," she said sweetly with a smile. "Welcome back to the tavern."

"W-was I gone that long?" he asked, looking around, making sure people he remembered being there were still there.

"Just a minute or two," she laughed. "Let's go get some desserts or something. I have a craving for something sweet."

"Don't you always?" He jumped again as pain filled his shin. "All right, let's go."

"Yay!"

Vallarya led Kenjo out of the tavern and down the streets. Keeping their heads down as much as possible, they avoided asking anyone where a proper sweet shop would be, instead choosing to wander around the port until at last, they stumbled upon one near the gates leading out into the country.

Display cases of various sweets lined the counters of the small shop. Brownies, cakes, and cookies of various sizes filled them to the brim. Both hands on the case with her face pressed against it, Vallarya eyed the cookies like a starving beast. Kenjo placed a hand over his face and looked the other way. When he noticed others in the shop staring at her, he nudged her back to reality.

Moments later, they were walking back down the street to the tavern, Vallarya happily munching on a cookie as big as her head. Kenjo kept looking around to see if any soldiers were paying attention to them. To his relief, none even seemed to bat an eye toward them.

"Ey, yo wan a bi," mumbled Vallarya through a mouthful of cookie.

"What?" asked Kenjo. "Can't understand you through the cookie."

She swallowed what was in her mouth before tearing a piece of it off. "You want a bite?"

"No thanks, I wouldn't want to take any of it from you with how happy you look."

"Here, say ahhhh," she said, jumping in front of him, opening her mouth for him to mimic her.

Reluctantly, his lips parted, and she shoved the cookie in his mouth.

"Now chew. How is it?"

"Ood," replied Kenjo, still chewing. The chocolate inside the cookie was delicious.

"What's that?" asked Vallarya, placing a hand to her ear. "I can't hear you through the cookie."

"It's good. Really good. Can I have another bite?"

"Nope!"

As they continued down the street, Kenjo kept trying to steal another bite. Vallarya remained light on her feet, twirling out the way as he tried, laughing as she took another bite, antagonizing him by waving it in front of him. She felt her back bump into someone.

"Sorry," she said with a bow, "I wasn't paying attention."

"I don't think he was either," said Kenjo as he pointed at the gathering crowd in front of them. "Let's take a look."

The two of them moved to the side of the street toward the shops and weaved their way through the crowd. Once at the front, Vallarya let go of the cookie as her hands rushed to her mouth.

Kenjo's hands began to form fists at his side as he realized what was going on. Standing before them in a circle made by the crowd were four soldiers. In between them, on his knees, sat a man with large white feathery wings sticking out of his back. His face was lined with bruises, one eye entirely shut from swelling. Blood had stained his clothes where he used it to try to wipe what came from his nose and mouth. One of the soldiers placed his hand on the man's chin and tilted it up to look at him before his knee connected to his jaw and sent him to the ground. He held his face as he rolled on the ground, writhing in pain.

"For all of you gathered here, it's a lucky day!" said one of the soldiers walking around, looking at the people gathered. He pointed at the man on the ground. "For today, you get to bear witness a choice given to all of these disgusting Angel-born. It is an honor usually reserved only for those in the capital. Come on, let me hear your cheers."

The crowd began to shout and clap. Boos and slurs could be heard being shouted toward the man as he was helped to his knees by two of the soldiers. A third grabbed him by his hair and yanked his head back, his face now skyward, sunlight beaming down on him from above. Shadows were beginning to be cast, and Kenjo's eyes moved between each one, thinking of what he could do.

He shifted, but before he could leap, he felt a firm hand grasp his wrist. Looking back, his father was looking at him, shaking his head. Kenjo looked toward the man again. Trying to pull his arm free, his father yanked him closer, lowering his head so he could whisper directly into his ear.

"What do you think you're doing?" Ryan asked sternly.

Kenjo, realizing he wouldn't let go, gave up his struggle. "Something that no one else is thinking of doing," he replied.

"Then it seems everyone else here is smarter than you. What do you really think will happen? There's a fraction of an army only a few minutes away. You think you can step into the shadows forever during a day like this? Take Vallarya and go back to your room."

"Why won't you let me save him?"

31

"Oh, I don't know, probably because I don't want you to die. Or your mother or Vallarya. And I quite like my life as well. Do you really not remember what your last stunt caused?"

"So you have chosen labor!" exclaimed the soldier. "Then you will no longer need your wings." He drew his sword as the two soldiers standing at his sides grabbed his wings and pulled them tight. A menacing smile formed on the soldier's face as his comrades played tug of war with the man.

"Dad—" mumbled Kenjo just loud enough for him to hear.

"Kenjo, if you won't go back to the room," he said, placing his hands on his shoulders, "then I want it to be ingrained in your head. You. Can. Not. Save. Everyone."

The soldier swung his blade down where the wing connected to his back, severing it in an instant. The soldier holding his wing raised it above his head to the cheers of the crowd, cheers that drowned out the screaming agony that filled the center of the circle.

He's lying to you, said a voice.

Kenjo looked around, the voice did not belong to his father or Vallarya. It was one of the calmest voices he had ever heard, as if the display before them stirred nothing in them. Not anger, sadness, nor happiness in any capacity; focused only on what Ryan had said to his son. *Although now it is too late, his wings are already clipped. Had your father not stopped you, you could have saved him. You feel it stirring in you, don't you? That burning desire to make the world better. I feel it too. Your father thinks this world is not meant for your kind. But he is wrong. This world needs your kind…*

The voice faded away to the back of Kenjo's mind, replaced by the cheering crowd as the second soldier helped up his other wing in triumph. Vallarya had covered her eyes at that point. With the crowd dispersing, Ryan grabbed their hands and walked the two back to the tavern. Kenjo didn't fight. All that was on his mind was the voice and what he had just seen.

Ryan practically threw them in their room. They stumbled over each other and fell to the floor as he shut the door in frustration. Kenjo hopped to his feet and helped Vallarya to hers, her arms quickly wrapped around his waist, her head pressing against his chest.

"No matter how many times I see it," she said, "I just can't get used to it. It isn't right. No one should be treated that way just because of their race. What is wrong with this country?"

"A lot," replied Kenjo as she pulled away from him and took a seat on the bed. "I'm actually glad we're leaving now." He took a seat next to her. "When we were standing there, did you happen to hear a voice in your head?"

She looked at him like he was crazy. "No, what do you mean?"

"Oh, uh, nothing. I think it was just one of the crowd. Let's just get some rest, ya?"

"Um… Ya, that sounds good."

*****

The next morning, the two of them woke to a rapid knock at the door. Opening the door, Kenjo was greeted by his smiling mother. His father was nowhere in sight. Stepping to the side, he let her come in.

"You two have twenty minutes," she said, pacing through the room. "I know you two were listening to the conversation. You knew we had to be at the ship before dawn."

"Where's Dad?" asked Kenjo as he changed into his leather gear.

"Down at the dock, talking to Baxter."

"Did he mention—"

"Oh yeah, he did," she said cutting him off. "You two are quite something. Quickly now. Vallarya, get out of bed!"

Vallarya jumped and fell off the bed, hitting the ground with a thud. McKenzie grabbed her armor and threw it at her, clapping her hands to rush her along before stepping out of the room with Kenjo, and closing the door behind them to give her privacy.

"When will you start to care about her?" she asked with a sigh.

"What do you mean?" asked Kenjo, beginning to turn red. "I already do care about her."

"Then why do you continue to drag her into these things? I'm not mad like your father is. I just want to know the honest truth, Kenjo. Why are you trying to—"

"Save people?" he cut her off. "Because I was raised on that. You, Dad, the teachers back then. You all wanted me—us—to grow up and be like that. And now all of a sudden, you don't want us to... Where is the sense in that, Mom? Why raise us to save and help people, and then when we do so, either stop or reprimand us?"

McKenzie could only look at him. Her mouth opened only to find itself closing again before words could come out. Again, it opened, and again, nothing came.

"What is it? Mom, please just say it. Give me a reason!"

"If you haven't figured it out by now after living nineteen years," she replied, turning away from him, "then why should I tell you?"

"Why wouldn't you? Why are you and Dad being this way?"

"Because it was wrong of us to raise you two this way! I know, I know, it's late. I know it's hard to change after everything you grew up on, but Kenjo...please just listen to us. Your father most of all. No more heroics. None at all until were settled down in Zell. Please."

She walked away from him, glancing back for only a second. Kenjo caught a glimpse of tears forming in her eye. He placed his back against the wall and waited for Vallarya to come out, thinking only that his father was going to spar with him again for making his mother cry. A few moments later, Vallarya emerged, holding his sword.

"You forgot this," she said, handing it to him. "And your bag... Is everything all right with your mom and you?"

"I... I don't know," he replied, taking the sword. He fastened the scabbard to his back, walking back into the room. He grabbed his bag, and the two of them headed to the docks where his parents awaited them.

Ryan's eyes were still full of anger from yesterday. McKenzie only greeted them with another smile as they climbed the wooden ramp onto the ship deck. Baxter stood at the helm, a beautiful wooden wheel engraved with the flowers of the merchant's guild grasped firmly in his hands. His crewmen hoisted the ramp up as Ryan got on and made his way to Baxter's side.

"Is that everyone?" asked Baxter

"Yeah," replied Ryan. "Sorry for being late."

"Eh, don't worry. I haven't forgotten all those times you were late in the past. It ain't nothing new for young'uns. Ryan, I have to ask something, though."

The crew raised the anchor, and the ship began to drift away. Sails unfurled and caught the wind. With the rising speed, Kenjo found himself clutching his stomach, Vallarya patting his back in an effort to help him.

"What is it, Baxter?" asked Ryan as he watched the harbor town of Gennegnan and the fleet of ships shrink in the distance.

"Those two. They hold the Hands of the Children, don't they?"

Ryan went stiff. "Why do you ask?"

Baxter let out a long sigh. "I wish you would have told me yesterday. I would have had us depart right away. It feels kinda good telling Samil and King Victor to go shove it this way."

Ryan relaxed and laughed at Baxter's remark. "Don't tell me he's gathering them up too."

"No. He's just killing them outright."

"W-what do you mean?" Ryan was shaking now, his eyes darting to Kenjo who was now on the ground, unable to stand, Vallarya holding him and trying to comfort him.

"Oi! Leman, come take the wheel for a bit. Ryan, let's talk in the captain's room for a minute. Even if it looks like they won't be listening to us, don't want to risk it if you are in agreement."

Ryan nodded, and Baxter led him across the deck as Leman began to steer the ship.

Baxter pulled out a long pipe, stuffing it with tobacco. He quickly lit it and took a puff. Leaning back in his chair, he rested his legs up on the desk between them. His quarters were lined with shelves full of various business ledgers all separated by the port they dealt with.

"Is Victor really killing them?" asked Ryan, his hands folded in front of him.

"I wish I could be as out of touch with the world as you, Ryan," said Baxter in between smokes, "and just focus on living. But. yes, Victor made it a decree. In Samil. the only one who will hold onto the Hands of the Children is good ole Daniel, Victor's right hand

and true judge of all of Samil's citizens. Everyone else is just a dead man or woman walking. Even the children."

"What about the villages?"

"Razed."

Ryan slammed the desk with his fists. "Damn it all! What the hell got into that boy's head? First he clips the Angel-born's wings, forces them into slavery or the army, then the conscription and hunting of Kryzen. Now this? How long has this been going on, Baxter?"

"I would say five years now. And the people don't seem to care, just like with the other two. He gives them privileges for ousting someone, for giving up your children and so on. It really did go to shit after your treason."

"Can you really blame me for it, though?"

"Before all this, absolutely," said Baxter with another smoke. He blew a ring into the air between them. "But now, I only wish you had taken more with you when you left. Anyways, I don't know what those two are to you. But Ryan, you, McKenzie, and them are a dying breed. And if this war happens, you can bet that he will cut down every last one in Zell and Ivofir."

Ryan looked at his hands, to Baxter, and then back to his hands as if they or he had an answer, an answer that could fix the country. He wished he could go back in time and change what he did.

"Ryan, if you don't mind me asking," said Baxter as he put up his pipe, "where have you been these past thirty years."

"Well…"

*****

A few hours later, Kenjo was sitting below deck on the bed assigned to him. He had grown accustomed to the sea and was no longer suffering from the motion sickness. Vallarya enjoyed teasing him for the duration of his suffering, though she never left his side and tried to take his mind off of it as much as she could.

During this time, his parents seemed to be avoiding them. Ryan had stayed at Baxter's side, conversing and catching up while McKenzie was busy sewing. Whenever they tried to talk to her, she just ignored them, shifting so that her back was to them when they tried to approach.

A crewmember came by and handed them some food that the chef had whipped up—tender meat and warm white bread to tide them over. The real meal was going to be ready after noon. After he left, they were both shocked to see McKenzie walking to them. She took a seat on Vallarya's bed, the same warm smile she always showed them whenever she wanted to talk.

"I wanted to apologize," she said, her eyes moving between theirs. "I spoke with Ryan. Things are a bit worse than he realized… than we realized. So I wanted to tell you something. Just a little bit of our past that we have never brought up with you two. Kenjo, do you know why your father and I never fully embrace when we fight?"

"Because you're going easy on us?" he replied with a downcast gaze, a slight anger forming in his chest at his words.

"Well… Yeah. But also because we can't."

"What do you mean?" asked Vallarya, curiosity filling her voice while worry formed on her face.

"From a long time ago, when we were RFs"—she let out a weak chuckle—"Thinking back on it, it's kinda sad how we let it happen. Even after all those years, we still had some naiveté. No matter how much experience you have, doubting your enemies for a second can be your undoing. And that brought us to our current predicament. Should we fully embrace, we die. Here, take my hand. Read my memories of that day…"

3

19ᵗʰ of Dryzesius; Mortal Year 482

Ryan

Snow crunched underfoot as Ryan led a group of warriors known at the time as Crimson's Vanguard. Although Ryan and McKenzie were the only ones still living of the original founders, their current companions had been with them for over fifteen years. All around them were snow-covered trees, branches buckling under the weight. If any more snow were to fall, they were certain the larger branches would snap and join the smaller ones on the ground below.

At Ryan's side stood a woman named Lorraine Boudet. A bit on the small side, even in her armor, she barely made it up to Ryan's chest. Although she was small, she was as equally strong as she was nimble. A beautiful ornamented shield was strapped to her right arm, a sword sheathed at her hip. Short brown hair reached to right above her shoulders.

Back when she first joined, Ryan was rather annoyed with her walking beside him. For as long as he could remember, he led the group at the front alone, save for McKenzie who rested inside of him on the battlefield. But she insisted that he needed a shield and that she would fill that role to make it easier on both of them. Eventually, he gave up trying to get her to quit and found it lonely if she were to not be there.

Behind the two of them stood a large man named Kaeso Veranius. He made Ryan feel small, a native of Zell. And although most Zellians had naturally large physiques, even among them, he was bigger than most. Fur armor was draped over his muscles loosely; a large war hammer slung over his shoulder as he walked. The only hair on his head was his long blonde beard, his bald head currently covered by a fur cap due to the snow.

Next to him, another Zellian, but much smaller, was Javier Arboleda. Brown hair stuck out from his hood, a beautiful golden bow in his hand, a matching quiver resting against his back. Every so often, he knelt down in the snow or ran his fingers along the trees, looking for any sign of the foe they were chasing. Javier had been with Ryan and McKenzie the longest; he was one of the best trackers in the world at the time.

"Yo, Ryan, why are we even out here?" asked Kaeso as they continued through the forest. "I thought we wiped all of the Nothingness out of Zell? Not to mention my balls are freezing here, man."

"You know, for that personal problem, you could just wear more instead of trying to show off your muscles," said Ryan over his shoulder. "After all, I don't think they care about those muscles of yours. They don't feel the same fear a normal person might facing you down. And I thought we did too. But some woman believes she saw something out here."

"We really should stop looking into everything crazy people give us. You saw how that woman looked when she told us about it at the Cathedral? That wasn't something to trust."

"Regardless of who said it," said Lorraine, "we can't risk letting the creature live if it is there. Although I hope it's not."

"We're definitely following something with claws," said Javier as he ran his fingers along another tree, outlining four different marks where the creature had dragged its claws across the bark.

The tree branches above them shook, snow falling to the ground beside them, each of them jumping to attention. Javier nocked an arrow, drawing back the bow. The tip caught fire. Loosing it into the tree where the snow fell, something jumped out of the way. Before it could make it to another tree, Javier fired again, hitting his mark. The creature fell from the sky.

It landed on all fours at first glance. It looked like a normal woman, slightly taller than Lorraine. As she moved, however, it became clear how different she was. Her face had a divine beauty to it as if the gods had sculpted her personally, thrown off only by the empty pitch-black eyes that stared at them. Glowing purple hair reached down to the snow. Tendrils of twisted flesh extended from between her shoulders, following the length of her body like a cape.

Another flaming arrow cut across the sky, embedding itself in the creature's left eye. She screeched, attempting to move away. She found herself blocked off by Ryan. Two of the tendrils on her back extended themselves and rushed toward him. He took them in each hand. With a quick tug, he pulled her to him. McKenzie manifested an arm and brought it to her head, sending her rolling into a tree as Ryan let go.

Before she could recover, Kaeso was upon her, swinging his hammer down on her. Tendrils rose to block the attack. The pushed back, throwing Kaeso off balance. She jumped at him, tackling him to the ground. Raising up a hand, purple energy crackled like lightning between her claws. The sound of crunching snow caught her attention. She turned to see an ornamented shield slam into her face, throwing her off of him.

Lorraine offered her hand and helped Kaeso to his feet. A blast of energy came flying toward them. Lorraine jumped in front of him to block the blast. It crashed into her shield. Smoke rose from the point of impact. Looking down, she found some of it burned off.

The woman was upon them again. Lorraine drew her sword as she blocked her attacks with her shield. Throwing the woman off balance with a pivoted swing, Kaeso capitalized on the opening, swinging his hammer into her side. Tendrils shifted in time to defend her from the blow, but she still went flying with the force, her back smashing into a tree.

Trying to get to her feet, another arrow found its mark in her good eye. She let loose a deafening shriek of pain. Another arrow flew into her throat, silencing the noise for good. Head slouched to the side, she lay still, her enemies breathing heavily as they walked toward her.

"What the hell was that?" asked Lorraine. "How was something like this still living out here? We killed them all!"

Ryan walked closer as Kaeso grasped her neck in his hand and lifted her off the ground. The flesh around her forearms was old, warped, and twisted. It was possible to see bone where the flesh had been pulled too tight and tore. Her index finger twitched.

"Kaeso, throw her!" yelled Ryan in panic.

Before he could, tendrils busted out of his back. As he fell backward onto the ground, the tendrils came free. His blood dripped down onto the white forest floor. The woman stood up on top of her defeated opponent, grinding his face beneath her bare heel. Placing a hand on the arrow in her throat, she yanked it free, the wound closing in seconds.

"To think my kind has been hunted down by you lot," she said as she stepped off of Kaeso, tossing the arrow aside. "We grew too soft, I guess. No matter."

A devious smile formed on her lips as she pulled the arrows out of her eyes. Tossing them to the ground as she healed, her gaze locked onto Javier who fired another arrow. It only found the bark of the tree behind her as she ducked under it. Sprinting past Ryan and Lorraine, she was upon Javier in seconds.

He raised his bow to block as she swung down with her claws. It split in half from the force. Tossing it to the side, he took an arrow in each hand, igniting the tips. He sidestepped her next attack. With a quick motion, he plunged them into her side; tendrils whipped around, severing his right arm at his shoulder.

Letting out a scream of pain, Javier fell to the ground. The woman laughed as she raised a hand to finish him. Ryan intervened before she could, forcing her back with a barrage of attacks. McKenzie manifested arms of her own to ward off the tendrils that struck at him. Their fight continued away from Javier, dancing in and out of the trees, claws and fists colliding with bark.

McKenzie grabbed a hold of two of the tendrils as they struck again. Ryan hit each one. McKenzie let go to block another set of attacks. The woman tried to pull the tendrils back, but they refused to budge. Spheres of red light held onto the tendrils near the tips.

"What is this magic?" she asked as Ryan took full control of the fight. Within seconds, each tendril was suspended where it had reached out to attack them. She struggled again to pull them free as Ryan and McKenzie battered her body in a flurry of blows.

"It doesn't matter to someone who's going to die here," replied Ryan coldly. The crimson armor around his arm formed into a blade. He swung. A blast of purple energy surged from her claws, colliding with his chest and taking him off his feet.

Another blast began to charge between her claws as she laughed. Lorraine jumped in front of Ryan and blocked the next attack. A third followed as she blocked it. The energy shattered the shield at the impact point, revealing the forearm behind the hole. Lorraine tossed it at her before she could let loose another blast, running after it before she could recover. Her blade flashed. The woman twisted her body, and the blade pierced her sternum instead of her heart.

Energy crackled between her claws. Lorraine groaned as she plunged them into her stomach. Lorraine grasped her wrist in both hands, trying to pull away. Ryan ran at them. The woman kicked Lorraine off her arm and into him. With a yell, she ripped her tendrils free, purple blood dripping from wounded ends. Breathing heavily, she jumped into the air to come down on Ryan.

Ryan pushed Lorraine to the side in time to catch his enemy's claws. Her middle finger, just within reach, scratched into his breast plate. McKenzie manifested an arm to strike. The woman pinned it to the ground in an instant.

"You will die!" she yelled, struggling against their strength. "You will pay for your sins. For their sins!" Her flesh turned gray as the claw began to dig in more, piercing through the plate. Ryan could feel it against the cloth underneath.

McKenzie separated entirely from Ryan, manifesting at his side, getting to her feet. Before the woman realized what happened, her claw was now grasping the snow where her arm was. McKenzie wrapped her arms around her neck, choking her as she pulled her off of Ryan. The woman scratched at her arms, digging into her flesh and drawing blood. She only winced in pain, trying to push the feeling to the back of her mind. Protecting Ryan was all that mattered.

A sharp pain filled McKenzie's leg, and she screamed. Her grip loosening, the woman seized her chance, pulling the arms free. She turned around to attack. The tendrils had regenerated from where she ripped them. Arching back, they took aim at her chest. Ryan embraced with her again, the tendrils piercing into their crimson armor.

Ryan didn't feel anything, however, just a slight discomfort as the tendrils wiggled in his chest. The armor had been broken. Looking over his shoulder, he found McKenzie suspended in the air, held up only by the tendrils that pierced through her upper body.

"You take their names to what end?" the woman asked, her face full of hatred in disgust as she gazed upon Ryan. "Why do you use the so-called Hands of the Children? To make the world suffer more? To make my kind suffer more? I curse you both. May you never embrace again!"

Energy surged along the tendrils. McKenzie screamed as Ryan buckled under the pain, falling to his knees. The woman placed a hand on his head and tilted it back to look at her.

"You. Are. All. Disgusting. Sinners—"

She was silenced as a crimson blade pierced through her jaw. Her body hit the ground. The tendrils went limp, and McKenzie fell. Ryan pulled himself along the tendrils to his wife, pulling them free of her before pulling them from his chest.

"McKenzie, stay with me!" he said, taking a hand in his, her head in his other.

Her eyes fluttered open for a second before closing again. "Is it over?"

"Yeah," he said with a smile through tears. "Yeah, she's dead."

"Good. Good... I...need...to...re—" Her voice faded away.

*****

McKenzie pulled her hands away from her son's, preventing him from reading anymore. "That's all you get to see."

"What happened after?" both he and Vallarya exclaimed.

McKenzie sighed as she looked back on the painful memory. "Javier was the only survivor of the three who went with us, although he never drew a bow again and became a teacher at the academy for the rest of his years. I rested inside of your father in a coma for almost two months."

"And how do you know you two can't embrace?" asked Vallarya. "From what we saw, there didn't look like any type of curse actually used. You two probably—"

"Pain racks are body the closer we get to fully embracing like you two do. We grew used to the pain from just embracing our limbs. But the closer we get to that state, it feels like a bunch of rope tied through our hearts, each one yanked at the same time until at last it tears. We've been around in the forty odd years since. No one can fix it. That curse is permanent."

"Why did you want us to see this, Mom?" asked Kenjo.

"Why? Because I wanted you to know more about us like I said before you started to read that memory." McKenzie smiled at him, the smile quickly fading as she looked at his eyes. He was seeing through it. "B-because I wanted you to see the real enemy of those who use the Hands of the Children."

"I can't save them all," he muttered under his breath. *She did this because of him,* he thought to himself. *To try and give me another reason to look the other way at the suffering of others.*

"What?" she asked, unable to understand his words.

"Nothing. Is it so wrong of me to want to save others, Mom? Like that Angel-born in the street the other day."

McKenzie twiddled her thumbs as she looked down at her hands. "It shouldn't be. But sadly…this world…well, at least Samil won't let—"

"You two say the same damn thing every time! Dad only punishes us for helping someone in need. Risking our lives comes with the job, but it looks like both of you forgot about it. Honestly, if you're keeping us from helping people, are you two any different from the ones you're trying to keep us from?"

McKenzie was at a loss for words. Kenjo was standing now, awaiting a response, but she couldn't think of one. His words had struck her in a way she wasn't expecting. He returned to the deck without another word. Vallarya silently followed after him. She wanted to comfort McKenzie, but she didn't know how. Instead, she bowed and left, leaving her alone in silence, a faint sob emitting from the room.

Kenjo crossed his arms on the side of the ship. Resting his head on them, he gazed out at the sea. Vallarya found her way to his side and followed his gaze.

"Maybe that was a little harsh," she said, a gust of wind blowing her hair into her face.

"Maybe," he replied. "Maybe it wasn't enough. They keep hiding things from us, Val. On top of punishing us, I just want to know why they raised us this way. The world was going to shit when we were young. Why raise us to feel the way we do and punish us for doing so?"

"I... I don't know," she replied, looking down the side of the ship at the sea directly beneath her. "I want to know as bad as you do. But Kenjo... When he stopped you in the street, I do believe it was the right thing. After all, if we were to die there, think of all those we couldn't save in the future."

Kenjo looked at her. Her eyes were still on the ocean as she fought the wind messing with her hair. Her eyes seemed to shimmer like the sea in the light of the sun. When her head turned to face him, he turned instantly to face the sea again.

"I'm not saying I agree with everything he did up to this point," said Vallarya. "But it wouldn't have been wise of us to do anything. Let's just try and give it a rest for now. Focus on what we're going to do at the academy. I'm sure your parents will tell us something eventually. Do you think creatures like that woman still exist? I really hope the Nothingness is gone, personally."

Kenjo's ears twitched at the sudden change in conversation. "You and I both know it isn't. The elders at the village said it. We were bound together via the oath. If they didn't exist, we never would have had to become wielders of the Hands. They're just hiding out there somewhere."

"You could at least say they don't for my sake," mumbled Vallarya, unsatisfied with his response. "Why can't you be nice?"

"Is lying really nice, though?" he asked with a small chuckle.

She slugged him in the arm before walking off. "I hope you get seasick again!" she yelled over her shoulder before disappearing below deck. One of the passing crewmen laughed as he went by.

Kenjo's face went red. The rest of the journey was going to be long. The next day, he was sick again as choppy water made the voyage rough. Vallarya only laughed at his pain the first day, comforting him on the second. Unanswered questions filled the silence between his parents and them; questions that they hoped would be answered as they approached the shores of the western nation of Zell.

4

2ⁿᵈ of Japhim; Mortal Year 523

Kenjo and Ryan

*T*wo months later, they were finally drawing close to land. Neither Ryan nor McKenzie said another word about their past. Instead, they opted to avoid their two younger traveling companions as much as possible, a silent rift growing between them over the duration of their trip. As they got closer to the port, Ryan noticed Samilian warships lining the coast. Smaller transport ships were anchored at the docks, unloading soldiers and supplies.

"What the hell is this, Baxter?" asked Ryan, running to the helm as the merchant ship prepared to pass in between two of the war ships. "This doesn't seem safe like you said!"

"That's still my plan, Ryan," he said. "Unless you really want me to cause a scene and get their attention."

"Explain yourself right now!"

"I told you they were at war. Victor wants to try and swing the vote in his favor. I have a schedule to keep. Otherwise, I would have taken us further up north where they haven't made landfall. Keep your heads down. Relax. And then I can get you, McKenzie, and those two children safely onto Zell's land. They won't sink us. Just relax."

Ryan took a deep breath to let out his anger. He watched as they came closer to the military ships. Gazing upon the emblem of the imperium that decorated the side of the ships, he remembered the days when he proudly wore it. It was another lifetime ago, long before Kenjo was born; now that emblem only gave him unease and a sense of fear.

The ships themselves were like titans of the sea. They were in development before he and McKenzie had left. Dwarfing the merchant and transport ships, they were built to establish fear in the enemy before their cannons even sounded. Six cannons sat upon the upper deck with ten more lining each side. Ryan could hear the hum of the beasts' inner workings as they passed by, raw mana feeding the quiet engine.

Passing the wall of ships with no hiccups, like Baxter said, they made their way to the leftmost dock where the military presence of Samil was less concentrated. A few fishing boats were returning to the docks, and another merchant ship was already there. Finding an empty spot, the crew threw down the ramp before getting to work.

Baxter was the first to depart the ship with his two assistants. Ryan and McKenzie followed next with Kenjo and Vallarya close behind. To their relief, no guards stopped them as they moved to the tavern that sat overlooking the docks. Taking a seat at the largest table they could find, they ordered food and drink. Baxter sent his assistants out to contact the merchant's branch in the area, all the while keeping their eyes peeled for anyone who seemed to be eyeing them.

The tavern was rather quiet, although it was nearly packed. Most seemed to talk in mumbles or hardly uttered anything at all. The only ones louder than that were the few Samilian soldiers that sat, filling their own gullets. Not one bit of it felt right to any of them; it was like the life had been sucked out of the townsfolk.

"Well," said Baxter, finishing off his meal, "the good news is that the stable here in Adana has plenty of horses for use. If their prices haven't changed since I was last here, they should be fairly cheap and get you wherever you need to go. Do you have that figured out?"

"Gonall," replied Ryan bluntly. "An old friend owes me a favor. Can have a fresh start there. And…just hopefully avoid this fighting altogether."

"From the way it looks here, this hunt for the Blades of the Mother is going to bring out war. The kings of Zell won't stand for them sitting on the coast much longer. And you know the people of Zell prefer conflict over diplomacy any day."

"Just gotta hope," said Ryan, finishing off his food. "They were improving in my mercenary years, trying a bit more to talk than punch the guy in front of them. You think it's safe to stay the night here?"

Baxter laughed as he waved down the maid for another drink. "I recommend you stay on the ship. Even the merchant branch here, I am sure, is rigged by Samil."

"Hey, Dad, do you mind if we go explore the town a bit?" asked Kenjo, finishing off his meal.

"Why would you want to do that?" asked Ryan, turning to his son, the first words they had spoken in months.

"First time in the west. This dock and tavern look just like they did back in Samil. Me and Vallarya wanted to see if the actual town was any different."

Ryan pulled him close to whisper in his ear, "Promise me no heroics if someone is in trouble. You look the other way. Promise."

"I…promise."

"Vallarya, make sure you two are back to the ship by midnight," said Ryan over his son's shoulder.

"Yes, sir," said Vallarya as she and Kenjo stood up to depart the tavern.

He led Vallarya out to the sidewalk. Hanging a left, they began their exploration of Adana. Soldiers were strolling down the streets. Any civilian in their path made sure to stay clear of them, stepping to the side and letting them go by, even though the natives of Zell were noticeably larger than their eastern neighbors.

Everyone stood at least a head taller than the soldiers, man and woman alike. Most were wearing leather, muscles being exposed to the sun from the gaps in the clothing. It was hard for Kenjo to picture them being suppressed by soldiers who were smaller in stature than the average citizen. But they were increasing in number by the minute as more and more unloaded for the transport. Adana was not going to be able to contain them all.

Reaching the end of the road, they found a guardhouse near one of the town exits. Taking a quick peek inside through the window, they noticed they were only soldiers sitting there, laughing and drinking beer. It was becoming harder and harder to believe that this town actually belonged to Zell. The soldiers were making it their own at every turn.

Vallarya took the lead, grabbing his hand and crossing the street. The two headed toward the center of the town. As they drew closer, they passed an old woman crying with her head buried in a handkerchief. Another woman they assumed was her daughter had her arm around her, trying to comfort her as she walked, tears clearly visible in her eyes.

A crowd was gathered in front of them. Memories of the Angel-born flashed into their mind. Pushing their way through the crowd as they did then, they arrived at the front. There were no Angel-born this time, just natives of the town, some of the previous guard who had been uprooted.

A public display atop of a wooden platform, three soldiers stood on the ground in front of it. Behind them hung five men still in armor. Blood had caked their bodies. The skin that was exposed, bruised, and split. Something had been ripped off their chest armor, a small hole exposing the skin underneath. The light in their eyes had faded, ropes wrapped around each of their necks, with their hands bound behind them.

A fourth soldier stood on the platform and took the lever at his side in both hands. With a nod from one of the ones below, he pushed with all his might. Kenjo began to step off, and he felt Vallarya grab his arm. She pulled him back to her side, shaking her head vigorously.

Turning from her, he looked back up at the wood stage and watched as the men descended, the wood taken out from under them. They did not struggle for long. Cries and screams could be heard from the crowd. Kenjo's anger began to swell. His hands formed into fists, and he began to pull away from Vallarya. It was Manfo all over again.

"We promised we wouldn't do anything," said Vallarya, planting her feet and pulling him back again. "There's nothing to save."

"There would have been if you just let me go!" he replied. Pulling his arm free of her, he began making his way back through the crowd.

"It's just like what your father said back then. We would only get so far. You know there is an army here. You know the soldiers have already taken control of this whole town. We can't do any—"

"Why are you taking their side now?" He turned around and found her shaking. She was angry. Whether it was at him or a mutual anger they had to the soldiers, he could not tell. He figured it was both.

"I'm not! Let's just go back to the ship. I think I've seen enough of the town."

He took her hand in his. "Want to see if they have a sweet shop here?"

Vallarya's eyes lit up. The shaking stopped at the thought of the delicious sweets. "Maybe we haven't seen enough of the town. Hopefully it isn't this depressing throughout."

Kenjo led her back down the street, turning off when they could. They found themselves passing by the woman they passed earlier. They were chatting in front of an alleyway, both having stopped crying since they saw them last. As they got closer, their ears perked up to listen in on the conversation as they walked.

"They didn't even give them a chance," said the older one.

"I know," said the daughter. "I know they didn't. But we have to stay strong. Nothing foolish, okay? Dad and brother wouldn't want that for either of us. Come on, let's just finish getting home. Hopefully, they will at least let us give them a burial."

Kenjo and Vallarya wanted to do something. Both of them wanted to reach out and tell them it would be okay, that they could make it right in some way. Yet knowing they lacked the strength to follow through on any comforting words they remained quiet.

Watching them continue down the sidewalk, they forgot about the others around them, and Kenjo felt himself pushed into Vallarya by a passerby.

Stumbling to regain his footing, he looked around for who did it. He continued onward down the street without showing any sign of stopping. Shaggy chestnut hair covered his head; a gray cloak reached down to his thighs. On the back of it was the crest of Samil. His lower attire consisted of gray leather pants and ornate silver steel boots.

Leather armor covered his upper body. Silver steel gauntlets matched his boots covering his arms. They reached up to his elbows with the outer portion forming a blade that reached up to his shoulder. Two unlit lanterns, one on each hip, hung from his belt.

"Watch where you're going!" said Kenjo.

The man stopped, a reaction that neither of them were expecting. Vallarya placed her hand on Kenjo's back, ready to embrace at a moment's notice. Kenjo tensed up as the man turned around to look at him. A gray mask covered his lower face. A purple flame was embroidered into it.

"Oh!" he exclaimed. "Someone in this town actually said something to me that wasn't a soldier. Well, ain't this turning into an interesting day."

The surprise in his voice made them uneasy. It was hard for them to tell if it was an attempt at humor or if he was being serious. With everything they had seen in the town, it was easy to be taken either way.

"Though I must say..." He began to study the two of them, his eyes moving from head to toe as he looked them over. Placing a hand to his chin, he continued, "You two don't look like you're from around here. You both look Samilian... Hmm, you look like a southern boy with your face a little rougher around the edges, almost chiseled. And you, girl...well, maybe a mix between northern and southern Samilian. Though with your beauty, you could easily pass as nobility, save for the oddity of your hair. You dye it? Or is that a natural mix of black and white?"

Vallarya ignored the question, watching him silently, her hand still firmly against Kenjo's back. She was holding her breath. Beneath her hand, she could feel Kenjo shifting, his heartbeat getting faster.

The man shrugged and began to take a few steps closer. He stopped himself a little out of harm's reach. "Hey, now, you two can relax. I can tell you're both uneasy. I was just having a friendly chat. No one in this town has said a thing to me without a shaky voice. And seeing nonsoldier Samilians here is quite a treat. Now that I look at you closer, you two have some interesting eyes, don't ya? You, boy, have a right eye of gold that almost glows compared to your duller red left eye. And the girl has the same colored eyes, but her left seems to glow. How curious... Such an oddity. See you around."

The man whipped around and walked away, waving his hand as he did so. Vallarya took her arm off his back and relaxed herself. Kenjo watched as he turned off the street and disappeared.

Vallarya exhaled. "That was very odd," said Vallarya, removing her hand from Kenjo's back. "It felt like we were talking to a professor from the academy back in Saussion. But he had a presence about him. It felt almost overwhelming but at the same time similar... It seemed lik—"

"My parents," said Kenjo. His heart was beating faster. "The presence of a Finger like in the memory. They had it, and so did Lorraine..."

They ran back without a second thought, not making eye contact with a soul, not looking back to the man in gray, unaware that his eyes had made their way back to them. Watching as they moved back to the ship, a small smile creased the edges of his lips.

*****

McKenzie was the only one in the lower deck at the time, finishing up the last bit of sewing that she began a couple of months ago. She jumped out of her seat as they came crashing down the stairs from the deck above. She rushed over to them once she regained her composure. Offering her hands to them, she helped them to their feet. Grabbing them each a cup of water, she handed it to them and took a seat next to Vallarya.

Her hands were shaking as she placed them in her lap. No matter how much she tried to get them to stop, they would not calm down. Before the two could notice, she decided to sit on them before speaking. "Please…don't tell me you two did something already. And if you did…just lie. Please"

Kenjo finished off his water before he began the retelling of their look around the city. With Vallarya assisting, they painted a vivid picture for her. McKenzie was starting to calm down, her hands shaking less and less as their words poured in, relieved that they held back in the square.

"There was this odd man we met," said Vallarya. "His armor was all gray, even his clothes. He had these really beautiful silver gauntlets and boots. And he had some type of fascination with our eyes and my hair."

"Silver gauntlets and boots…and gray… Did he have lanterns at his hips?" asked McKenzie as she grabbed Vallarya's shoulders. There was panic in her face. Her hands were trembling.

"Y-yes. McKenzie, why are you trembling? What is it?"

McKenzie pulled her hands away and sat back down. Burying her face in her hands, she tried to hide away from the world. They watched as the strong woman with the kindest smile became a shaking mess.

Ryan came below deck, chatting with Baxter. The moment he saw McKenzie, his eyes locked onto Kenjo. In the blink of an eye, he had his son by his collar up against the wall of the ship. Kenjo struggled, placing his hands on his father's wrists in an attempt to pull them away. Black gauntlets formed around his hands as he continued his struggle.

He was almost free when his father's hands clamped down even harder, red gauntlets now covering his. Armor formed around Kenjo's knee, and he brought it into Ryan's stomach, taking his breath away as it forced him to let go. He coughed as he fell to the ground, trying to regain his breath.

"D-Don't you worry," said Kenjo, rubbing his neck where his father had grabbed him, his gauntlets fading away. "All we did was watch more people die like you wanted."

Ryan moved to grab him again.

"That's enough, Ryan!" yelled McKenzie, standing up, waving her stubby arms. Ryan froze in his tracks and dispersed the armor so her hands could return to normal. Never in his life had he heard her so angry. "They did nothing this time. This time...it found them by pure chance. He found them."

"Who?" asked Ryan as his fists relaxed. "Who ran into them?"

"Lucios."

Ryan's eyes widened. The anger that was once present dispersed. He now shared the same fear as she did. "L-Lucios? You're sure?"

"From what they have said, he looks just like we remember. What shoul—"

"Kenjo and Vallarya, stay here on the ship. Help Baxter with whatever he needs..." He trailed off as he looked to Baxter. Baxter had been silent this whole time, a letter in his hands, a crew member at his side whispering in his ear.

"Ryan," said Baxter, "someone left a message for you." Baxter handed him the letter. Ryan unfolded it and skimmed the words written on the parchment.

"McKenzie, we're leaving," he said, crumpling the letter into a ball. "Kenjo, Vallarya, as I said before, stay here and help Baxter. Baxter, if you will find something to keep them occupied."

It was as if a switch had been flipped in McKenzie. She was no longer shaking. Her eyes were no longer filled with fear. She nodded at him and followed him toward the stairs. Vallarya was amazed at how quick her stance changed, shrugging off the emotions she was feeling only moments before and replacing them with nothing but determination.

"Who's Lucios?" asked Kenjo as the two began their climb to the upper deck.

"Someone you need not concern yourself with," said Ryan.

As they disappeared, Baxter looked at them with a smile. "Well, I do have some boxes that need moving around here. And I think the crew deserves a break after the voyage, eh?"

The two only sighed as they began the menial task.

*****

Ryan and McKenzie moved with a brisk pace, their eyes constantly moving to observe their surroundings. Soldiers were patrolling the nighttime streets. It was clear they were staking out the ship. Ryan stopped suddenly as he saw the one who called for him. Leaned against the wall of a building, arms crossed in front of him, with two lamps on his hips.

Under the torch-lit streets, it was hard to distinguish his face, but they already knew who it was. He motioned for them to follow him as he walked down the street. They followed at a distance, watching for any signs of a trap or trickery from him. There were very few civilians walking the streets. Most who were out were soldiers, everyone they passed freezing at attention like statues. Only their heads moved, following the three of them.

Lucios led them to the back of the town up a stone staircase lining a hill that overlooked the building below. Three benches were arranged in an U-shape, allowing those who climbed the steps to gaze out at what was currently a sleepy town. It was a peaceful façade, at first glance anyone whould be unaward of the sleeping army housed within.

Placing the lanterns at his feet, he took a seat on the middle bench, crossing one leg over the other, stretching his arms out along back of the bench. A purple flame lit in the lanterns beneath him. The flames parted in the middle, forming a mouth. They looked like they were laughing at them.

Lucios turned his head to Ryan who looked at him like he wanted to kill him. "You know, ole boy, you don't need to be so on edge. I'm not going to attack you. We both know if it was going to happen, it could easily have just happened on the street back there with all the soldiers around."

"What do you want to talk about?" asked Ryan. He glanced over at McKenzie who remained by the stairs, watching for any sign of trouble.

"Life, really. Is it so wrong of me to want to catch up with my old friends?" he asked, looking between the two of them. "After all, it's been thirty years or so since we have actually talked. With you two committing treason and what not, it still is hard to picture, you know."

"What is?" asked Ryan as he continued to glare at him, thinking all of this was just some kind of trick.

Lucios's frame was illuminated by the moonlight as he gazed over the town.

"You two were the greatest of us. You had no equal during the Age of Heroes. The Blood Rain ended because of you...and you threw away two hundred years of fame in an instant..." He shook his head as he shrugged. "I am sure you two had your reasons."

Silence followed between them. Ryan took a seat on the left bench, joining him in looking out at the town.

"So," said Lucios, finally breaking the silence between the three of them, "how have you been? I mean it, how have the past thirty years treated you two...from what I can tell, you look well. Both of you still look like you did the last I saw you."

"Is this really why you made us come out here?" replied Ryan as he crossed his arms in front of him, his foot beginning to tap, growing annoyed.

"Well, no, but business can wait till we're done chatting, can't it? Humor your old pal."

Ryan let out a long sigh. "We've been good, Lucios, as good as ones wanted by the law can be. The first couple of years was spent looking over our shoulder for anyone who recognized us before we settled down and knew you would never find us."

"That does sound terrible. Not that I would be able to relate to that in the slightest. But the idea of it is none too pleasing. You two finally have kids yet?"

"We thought about it but ultimately held off," Ryan said as he glanced to McKenzie who was looking at him. She took a step closer to the two of them.

"You two have been together for over two hundred years, and you still don't have kids?" he asked, the bewilderment on his face made plain as day in the moonlight.

"They wouldn't be immortal like us," McKenzie chimed in, now standing next to Ryan. "We would have to sit there watching them age as we didn't. One day, they would look just like us. The next, they would be approaching us with a full head of gray. It wasn't something either of us wanted to go through."

"Oh, I see," said Lucios as he placed his elbows on his knees and leaned forward. "Immortality really is a blessing and a curse all at the same time, eh? At first, it's a blessing all the time in the world to do what you want. Then it becomes a curse as the world around you changes, people coming and going. Even the others at the academy in the capital can't agree on it being one or the other." He chuckled. "I personally don't envy you wielders of the Hands of the Children."

"What about you, Lucios? How have the past thirty years treated you?"

Leaning back again with a smile, Lucios replied, "It's been really great. Megan is pregnant with our fourth child. Should be due by the end of summer. And I got promoted. I now sit as one of the five Fingers grasping the throne. Came with a good pay raise too. Only thing that's been bad is I am sitting on the other side of a world, edging ever closer to full-blown war. I want to be there for Megan, you know? I just wish these damn Zellians would hand over the blades so we can go home."

"Are they the only reason for this war?" asked Ryan, hoping he could get a clear-cut answer from him.

Lucios just shrugged as the smile faded from his face. "Truly, I believe so. From an analytical view, I can guess for nothing other than power. After all, you and I both know what they are capable of in proper hands. No smith has been able to replicate them. But beyond that, I don't know his end game. He started gathering up those who could wield the Hands of the Children." Lucios took a long pause. He was thinking about something, his gaze off in another world. "And he had every last one of them killed. We destroyed every village in Samil that could create them."

"What the hell has gotten into him?" asked Ryan, practically yelling. He was no longer cautious of Lucios, all of it replaced with anger. "Back then, he gave two shits about the Blades of the Mother.

He hardly cared for his own! And now he's willing to go to war over them?"

"It's been thirty odd years since you saw him. That young boy you remember is gone, Ryan. He's a much different king now. The kingdom we shed blood for together is gone."

"And you are okay with this?" asked Ryan, looking at his friend like he was a younger brother.

"I am but a Finger following the will of the hand I am bound to. The hand being that of the king of Samil. And I personally can't completely fault him for falling off the deep end. The one he admired most betrayed him and disappeared, becoming the most wanted person in the world. Er…two most wanted people in the world. Eh, no, we'll just make this about Crimson. You two preferred that name, ya?"

Ryan was about to reply but held his tongue. It was true that they had betrayed Victor, turned their backs on the kingdom they served. But to think it was all their fault made him uneasy. *Was the world really in this state because of what we did?* he thought to himself.

"Anyways," said Lucios, breaking up his thoughts, "on to business. The western gate leads out to a nice open plain, a perfect place for someone like you and me to talk it out. As I know you won't surrender yourself, it will keep the civilians out of harm's way. I'll make sure the soldiers have no part in it. However, if you don't show up tomorrow—say, by ten—I will have the full might of the army storm that ship. And the cannons lining the coast will all be trained on it. I give you this last night together as a courtesy for us once being friends. Megan wouldn't forgive me when I tell her about this if I didn't. Even with you lying to me about not having a child of your own."

Ryan and McKenzie both were taken back. "What do you mean?"

Lucios stood up, grabbing the lanterns and fastening them to his belt. The flames inside still seemed to be laughing at them. "That boy, when he was at the hanging earlier today, he had a look in his eyes that reminded me of you a couple decades ago. I knew in that instant that he was your child. I wish he could've met my girl. She would be slightly younger than him. But I bet they would've been great friends."

Lucios walked toward the stairs without another word, stopping when he got there. "Oh, I almost forgot, make sure to bring the blade you stole. That has more value than your life ever will again to Victor." He disappeared down the steps with a wave and a smile.

McKenzie took a seat next to Ryan. Placing a hand on his, she squeezed it tight as they looked together out at the town.

"Keeping the civilians out of harm's way," said Ryan. "A true knight of Samil. He hasn't really changed at all."

McKenzie laughed as she turned to look at him. Placing her free hand on his cheek, he turned him toward her. "I have a favor to ask of you, my love."

"Anything."

"Talk to Kenjo. Not as a teacher or a master would to his student, but as a father to a son. I plan to have some girl talk with Vallarya as well. You may not see it, but there is a rift growing between you two. I won't allow it in this family any longer."

"I doubt he will care to listen." His eyes drifted downward, unable to look at hers any longer. "I shouldn't have done what I did earlier."

A single tear slid down his right cheek, catching the moonlight; it almost seemed to gleam. McKenzie wiped it from his face as she smiled. "He's just putting on the tough face he got from you. He's a smart boy, and with Vallarya, well, I can think of no better *Other* than her. Even if you have to humiliate yourself, talk to him because—"

He cut her off with a kiss. Time felt like it had stopped. The world itself still, its problems, its people all melting away as they focused on each other. They both felt it deep down, but neither could muster the strength to say it. Tomorrow was going to be the end of their journey.

*****

Ryan sat across from his son in the mess hall of the ship, a glass of whiskey pressed against his lips. Placing the glass back down as

60

his throat burned from the contents, he looked at Kenjo. His mouth opened. No words came out. Instead, he took another drink.

A few more minutes of silence passed before Ryan could think of what he wanted to say to him. "I want to apologize for how I have acted to you over the past few months. No, the past few years. I let my anger take hold of me before thinking."

"You think so?" replied Kenjo as he rolled his eyes. "I mean, thanks for apologizing, but I don't know what you want from me. Do you want forgiveness?"

"I don't know what I want from you, really. I guess I just want to talk to you. And the moment you don't want to hear any more of what I am saying, you can get up and leave. I won't stop you."

Kenjo shifted in his seat. Ryan reached out toward him but placed his hand back on his glass, a smirk crossing Kenjo's lips.

"Won't stop me?"

"I—"

"Please say what you want to, Dad. I just wanted to test it. Had you really let me go, I feel there would be nothing important for you to say to me."

Ryan tapped his fingers on the glass in his hands, watching the whiskey move ever so slightly with each tap. "Can I just ask, are you really oblivious to the laws of Samil now? Do you have no problem flashing that you are a Kryzen, that you or Vallarya are Hands?"

"No. I am well aware of them as is Vallarya. But it comes with the job, doesn't it? We are meant to be heroes to the people, to fight the fights they can't, to make the world better when others make it hell. Risking our lives, we have no qualms with it."

"And when the whole nation comes down on you?"

"We'll fight together like we've always done until the very end. Be it criminals, Royal Fingers, the king himself, or even Nothingness." Kenjo's eyes gave off a glow as Ryan looked at him. Was it determination? Was he promising something to him? He couldn't tell, but there was a sense of calmness that radiated from his eyes.

Ryan took another drink as Kenjo continued, "I hope before our time is up to have left an impression on the world like Crimson did. During the Age of Heroes, of course, not the events thirty years ago."

Ryan spat his whiskey on the floor at his words. He became choked up as he coughed against his burning throat and the liquid ending up in the wrong pipe.

"C-Crimson, huh?" said Ryan once he regained his composure. "Why him? There were plenty of others who stood against the Nothingness back then."

Kenjo laughed. "True, but there was only ever one Crimson that led them all."

"What? That's true enough, he was quite something back then," Ryan said as he finished off his whiskey.

"Did you two ever meet him?" asked Kenjo, his eyes now full of boyish wonder.

"We worked alongside him throughout the age. But they were fleeting moments. We never really got a chance to get to know each other. We do share the same armor color when we embrace, though. That was always a cool thought when we were young. Anyways, I really do wish you two together could lead a peaceful life."

"A peaceful life?" Kenjo looked at him, confused. "What kind of peaceful life is really left to us? We were chased out of the village when I was eight. Vallarya was only six. I wasn't even supposed to be her Anchor. And now here we are on the other side of the world because of what we did. Samil is hunting down those with the Hands. There is only a fight left for us, no matter where we end up."

"You're starting to sound more like a warrior than a hero."

"Is it really that different?" asked Kenjo, crossing his arms and looking away from him. "They fight all the same."

Ryan shook his head. "Oh, don't be dumb on me now, Kenjo. You know deep down they aren't. Heroes fight only when it's necessary. Warriors live for it, relish in it, bask in any glory that may come after. Heroes can go with or without glory. I may not have really had a chance to get to know Crimson, but I know he didn't do the things he did for the fame or the money. Is that what you want it for?"

It was Kenjo's turn to shake his head as he sighed. "No, not at all. Dad, can we spar tomorrow after we get away from the town?"

"That's your next question?" asked Ryan, surprised. "I figured you would have wanted to know about Lucios."

"I do, but I would rather have that be my reward when me and Val win."

"Oh, you think you can finally win?" Ryan erupted into laughter. Wiping a tear from his eye. he looked at him. "You two can try all you want, but you'll be better off just asking me for it now. You won't ever get an answer this way."

5

3rd of Japhim; Mortal Year 523

Lucios

Lucios stood with his back against the wall next to the western gate. Lighting his cigarette, he took a long drag, blowing smoke into the air as he pulled it away. He checked his watch. They had twenty minutes left before he would give the order to destroy the ship.

A snickering filled his ears. He unhooked the lantern on his right hip and lifted it up to eye level. The purple flame inside was laughing, flames parting above the mouth to form eyes.

"Someone's excited," said Lucios before taking another smoke. "Though you may end up only able to light another cigarette. I don't know if they'll show."

The flame went quiet as it rearranged to form a pouting face.

"I'm joking. They'll be here. And you both will be able to burn as much and as bright as you want."

Lucios looked around. The blades of grass danced with the wind. It hadn't rained for a couple of days, making it very easy to burn and a perfect spot for him to take down his mark. Tossing down his cigarette, he stomped it out and checked his watch again. Ten minutes were left.

He sent a letter to Megan earlier that morning, hoping that it would tide her over until he could come home and be there for her. With her being due in the fall, he really didn't want to miss his child's birth. Although he did figure she would be extremely upset with him, regardless, due to what was happening today. Ryan and McKenzie had done a lot for them in the past. Part of him wanted to let them go, but he knew it would only come back to bite him and his family if he did.

The gate finally opened. Ryan and McKenzie stepped out. As the gates shut loudly behind them, Lucios waved them down in greeting.

"I was just telling these flames that you two were always on time," said Lucios. "They seem to have forgotten you... Hmm, I don't see the sword with you. Where is it?"

"It's in better hands," replied Ryan. "Besides, my old friend, you won't be getting your hands on it, even if we had it with us."

"Ah, I see..." Lucios shrugged walking away from the wall, turning around when he felt he was far enough away. "I guess there's nothing else to say. We all know why we're here."

Lucios readied himself, placing one foot behind him, both hands in front. He pushed off the plain between them and crossed in seconds, silver gauntlets colliding with crimson red armor. Ryan grounded his feet and pushed him off. An arm from McKenzie shot forth, grabbing his foot, and pulled him down. The blade on one gauntlet flipped in place. Reaching down, he sliced at the hand, causing McKenzie to pull back.

Jumping to his feet in time to meet Ryan's fists again, shifting his hand, the other blade deployed. He sliced at his stomach. Another limb manifested, darting forth, it parried the blade swing. Ryan capitalized on the opening, connecting his fist to Lucios's stomach. He staggered back from the blow. The sound of breaking glass filled the air, and Ryan leapt back.

The purple flames in his lanterns broke free, one running along the lengths of his arms, setting his hands alight as the blades flipped back. The other went down his legs, lighting both his boots and the ground on fire. The flames along his boots erupted, propelling him forward.

Ryan stepped to dodge. Lucios followed up quickly, hitting Ryan's side. Flames erupted and sent him off his feet.

Lucios jumped up, descending with a kick. Ryan rolled out of the way, another explosion incinerating where he previously was. By the time he got to his feet, Lucios was already on top of him. Hit after hit making contact, explosive flames following every hit, McKenzie regenerated their breaking armor after each attack.

Forming an extra set of legs to help Ryan maintain balance, an extra arm reached down and sprung Ryan into the air. His fist came down on bladed wrists before Lucios pushed him off, laughing at him as the flames circled around them, forming an inescapable ring.

"Have you two really not aged as well as I thought?" he asked. "Even your magic isn't working on me. I'm not even a Kryzen!"

A gout of flame shot out, forcing Ryan back again. Lines of fire reached out from his hands, arching into the sky like great serpents before descending on their target. Ryan stayed light on his feet, hopping from place to place. Flames followed shortly behind, the ground he could safely tread shrinking by the second.

"Ryan," said McKenzie as she formed a leg to help her husband dodge again, "we can't keep this up."

Ryan dodged another stream of flame; this time, Lucios met him at his landing point.

His fist connected with his head, sending him to the ground. Deploying an arm blade, he thrust down at his stomach. Alight with flame, it pierced through the armor. McKenzie formed a hand, shoving the blade out his side as Ryan groaned in pain.

Lucios, caught off guard by the move, felt the full force of McKenzie's foot sending him through the wall of flames next to them. She pulled Ryan up to his feet before embracing with him once more. He clutched his side, the blood from the wound beginning to paint his palm.

"Are you that worried about them?" asked McKenzie.

"Is it that easy to tell when you're next to my soul like you are?" he replied, eyeing Lucios. He was just standing there, waiting for them to move, only a knee-high wall of purple flame between them.

"I think it's okay to let them be."

"What?"

It felt like she was hugging him now, her arms wrapped around him in comfort. "Think about how easily your magic worked on Arthur back at home. Arthur was a Kryzen. Lucios isn't all he was in his wards and those damn lanterns. Arthur had far more protecting him, but you affected him with a single touch. Kenjo and Vallarya did far more than you think in that short time."

Ryan's eyes widened as his wife's words repeated over in his mind. A smile formed across his face, his eyes glowing with a light that hadn't been there since he abandoned Samil. "Then McKenzie...let's fight the pain long enough to get rid of one more enemy for them."

"I'm with you."

Lucios watched through the distorted air from the heat of the flames as Ryan's armor regrew, covering up his wound, the crimson plates now forming around his head completing the suit of armor. Before him now stood the legend he remembered—the hero known as Crimson.

He grinned. Today would be the day he surpassed his old friend. Lucios crouched down, ready to push off with another blast of flame. A low growl ran through the air, followed by a shriek that lined his skin with goosebumps. His heart began to beat faster, not out of adrenaline but out of fear, his body afraid before he even knew why.

Refusing to be held back by fear, the flames propelled him into the air at his command. The blades on his arms deployed, his boots propelled him once more this time towards Ryan. They found nothing but air as he ducked. In that split second, McKenzie grabbed him by the wrists. Suspended there, Lucios came to understand why his body was afraid.

Ryan's fists struck Lucios's core as McKenzie let go. He went flying across the plain from the impact, rolling numerous times before finally coming to a halt. Lucios could barely breathe. His ribs were broken, pain surging through his core as he tried to get up. Looking toward his foe, he took in the twisted sight.

Standing amongst purple flames that flickered against his crimson armor was a demon. Three horns stuck out of its forehead. The stained-glass plates that covered his body, merging with flesh, were now a shade of gray. Red eyes glowed brightly from deep within his eye sockets, a piercing gaze that made his heart beat faster and faster. His fingers had turned into large twisted claws.

McKenzie's upper body had manifested, sticking out of his back, arms draped around his neck, crossing over his chest as her head rested against his. The flesh of her arms was gray, twisted and torn, revealing the bone beneath. A tattered crimson veil covered her face. Her eyes pierced through the cloth with the same red glow as his.

The ground around them began to decay; even the flames were snuffed out by an invisible force. With each step, more of them disappeared. Grass that had been spared the wrath of Lucios's flames withered and decayed as they stepped ever closer to him. The growl began to crescendo into a roar as his jaw unhinged itself beyond normal limits. It was hard for Lucios to even picture that they were inside of that armor.

Taking a deep breath, he pushed up with all his might to his feet. He swayed in place for a moment, putting his arms in front of him as the monster charged at him. Flames snaked outward, only to be snuffed out before they could hit their target. The monster swung a fist. Lucios brought up his blade to catch it. The blade shattered to pieces as it connected. Unable to pull away, it made contact with his. He felt his fingers break first, then his wrist before the rest of his left arm.

Lucios screamed in agony before he was punched in the chest and sent back to the ground. "I'm sorry... Megan." He coughed blood onto the grass. He no longer had the strength to stand up. On his knees, he looked up to the beast who only responded with a roar, and spit caked his face. "It looks like...you'll have to raise our next child on your own."

*****

68

Kenjo stood in the middle of the lower deck on display for Vallarya, pulling at his collar to try and stretch it out as it choked him a bit. He pulled up his face mask and popped his hood up, concealing the upper half of his face with a shadow. Vallarya put a hand to her mouth, trying to hide the laughter that followed.

"Looks a little tight on you," she remarked, wiping a tear from her eye. "Can you even breathe?"

"Well enough," he replied, pulling at his armor. "You enjoying the view?"

"Very much so. Looks like you need to lose some weight."

"It takes time to adjust to the body," said Kenjo, unamused with her comment.

"I know, I know. I was only joking. Your mother did good. You can't even tell she weaved the Zishagale silk into your armor or cloak. That new sheath for your sword looks really nice too. Although I must say I miss the alternating colors. How do I look?"

She hopped up from the chair she was sitting on. McKenzie had made her a black cloak to match Kenjo's. However, hers was trimmed in gold. While Kenjo's silk was weaved into his armor, she made Vallarya's from scratch—a long-sleeved black dress hemmed with gold that reached down to right above her knees with a pair of matching boots. She danced around the room with grace.

"I-It looks… Uh…good," he stammered, tearing his gaze away from her.

"I thought so too." She smiled at him. "We have to make sure to thank her. She put these together so quick."

"She was a master after all."

"Yeah, yeah. Come on, let's go get some air."

Kenjo followed her up the stairs, the smell of fish filling their nostrils as fishermen began to unload their catch. Baxter was in town along with the rest of his crew, taking care of business at the merchant's office. They had complete run of the ship.

"We could steal the boat," said Kenjo as he ran up the helm. "Go wherever we wanted."

"Yeah," said Vallarya, bounding up the steps. "I don't know the first thing about sailing boats, let alone maintaining them. I doubt

we would make it very far. Plus, we just got here, Kenjo, this is ho—
Is that smoke?"

Kenjo looked at her as she pointed off into the distance.
Following her finger, he caught sight of the purple smoke rising up
into the clouds from just beyond the town walls. "What the hell?"
He looked around, but no one seemed to notice. Citizens and soldiers alike were not reacting. "We can't be the only ones seeing this."

"Wanna check it out?" asked Vallarya. But Kenjo had already
leapt off the ship and onto the dock, running at full speed toward the
smoke. "All right. You could at least say something before we do!" she
shouted before jumping off the deck and sprinting after him.

Pushing open the unmanned gates, the two of them made it to
the other side and looked around. Grass was burning underneath the
heat of purple flames. As they made their way closer to the small fires,
they found a massive patch of burnt ground in the shape of a circle.

A growl could be heard some ways off that made them go still.
Their eyes moved from side to side as they looked for its owner.
Another growl, and their hearts skipped a beat as their eyes rested
upon a small hunched shape in the distance. It was moving slightly.
Another growl came out, confirming their suspicion that it was the
owner.

With slow and steady steps, they made their way closer to the
shape. Vallarya tugged on Kenjo's arm to stop him as they exited the
burnt ring.

"What is it?" he whispered, looking back at her.

"The grass here isn't burnt. It's just dead."

"Huh?" Kenjo looked down to see what she was talking about.
Withered and shriveled grass buckled under his steps. Even the soil
beneath was dead; a few birds and squirrels were scattered about lifeless, bodies unscathed as if they had just dropped dead. Looking forward toward the moving shape, he noticed all of the ground up to it
had decayed.

"Something feels awful. We should turn back. Let's just wait for
your parents back on the ship, tell them what's going on," Vallarya
said. But her feet moved after Kenjo as he continued on closer to the
creature.

A scream escaped her mouth when they could distinguish the shape—a body of twisted flesh and glass plates of armor. Its claws were holding down a body as its mouth of jagged teeth ripped a piece of its prey free. It turned to face them, a low growl emitting from its throat as the piece fell from its mouth.

"Why does that shade of armor look so familiar?" asked Kenjo. His legs were trembling as he pointed. The creature was already up and running at them. Black armor formed around his arms as he crossed them in front of his chest to block its attack. The force of the blow sent him tumbling across the grass.

The rest of his armor formed as they fully embraced. Wasting no time, the creature was already upon them the moment they got back to their feet. With a leap, it took them to the ground. Kenjo attempted to push it off as its snapping jaw tried to get his head. Twisting his body, he turned and threw the creature off. He hopped to his feet as it pushed off the ground, coming for them once more.

This time, it remained on two legs. The way it fought was familiar to them, keeping up with its strikes, deflecting each one with his palms in an effort to find an opening. Every time, when he thought he had one, the creature had already covered it with another strike of his own. The creature was in full control of their dance of fists.

"Kenjo," said Vallarya, maintaining their armor as she studied their foe. "Why is the monster fighting like it's fought you before?"

Kenjo deflected another swing. As he did so, a fist extended from the creature's chest, connecting with his jaw. He staggered back, shaking his head. He watched as the upper body of a woman stretched out of its back, wrapping its arms around its neck as it rested her head atop the creature's shoulder.

"That's because," said Kenjo. His heart was beginning to beat faster as the words began to form in his mouth. "We have fought them before...countless times."

"No, no, no, no, no. You're joking, right?" she asked, her voice full of tears as it dawned on her. "What... What do we do?"

Both of them were unaware that the creature before them was but an empty vessel, a doll of sorts that was once his parents and her adoptive ones. They sat in an eternal darkness, only able to see each other, unable to control the actions of their previous bodies. One would cry out for help, only to be answered by a woman's laughter.

If you still seek to save, to protect, and help, then you must not falter now. The enemy before you is a monster. Nothingness in the flesh. Destroy it like you were raised to do.

Kenjo and Vallarya were caught off guard by the voice. It was the first time she had heard it, but Kenjo remembered it was the same voice that spoke to him back in Gennegnan. A wave of calm washed over them. Kenjo stepped off to the shadow cast by the creature. His back to him, he kicked the back of its knees, causing it to fall slightly, and followed up by a swift punch at the side of its head.

His fist was caught by one of the woman's hands. He was unable to pull his hand free as the creature turned to him. With his free arm, he tried to fight off the creature's following assault. Vallarya created arms of her own to help. They fell behind, unable to keep up. Blow after blow assaulted his body, only stopping so he could toss him across the plain and into the town wall.

Kenjo gasped for air as he slid down the wall. Both he and Vallarya struggled to shrug off the pain that wracked their bodies. He stood up, he blinked, and the creature was upon them again. They narrowly dodged the claws as they went over his shoulder and pierced into the wall behind him. Moving quickly, he feinted a swing. As a hand went to grab it, he put his all into another, hitting directly against where its nose would be and sending it to the ground.

Vallarya pinned it down as Kenjo began his assault, blow after blow, connecting with the creature's head as it growled. With a roar, the woman grabbed Kenjo by the sides and lifted him upside down into the air. Kenjo undid his cloak, throwing it into the air above them as she tossed him away.

The creature was back on its feet. Before it could move, Kenjo struck again. His fist engulfed in a golden light smashed into its chest, breaking through crimson plates, twisted flesh and bone.

Kenjo was falling head first into silent darkness, Vallarya falling with him. Looking behind them, he saw the sky illuminated with a golden light. Turning his gaze back down at where he was headed, he could see two figures huddled together. One of his arms moved on its own, reaching out for them. Vallarya followed suit, the figures below them looking up at them before they touched. It was Ryan and McKenzie.

Ryan reached for his son's hand, McKenzie for Vallarya's. As they took them, they felt a warmth surge through their bodies that made them smile.

"We have to go," said Kenjo. "Come on, let's get you out of here." He tugged, but his father wouldn't budge. He only continued to smile at them.

"Mrs. Alexander, come on!" yelled Vallarya. She remained as still as a statue as Vallarya struggled against her, trying with every ounce of her strength to pull her up off the ground.

"You already know we were meant to die if we ever embraced completely again," said McKenzie as she placed her other hand on Vallarya's. "I wish it never had to come to this, but we wouldn't have beat him without doing so."

"Why didn't you just take us with you?" asked Kenjo through tears and growing anger. "We could've done it together, beat him, and left!"

"Because you shouldn't have to deal with our mistakes," said Ryan as he pulled his hand free of Kenjo's and took his son by the wrists. He looked him dead in the eyes. "Don't be like Crimson. Be better than he ever was."

Ryan and McKenzie both let go, and the two of them felt themselves being sucked back into the sky. They tried to fight it, swimming against the force reaching for the two below them. But the more they struggled, the further away they got. The last image of them was their smiling faces as they were once again consumed in the darkness.

Kenjo pulled his arm free. The creature fell back and hit the ground with a thud. They had no time to relax as they heard the gate begin to open. Grabbing his cloak, Kenjo looked for an opening and stepped from shadow to shadow all the way back to the ship where Baxter stood at the helm, looking over a few things before departure.

"What the hell!" yelled Baxter, jumping in fright as Kenjo stepped onto the deck and collapsed. Vallarya separated from him and looked up at Baxter. Her eyes were red from crying. "What's the matter? Where are Ryan and McKenzie?"

"Gone," said Kenjo, slowly sitting up.

"I…see." Baxter sniffed as he fought off growing tears. "Then you two need to get going."

"Huh?" asked Kenjo, thrown off by his comment.

"I promised them I would get you two on the road to Gonall. Go to the stables near the north gate. I have some crewmen there. Horses and packs are waiting for you." Baxter offered his hands to help them both to their feet. "Look, I am sorry for your loss. I wish I could be of more help that I could comfort you kids. But you need to go before the soldiers get here. Go. Come on, go, you two!"

Baxter was practically shoving them off the ship with his final words. He waved goodbye to them as they ran up the stairs and into the town. They glanced back at the ship, watching as Baxter returned to the helm. A sound like thunder boomed across the sky. The merchant vessel shook violently in place before exploding. Splintered wood and cargo flung all over the docks.

Kenjo grabbed Vallarya, and the two of them sprinted for the stables to make their escape. The ones who had helped them get to Zell were left behind, no longer able to guide them…

6

28th of Grehl; Mortal Year 523

Jasmine

asmine sat on the rooftop of the merchant's hub in the financial district of Samil's capital, kicking her legs out in front of her over and over as she grew restless, waiting for the person she was after to leave the building. According to Cardinal, there was reason to believe the merchant, Oscar Oddarsson, was helping to finance a growing rebellion. He would have seen to it himself, but with the war on the horizon, he had enough on his plate, making sure the nation could afford a globe-spanning war.

So the job fell to the girl who was growing only more and more impatient. Finally, she heard the door open and she stopped moving. Listening to the sounds below her, she looked down and found her mark. Oscar was the one in the middle, slightly shorter than the other two on his flanks. She watched as he and another two started walking down the wet cobblestone street toward the housing section, casually discussing their plans for the weekend.

Getting up, she moved to the edge of the roof. Silk strands of starlight wrapped around her arms down to her hands. Pointing her hand to the roof across the street, a string shot out and attached to the roof, pinning the other end of the string to her roof. She stepped onto it and walked across. Luckily for her, no one was around to witness the feat, appearing as if she was walking on air, the thin strand barely visible to the naked eye.

Once she was on the next roof, the string dispersed, and she continued on, attaching new silk strands to each roof she needed to cross as they continued through the district. By the time he reached his house, he was alone, his partners already having split off a few streets back. Attaching a new strand to the top of his house, she ran across it. Positioning her foot as an anchor, she rotated upside down on the silk, strands of starlight now reaching down from her thighs to the bottom of her boots.

She lowered herself down on a new string until she was level with his head. As the merchant unlocked his door, he heard a whistle and turned around to find her dangling upside down. A small smile formed across her face as silk shot from her arms and sealed his mouth. Clawing at the silk, he scrambled inside, nearly tripping on the way in. Before he could shut the door, she stopped it with one arm. Swinging it open, she kicked him in the chest, sending him to the ground with a thud.

Jasmine closed the door and locked it. Picking him up, she sat him in a chair in his living room and wrapped him up in silk. Completely bound to the chair, he struggled for a few minutes before finally accepting his fate and looked at her with fear-filled eyes.

"Now it seems like I can talk to you," she said as she pulled away the silk on his face.

"Wh-What do you want?" he asked, sweat beading his brow. "Money? Got that here. Valuables? Got that too."

"What is with you merchant types always doing this? And here I thought life wouldn't be so cliché." She let out a sigh before continuing. "I come here on business as a Royal Finger."

"A... Royal..." His eyes began to widen. "Finger..." Oscar started to thrash violently in the chair, hoping that he would finally break free.

"Just give it a rest. You won't escape that. You don't even have an ounce of magic in you."

He didn't listen, only stopping when the chair finally tipped over, and his head hit against the wood floor. Jasmine sat him upright and reapplied new silk, this time pinning the chair to the ground so he couldn't fall. Pulling another chair around, she sat it in front of him and took a seat. Crossing one leg over the other and crossing her arms, she looked at him, waiting for him to stop. He, once again, didn't.

"You are going to pull something if you keep that up. Look, I'm not here to hurt you. Truly. Just answer my questions, and I'll be gone."

He stopped thrashing and looked to her. With a hesitant nod, he decided to hear her out.

"Good. Now then, uh… Where are they?"

"Who?"

"No point to play dumb. Not after this fit you just threw. The ones you finance. The ones who have 'plans' for a rebellion or something."

"I don't finance any such thing. *My* finances are well placed in proper investments that would not have a chance of coming back to me like this. I can give you some names of someo—"

"Yeah… No. Not doing this running in circles bit."

Jasmine stood up, and the strands of magic silk began to glow. *I really hate doing this,* she thought to herself. The merchant felt something begin to crawl on his legs, and he looked down. A spider the size of his hand was crawling up each leg. Large glowing red eyes stared up at him from bodies of dim white light. Their climb was unfazed as he began to thrash again.

"You're going to aggravate them," she said, watching her spiders spread their legs onto his stomach. "Just tell me, please. Don't make them go further."

He struggled even more, and soon, the two spiders' legs could be felt passing over his throat, then his cheeks, and he began to scream. When his face was hidden behind the spiders' bodies, he surrendered. The two spiders instantly disappearing as Jasmine took a seat again. Taking a deep breath, the merchant gave up all he knew, and Jasmine undid the silk before disappearing into the night with a thank you.

Oscar slowly stood up as he watched the door, making sure she was not coming back. Checking himself once over for any more spiders, he moved to his liquor cabinet and produced a bottle of unopened whiskey. He grabbed three glasses from a kitchen cupboard and placed them on the counter.

"You could have helped me, you know," he said as he topped off the third glass and placed the top back on the bottle.

"Is there a third here?" asked a voice.

"One for you," he replied, pushing the glass across the counter. "Two for me. Now why didn't you help?"

"I am not foolish enough to fight a Royal Finger like this. Not one I don't know anything about. But since you gave up everything, looks like I don't have much of a choice. There's no doubt where she's going next, so I must be off before she gets there."

The glass was picked up by a materializing black glove. The rest of the voice's owner came into view as the glass pressed against his lips. A man of average build wearing black robes with a white sash and a left sleeve of white appeared before him. Placing the glass back on the counter, he headed for the door.

"Try not to let things slip again," he said, pulling a hat out of his coat pocket and adjusting it on his head. "You lucked out with her being so kind. But who knows what the next one might be like? Maybe I'll even pay you a visit for spilling all our info out."

"Don't even joke like that."

"You're right. You're too good of bait to make a visit like that worth it in the end. See ya around, Oscar."

The man laughed and shrugged as he left the house. Closing the door behind him, he broke into a sprint, trying to get to Jasmine's destination before her.

*****

Jasmine crept silently along the rooftops as she approached the lone shop at the southern edge of the shopping district. Most general shops stuck to the center streets, competing with one another on a daily basis. Out on the edge, specialists usually worked in their shops while having a different building attached to do their actual business. Her destination was no exception to this rule, an alchemist's shop with a supposed hidden entrance to some type of rebel hideout.

Making sure no one was around before jumping down to the street, she approached the shop casually. Opening the door, she took in the sight of the lamp-lit store. Along one wall, countless books filled the shelves arranged in alphabetical order. On the opposite wall sat vials, jars, and all the other glass containers you could imagine. In the middle of these two sat a long counter nestled against the back wall. The shelves behind it filled with various items all for use in the practice.

Behind the counter stood a man in his brown robes with a white sash over his left shoulder. He scratched his head of gray hair as he noticed his new customer. Placing a hand in front of his mouth, he cleared his throat. Another man came from a door nestled out of view between the books and the counter. He placed a box of glass containers on the counter before going about stocking the shelves.

"How can I help you, missy?" asked the shop owner, his eyes following her as she began to look over the bookshelf. He studied the girl in black and yellow. With her clothing, he had chalked her up to being a mercenary of some sort. Long black thigh-high boots reached up her legs. Her battledress fell down to her shins, two long slits on each side to allow more freedom for her legs. Long-sleeved gloves reached from her hands to midway on her upper arms. The dress covered up to the base of her neck where blonde hair rested against it, long bangs and a high ponytail that reached halfway down her back. Her yellow eyes glowed slightly, like the web patterns that decorated her clothing.

"Well," Jasmine said as she ran her fingers along the book spines, "there were two things I wanted to ask you about. First, I am interested in getting into alchemy and was wondering the best place to start."

"*Oh ho!*" exclaimed the old shopkeeper as his face lit up. "An aspiring student! Well, I'll be damned, I haven't had a new alchemist wander in here in a long time. You're going to want the third book in the A section and the sixth book in the B's. Those are good places to start for beginners. Do you have any supplies?"

Jasmine stood up on her tiptoes to reach the book he said in the A's and pulled it down. *Alchemist's First: A Complete Guide from Beginner to Master.* "No, I don't have anything at the moment. A friend of mine mentioned this place, and so I figured I would stop by after my classes." She counted off the books in the B's and found the one he mentioned: *Beginner's Guide to Alchemic Exchange.* "I'm impressed you know exactly where these books are just like that."

"He doesn't get out much," said the young man finishing up his stocking before returning to the back room.

Jasmine giggled at the remark before approaching the counter, surprised when she saw that while she had been finding those two books, the man had already formed a box of supplies and stood eagerly waiting for her.

"With the purchase of those books, I'll throw in this set of supplies," he said, smiling. "Those two are very good starting points for everything. To get through most of the introductory experiments, everything in this box will be enough. And once you're done with them and you find the field you want to focus on, you can come back and get those that are more tailored for you."

"Oh, you really don't need to," she said, placing the books on the counter and reaching for the small bag on her side. "How much do I owe for these?"

"Twenty gold coins."

"Twenty gold! For these books? I thought the average price of books didn't even break five?"

"Ah, yes, for the average literature. But for alchemy books, the market is a little different, my dear girl."

"Hmm..." Hesitantly, Jasmine pulled the twenty coins from her bag and counted them out before him. "I guess that's fine then. Here you go. Thank you very much for the help."

"Anything for an aspiring alchemist," he said as he slid the coins closer to him and counted them again. "Now you said you had a second reason for being here. How can I help?"

"Well, I think you can. Oscar said you white sashes liked to work out of here."

In an instant, the smiling face of the shop owner disappeared. His face went dark as his skin began to pale, the coins in his hand spilling out onto the counter and the floor.

"O-Oh...did he now?" He was shaking, his once happy tone now replaced with constant stuttering. "W-W-What e-else did h-he happen to...s-say?"

"Nothing that you're not telling me right now," Jasmine said as silk strands of starlight formed along her arms. She sealed his mouth as she leapt over the counter. Binding his arms and legs, she knocked him unconscious and moved to the door that led to the back.

Footsteps could be heard on the other side, and she slammed the door open. Running in, she found a large lab filled to the brim in materials and vials, some still full of their experiments. This whole time she had been playing the role of a customer, the ones she sought were working right next to her. Looking at the end of the room, she saw two people escape out another door in the floor.

Moving as fast as she could through the cluttered room, she shot her silk out to one of the doors before they could shut it. Grasping it in both hands, she pulled as hard as she could, continuing her advance. The people running from her let go, and the door slammed against the ground with a loud bang. Chasing after them, she made her way down the stairs and into an underground tunnel. Following the lit torches that lined the stone walls, she decided to stop running.

Six spider legs of the same white starlight as her silk sprouted from her back. Jumping up to the ceiling, she skittered along the top down the tunnel. The further in she went, less and less torches were burning the way forward. As she approached the end, the tunnel opened into a large room. Below where she was, there was a ledge with a single ladder that reached down to the dirt ground.

Inside were various tables sat about, and the whole room was almost as cluttered as the lab. Various papers lined each one on some weapons and armor laid down. On others appeared to be potions and other chemicals in their own containers. Twenty people were running around hastily, putting on armor and grabbing weapons.

Jasmine noticed the young man from the shop talking to some-one else who was barking orders at the rest. The same white sash that had adorned the old man upstairs was being worn by each of them, and the assistant had finally put his on before putting on his own armor. Dropping down from the ceiling, the legs disappeared as Jasmine thought of the best way to approach them from her ledge.

"You know," whispered a voice into her ear.

Before she could react, she felt a foot against her back and soon found herself rushing to meet the ground. "Your kind doesn't belong here. This place only has death for you, dear girl."

She rolled out of the way as her attacker leapt down after her. His long sword piercing through the ground where she just was. Leaping to her feet, she reached her arm behind her back and pulled forth a baton that fit perfectly in her hand. Not even a second later, it had grown into a full Bo Staff. Her attacker smiled as he pulled his sword from the dirt. Removing his hat, he tucked it into his robes before rushing toward her in a flurry.

Staff met sword as they danced around the room. The further in they got, Jasmine started to find herself surrounded as the other rebels readied to join in. She began to move faster, only barely able to keep up with the assault from all of them. Sprouting the legs from her back and forming silk along her legs, she pushed up off the ground. Balancing with one hand on her staff, she was upside down as spider silk shot toward the ceiling, pulling her up and away from the group below.

"You must really like spiders, eh, dearie?" asked the man in the black robes. "I'll make sure you're buried with plenty of them. Let them make your corpse into a fine nest."

"We really don't have to fight," she said as she felt her feet touch the ceiling. Her spider legs began to push against it, bending as they gathered up more force. "I mean it, you can all just throw down your weapons. No one has to get hurt. Please don't make me do this."

"Well, since you asked nicely, I guess we should, eh?" Her ene-mies let out a laugh.

"I really don't want to hurt you."

"No, no, the little Royal Finger doesn't get to ask for anything here nor does she get to leave. The more of your pathetic excuses for protectors we get rid of. The easier our life becomes, the better Samil becomes."

Jasmine sighed before taking a deep breath. She aimed her staff for the center of the group below. Pushing off, she approached them at full force, the black robes barely jumping out of the way in time as the force of her impact cracking the ground underneath. An army of starlight spiders began to crawl out the cracks, growing in size as they stepped onto the ground. They leapt onto her foes, taking them down to the ground and beginning to wrap them up in a massive web.

Jasmine saved the robed man for herself. Lunging toward him with her staff, they began to trade blows again. She placed him on the defensive with an endless barrage. When he began to push back, she switched it up on him. Ducking low, she swept his legs out from under him. Shooting silk from one arm, she pinned a leg to the ground while she leveled her staff to his head.

Before she could bring it against his skull, the lanterns in the room were extinguished, leaving only the faint glow of her spiders to fill the room. She felt her silk get cut and slowly stepped back. Looking all around the darkness seemed unnatural. Her spiders were now no longer illuminating anything other than themselves as if the area around them was feeding off their light. Eventually, she could no longer see them.

Another step, and then he struck. His sword cut straight through three of her spider legs, and she let out a scream of pain. Before she could react, she felt him grab the top leg of the remaining three. He sliced the bottom two before kicking her in the back. She staggered forward from the blow, only to meet another two kicks that sent her tumbling into her spiders and their web.

"Hmm, these were connected to you more than I thought," he said as he picked up one of the spider legs he removed. "I didn't expect that scream of pain, nor did I expect them to still be here after severing them from your body. These sure are sharp, aren't they?"

Jasmine struggled to her feet, using her remaining spider leg and staff as a support. She began to feel the pressure of his feet against the web. Then it was gone. Her senses began to dull, and she could no longer feel him walk on her web. She couldn't even see the spider leg still attached to her body. Standing upright, she readied her staff only for it to be knocked away from her. Suddenly, a sharp pain filled her stomach.

The darkness parted just a little to show her own spider leg piercing into her body. He twisted it a little before placing his sword against her neck. Even with him so close, she couldn't sense him. It was if he was just a figment of her imagination. But the cool steel against her neck was not imaginary.

"Ah, how well the trap was set," he said with a laugh. "Little bit of seeds for ole Cardinal. He sure lives up to his namesake so willingly pecking at them. And then he gladly sent a young Finger out to get us. You're not the first and you certainly won't be the last, dearie. Slowly but surely, you corrupt savages will be removed, and the nation of Samil will no longer be tarnished by false heroes…and their equally false king."

Jasmine felt the blade press deeper against her skin. Trying to control one of her spiders, she found the connection had been severed by the darkness. They skittered along her web as blind as her until one bumped into her leg. It crawled up her body, onto her back, and she began to feel the connection between them form again.

He twisted the leg in her one more time for her to suffer. As she screamed in pain, he had sealed his fate. The spider crawled onto her shoulder and quickly leapt in his direction. Jasmine pulled away, and the blade sliced into her cheek. Her vision slowly returning. She watched as her opponent grabbed at the spider on his face and slammed it to the ground. As her senses returned, she felt the rush of magic as the link between her and her spiders returned. With a simple thought, they skittered toward him, biting into his arm to force him to drop his blade before weaving him into a cocoon of starlight silk.

"We are…not…false protectors," she said, finding each word harder to say than the last. "The king is going to make this world…a better place. We're going to help him. You are the only savage trying to ruin what we're striving toward!"

The black-robed man furrowed his brow in anger. Had webbing not already covered his mouth, she was quite sure he would have been heard all the way back at the shop. But she could still hear his muffled shouts up until he was completely hidden in silk.

Jasmine took a deep breath and fell down to one knee. The spiders began dispersing one after the other. Her eyelids were far heavier than she remembered. Falling forward, her hands and remaining spider leg held her up for seconds longer. The leg vanished as she no longer had the strength to stay up, collapsing into the bloody web beneath her.

*****

Jasmine opened her eyes to sunlight coming through a large ornate window; above her, a large mural depicting a battle from long ago. She rolled to her side and looked at the cream-colored walls, then out the large window. It was sunny out. *Is it really already daytime?* she thought. *I could have sworn it was only going on midnight.*

And then she remembered what had happened and sat up quickly, tossing the covers off of her, only to be met with pain in her stomach. Looking down, she lifted up the shirt she was wearing only enough to see the bandages that wrapped around her body, covering where she was stabbed. Lying back down slowly, she focused her gaze back to the ceiling. It was much more comfortable lying there, unmoving. Though she was unsure of where she was, she was in no condition to find out at the moment.

Her back was still hurting from where the robed man had removed her legs. The wound in her stomach felt like it was closed but still hurt just as bad as it did when he initially stabbed her. He wasn't wrong; her legs really were as sharp as any blade. The twisting only had made it worse, but she was alive; the rebels had been taken care of, and no one was dead. She found herself smiling at the thought.

A knock at the door rang across the large room. Shifting her head, she looked toward it and saw a woman in a white nurse's uniform of the castle walking in, carrying a bowl filled with water in one arm and fresh bandage supplies in the other. She hadn't realized Jasmine was awake until she pulled at the bandages and she let out a small groan. Jumping back, she placed a hand over her mouth to muffle her surprised scream. Then she ran out the room.

Minutes later, she came back in, this time with another young woman who looked not much older than Jasmine—short orange hair with long spiked bangs that covered her forehead and caressed around her light tan face. Her hands were pressed up against her cheeks as she smiled. Jasmine knew the smile couldn't be helped, and in a moment, she jumped on the bed, hugging her. The nurse tried to pull her off, saying that she was going to open her wounds up again.

She reluctantly let go and sat on the edge of the bed as the nurse went about switching out Jasmine's bandages. The young woman who hugged her was named Aliya Sharp, someone who had been like a big sister to her since she joined the guard five years ago at the age of twelve. Though they no longer worked together, every moment they were not working they tried to spend together.

"I'm so happy you're awake!" she said with an even bigger smile. "When they said they found you in a pool of your own blood, I feared the worst."

"Oh, come on, Aliya," said Jasmine. "Do you really think that's enough to take me out?"

"Anyone lying in a pool of their own blood usually has a very high chance of being dead. Also, you know that's not my name anymore."

"Oh, right, I'm sorry, still not used to it just yet." Jasmine winced in pain as the nurse finished tightening the bandages and got up to leave the room. "It's Forsythia now, right?"

She nodded. "Mm-hmm, that's what I go by now. What everyone, save for you and the family back home, calls me."

"I'll try my best to remember it... Where are we?"

"My room, though I haven't fully moved in yet. I'll be out for the next two days taking care of business. So I decided to have you stay here and recover. Don't worry, you're not being a nuisance. You're a Finger after all, so the nurse doesn't have anything against helping you. She's quite happy to assist someone like you compared to the others."

"I'll be gone before you get back."

"I just said not to worry, sis. Come on now."

Jasmine giggled at the annoyed face Forsythia was making. "Did we get everyone I left down there into custody?"

"Twenty people were rounded up and escorted to the dungeon."

"Wait," said Jasmine as she thought back to last night and counted. "There should have been twenty-one. Was there anyone in black robes with a single white sleeve?"

Forsythia shook her head. "According to the guards who arrived first, there was an open web cocoon near you. Looked as if something broke out of it."

Jasmine looked down at the covers over legs. He had escaped after all of that and was still out there able to do exactly what he planned to. Forsythia moved closer and placed a hand on her now shaking hands. She looked up at the gentle smile staring back at her.

"Are you going to be okay?" she asked.

"Yeah, I think so," she said. "Just there's someone—"

Jasmine went on and told her of the fight down in that room. How she began to lose her senses and how the darkness seemed to be eating the light she and her spiders produced. She mentioned how he was planning on luring more after her and how he had already killed some of the Royal Fingers already.

"That would explain why some of them have gone missing without a trace," Forsythia said when Jasmine finished her story. "I'll talk to Cardinal about it later. Make sure he's careful about which seeds he pecks at."

Forsythia got up and moved to the window and looked out over the town below. The castle room they were in was nestled on the west side, facing toward the residential district. It was peaceful—a blue sky without a cloud in sight, and a gentle sun cast its rays down on the people going about their day.

"Don't end up like them, Jasmine," she said in a sullen tone. "I don't know what I would do if we found you and you didn't wake up next time. Plus"—she turned around to face her—"you can't join my group if your dead."

"I won't end up like them, that's a promise," Jasmine replied, placing a hand on her stomach as she lay back down. "What do you mean by join your group?"

"After a couple more months as a Sovereign Finger, I'll be in charge of my own group on the same level as the others. When that comes, I'm going to put in a request to Cardinal for you to be transferred so we can work together again. Sound good?"

"That sounds amazing," she said, her face beaming with happiness at the thought. "To work alongside you again would be like a dream come true."

Forsythia walked over to the bed and hugged her again. Saying her goodbye, she moved to the door. As she grabbed the handle, she stopped. "What he said to you doesn't bother you, does it?"

"About us being fakes and corrupt? No, I know we're doing the right thing. Every great thing has haters as much as it does admirers. The murders he has committed and plans to continue? I don't plan to let that go unanswered or continue for long. As soon as I get out of this bed, I'm going to get back out there and find him."

"Good to hear. Take care of yourself." Forsythia left the room and gently closed the door behind her.

Jasmine looked up at the ceiling again, the white sleeve brandishing a black blade dancing across her thoughts. She was perfectly content with not seeing him ever again, but so long as he was out there, she knew it would be inevitable. And the longer he was, the more at risk Royal Fingers would become, not to mention it posed a risk to Forsythia as well.

She closed her eyes for what she thought was only a moment. When she opened them again, the sun was setting. The nurse who had replaced her bandages earlier came back in, this time with a tray of food sitting on top of a box. Jasmine sat up as the nurse placed the box on the ground and put the tray on her lap. Before her, a warm bowl of soup and two slices of bread were on display. Jasmine grabbed the spoon that sat next to the bowl and stirred it, finding pieces of finely chopped meat hidden among the noodles and vegetables.

Taking a spoonful, she blew on it before placing it her mouth. It burned a little, but the great taste quickly replaced the pain. Grabbing a piece of bread, she dipped it in before taking a bite, a harder crust surrounding the soft bread. The combination of the three tasted amazing as she took another bite. The nurse closed the large blue curtains over the windows before striking a match and lighting a lamp on the bed's nightstand.

She reached down into the box, and Jasmine heard the clattering of glass as she pulled a book from it. Jasmine finished off her food and watched as she placed it on the nightstand. In big letters at the top, it read *Alchemist's First,* and she almost spit.

"Where did that box come from?" she asked as the nurse took the tray from her lap.

"An elderly gent," she replied. "He was the one who found you and got the guards to come in the first place. He then insisted that this be given to you, almost getting arrested for his attempt to trespass into the castle."

"Oh my, my performance wasn't even that good. I guess he really was excited to find someone interested in the craft."

"Do you want me to take it away? I don't mind tossing it for you."

"No, no, it's fine. Really. It wouldn't hurt to take a look, especially with him going so far."

"Very well. This will be the last time I come in tonight. Do you need anything else?"

"No, I'll be okay. Thank you very much."

The nurse bowed before leaving her alone in the room. Jasmine opened the large book and began reading. Page after page was turned, and she began to lose track of time. She was engrossed in the words and the multiple illustrations that depicted so many possible outcomes and explained what went wrong or right to arrive there, finally stopping when she passed out with the book open across her chest, two hours before dawn greeted her.

7

7th of Japhim; Mortal Year 523

Kenjo

Kenjo stood in an empty room illuminated by a single hanging lamp in its center. All around him, all he could see was darkness. With nowhere else to go, he moved toward the lamp, each step feeling heavier than the last. Finally, underneath the lamp, he bent over, trying to regain his breath. Looking up, he found Ryan smiling at him.

Tendrils of darkness began to move along his body. Kenjo reached out for him, Ryan, in turn, reached for his son. Kenjo's hand passed through his, unable to stop. His hand hit against his chest and carved out a hole. More tendrils burst forth, wrapping his entire body before constricting and disappearing from view.

Kenjo screamed, but there was no audible sound. He lifted his foot to run after him, but something tugged back on his ankle, struggling against it until it yanked him to the ground. Tendrils sprang forth and latched onto his shoulders. They dragged him back with increasing speed until at last, he felt the sun kissing his face. Breathing heavily, he rubbed his hands along his shoulders and ankles, finding them untouched.

Vallarya was sleeping next to him in her own sleeping roll. Her hair, a mess, covered most of her face as she slept peacefully. Looking around, he found their campsite was undisturbed. The horses remained hitched next to the tree beside them, the large scattered rocks blocking them all from view of the main road.

Getting up, he moved to the horses. Digging into their saddle-bags, he pulled out a snack for them, a special blue apple that the merchants had recommended. Apparently, it had the ability to keep the horses fed and hydrated for three to four days off of it alone. Feeding them one each, he then grabbed a pan and ingredients for their breakfast.

Making a fire, he got to work, the aromas of his craft filling the air and rousing Vallarya from her slumber. With a long stretch and a deep breath, she hopped out of her roll to join him at the fire. Minutes later, Kenjo made three plates, handing her one of them before grabbing his own and taking a seat next to her.

"Did you have that same dream again?" asked Vallarya before blowing on the food in her hands.

"Yeah," replied Kenjo. "Fourth day that I've killed them... Fourth day that I couldn't save either." He shoved food into his mouth to try and clear up the images forming in his head. "How did you sleep?"

"Well enough when I finally made it there. Kind of like yours, but it's not your parents in it. Instead, it's you. You're the one I can't save." Vallarya looked at him with concern and then noticed the third plate. "Is that for our guest?" she asked, pointing at it.

"Oh," said Kenjo, placing down his food before getting to his feet. "Yeah, it is. We should probably get it to her before it gets cold."

The two of them moved to the other side of the large tree beside them. Behind it was a girl. Her head was down, asleep, a blue cloak wrapped around her like a blanket. Weathered brown leather boots protected her feet, the lightly tanned skin of her legs exposed up to her skirt. Kenjo placed the plate down in front of her. Furry wolf ears sticking out of the top of her head twitched at the sound.

She had shoulder-length hair as black as Vallarya's. As she looked up at the two of them, her bangs fell and covered one of her eyes. She looked down at the plate and then back up at them.

"I appreciate the thought," she said, a high-pitched tone to match her petite body. "But with my hands bound like this, it's kind of hard to eat."

"Do you think it's wise for us to release you?" asked Vallarya, kneeling down beside her.

"Well. If I were in your shoes, I wouldn't, but look, I wasn't doing anything wrong!"

Vallarya tugged at the ropes, releasing her hands. "You have been following us since Adana. Not to mention last night when we caught you, you were bent over my friend here while he was sleeping, so close to his face that you were breathing on him."

"Oh, did you wish it was you that close to him instead?" she asked, reaching for the plate.

Vallarya snatched it away from her before she could lay a finger on it.

"Okay, that was a bad joke. I'm sorry." The girl placed her hands together in front of her and bowed forward.

Vallarya sighed and handed her the plate "Here. Eat it while it's still hot."

"I'm surprised you remained quiet the whole night," said Kenjo as she ate.

"Th... Orses." She swallowed the food in her mouth before continuing. "The horses don't make for the best conversation partners after a while. And I figured you two would just ignore me."

"Why were you following us?"

"Oh, um..." She fidgeted in place. Three long black tails hidden behind her began to sway. "Because it sounded like it would be fun."

"Excuse me?" they said together.

"Yeah, I know it's silly, but that's the truth. After watching you two defeat that creature of Nothingness, I felt this force telling me to follow you. And I did without a second thought. I was close last night because I wanted to get a good look at you two. Alas, I didn't expect you to grab me from inside his body. That was creepy."

"Not as creepy as what you were doing."

"That's fair."

"And why do you have those lanterns?" asked Kenjo. She looked down at the metal hooked against her belt.

"Oh, snagged it from the guards as they took the bodies away," she said with a smile. "You know, with you having the Hands instead of asking me all this, you could just read my memories."

Kenjo looked away at her words. Standing up, he grabbed her empty plate and walked back to the camp. He began to break it down so they could continue their travels.

"Did I say something wrong?" the girl asked as she got to her feet, watching him as he moved.

"No, not exactly," said Vallarya. "But now we know you are a scavenger or a thief. Either way." She shrugged. "What's your name?"

"Kaldana. Kaldana Dawson."

"I'm Vallarya Aberdanth, his name is Kenjo. Don't worry, he's a lot nicer than he seems. He just doesn't like to talk to new people too much."

"I thought it might have been my appearance. Good to know it's just him."

Kaldana stretched as she walked with Vallarya to Kenjo who was stomping out the fire. She jumped onto one of the rocks, and then with a leap, she was gone from sight.

"Well, that's good," said Kenjo.

"We should probably get going too," said Vallarya. "Gonall is still at least two weeks away. And well…after what happened, I don't doubt if people are looking around for us."

"Hmmm, ya, let's get out of here."

"Wait for me!" yelled Kaldana as she came back from behind the rocks atop a horse.

"You stay back."

"Hey, look, I'll follow from a distance. Won't bother you two unless it's important. Do you want to tie my hands again?"

Kenjo looked to Vallarya who only responded with a shaking head and a shrug. "All right, you can follow us until we get to the next town."

"Yay!" she exclaimed, practically jumping from her saddle.

The three moved from the campsite back to the main road. Following the map they were given, Vallarya led them to the town of Caprae. They passed few people on the road, much to their relief. At one point, they encountered a traveling merchant who was able to help them restock some of their supplies. When night came, they found a spot to camp off the main road.

Kenjo practiced his swordsmanship in the light of the campfire. He was thinking he was growing rusty after not using it for so long. Vallarya happily acted as his sparring partner while Kaldana watched from the other side of the fire. She said nothing, just watching their movements like they were performers on a stage.

When first light hit, they departed again after breakfast. They continued this for another three days until they arrived at a small village of Caprae that stood between Adana and Gonall. No soldiers of Samil were in sight. It seemed that the army had not spread this far inland yet. As they approached, the guards of the city crossed their halberds to deny them access.

"Hold it there," said the one on the right as he raised his hand. "State your business."

Kenjo was rather caught off guard by the question. After all, the "guards" were mostly dressed in basic leather that could hardly be called armor, a breast plate, some leather pants, and boots. The halberds seemed to be of shoddy quality. A quick glance could reveal that the blades were dull and rusting.

"We're just travelers passing through to Gonall," replied Kenjo. "We came from Adana. At most, we were hoping to stop by and maybe rest at an inn here if there is one instead of out in the wilderness."

"From Adana? That entire place is occupied by the Samilian army. How did you get out of there?"

"We had help and some fast horses. Now may we come in?"

"Yeah, all right, just don't cause any problems while you're here or you will be thrown out without another word. Stable is on the left side as you go down the main road. Inn is smack dab in the center of town. You won't miss it."

"Thank you."

The guards raised their weapons and allowed the three of them to pass inside. Vallarya took the liberty of talking to the stable master in town and got stalls for their horses. Grabbing their packs, they made their way to the inn, quickly finding that it was much different here. However, just like Adana on the coast, it paled in comparison to the towns of Samil.

The roads were made of dirt. Many of the buildings seemed to have damaged signs or missing portions of their walls, patched over with sheets or other cloths. The entire placed seemed like it was going under, save for the inn—it was the only place whose sign remained undamaged. The building itself seemed completely intact as well.

"Guards look like crap," said Kenjo. "Town looks like crap, but the inn looks just fine."

"Well, at least they have their priorities right," said Vallarya as she moved closer to the door. "Sounds like they're having a riveting time in there."

The sounds of music and voices became more noticeable as they drew closer. *Was the whole point of this town just a good time at an inn?* they wondered as they pushed open the door. And their idea of it all went out the window along with a chair. The sound of shattering glass put an end to the cheery music.

In the center of the floor, tables were smashed, people draped over them, unmoving. On the outer edges of the room, tables turned on their side were being cowered behind. Some brave souls peeked their heads around the side to watch the drama unfold while most kept their hands over their heads and ears. A few children could be heard crying.

Kenjo and Vallarya only blinked in disbelief as a man standing in the center kicked another into a wall, leaving an indention where he hit. He wore brown boots and black pants; a white long-sleeved shirt covered his upper body. It was torn and covered in blood stains. Difficult to say if it was his or one of the other guys in the inn. On his waist was sheathed a sword, and along his belt were vials of some gray material. His messy blonde hair reached down past his shoulders.

A patron approached him sporting a dagger. The blond man grabbed him by the arm as he dodged the thrust, disarming him before tossing him through a nearby window. Without a moment's hesitation, he leapt out after his opponent, pinning him to the ground before beating him unconscious.

"Um," said Vallarya as the rest of the patrons started running for the door. "Maybe we came at a bad time?"

"Should we tell the guards?" asked Kenjo as the two of them moved to the window.

Outside, the blond man stood with a foot on his bloodied opponent. Four other men surrounded him, each wielding crude and warped axes.

Drawing his sword with one hand, he quickly popped open one of his vials with the other hand. Holding onto the cork, he darted his eyes between his opponent's hands and feet, waiting for any of them to make the first move. When there were no takers, he opted to make the first move himself. Quickly turning around, the cork shot from his hand, propelled by the gray substance in his vials, hitting him between the eyes with enough force to send him off balance. Before he could recover, his blade pierced his heart.

Pulling it free, he swung around to block an attack. The three moved around him in formation, striking simultaneously. They aimed for different spots to throw him off. Yet, it appeared to them as if he were playing with children. His body dodging one way, his blade shifting to block other swings with ease. The next swing he parried, the substance in his open vial moved, creeping up his body, down his arm, and onto his sword.

The substance jumped from the blade like it was being sprayed into the eyes of his three opponents. They screamed in pain, tears streaming down their faces as they staggered backward. Before they could see again two of them were cut down, the last stepping back as his grip loosened; through his irritated eyes, the man before him seemed almost demonic.

He was cut down where he stood without even a whimper. The blond man began waving his hands, and the substance moved along with him, swirling around him before returning to the vial. Grabbing the cork, he closed it off before triumphantly dusting his hands. He stood up with a smile that quickly faded away, a rusted blade of a halberd resting against his shoulder and neck.

"That's not good," said Vallarya as Kenjo moved past her. "Annnnnd you're already out the window. Damn it, Kenjo."

"Does he do that often?" asked Kaldana, eyes widening as she watched Vallarya's hand disappear.

"Yeah. He won't learn."

Kenjo rushed forward as the man broke free of the guard's weapon. Spinning around, he brought the blade to where the guards head was but met a black gauntlet instead.

"Sorry," said Kenjo as he began to push the blade away. "I don't know about those others you killed, but this guy here is just a guard doing his job. Can't let you hurt him."

"And who the hell are you?" he asked, pulling his sword free before stepping back. In a blink, he had popped open two vials the corks resting between his fingers.

"Just a traveling hero on his way to Gonall," he said as the rest of his armor formed around his body. "You can call me Kenjo."

"Gonall... Why would some unknown hero be headed to a bunch of ruins? Unless you're no hero at all, just another grave robber! You came to take the remains, didn't you? The scraps left by those bastards!"

"Wait, what?"

There was no answer as the substance began to swirl around the man's sword. He lunged forward with a thrust. The substance shot outwards, doubling the length of the blade. Kenjo stepped to the side as the attack moved past him. That close to it, Kenjo was finally able to tell what the substance was. It was ash.

Another swing came across. Kenjo ducked down and pushed the blade upward with one hand as he struck him in the stomach with another. The ash redirected straight down, forcing Kenjo back before he could swing again. Now the ash began to swirl around him, covering his movements from sight until he was right on top of him.

Vallarya saw the next swing and blocked it with a sharp limb, exploding it outward. It disrupted the flow of the ash and exposed him. Kenjo moved quickly: Two swift jabs—first to the stomach, second to the head, sending the blond man down, pinning him to the ground as he took his forehead in his hand. The memories of their foe beginning to unravel like a beautiful tapestry.

*****

His memories began to flow through him. As his life began to play before them, they watched as the boy known as Arlo Maccalus grew. Trained by his father to be a fighter since age five, born a Kryzen, he adapted to magic quickly and picked up ash-weaving from his mother. Through his eyes, the capital city of Gonall was the most beautiful thing he had ever seen.

They caught different glimpses of Zell as a young Arlo followed his father to the capital, Rastoram, once every year for something known as the Meeting of Kings. His father showed him everything, taught him how to be a swordsman and a politician in a nation slowly adapting the diplomatic policies seen in the rest of the world. They groomed him to be a prince worthy of his title. When he came of age, his father would be more than willing to pass down the crown and not wait a second longer.

Time passed on, and Arlo became one of the most well-known and capable warriors in all of Gonall, bringing back countless trophies of his defeated enemies. And whenever he held court or made a public announcement, there was not a single person in the kingdom who hated him nor opposed him. Everyone adored him, giving him gifts and praise whenever they saw him. But even with it all, he remained humble, never once boasting in his life, except to his friends. And even then, it was only for things he knew.

At one point, his father offered him the crown. But Arlo refused it, believing that his old man was still more than capable of leading the kingdom. Instead, he remained in the military, racking up more impressive feats and accomplishments. He did promise him, though, that after another year or two, he would put the life of a soldier behind him and gladly accept the throne.

*****

It was an early morning. Arlo sat atop a horse in his gleaming silver armor, freshly polished the night before by his aides. Behind him were his loyal companions, the group who had been with him since the first day he joined the Gonall military. Arlo's hand tightened around his lance as he looked back at them, each one responding with a nod as they felt his eyes upon them. Closing his visor, he kicked his horse into a gallop, and they were off.

The group of eight stormed across the plain that stretched out in front of the kingdom. Their target was the artillery line that sat positioned on hills raining hell down on the forces below. The crews were caught off guard, their exposed flanks laid bare as they crashed through them, running down each and every one before the army sieging the castle could notice.

"Sergio and Yale, man these two cannons!" said Arlo, pointing at the ones situated in the center. "Maria and Roberto, dismantle all the others! Liam, Volumnia, and Loreia, watch our sides for anyone who may be coming that way!"

They all responded with a "Yes, sir!" before getting to their assigned tasks. Arlo sat his horse behind the two cannons, watching the battle unfold before him. The artillery that they had just commandeered had already done their job, tearing massive holes through the walls and breaking open the main gate.

Samilian soldiers began slipping into the kingdom as they broke through the defensive lines erected by the Gonall army. Trampling over defeated foes, they began to push their way deeper into the kingdoms heart. Arlo felt anger unlike any before well in his chest. The ash lands that surrounded the castle were becoming tainted by the amount of blood that hit the ground with every fallen soldier.

The cannons fired with a booming thud. The balls pierced through lines of attackers, catching fire midflight before exploding, creating massive dents in the blocks of unaware soldiers. Loreia came galloping up to him as they released another two shots.

"Prince Arlo, we got Angel-born incoming!" she said quickly. "Back from where we came from."

"Good," he replied. "All right, everybody. Sergio and Yale, fire one more volley, then dismantle the cannons. The rest of you on me!"

Arlo charged back down the hill toward his flying enemies who swooped down low as they drew closer. Angling his lance, he thrust upward at his foe, connecting with his abdomen. His foe was far heavier than he expected. He let go of the lance before being taken down with the weight of the lifeless body.

Mechanical wings, an engineering marvel of Samil, had replaced the once feathery wings that stuck out of their backs. There was no denying that they flew with an increased speed and probably better than they would ever be able to. But the bad taste left in Arlo's mouth was quickly spat onto the ground as he looked to his enemies.

Another foe swooped down from behind. Catching him off guard, the Angel-born grabbed him, lifting him off his horse. Arlo pulled a knife free from a holster on his leg, stabbing it into his foe's arm, forcing him to let go. Falling to the ground, he rolled to his feet as he came at him again.

Arlo drew his sword, parried the first swing, and then brought it against his exposed chest. As he fell down, lifeless, he looked around at his companions. They were unharmed, Sergio and Yale rejoining them as they charged back across the ash plains toward the castle.

Angel-born had already commandeered the walls, cutting down the unexpecting soldiers. Making their way into the courtyard, Arlo sent Sergio and Yale as reinforcements to retake the walls while he and the others went along the inside perimeter, bringing their wrath down upon any who got inside.

The Gonall army rallied behind Arlo as he and his companions began to push back the enemy, ash weavers sending volley after volley of exploding ash down into the ranks to assist. Arlo fought his way to the main gate; the forces were being repelled, and victory finally looked within reach. Blue flame cut across his vision, his horse reared, and he tumbled to the ground. An explosion went off, and he went flying into a building.

His head was spinning as he looked around. Blinking his eyes, he slowly regained focus, looking where he was moments ago. A new foe stood there, a lance alight in blue flame at his side. Four metal wings of blue stuck out of his back, flames still burning at each of their ends. Soldiers charged at him, only to be engulfed in blue flame that appeared as if from nowhere.

Maria and Roberto charged at him next. Instead of flames, the foe used his lance, blocking both of them with a simple spin, effortlessly pushing them back, their arms dangling as if the movement had broken them. In moments, his lance had pierced through each of them, their lifeless bodies sliding to the stones below.

"No!" screamed Arlo, getting to his feet. Ash encircled his arms as he charged, grabbing a sword from the ground it wrapped around as they clashed. Magical blue flame and ash collided, a blast throwing Arlo back. The lance swung around, shaft catching him in the side, flinging him to the ground.

Before his enemy could finish him off, Liam and the others arrived. They surrounded the Angel-born who only sighed as he looked over all of them. In the fight that followed, there was no chance for them. He fought with the ferocity of a beast and the might that could only be compared to that of the gods. Flames erupting wherever his lance made contact, Arlo's companions were burned away in moments, not a trace left. The cerulean flames of his enemy swirled around him. He inhaled, and the flames moved with him.

His foe flew into the sky and jetted toward the keep for the throne room. Arlo scrambled to his feet again, fighting back the tears. Grabbing his sword, he made his way back across the courtyard and sprinted up the stairs, his heart beating faster and faster. The royal guard surrounded his parents, but after what he had just seen, he knew they would not be enough before that Angel-born. Deep down, he didn't know what he would possibly do when he got there.

Pushing open the throne room doors, he watched his father get disarmed. A kick sent him down onto his throne, lance piercing through both king and throne. Arlo sprinted across; with a swing, he forced the enemy to let go of the lance.

Without his weapon, the Angel-born quickly disarmed the Arlo blinded by rage and fury. Consecutive blows found their way to his core; picking up his sword, he ran it through his stomach and pushed him all the way to a stone pillar, impaling him against it. Arlo groaned in agony, trying to pull the blade free, but it wouldn't budge.

His enemy grabbed his lance, and the keep began to shake. His wings flapped, and he took off again, flying through the hole he made when he entered. Arlo watched helplessly as the blue-winged foe disappeared from sight. Stone fell from the ceiling, and he looked up, eyes widening as the entire keep started to crumble down.

*****

Kenjo stopped viewing the memory and got off of Arlo. Vallarya began to separate from Kenjo as Arlo decided to come after them again. Kenjo caught the blade in an armored hand and locked eyes with him.

"I'm done fighting you," he said as he started to push the blade away.

"We mean it," said Vallarya, stepping out from behind him. "Just put the sword away, okay?"

She tilted her head and smiled. Arlo noticed the missing left hand of hers and began to realize what they were. With a nod, he pulled his sword away as Kenjo loosened his grip. Sheathing it, he began to recall all of the ash to his vials.

"You two are wielders of the Hands?" he asked, closing up the last of his vials.

"Yep," replied Vallarya. "And you are the prince of Gonall, correct?"

"If you read my memories, then you already know that answer."

"Just like you knew the answer to your own question before you asked it."

Arlo went silent at her remark and noticed the guards beginning to gather around them. His hand instinctively moved to the hilt of his sword as he studied their movements. Kenjo was readying himself to stop him as Vallarya stepped out.

"How are all of you doing? Anything we can help you guys with?"

"The killer there," replied one of the guards, presumably, he was the captain as he was the only one in full armor. "Hand him to us. He has some murders to answer for."

"We already took care of it. He's not a threat to you, just to all the others he killed."

"And why should we listen to some random strays who wandered in?"

"Last I checked, the words of Hands carried weight as great as kings if not more anywhere in the world."

"Hands you don—"

Vallarya cut him off by phasing a part of her body into Kenjo. When she knew he wouldn't say another word about it, she pulled her self away. "Very…well. But if you are not out of the town by sunrise tomorrow, we will arrest all three of you."

"Good luck with that," murmured Kenjo under his breath as the guards turned away to leave at their captain's order. "We need to talk, Arlo. I think you still left some tables intact in the inn."

Kenjo walked away without another word, and Vallarya followed after him. Arlo hesitated before deciding to go after them. When he arrived, he found the two of them sitting at the only upright table in the room. Kenjo motioned for Arlo to take a seat at the table. He nodded as he sat down and began to study them. What struck him the most was their eyes; no Hands he had ever met had eyes like theirs, let alone anyone else he had ever met.

"So what did you want to talk to me about?" asked Arlo as he placed his hands on the table. "A prince of a destroyed kingdom isn't worth much."

"My master wanted us to go to Gonall," said Kenjo. "He said a friend there owed him a favor. And so here we are, on our way there…but now we're both kind of lost. Maybe you could help."

"Who was your master?"

"Ryan Alexander."

"The Ryan Alexander!" exclaimed Arlo. The surprise and excitement that filled his face made it seem as if the fighting that had happened moments ago never occurred. "Where is he now?"

"He... He's..." Kenjo's hands began to clench as he tried to form the words. But thinking on it immediately brought only pain.

"He had to leave before we got here. He didn't tell us where he was going," said Vallarya as she placed a hand on his. The touch felt calming, causing him to loosen up and stop them from trembling. "Arlo, you seem to have some admiration for him from both the way you reacted and the memories we read. You wouldn't happen to have been his friend?"

Arlo began to wave his hands in front of him. "No, no. The honor of being a friend with him belonged to my father. Ryan was a great hero, and not to mention the savior of Gonall back in the day. But that was before my time. Back when my father was still in his prime."

"I see... Savior of Gonall. That's a story he never told us. I guess that would lead to quite a favor... Arlo, do the other kings know of Gonall's fate?"

Arlo's excitement quickly faded, and he went pale. The memories of the fall flashed throughout his mind. His friends, family, and comrades dying, all dead by the time the sun had set. A single tear began to form in his right eye. "Somehow they don't. Otherwise, war would already have begun. Furthermore, the kings aren't all together in Zell. The time for the annual Meeting of Kings is another month away. Since the initial demand of Samil for the Blades of the Mother started, the kings have been holding council separately, trying to figure out exactly what their people want before making their final call, the call that determines if we go to war or just hand over the blades peacefully."

"Is there no one that you can talk to about this?" asked Vallarya confused. "How can a kingdom just be destroyed and an entire nation not know of its fate?"

"The kings, especially the Lord King, are exactly who I need to talk to. But I haven't been able to make it there since I made it out of the rubble."

"Why's that?"

Arlo stretched and then went and grabbed the body of one of the men he killed earlier in the tavern. Dragging it back to the table, he lifted up the man's right sleeve, revealing his tattoo—a human skull, two swords stabbed through each of its eyes, and another through the top.

"Bandits would be the best way to describe it," he said, pushing the body away and taking a seat. "They moved into Gonall after all was said and done. Not only that, Samil is paying them to hunt survivors of Gonall so they can hide all trace. Though I must say I think they are growing desperate for me, this was more than usual."

"So Samil just up and left after taking it?" asked Kaldana, joining them at the table. The contents of her arms spilled out over the table, coins and trinkets clinking against the wood and each other. Her ears twitched underneath her hood, and she noticed she caught Arlo's attention. "What? Is there something on my face?"

"What... No, no. Who are you exactly?"

"Have they not introduced me? Here I was, thinking we were friends." She looked to them and was only met with unamused faces. "Oh, they're just being shy. Anyhoo, my names Kaldana. Nice to meet you."

"I'm Arlo. If you don't mind me asking, what are you doing with all of this?" he asked, picking up a necklace with a circle locket at the end. Popping it open, he revealed the faces of two children. Closing it up quickly as the memories of that day rushed into his mind, he dropped it on the table with the rest.

"Sorting through the loot," she said with a laugh. "They don't need it anymore. Plus, I am hungry for some actual food instead of what this guy has been cooking."

"Hey!" yelled Kenjo.

All Kaldana did was laugh as she separated the spoils.

"Can we not just avoid Gonall on the way to Zell?" asked Vallarya, suppressing a chuckle, causing Kenjo to glare at her. "I know, Gonall probably means a lot to you, but going around and making it to the capital would be better, no?"

"They have eyes all over that ground is the problem. We can go around if we cut way across, but that would take weeks. Weeks that could make me miss the Meeting of Kings. Going through them would be easiest. There are some escape tunnels that reach from the border with Gonall all the way to the keep. I'm going to use one of them to sneak in."

"Were you planning on facing them alone?"

"When my body fully recovered, yes. These bandits of the Skull Scabbard as they call themselves aren't that strong."

"And yet you can't sneak past them," muttered Vallarya under her breath.

"What was that?"

"Oh, nothing," she replied, waving a hand as she stood up. She walked over to the bar and began to talk to the tavern keep about lodging. As she did so, the doors swung open, and a young boy in tattered clothes stumbled a few steps before collapsing.

Jumping up, Kenjo ran over to him and turned him on his back. Supporting his head, he began to study his body: He looked no more than thirteen; multiple wounds lay underneath the holes in his clothes, dried blood caking around his exposed wounds covered in fresh blood caused by his movements.

The tavern keeper yelled at them to take him upstairs. Kenjo listened, lifting him up and following after him to a designated room. Vallarya came in seconds later with a bucket of water and rags. Arlo and Kaldana eventually made their way to the room, finding the two of them tending to the boy. Moving toward the window, Arlo peeked through the blinds and watched the silent town.

"When did he stumble in that the guards didn't notice him?" asked Arlo.

"I think this whole little incident you caused had them all focused on you that they forgot about the gates," said Kenjo. "Just look out back...or downstairs."

"Uh-huh. Well, I can tell you one thing. Our little mystery boy came from Gonall."

"What makes you say that?"

"The scars on his arms. That pattern of three cuts going from hand to shoulder. That's how they mark their prisoners. Reminder of their property, but a boy that young escaping them seems nigh impossible. Unless he has a ridiculous amount of luck."

As they finished cleaning his wounds, the barkeep came in with bandages so they could wrap up the wounds. Once he was bandaged, Vallarya put her hands on his. A gentle gold light emitted from hers, sending pulsing waves radiating through his body. He was still breathing, but he was not moving.

"You know healing magic?" asked Kaldana, hopping to her side, eyes wide in amazement.

"Only a little," she replied as the light faded. "Just enough to help the flesh mend."

"That's still incredible! So few actually know it outside the churches."

Arlo walked away from the window and headed toward the door. "I'll be downstairs if you have any other questions. Otherwise, I wish you good luck with the boy," he said as he passed by them. Once he was in the door frame, he glanced over his shoulder and looked at Kenjo. "Thank you for stopping me from killing that guard."

"Ah, he actually said thank you," giggled Vallarya as she wiped her hands on her skirt. "He doesn't seem too bad after all. I got us rooms, by the way, Kenjo, so we can actually sleep in a bed. The boy should be fine. Goodnight, Kaldana."

Vallarya left the room, leaving Kenjo and Kaldana alone with the boy. She was still fixated on the healing light that was pulsing beneath the bandages. Once they had all died out, she stretched and headed for the door. A firm hand grasped her shoulder, stopping her in place.

"No, no," said Kenjo, "you're staying right here with him."

"Excuse me, what?" she nearly yelled, turning around to face him. "He's not my problem."

"No, but as we are friends, it's time for your share of duties."

Kenjo's serious face left Kaldana unable to fight back. With a pout, she took a seat in a chair next to the bed. Crossing her arms in front of her, she growled at him until he left, a smile on his face as he closed the door.

*****

When morning came, the boy had finally woken up. He sat up with such force Kaldana thought he was going to do a flip out of the bed. Immediately falling back, clutching his sides in pain, he turned his head to look at her through half closed eyes.

"S-Sister?" he asked. "M… Mary is that you?"

"Oh, goodie, you're delusional," replied Kaldana. She stood up and swung open the door. "*Kenjo!*" she screamed loud enough for the entire tavern to hear her. "*Kenjo!* The boy's awake!"

A door opened, and he stepped out into the hallway. His hair was a mess. She found it odd seeing him out of his armor, just wearing a normal white cloth shirt and pants.

"Why are you yelling?" he asked through gritted teeth. "We are not the only ones here."

"Thought you would like to know. You didn't tell me where you were sleeping. Otherwise, I would have come woken you up quietly."

Kaldana stepped to the side to allow him to pass. Kenjo walked into the room and found the boy with the blankets up underneath his nose, shaking in fear as he came closer to him. Taking a seat, he smiled at him.

"It's all right," he said, "no need to be afraid. What's your name?"

The boy only shook more, pulling the blanket up to cover his head. He remained silent.

"You're great at this," said Kaldana, bursting into laughter. "Oh, I bet she's better at this. Good morning, Vallarya!"

Vallarya stepped into the room and took a seat on the bed. With a shrug, Kenjo got up and left the room. Minutes passed, and he eventually returned to the room with a large tray of food in his hands. The boy was still under the covers as the smell began to fill the room. Kaldana's mouth began to water at the sight as he placed it down at the corner table.

"Are you hungry?" asked Kenjo, slapping Kaldana's wrist as she reached for the food. "If so, I've got plenty here. Eat with us."

The blankets slowly lowered until his face was revealed. He glanced over at the food, his hungry eyes widening as they moved side to side, looking at the options. Trying to get out of bed, he swung a leg out. Groaning in pain, he pulled it back in and began to rub it.

"Don't worry about moving," said Vallarya. "You're really hurt. What looks good to you? I can dish you up."

The boy pointed weakly at the food. First at the eggs, then the toast, and then at an apple at the end. Vallarya gathered them all up on a plate and offered it to him. He took it without a second thought. In mere seconds, it was gone, and the plate had been licked clean.

"T-that was impressive," said Kenjo.

The boy blushed in embarrassment at the comment. "What's your name?"

"Elijah."

"And what are you doing here? Where's your family?"

"Looking for help. My sister and I were captured by bandit's when we entered Gonall's land. When we saw the castle destroyed, we didn't know what to do. One of the other prisoners helped me escape, and I ran as fast as I could. My mother and father are at home. They don't even know where we are."

"I'm so sorry to hear that," said Vallarya. "Is your sister still there?"

"She... She should be. Along with all the others."

"How many do you think?"

"Maybe thirty, I don't really know."

"Looks like we're going to Gonall after all, Val," said Kenjo as he stood up and went back to his room to grab his gear. Throwing on his armor, he checked over everything before fastening his sword to his back. He returned to the room and stopped in the doorway as he noticed all of the eyes on him.

"What do you mean you're going there?" asked Elijah.

Kenjo looked at him blinking a few times, a sparkle now shining in the boy's previously dull eyes.

"There's people in need, bandits running amok, taking prisoners. Something that sounds just up my alley to take care of. Come on, you two."

"W-wait I have to go?" asked Kaldana, pointing at herself. "Why do I have—"

"Because we all have to be out of here," he said, cutting her off before heading downstairs. "Plus, you were just going to follow us anyways."

Kaldana sighed as she chased after him. Vallarya looked to Elijah and smiled at him. Standing up to leave, something grabbed her hand. Looking down, she found Elijah clinging to it.

"We'll speak to the tavern keep to make sure you can stay here until we come back. When you see us again, we'll be with your sister."

"You…you promise?"

"A hero's promise, Elijah. Take care now."

The three of them headed downstairs and found Arlo sitting at the bar, eating. Approaching him, they found he had changed into some fresh clothes and had some actual armor on. Though it was still not gear-worthy of a prince, it was nonetheless better than any of the gear the guards of Caprae had.

"Arlo," said Kenjo, "we're going to Gonall."

Arlo spat his food at the words and looked toward them. "What did you just say?"

"We're going to Gonall. The boy we helped, Elijah, he says there were around thirty prisoners there, including his sister. We're not going to let that stand. Do you want to come?"

Looking into their eyes, Arlo knew there was no lie in his words. He looked to the two girls who only shrugged and nodded. Their eyes, however, burned with the same determination as his. "Yeah. It was my home after all. Plus, you'll probably need me."

"Glad to have you."

8

The sun was beginning to set when the group finally reached the mountains that formed the southern border of Gonall. The dirt road they traveled along had been carved through the mountains long ago, worn down rocks towering over each side. Once on the other side, Arlo led them along the western side off the beaten path and toward a house in the distance. It was in his mind to find cover for the night and, as a prince, figured the owners may be willing to help.

As they got closer, the layout of the land and house came to resemble a farm. Arlo hopped off his horse and walked to the door. Kaldana's ears twitched under her hood. Her attention pulled away to a rustling bush from a field nearby. It went still, and she shrugged, turning back to find Arlo talking to a man in the door frame. He waved to them, and the group dismounted.

"Hey, Kenjo," said Kaldana, handing her horse's reins to him, "can you take care of her for me? There's something I want to check."

"Um, sure," replied Kenjo, taking them from her. "Be quick."

"Will do."

Kaldana ran off as Kenjo and Vallarya tied their horses up to the wooden rails set up along the porch, handing them a small snack before heading inside to join Arlo. He was sitting in a living room illuminated by candles on the wall. The owner of the house was sitting in a chair opposite him.

A scruffy beard covered his face. He eyed Kenjo and Vallarya as they came in and stood on each of Arlo's sides. He scratched his head of thinning hair.

"Well, my young guest, we had originally left Gonall after the fall. But after some time, we decided to come back and check on the farm. Seeing that it was untouched, we started living here again, the Samilian army nowhere in sight."

"Have you not reached out to anyone about what happened?" asked Arlo.

The man shifted. His eyes darted to the kitchen then back to him. "We were forced to flee. We came back and just started getting our lives back to normal. Surely there would have been others, including yourself, that could have reached out."

"I-I was recovering," said Arlo, gripping the arms of the chair tighter. "If it wasn't for bandits constantly trying to attack me, I would have recovered sooner. Don't worry, I'll be letting the kings know what is going on. And little by little, things will go back to normal. Hopefully."

"Ah, thank you. You're truly worthy of your title, Prince!"

Arlo's body went limp. His eyes fixated on the man as if he was burning a hole into him. "I never said I was a prince."

"Of course you did!" he exclaimed. His eyes darted to the kitchen, then back to the three. "When you introduced yourself."

"No, I—"

The door busted open as Kaldana and a man came crashing through. Purple flames enveloping her gauntlets, she pushed her hands against the man's face, his screams of pain muffled by the palms covering his mouth.

"Kaldana, what the hell?" asked Arlo hopping up.

The man across from them rushed at him, a dagger in hand. Vallarya moved, grabbing the man's wrist before the dagger could contact her unaware friend. Kenjo followed her, delivering a swift blow to the man's face and taking him off his feet.

"What is this?" asked Arlo as he turned around at the sound of his body hitting the ground, turning back just in time to see someone rush at him from the kitchen.

A cork shot out from one of the vials and struck him in the nose. Thrown off balance, Arlo took the time to draw his sword and run it through him before he could recover. He lifted up the man's sleeve and revealed the same tattoo the men who attacked him in the bar had.

"They're here..." said Arlo. "I knew I shouldn't have believed he was a survivor."

"Had it not happened like that, I would have warned you guys about the fields," said Kaldana. "The crops are all dead. The soil is poor too. None of it has been maintained. But, oh well, looks like we had to get this place all messy."

"With them taken care of. however. It means we can rest here. Let's just make sure the house is empty. Kenjo. do you mind taking first watch?"

"Sure. that's not a problem," he replied. "Are you all right?"

"Of course!" Arlo exclaimed, walking away and into the kitchen to double check for any others.

The night was peaceful as they rested. Kenjo remained on watch until Arlo switched with him so he could sleep. In the morning, Arlo was the first one up and immediately ran outside with his breakfast in his mouth.

Arlo searched along the ground as the rest kept watch. His foot stomped at various places until he felt the faint echo from the hollow ground beneath. Lifting the gray grass slab that covered the hatch, he revealed a large hole with a wooden rope ladder, checking the stakes that anchored it to make sure it could support his weight before preparing to descend.

Kenjo heard something move. Turning around, an arrow flashed into his vision. A shadowy limb reached out of his chest and caught it, the tip of the arrow stopping right before hitting between his eyes.

"That was close," said Vallarya, tossing it aside. "Watch out!"

Kenjo rolled out of the way as another two pierced into the ground where he was. A lone archer knelt atop the farmhouse. Nocking another arrow, it was loosed a second later. Kenjo swatted it away, his gaze unmoving from his attacker.

They weren't dressed like any of the other bandits. Concealed beneath black armor and a cloak, a scarf pulled up around their lower face, white stripes running vertically along it, purple bangs could be seen covering their forehead. A stream of ash crashed into the roof where they were forcing them off before it returned to Arlo.

As they landed, Kaldana was on top of them, swinging unarmed, emerald green gauntlets gleaming in the sunlight with each attack. The archer dodged nimbly; for the attacks they couldn't, they used their bow to deflect it. Throwing her off balance before knocking her to the ground with a swift blow against her head, the archer knocked an arrow and pointed it at her head.

Kenjo tackled them from behind. The arrow flew, striking the ground right next to Kaldana's head. With a breath of relief, she hopped back to her feet as Kenjo rendered the archer unconscious with a swift beating to the head.

"There's no way that was a bandit," said Kaldana.

"It doesn't' matter," replied Kenjo. "Arlo, are we good?"

"Yeah, the ladder's secure," he replied. "If you're not going to kill them, at least tie 'em up. I don't want an arrow hitting my back now."

Kenjo nodded. Pulling some rope from his pack, he bound the archer and left them there before joining the other two in the tunnel, closing the hatch behind them, leaving nothing but an undisturbed ground. The tunnel was pitch black. Kaldana clanked her lanterns together, and the purple flames inside went ablaze, illuminating the path ahead of them.

They walked the tunnel for the next two days, keeping an eye on their watches to keep track of the time of day above them. The two days in the tunnel were quiet. It had seemed that no one had discovered the tunnels themselves and that the ones they left alive on top had no idea where they had disappeared to.

Arlo had said that these tunnels spread out in multiple directions from the keep, all leading to the outskirts in case an evacuation was ever necessary. It was these very tunnels that any and all survivors of the fall of his kingdom would have used. And even though he had not met any in Caprae, he held out hope they were out there hiding on their own.

A disgusting smell filled the air. The low buzzing could be heard ahead of them. They found themselves covering their noses as they trudged ahead, the stench becoming stronger with each step. Kaldana froze in place, causing those following behind her light to stop as well.

"What is it?" asked Kenjo from beneath his hands. He peered over her shoulder, squinting to try and make out what made her stop.

"Bodies," she whispered. The flames burned brighter, bringing into view the mass grave that lay before them.

Arlo stepped forward sluggishly, his feet barely leaving the ground. He collapsed to his knees, his arms shaking as he reached out to the dead. "How?" he asked weakly. "How could this have happened? I led them to the tunnels myself before I joined in the battle. No one followed… No one should have known…"

"Arlo," said Kenjo, placing a hand on his shoulder, "we need to keep moving. We need to rescue those that we still can. Prevent any more from joining them down here."

Arlo said nothing as Kenjo helped him to his feet, following them without another word as Kaldana led them the rest of the way. Stepping over the bodies in an effort to not disturb them, Kenjo clenched his fists. He was just walking through another reason to hate the people who ruled Samil, another truth kept out of the textbooks at the academies.

Finally reaching the ladder, Kenjo climbed up and strained against it as he pushed it open. The hatch hit with a thud, and the sound of a bell could be heard ringing as a chorus of humming filled the air. Making sure no one was around, he stepped onto the ground above and helped the others up to join him.

"Did the alarms just sound?" asked Vallarya. "Where's all the bandits?"

Kenjo led the group out from the alleyway. All around them was nothing but rubble. Buildings were caved in or entirely destroyed. Their components scattered about, littering the streets. The walls could barely be called that. The large holes torn in them from the siege were still present, the ash plains stretching out before them as they peered through.

"This place is deserted," said Kaldana, pushing over a brick. A tattered flag of Gonall was beneath it—two hands placed together on what she believed was ash falling between the fingers while more of it rose above into a ball. "You guys have a weird emblem."

"It's not weird when you grow up underneath that emblem," said Arlo as he continued on. "It's supposed to be like a cycle. The hands of the youth shape the ash into what they will while the bodies of the old are burned to ash to be used. Their souls release from their bounds into the After."

Passing into the courtyard, the memories of the blue metal-winged Angel-born flashed into his mind. The deaths of his companions all replayed themselves over and over again. Kenjo felt tears form in his eyes. As they slid down, he wiped them away. He was beginning to feel the same feelings as Arlo. Vallarya wanted to comfort him but felt the same sadness building up inside her as well.

"I thought we weren't supposed to feel from just seeing them," said Vallarya. "Why are we feeling this?"

"I don't know," replied Kenjo, noticing him trudging onwards. They followed him to the keep.

From the memories, they could piece the walls back together, but with a blink, they returned to normal—a door hanging on one hinge, the other buried beneath stone. With weighted steps, Arlo climbed the steps to the throne room. Sadness and the sense of failure welling within him dispersed at once, replaced with a burning hatred as he noticed the throne had been replaced, the sun bearing down on the back of the new throne's owner.

A white bell was at his side being rung by a bandit. He stopped when he noticed them enter. The humming continued on as the others stepped into the room. Their eyes made their way to where it was coming from. A massive being of solid muscle relaxed on a throne of hides.

Numerous scars covered his body. Two large ones covered his chest in the shape of an X, while smaller ones adorned his side and collar. Armored gauntlets and greaves adorned the rest of his body while his head was covered by a large metal skull. Bear pelts were tied around his waist, and his left hand fingered a large mace. The humming came to a rhythmic stop as he finished his tune.

"I can tell my men were worthless," he said. "Even that archer the sovereign left for us."

"That throne doesn't belong to you," said Arlo, drawing his broadsword. "Get your ass out of it now."

"If you insist, I'll stand, only because I can't kill you three if I just sit here."

As he stood up, all of them felt their hearts begin to race. When he was sitting, it did not do justice to the man who towered above them. With a single step, they felt the ground tremble beneath his weight, tremors following every one after.

"What the hell is a giant doing here?" asked Kaldana. "I thought they remained in Ivofir!"

And when he began to run, it felt like an earthquake went off. Leaping out of the way, Kenjo drew his sword. The mace crashed down where they were, leaving an impact crater where it hit. The three moved to surround him, forming a triangle around him.

"I don't sense any magic coming from him," said Vallarya.

Arlo popped all the corks out of his vials and began to swirl the ash around him. Kenjo stepped in behind his foe and prepared to strike at his leg when he kicked backward with one foot like a mule. It collided with his chest, sending him flying into the remainder of the wall next to the throne. He pushed himself out as the giant became enveloped in ash.

An ear-bursting shout erupted from inside the ash, causing it all to be scattered to the ground. The man, unfazed, turned his attention to Arlo and began to attack. The shaking ground didn't help when he was trying to dodge. Each moment, he drew closer and closer to slipping until he finally did. The man raised his mace above his head and brought it down on the hard ground as Arlo barely rolled out of the way.

"I retract my previous statement, Kenjo," said Vallarya. "That was definitely magic that only a Kryzen could muster."

"Well, that's good to know," he groaned. His entire core was in pain from the hit. "Are you doing okay?"

"I'm not in any pain. But I can only make one limb now while maintaining full embrace with you. I'm sorry. I wasn't expecting that kick."

"Don't be sorry. That was far quicker than I expected too. He's not in a good spot anymore to step to either. Let's try and save the prince."

Kenjo ran forward as Arlo continued to dodge the man's swings. Even as Kryzen, the enemy before them had physical strength beyond theirs. Sliding between his legs, Kenjo swung his sword, cutting through the metal greaves like butter and slicing through some of the flesh underneath.

Looking down, he noticed the blood dripping as the man stumbled a moment, taking in what happened. Kaldana and Arlo went in to attack while he was off balance. Before they could hit him. another shout erupted from him, sending both Arlo and Kaldana backward.

"Are the shouts his magic?" asked Kenjo.

"It's anti-magic. That's why we can't sense it. I can't make any more limbs now. Another hit, and we won't be fully embraced anymore. Arlo's ash isn't responding to him anymore."

"Arlo! Kaldana, are you okay?"

"No," said Arlo, getting up. "Do I look okay to you, pushing myself off the ground like I did?"

"Well…you could at least get up. That's something."

"Bite me," Arlo responded as he jumped out of the way of another swing. As the man was pulling his mace from the ground, he ran forward and attacked the leg Kenjo hit earlier. Cutting into the opening, he began to weaken it even further and could hear him grunt in pain.

Kenjo stepped into a shadow and met Kaldana at his unharmed leg. Blade and a flaming fist dug into it. He shouted again, this time severing the embrace between Kenjo and Vallarya. The black armor from the embrace was gone, but Vallarya remained inside of him.

Arlo hit against rubble as Kaldana hit her back against the steps of the throne. Both could only watch as their foe approached Kenjo. Towering over him, unfazed by his wounds, he raised his mace high and prepared to bring it down.

"Can you give me gauntlets still?"

"Yes."

The shadows lined up as he raised his arms. Kenjo stepped and stood on his shoulder as the mace demolished where he previously was. "I feel like he needs to get a new weapon. He can't hit a damn thing with that mace." Kenjo stabbed his sword into the giant's shoulder, forcing him to drop the mace he grasped at him with his other hand. Jumping off, Kenjo ran forward before he could react and took a full swing at his right leg, severing the connection between leg and foot.

As he fell down, he balanced himself up on his knees and his good arm. Kenjo stabbed his sword into the ground and ran forward. He placed both hands on his head, peering into the empty sockets of the skull helmet as black and gold lines of energy began to spin around them.

*****

The giant man before him was named Maximus, born to a father and mother who even dwarfed him. In the northern continent, he was raised among the giants. When they discovered he was a Kryzen, they decided Zell would be the best place for him to be raised. And at the age of five, he arrived on the shores with his parents and, shortly thereafter, started a life in a small village a little further inland. Once he was old enough, they would bring him to the capital and present him to the king and find him a place worthy of his talents.

But that day would never come. When he was twelve, his village was attacked by a dragon. It was in his anger on that day that he began to understand exactly what his magic was and why his seemed so different from others like him. For even the flames of the dragon dissipated upon his shouts. Picking up his father's mace from where he died, he moved forward as the dragon continuously breathed fire. When it finally stopped, Maximus stood before him and, with a swing, dislodged his jaw and sent him staggering, attempting to fly away, knowing there was no chance to beat him. He flapped his wings once before another shout filled the air, and it began to lock up, looking down at him with fear that betrayed the appearance of a dragon.

Maximus crushed his skull into a pulp before returning to his parents' bodies and collapsing next to them in tears. Shortly thereafter, he met a wandering party from Samil. They took him in, offered him a place to live, and eventually took him to Samil. And it was here that Maximus, The Dragon Slayer, would lose everything that he was.

He met a Finger who never mentioned her name but who also specialized in anti-magic, making him respect, admire, and aspire to be like her. Her blue hair was a guiding light in the years that followed. It was odd to the two looking at his memories, for no memories of night ever appeared. It was only those of his time in the day. Eventually, though, he snuck out one night and stumbled upon a room that looked as much like a torture room as it did a scientist's lab.

In one of the books, he discovered sketches of himself from countless experiments they had done, one of the first sketches of which was noted after the effects of memory wipe. In a fit of rage, he trashed the lab with a shout more powerful than the one he used to disrupt the dragon's magic. Running off into the night, he made a break for it.

It took only two hours for the guards to find him, though they themselves could not apprehend him. Ten guards were killed before his teacher was able to make it to him. Beginning to cry at the sight of her, he lowered his guard to let her approach. Then before he noticed what was happening, he felt his body weakening as she used her magic on him. And once again, the memory cut out. The next time he was awake, he was in his bed. And memories of day were all they could see again.

Each day from then on seemed to get more and more violent. He began to show more ferocity in combat and began to garner a following of friends and admirers. It was shortly after this it was decided to send him back to Zell. There he became a bandit, created his group known as the Skull Scabbard, and began raiding and pillaging villages for over the past fifteen years.

But the way he did it made him seem more like ghost story more than anything, attacking only every so often not to draw the eyes of the kings, and hiding out in the hills or forests until he felt the time was right again to strike.

After the fall of Gonall, an envoy of Samil came and gave him a letter, telling him the ruins were now his to rule over to protect and watch, to become a set of eyes for them. The envoy did two more things in this, one giving him the silver skull helmet he now wore, while also taking his most able soldiers and leaving behind an archer who would help him defend. During this time of raiding, he was tasked with finding more to join his ranks, and every couple of months, the envoy would return to collect them.

Kenjo began to wonder if he set up Maximus to fail or if he believed in his strength that much that even green recruits would be just as effective with him and that archer. Before they arrived, he had taken more recruits resulting in Gonall being as undefended as it was. As the memories continued, they saw the terrible treatment of Elijah and the other prisoners. They also watched as he removed an eye from one of them for speaking out against him.

Then they arrived at today and Kenjo found himself back in reality. Maximus was breathing heavily as his blood began to pool underneath them. He was unable to move, his body shaking as it started to give out on him. Kenjo felt control of his body taken from him; his right eye engulfed in golden flame. With a will of its own his body moved towards his sword.

Kenjo yanked his sword from the earth and without another word embedded it in his enemy's metal skull. Pulling the sword free, he hopped back to give the giant enough room to fall, no longer moving. Wiping the blade clean on the bear pelts he sheathed the sword, the light dimmed, and his eye returned to normal as he regained control. Looking to Maximus, his hands began to shake.

"Are you okay?" Arlo asked as he placed a hand on his shoulder. "Watching you Hands work is the strangest thing, no matter how many times I have seen it back in the court. Though I must admit this is the first time I've ever seen it on the battlefield."

"I... I don't know," replied Kenjo as he stood up. "I... I don't think I wanted to kill him, not after seeing his memories. He was just a victim of Samil. But the more I think about it like that, the more I just hear this voice saying it was okay. It was necessary..."

"Uh-huh... Well, that sounds like crazy talk for those who have the Hands. When we get to the capital, we can find another one who uses the Hands to have a chat with you. But for now, let's focus on what's in front of us."

"He's dead, though, shouldn't we focus instead on the prisoners?"

Kenjo's words fell on deaf ears as he watched Arlo bring his sword to Maximus's neck. Raising it high, he brought it down, sheathing his blade. Arlo stretched before beginning to drag the head through the ruins as they went back out to the courtyard to find the prisoners.

"What... What the hell are you doing?" asked Vallarya as she split from Kenjo.

"Taking my...our trophy."

"Excuse me?"

"Oh, right, you're Samilian. Guess they didn't teach this to either of you in school," Arlo began to grunt in between his words as he found the head to be far heavier than he originally thought. "Basically, power, might...that kind of thing, means a lot here. Trophies, heads, they are great symbols of respect to be shown off, especially the head of a giant like this fella. So as disrespectful or disgusting as it may look to you...to me, this is quite normal."

"Gross."

"Indeed. Now let's go get those prisoners. I really don't want to be here any longer than needs be."

The four of them eventually found them locked behind cages where the markets used to be. They began to cheer as they saw Arlo's trophy and began thanking them all with tear-filled eyes. Handshakes and hugs came from all of them. Checking over each of them to make sure they could still walk and had no open wounds, Kenjo made his way down the line until he met the girl who lost her eye.

Her dress was ragged and torn at the bottom right above her ankles. Dirty bandages covered the right side of her face where her eye once was. Frizzy shoulder-length brown hair helped hide some of the scars she had along her neck and shoulders.

"Excuse me," he said, "you don't happen to know an Elijah, do you?"

She perked up, her eyes filled with questions as she looked at him. "I have a little brother with that name... Is he...?"

"He's perfectly fine. Well, he was when we left. He's the reason we're here now. I'm sure he'll be excited to see you."

Tears filled her eyes as she hugged him. The happiness she felt overfilled her. It had been some of the worst months of her life, and they were finally coming to an end. "Thank you so much!" she said as she pulled away from him and joined the other prisoners who were ready to leave.

"Oh, we're getting everybody today, aren't we?" said Arlo as he looked at the archer who was standing in the way with her bow drawn. "Look, he's clearly dead, just let us pass by, and you can go about your sad excuse of a life serving Samil."

The archer eased up on the bow as his words filled her ears. Seeing Kenjo pop up from behind the head, he instantly drew back again, taking aim between his eyes like he did when they first encountered each other.

"You know you tried that once already," he said as he felt Vallarya merge back into him. "Do you really want to go through that again?"

Vallarya waited to grab the arrow the moment it came close. But the arrow never came. The archer lowered his bow, placing the arrow back in his quiver, and his bow around his body. He walked up to him, as he did so Arlo moved his hand to the hilt of his blade, about to draw it. He let go as the archer kneeled before Kenjo.

"I surrender," he said, a feminine voice coming from beneath the mask. She looked up at Kenjo with bright blue eyes. "And I ask to have a place in your service."

"Excuse me?" asked Kenjo.

"You three killed Maximus and beat everyone else on the way here. I failed, they failed…there is no life to return to after this. Even with you sparing me, I do not have a life to live for my failure if I go back. So I ask of you, may I serve you? If you do not trust me, I understand, in which case—"

The archer reached out and grabbed Kenjo's hand. Vallarya began to form the armor around his arm as Arlo drew his sword. The archer guided his hand to her forehead.

"Read my memories, like you can with everyone else. If you cannot trust me after that, then crush my head in your hand."

"You two looked at me like I was weird," said Kaldana from behind them. "But that one, I would say, is really the weird one."

Kenjo's hand shook for a second in hers. But the archer seemed to not notice it, her eye unmoving from his. Vallarya separated from his body and pulled her hands away from his, taking them in her own.

"If you're willing to do that," she said as she pulled him up, "you're no enemy of ours."

"Did you even—"

"No," said Kenjo before she could finish her sentence. "We didn't read your memories. You want to serve us. You willingly placed a hand that could kill you on your head. I don't see the need. But do be warned, you slip up once and bring any harm to us, you will wish you went back to Samil."

Kenjo beckoned to Arlo, and the two began to push the head again. Vallarya led the group on the journey back to town. It would be a couple of days, but they were able to split their supplies spread out enough to help everyone. The archer turned out to be incredibly useful in these days as she returned with game for them to eat at night, leaving their original supplies for the daylight hours if someone was hungry or thirsty.

When they got back to town, the prisoners all headed for the inn, save for the archer who remained at their side like a guard dog. She followed the three of them as they put their horses in the stable.

"So…is there a reason you're pushing this head?" asked the archer, her first words since pledging her services.

"Bringing it before the kings of Zell," said Arlo. "Trophies are important to us here. This is a good one, especially with this interesting skull helmet. Now I have a question for you. Now that we're back in town, do you know how they did it?"

"Who did what?"

"How they got through Gonall the way they did. There was no way it could have been possible, not bandits. Not the Samilian military, not the way they did."

"Well…"

The five of them made their way back to the tavern and found Elijah and his sister having a teary-eyed reunion. When he saw them, he sprinted over and shook their hands, saying, "Thank you" over and over again, never thinking that the previous one was enough. The town guards headed over due to the large commotion. They soon returned to their duties as they heard their story and saw the head of Maximus staring at them on the outside.

"What do you mean they betrayed us?" yelled Arlo as he slammed a table.

Kenjo and Vallarya looked across to find him talking with the archer.

"Burrium, the kingdom of Iron," the archer repeated, unfazed by Arlo's outburst. "It's Samil's now."

9

15th of Japhim; Mortal Year 523

Kenjo

Kenjo ate his food slowly as he stared across at the group of people sitting at his table. Vallarya and Arlo he expected. But deep down, he had hoped Kaldana and the archer, Luna, would have left them by now. Kaldana stayed simply, as she put it, "to see the things that they would get up to;" she was fascinated by them. And any attempt Kenjo made at trying to get her to leave was brushed aside.

As for Luna, she was adamant about her oath she made to them back in the ruins, swearing to go wherever it is they went. He didn't have much problem with her, however. Luna was quiet and only spoke when she was spoken to, giving little room for added conversation. Her light-brown hair reached to her shoulder blades. Bright red bangs reached down to her cheeks. As they finished eating, she gathered up all of their dishes and took them to the tavern counter.

Today was the day they were leaving. Kenjo and Vallarya couldn't have been happier. Arlo was on edge, though. Ever since Luna told him about the Burrium's betrayal, he had been in a fit of rage. Had Kenjo not stopped him that night, he would have left then. But with a few words and the aching in his body, he was brought back to reality, facing the fact he was not in the shape yet to make that kind of travel alone.

Instead of leaving during the night, Arlo spent his time in his room, thinking of what he would do to make the king suffer. If what Luna said was true, that was. Truthfully, Arlo didn't want to believe her. She was the enemy, without a doubt. But the more she spoke of it, and after seeing that the ones who escaped into the tunnels were butchered, he believed it more and more. He was the first to leave the tavern and went to the stables where the stable owner had fitted his horse with a wagon to carry Maximus's head for them.

When the others arrived, they found him loading everyone else's horses. Noticing them, he yelled for them to hurry up, motioning wildly with his hands before paying the stable master and hopping onto his own horse. Arlo led the group out the gates and back toward Gonall. The day treated them well, scattered clouds dotting a blue sky. A cool breeze blew against them as they traveled the day away.

At night, they took turns keeping watch so the others could sleep, though Luna always volunteered to do it when it was someone else's turn. After a couple of nights like this, Kenjo decided to do something about it and ordered her to sleep. She wanted to object, but she never said anything. Instead, she bowed and walked away. Luna went and lay by the campfire as Kenjo took over for her.

They were now resting at the outskirts past Gonall. Arlo asked that they didn't spend the night in the ruins unless it was raining. Respecting his wishes, the group traveled a few miles north of it, setting up camp on a hill that rose up as high as the walls once stood. Kenjo gazed out in the direction they were heading. Before him lay plains and rolling hills as far as he could see.

"Hey, Arlo," asked Vallarya as the group was eating dinner. "Back in Samil, we were taught that the land was gray here, and in your memories, you grew up playing along the gray plains. So why is the grass beginning to turn green?"

"Because the weavers are no more," he replied. His voice was distant. He placed his plate down and tore up some of the grass beside him, lifting it up to his face to examine it in the light of the campfire. "With no one left to maintain it, the land is returning to normal. The ash lands will be just another plain by year's end."

Arlo tossed the grass away and went to sleep. Vallarya and the others looked on at him with sadness. Kenjo felt something growing in his chest; it was another part of the world Samil was ruining. Even though they had left the land after the battle, they had scarred it beyond repair. He wished there was something he could do as he took a seat on the edge of the camp, taking first watch.

The plains below were shrouded in the dark, and it began to remind him of the darkness that surrounded his parents. He was half attempting to step away from the camp, stepping and stepping until his body wouldn't anymore without hurting him. Approaching footsteps stopped that idea. Kaldana took a seat next to him and tried to figure out where he was looking.

"Hmm, I don't see anything interesting out there," she said, squinting her eyes. "Not a thing."

A heavy sigh came from Kenjo before he spoke. "Why aren't you asleep?"

"Not tired, bored really. Everyone else is asleep. Saw you alone out here. Thought you might like some company."

"You should get so—" He stopped as he turned to look at her. She was holding the purple flames from her lantern in her lap. They danced around her palms, laughing as she tossed them up. The flames didn't burn her nor did her clothes catch fire.

"What was that?" she asked, turning to him, the flames landing back in her hands.

"N-Nothing," he said, entranced by her and the flames. "Can you not feel them?"

"They are warm and gentle. Not to my enemies, though. And I can assure you that creature you killed back then felt the flames before you arrived. But like this, when there is no enemy around, they only want to be friends."

Kenjo thought of his parents fighting Lucios. "What kind of weapon is that exactly, Kaldana?"

"A Blade of the Mother," she replied.

Kenjo's heart skipped a beat, the conversation he listened to between Baxter and his parents playing over in his mind. "Samil's hunting for them…"

"They sure are, and this was theirs to begin with. Boy, will they be upset when they realize it." She burst out in a laughter as she opened the lanterns and let the flames go back inside. "It was always meant for me to begin with…"

"What do you mean?" Kenjo asked, surprise filling his face.

Kaldana didn't reply. Instead, she just shook her head and gazed up at the moon, her ears twitching underneath her hood. Figuring she wouldn't give him an answer, he changed the subject. "Tell me why a Muzilian is here."

She glanced over at him. With a smile, she looked back to the moon. "Long story short, I snuck onto one of the ships heading out here from back east. I wanted what was rightfully mine and followed them here. Blah, blah, blah, here we are. Back home, people aren't very kind to Muzilians of any kind. This was a sort of freedom on its own, but even here, I don't want to put my hood down. Had you not tied me up and made me defenseless, I would never have let you in the first place."

Kenjo leaned back on his elbows to prop himself, turning his gaze to the moon as well. "You don't have to keep it up around us you know."

"I'm more comfortable this way," Kaldana replied, lying back. She placed her hands behind her head, her eyes following a cloud as it passed over the moon.

"You should take it down once in a while"

"Why? You got a thing for girls with wolf ears or something? I didn't take you for that kind of guy. But then again, now that I think about it, maybe you do have a thing for more exotic girls. I mean, Vallarya has some very interesting eyes." She burst into laughter once again as his face turned red.

Her laughter cut off abruptly as she began to sniff the air. A new scent filled her nostrils as her nose guided her upright. Looking around, she pinpointed the direction and hopped to her feet. Kenjo watched her, trying to figure out how much of an animal she was really like.

She was like a hound on the chase, Kenjo reluctantly following behind in case it was to be something serious. At the bottom of the hill, they found a lone horse eating away at something. It wasn't one of theirs. Two small bags were attached to its saddles.

"This smells slightly familiar," said Kaldana as she got closer. "This definitely came from Caprae. Though I don't remember anyone leaving shortly after us."

The two were at the horse now and began going through the bags—traveling rations, a change of clothes for a man and a woman. Though, judging by the size of the clothes, the man was smaller. Kenjo held up the shirt close to Kaldana and figured he was barely taller than her. When she noticed what he was doing, she snatched the shirt and stuffed it back in the bag with a scowl.

Kenjo laughed before looking around the horse once more.

"It wasn't that funny," Kaldana growled.

"Who are you talking to?" he asked, confused.

"You! You were still laughing!"

"I stopped laughing before I got to the other side of the horse." As he finished, he began to hear the laughing too before it stopped, its owner realizing they had been caught. "Kaldana, you don't smell anything else, do you?"

She sniffed the air and took a couple steps closer to the hill. Her foot hit something, and she tripped. Kenjo ran to her and helped her up. She held out one of her lanterns in front of her. The flame began to burn brighter, illuminating the ground around them. There was a lone blanket covering what appeared to be lumps on the ground.

"Get out of there," barked Kenjo.

The blanket sat motionless, and not a peep could be heard coming from it. "I'll say it again. Get out from underneath there or we'll set you on fire."

"We will?" asked Kaldana, looking to him, confused.

Kenjo glared daggers at her. "Play along," he whispered.

"Come out from under there or I'll cook you up for dinner!"

130

Kaldana looked to him with a smile and a thumbs up from her free hand. Kenjo only sighed as his hand covered his face.

It was enough, however, to get the two figures hiding under the blanket to come out, standing up at attention, waiting for them to say something in silence. They were scared stiff, their eyes focused skyward, refusing to make eye contact with Kenjo as he got closer.

Kaldana held the light a little closer to their faces, and the tenseness in Kenjo subsided in an instant as he saw who it was. Elijah and Mary were standing before them, both still awkwardly gazing to the sky as Kaldana and Kenjo stepped back to take in the sight.

"Care to explain to me why you two are here?" Kenjo asked, crossing his arms in front of him.

"*Oh!*" exclaimed Kaldana as she realized who they were. "It's the one-eyed prison girl!"

They finally tore their gaze away from the sky, looking first at each other, then finally at the two who found them. Elijah hesitated as he looked at the scowl forming on Kenjo's face. Taking a deep breath, he thought of what to say.

"We wanted to go to the capital and seek an audience with the kings," he began. "And since you guys were already heading off that way, we figured we would tag along behind, close enough to be safe with you guys around, but far enough for you not to realize we're here. Though we messed up that last bit."

"Why didn't you just ask before we left?" asked Kenjo as he rubbed his forehead.

"Thought you might say no… Can we stay?"

Kenjo walked off without another word. Heading back to the hill, he checked to see if everyone else was still asleep. Throwing another log on the fire, he moved to the edge of the hill and took a seat again, turning his direction back toward their destination.

"Uh…was that a yes? Or a no?"

"Dunno. We're gonna go with yes," replied Kaldana, beaming with life. "Grab your horse and follow me. We have a fire going. Find a nice spot near it so you two can stay warm tonight."

The two did as they were told and followed the cloaked girl up the hill to their spot. Tying the horse down near the others, Elijah and his sister, Mary, grabbed their blankets. Finding a spot next to the fire, they lay down and closed their eyes without another word. Kaldana, however, still refused to go to sleep and, much to Kenjo's annoyance, took a seat next to him again.

She didn't speak this time, though. Just sat there, quietly playing with the two flames. When the silence between them had gone on long enough, she spoke, "Hey, Kenjo, why didn't you give them an answer?"

"I didn't feel like wasting words on them. How long are they with us for?"

"Oh, seeing as you didn't give an answer, I did. So I said yes for you, and they'll be joining us all the way to the capital!" She smiled at him again.

Kenjo gritted his teeth. "Fine, fine. Vallarya probably would have argued for them to stay anyway. I expect you to watch after them both."

"But you're here. And so is Arlo and Luna. Aren't you strong enough to protect us all?"

"I'm not the one who willingly let them tag along," he said, glaring at her. "Plus, like you, they're just following someone they're impressed with."

Kaldana's mouth opened as she raised a finger to him. But she had no response. He had hit the nail on the head. She was only there because he had slain a creature of Nothingness. Going back to playing with the flames, she dropped the conversation.

"Are you a Kryzen, Kaldana?"

Her hood twitched at the question. The back of her cloak touching the grass moved back and forth slightly before resting. "Will something happen depending on my answer?"

"No. I just like to know who I'm traveling with."

"Why don't you just use your magic? You are a wielder of the Hands, aren't you?"

"I…" He stared down at his hands as he thought back to the moment he killed his parents and Maximus. Although it was hard for him to picture an alternative, no matter how many times he replayed the events in his head. Vallarya nor he had made those calls. "I honestly don't know anymore."

Kaldana eyed him, confused. Her head cocked to one side as she tried to figure out what he meant. "What do you mean you don't know?"

"It means I don't know if I really wanted to kill Maximus. We read his memories. He was just a tool, a boy made into a weapon by those bastards in the east. But something was telling us it was the right thing to do. We wanted to doubt it, but it just kept saying, 'Don't worry.' One less problem for the world to deal with. Our bodies acted before we could do anything about it."

"Is that why you didn't read Luna's memories then?"

"Y-Yeah. If someone didn't like what they saw... I feared what would have happened to her. I don't want more blood on my hands than necessary."

"Well, you got some problems I can't help with, don't ya? Man, traveling with you all is going to be quite the adventure, I can already tell!"

Kenjo wondered if she ever really took anything seriously. He did not know the answer, but something about the way she acted calmed him. Every one of them was serious about the next step they were taking. The world was on the brink of war, but here she was, bouncing fire in her hand with a smile on her face.

Placing the flames back in their lanterns, Kaldana stood up. Brushing off her cloak and skirt, she turned to walk back to the fire. "I am a Kryzen, Kenjo. And don't worry, I'll watch after those two until we get to the capital. Thanks for talking with me. Goodnight."

Kenjo continued his watch in silence. About two hours later, Arlo tapped his shoulder and switched out with him, allowing him to get some rest. Finding a spot next to Vallarya, he lay down on his side and quickly fell asleep, finding himself in the same darkness once more, wrapped in the tendrils along with his father.

The next morning, he explained the situation with their tag-along, and the group set off after breakfast. Arlo led them down the roads with Kenjo and Vallarya close behind. Elijah, Mary, and Kaldana filled out the middle with Luna being the eyes in the rear.

No one traveled the roads that led out of Gonall's territory. It was peaceful and quiet, yet at the same time, a wave of unease settled over them.

They passed into the northern mountains by dusk. The weather had changed drastically since their day began. Storm clouds hid the sun, and it was completely gray in all directions. When they felt it begin to sprinkle, they stopped and set up camp. Underneath a large rock sticking out the side of the mountain, they made a fire, and Vallarya began to cook dinner.

The rain picked up to a full-on downpour an hour later. Lightning streaked across the sky as thunder echoed through the mountains. Mary stayed close to the horses and kept each of them calm. She seemed to have a way with the animals. With just her hand and a few words, they calmed down instantly. Elijah brought her a bowl of the stew Vallarya made before returning to the group next to the fire.

"Well, this will put us behind a few hours," said Arlo as he finished off his stew. He took a swig of his waterskin before continuing. "Hopefully, this will all be cleared up before morning."

"Does it rain like this often around here?" asked Vallarya, pouring more stew into Kenjo's bowl and her own.

"During this time of the year, it's less common. Though for the most part, unless a Siv is involved, it doesn't last more than a couple hours."

"What's a Siv?"

"You guys don't have them in Samil?" he asked looking as if he couldn't believe what he had heard.

"I've never heard of them before. Anyone else?"

Luna, Kenjo, and Kaldana all shook their heads. Elijah and Mary, on the other hand, knew exactly what he was referring to. A Siv was a large bird-like creature with scales instead of feathers. Each scale looked as if it had a mini-storm raging inside of it. A large curved beak stretched out from its head. The tip of it shone like lightning. The beak was something collectors coveted, fetching ridiculous prices at auctions, and going for prices in stores that only the wealthiest could afford.

A Siv's scales, though, those were coveted by everyone else. Sturdy material, able to be melded into any armor from the simplest cloth to the heaviest plate. Craftsmen would spend their fortunes for your supply just to have a chance to make something out of them. Arlo went on to mention his father wore such a garment when he was younger. But it was lost some years prior to him being born, apparently in a battle he never went into detail on.

As dusk turned to night, the rain continued to pound away at the earth. Luna took first watch as the others set up their sleeping rolls and attempted to sleep, the thunder waking them up every time they closed their eyes as if on cue. Vallarya sat up at one point and found Kaldana shaking on the other side of the fire.

In an instant, she could tell it wasn't cold that was causing her to. For the thunder boomed again, and she almost jumped out of her skin. Her hands were on her head, and she tried to bury herself in her knees. Vallarya stood up, taking her blanket and sleeping roll over to her. Laying it down, she took a seat on it before wrapping her blanket around the two of them. Kaldana looked up to her and was greeted with a warm motherly smile. Little by little, her shaking began to stop.

"It's going to be okay," Vallarya said.

"I know," replied Kaldana as she looked toward the fire, embarrassed. "I'm not a little girl who's afraid—"

"Don't lie."

"It's not a lie! I'm not afra—Eeeeek!" Kaldana buried her head into Vallarya's arm as another thunderous boom went off.

Arlo chuckled and was soon met with a murderous stare from the scared girl.

Luna came back to the fire, an arrow nocked on her bow. Her hood was pulled up, droplets of rain falling to the ground as Arlo nudged Kenjo. Kenjo groaned as he looked around. He had just made it to sleep.

"Everything okay?" Arlo asked as he reached for his sword.

Kenjo sat up and waited for Luna to speak.

"Does that bird...um, Siv, was it? Does it happen to make any particular noise you know of?"

"Uh… I don't recall I never actually hunted one myself. And stories from hunters in Gonall stopped a long time ago when they stopped coming to our lands. Why? Are you hearing something particular?"

"Listen to the thunder carefully. There's something in between each clap. Kaldana, can you hear it?"

"W-why are you asking me?" she asked jumping from her position as it boomed across the sky again.

"I just thought—"

"Nope, don't hear anything extra," she replied hurriedly, returning to the comfort of Vallarya's arm.

This time, it was loud enough for everyone to hear—a spine-chilling shriek that put everyone on edge. Kenjo drew his sword and hopped to his feet. Another shriek filled the air. It was drawing closer.

"Speak of the devils, and they shall appear," whispered Luna as she ran to the edge of where the rock covered and began looking around for the owner.

"Oh, you're not trying to blame me for this, are you?" said Arlo, worried as he ran to her side and joined her in searching for the shriek's owner.

Kenjo moved over to Vallarya so they could embrace as fast as possible. Elijah and Mary remained where they were trying to calm the horses. The two of them struggled against their fear. They began to tug and buck; another shriek was all it took. One broke free and bolted past Luna and Arlo.

Mere seconds into the rain, it was lifted into the air, dropped a moment later in front of them. The horse crackled with electricity, its body broken from the fall.

"Arlo, *I hate you!*" yelled Kaldana as she stood up, looking all around, trying to find where it would come from next. She didn't know if she was more scared of the thunder or the shrieking as she remained as close to the fire as possible.

"I did nothing, you scared little girl!" he yelled back, popping a cork from a vial in his hand. Arlo still couldn't see anything, shifting himself ever so slightly to get more view of the sky above. However, the Siv remained cloaked in the veil of night.

Kenjo walked past them and out from under the rock. The gentle tap of the rain against his armor sounded a rhythm that echoed between his steps, every couple of drops followed by the boom of thunder and streaking lightning. Eyes darting back and forth, each step slower than the last, he tried to find the creature before it found him.

"Duck!" yelled Luna as she loosed an arrow.

Kenjo dropped, and the claws of the Siv passed right over his back. It let out a shriek as the arrow struck its leg. It circled back around and landed in front of them, one claw landing atop the horse's corpse, the other digging into the ground.

Bright white eyes eyed them carefully. It's scales shone brilliantly, lightning bouncing back and forth across each one. It spread out its wings, making it appear to have doubled in size. It rivaled some of the dragons they remembered reading about back in the academy. Luna fired another arrow at its face. Its wing came down and it bounced right off.

The Siv noticed the other horses as they neighed and reared in fear. Turning its attention to them, it clawed at the ground as if it were about to break into a sprint. Kenjo ran at it, bringing his great sword against its head. It staggered from the impact as the blade bounced off. It did nothing to the creature, but it brought its attention back to them.

It parted its beak. Lightning formed between the two halves and loosed it at Kenjo. It struck against his chest, and he fell to his knees. The rain was making it worse as the lightning surged across his body. He began to hear Vallarya pant. She was constantly trying to repair any damaged armor, and it was draining her.

Arlo ran forward, ash swirling around his sword arm. He sidestepped a bolt of lightning and jumped at the Siv, throwing his sword at it, the ash trailing behind. A wing came around and smacked him out further into the rain. His sword impacted with the Siv's chest, the ash rushing forward in a spiral, sending the Siv crashing against the mountainside. Recalling the ash, he ran to Kenjo's side and helped him up, the lightning surging through him finally dispersing.

"I think I forgot to mention the part where he can shoot lightning," he said.

"You sure did," said Kenjo as the two of them ran side by side toward the Siv before it could recover.

"Well, by how I described it, I figured it might be implied!"

Kenjo was about to curse him out but was stopped by the sweeping wing they blocked. Planting their feet firmly in the ground, the two of them pushed back against it. Luna ran around the side and unleashed two arrows, each one aimed for the Siv's left eye. One bouncing off its scales, the other found its mark. It reared back in agony with another shriek, lightning crackling in its beak. The bolt of lightning shot straight into the sky.

Its gaze was now focused solely on Luna as it pushed the other two away with a power flap. The murderous intent of its one glowing white eye burned into her mind. Aiming her bow, she loosed another arrow. It whizzed into the valley as the beast ducked underneath and charged at her. She jumped out of the way as an electrified beak pecked at where she stood. A bolt of lightning quickly surged toward her, forcing her to move the moment she hit the ground. The Siv was acting faster. It knew what it was fighting was no longer an easy snack.

"Arlo, I know you haven't hunted them before, but do you know of any soft spots on it?" asked Vallarya, trying to study the bird as Luna dodged it.

"The eyes," said Arlo as he popped open two more vials. A large amount of ash began to swirl around his arm. "And right where its feet connect to its legs. I noticed Luna's arrow is still sticking out of one. We're gonna have to cut them off. And I would argue you guys have the best sword for that, not to mention mine's still over there underneath our friend."

"Can you send it off balance again?" asked Kenjo.

"Yeah, follow me."

Arlo ran forward with a quick punch. The ash flew forward like a wave and crashed into the unsuspecting Siv, putting it on its side.

Kenjo moved as quick as he could with all his might. He swung the blade where Arlo mentioned and cleaved the foot from the leg. A massive shriek filled the air, and a bolt of lightning loosed from the tip toward Elijah.

Elijah was frozen in fear. All he could do was put his arms up. His eyes shutting closed, a few seconds passed, and he began to open his eyes. A warm purple light illuminated the area in front of him, and he slowly lowered his arms to see Kaldana standing before him. A circle of purple fire blocked the bolt. The two flames danced around the circle, crackling as a snake-like flame arched back to the Siv, setting its one good eye and the right side of its head alight.

"*Woooeee*, that was quite shocking!" she said, laughing as she closed the lanterns, the flames firmly back inside. "You two okay?"

Elijah could only blink at his savior.

"I'll take that as a yes." She was smiling brightly, and Elijah was starting to feel something stir inside of him as he looked back at the girl.

The beast fell silent, but Kenjo wasn't going to take any chances. He removed its other foot and stabbed the bird multiple times wherever his blade would go through. Once he was satisfied, he returned to the warmth of the camp.

Everyone ended up okay. However, Vallarya had received the worst of it. After the armor dispersed, she remained within Kenjo to recover. The storm was beginning to die down as Arlo took over watch for Luna. He didn't express it to the group, but he was barely able to contain his excitement. The rush he had right now from taking down the Siv rivaled that of them killing the giant earlier.

Kenjo lay down on his sleeping roll, rolling onto one side to try and sleep. Kaldana had moved hers beside his. Even though she wasn't shaking, she wanted to be close enough that she could still feel Vallarya's presence. Her back to him, she closed her eyes, trying to think of better things.

Something brushed against Kenjo's back, and he glanced back to find Kaldana's tails wagging. With a sigh, he put some space between them, closing his eyes once more to try and sleep, only to find she had moved closer once more, the tails brushing against him again.

After another attempt, he gave up trying to get away, sleep eventually taking him.

When they woke, Vallarya cooked up a breakfast with Mary's help. Then Arlo taught Kenjo and Elijah how to skin the Siv properly. Although he had never hunted a Siv, he had hunted other creatures with similar scales that were native to other parts of Gonall. And here, the experience applied itself well. Before noon, they had piled the scales inside the wagon that held Maximus' skull. He placed the beak on top of the pile, and they left the rest of the Siv to rot.

Vallarya was thinking about taking some meat, but Arlo was quick to shut down that idea. Elijah and Mary agreed with him, letting her know that no matter which way it was cooked, it couldn't be made to taste good. Even the animals who normally feasted on meat would leave it alone. The only living creature that would ever be able to stomach the meat of a Siv was something that was about to die of starvation.

With the sun high in the sky, they got a late start on their travel. Kaldana's horse was the one that was killed by the Siv, so she found herself sharing Vallarya's horse for the next leg of the journey. They passed through the mountains by the time night fell, deciding to put some distance between them and the mountains. They made camp a few miles north of the entrance to the pass.

Before them stretched a dense forest, which Arlo stated was the Forest of Calelem, named after the great hero and king of Adristan who signed for his people when Zell first became the united nation it was today. Rumor had it that even after he passed, the ghost of Calelem still wandered the forest, watching over traveler and animal alike.

"On the other side of this forest is a town," said Vallarya to Kenjo as she looked over the map. Kaldana glanced over her shoulder, curiosity plain on her face.

"Gitving," said Elijah.

"You know it?"

"It's where me and Mary are from," he replied. It started to sound like he was losing his voice. "I-It's where Mom and Dad are…"

"It's where they are waiting for us," said Mary, finishing her brother's comment. "They actually never knew that we left. That's why little Elijah here is beginning to lose his voice. I bet he's thinking of all the terrible things Dad will do."

"Quiet, Mary!" Elijah was flush with embarrassment. He glanced over and found Kaldana giggling, and he began to turn even more red.

"Unlike him, though, you guys will probably get a royal treatment. You all are practically heroes. And our parents honestly are really big fans. I think had my dad not been raised to work the axe like he does, he would have tried to become a hero or at least a merc himself."

"I think you are mistaken," said Kenjo as he shook his head. Vallarya was in agreement, her head shaking along with him. "We're no heroes."

"Huh," said Arlo who had been silent that whole exchange. He looked back at them around the wagon side as his horse continued heading the charge through the forest. "I could have sworn you called yourselves heroes back when we met."

"You must be mistaken," he replied.

Arlo turned around, unamused; he began to whistle a tune to himself.

"Well," said Mary, "you're heroes in mine and Elijah's eyes. That will suffice for them, hopefully."

Kenjo felt a small warmth in his chest as a small smile formed on his face at her words. He wondered if Vallarya felt it too, but he didn't want to ask at that moment, trying to keep his feelings under wraps from the others. His head turned to the right, and he found himself unable to pull away.

Through the trees, he could see something that looked like an elk from back home. Two creatures he believed were doe stood on either side of it. They nibbled on the grass below them. Long branches in the shape of a large hand slowly stroked each of them. He followed the hand up the length of twisted branches to the body of the humanlike creature that kneeled there.

A green mist swirled in between the wood that formed its body. The mist formed small circles to act as the eyes of it's wooden head. Wood parting to form a mouth, it smiled at the creatures below it. The large tree man looked up and locked eyes with Kenjo. Its smile faded away. The mist rearranged on its face; it almost looked sad. Standing up, the being turned and began to walk away into the forest, the animals following after it.

"Wow, usually, you can't see him this close to the road in the middle of the day," said Elijah. His eyes were wide and brimming with amazement.

"Was that Cal—"

"Yep. That was him all right."

"Did he look sad to you?"

"Huh?" asked Elijah, looking to Kenjo. "What are you talking about? He can't make any faces. He's just like a tree. A walking one, that is."

Kenjo was about to argue back but decided to keep his thoughts to himself. For all he knew, he was possibly crazy and just seeing things. Part of him, however, couldn't deny that the spirit of Calelem was looking at him with sadness.

It took them a whole day to pass through the forest. When night fell, they had arrived at Gitving, and it felt good to actually see other people again. The town itself was small but almost double the size of Caprae. The guards at the gate were outfitted in full suits of armor. Their weapons looked sharp and gleamed from a recent polishing. They seemed like the type criminals would be afraid of, unlike the ones back at Caprae.

Arlo handled the talking when they were stopped by the guards at the gate. Not mentioning anything about being a prince, instead, he showed them the trophies hidden in the wagon. Those alone allowed the group in without a second thought. Kenjo was baffled by how easy it was. Back in Samil, had you brought these types of trophies around, you either would have been detained or questioned extensively before maybe getting inside most towns near the capital.

They headed to the stables and hitched their horses. Arlo was able to purchase a cover for his trophy wagon and said he'd come back in the morning to help hook it up. They began to take a look around, Elijah and Mary taking the lead on this one as they delved deeper into the heart of the lumber town.

A whole quarter of the city was strictly dedicated to workshops and warehouses for the lumberyards. With the forest so close by, it made sense for them to be so focused on it, but it was strange to the three Samilians that the trees near the road showed no sign of being used for lumber. When they brought up the point, Elijah was quick to educate them. The lumberjacks of Gitving focused on the parts of the forest near the coast.

Although it led to an increase in overall travel time, everyone knew it was well worth it. The quality of the wood near the coast was better, and there were less creatures who called that part of the forest their home. Had they decided to go the opposite way or delve into the forest next to the main road, they would have caused a lot of problems; problems that would have been met by countless beasts, courtesy of Adristan's love of them.

From dawn to dusk, the lumberjacks worked. At night, they retired to either the tavern or their homes to rest or drink away the pains of the day and ready themselves for another hard day at work tomorrow. Elijah and Mary's father was one of them. Right now, he was probably sitting at home with their mother, unthinkable anger welling up inside of him.

"We don't need to waste money on an inn tonight," said Elijah happily. "There's plenty of room at our house."

"Are you sure we won't be a bother?" asked Vallarya.

"Not at all," said Mary, now with a skip in her step. "There's plenty of room for everyone. And after we tell them everything, I am sure they will have no objection."

"Anyone against it?" asked Kenjo, liking the idea himself.

When no one objected, Elijah led them to their house. Their large brick house stood and dwarfed their neighbors. Engraved wooden doors led into the four-floor building that was before them. Trimmed bushes and various flowers lined the paved walkway that led to the door.

"This doesn't look like it belongs here," said Kaldana as she moved closer for a better look.

Arlo's mouth was agape as he took in the sight. "It seems like something from the residential area back in Gonall. Why do you guys live in a house like this in this town?"

Elijah scratched the back of his head, "Well, Father's actually the current boss of the whole lumberyard. And seeing as this is the biggest lumber business in the southern part of Zell…it led to a little splurging on his part."

"Explain to me why you guys were traveling to Gonall if you guys lived in a place like this," said Kenjo. "It seems like you could have every—"

"You would think," Elijah said. His happy tone had gone cold, and he was looking at the ground. "But that's not the case. And I am sure all around the world, there's people in a similar situation. Every day here is just another push from Father to join him at the lumberyard, work my way up, and eventually take his place. But I don't want to look at wood being cut up for the rest of my life. I heard that something special was going to happen in Gonall soon from a passerby. It was… Um…"

"It was going to be the revitalization ceremony," said Arlo, clenching his fists.

"Right, that was it. Mary caught me when I tried to sneak out. She insisted she go with me to make sure I remain safe… And, well… I already told you the rest. I am sure our parents sent people out to find us too. Dad probably would have went himself if he wasn't critical to this town." Elijah let out a long sigh. "Okay, here goes."

Elijah and Mary walked to the door, the others close behind. They knocked simultaneously; a loud gulp followed from both of them. Moments of silence passed between the group. While the two who knocked held fear, the rest were quite eager to meet the owners of the house.

The door swung open, and out came a rather muscular man. A long white-sleeved shirt fit him a little too snug. The slightest stretch easily would have popped the buttons if not tear it. A well-trimmed beard covered the lower part of his face. Short and curly brown hair sat atop his head; there was no doubt he was their father.

"E-Elijah? Mary?" he asked in disbelief, rubbing his eyes to make sure he wasn't seeing things. The two gave him a weak smile. "Elijah! Mary!" he yelled, scooping them both up in his arms and squeezing them tightly. Tears were streaming down his face, a large smile of white teeth that gleamed even in the evening torchlight.

"Why are you being so loud, dear?" asked a woman walking into the doorway, drying a plate with a rag. Their father turned to her to show her the wonderful gifts in his arms. The plate slipped from her hands as she jumped at them, arms wide. Their heads were assaulted by a barrage of kisses. It was beginning to be hard to tell who was actually suffocating the two more.

"Mom," said Elijah as she kissed him again. "M-Mom, you can stop now. There're others here."

"No, not happening!" she replied, squeezing him again. She looked Mary over and noticed the bandage over her eye. "What happened? Where have you two been this whole time?"

"Can we just go inside? We're all tired and hungry, and we can explain everything."

"Oh, you're damn right you will, mister," she said, looking over the group behind them. Her gaze made them feel like she was their mother too.

Mary and her mother worked in the kitchen to prepare a meal for all of them. Elijah was stuck cleaning up the broken plate. The house was gorgeous on the inside. In the living room sat a large fireplace, and three couches gathered around a large wooden table. On the right side of the room was the staircase that led to the second floor as well as a hallway to another room.

To the left sat the dining room with a beautiful table covered with a red silk cloth. Emblems of Zell were embroidered into the ends. And there were plenty of chairs for each of them. Mary went about setting the table as her mother began to bring out various dishes and lined the table with them. Bread, chicken, fish and an assortment of vegetables filled the middle of the table. Before they sat down, the father went around and collected everyone's cloaks and hung them in a closet.

Kaldana refused to hand hers over, and when she sat down, Kenjo gave her a disapproving sigh. But she didn't care as her attention was directed to the food in front of her. They all dished up and dug in before the real conversation began. With both Elijah and Mary being scolded beyond belief, the others remained silent, continuing to munch on their food as the table grew awkward. The two of them were facing an enemy none of them could help with.

"You're not going to the capital," said their father as he took a drink of water. "Not after all of this. Not after what you let happen to your sister."

"Dad, it's not his fault," said Mary. "Everything that happened to me has nothing to do with him."

"No... Had he not wanted to leave and just did as he was told, it never would have happened. Don't try to defend him. Regardless, my decision is final. Elijah, you will stay here."

Elijah was squeezing his silverware so tight his knuckles were starting to turn white. Kenjo took notice and poked at Vallarya who then looked to Elijah. Putting down her silverware, she picked up her napkin and wiped her mouth.

"Excuse me, sir," she said, placing the napkin back in her lap.

"Yes, miss?"

"I apologize ahead of time if I am stepping out of line. I know you don't really know us, but we are going to Zell. If Elijah wanted to tag along, I can assure you that we would take care of him."

"He is staying here, young miss. I'm sorry."

"If you don't let them go now, he will sneak out again before you even realize it," she said.

Elijah eased up on his silverware and looked to her, his eyes wide.

"And should he sneak out without us, who knows what he may run into on the way? We fought bandits, a giant, and a Siv just to get here. He would be safest with us instead of trying his luck alone again."

Vallarya's sincere words came across like a spell, each one trying their hand at breaking down the wall around his father. Elijah looked to Mary before they both looked to their father who, in his own sense of loss, looked to their mother. A big sigh came from them both before he replied, "They're the only kids we have left. I can't—"

"You have the word of us Hands," she said, picking up Kenjo's arm and merging their arms together. "Again, I promise you, sir and madam. They will come back to you unharmed."

Elijah's father was looking down at his plate now, unsure of what to say until he felt his wife's hand on his. "We will consider it. You will get an answer in the morning. Elijah, can you show them to the guest rooms?"

They finished their meal. Vallarya and Kaldana helped with clean up. When they were done, Elijah guided everyone to the third floor where the guest rooms were, assigning one to each of them. He wished them all goodnight before heading back downstairs.

Kenjo heard a knock at his door moments later. He cracked it open just enough to see Vallarya's smiling face. Opening it wider for her to come in, he shut it quietly behind them. They sat on the edge of the bed together. There was nothing but silence between them in that moment. She placed her hand on his and smiled at the sight of it.

"I feel like we haven't actually had any alone time since we left Adana," she said. "Not any quiet moment we could really talk to ourselves. Ever since that day, we've been constantly moving, it feels like. We ran into Kaldana…er, we caught Kaldana. Then Arlo and Luna. I was starting to forget what this was like. Makes me miss Saussion a lot more than I realized."

"It really has been some time, hasn't it?" he said, his eyes cast downward at the floor. "I do hope we can reach the capital without any more events transpiring. A giant and a Siv—it's real hard to believe we even fought those things."

Vallarya let out a small chuckle. "Yeah, it really is. The others back at the academy would never believe it. I wonder how Amy and Martin are doing."

"I can only picture Amy at a loss of what to do without you there. And Martin is probably still passing every single task he's given with a perfect score." Kenjo laughed. "I bet Roger is still trying to beat the Master at Arms."

"Mm-hmm," she nodded in agreement, unable to contain her smile. "Roger was really upset when you managed to defeat Master Wilfred. I do hope Amy makes it."

"She probably won't."

"Don't joke like that," she said, punching him in his arm. "All that aside… Kenjo, are you okay?"

"Of course," he replied his, smile quickly fading as he looked at her. "Why? Do I look like something's wrong?"

"You know what I mean, Kenjo. We haven't said a word about it. You know I'm here for you. I always will be. You can say what—"

"I'm fine," he said, cutting her off. "Perfectly fine."

This time, his hand found its way to hers, and their fingers slowly intertwined. He began to squeeze her hand, and then she felt it begin to shake. Looking at him, she saw tears sliding down his face. For the first time since that day, he couldn't stop thinking about it. He couldn't get his mind off of what he had done.

It flashed over and over again in his mind. He was pulling his hand free of his parents' chest, their blood flowing down his forearm, dripping down his fingers to the dead ground below. That hauntingly calm voice whispering like a monster in his ear that everything was okay. But that voice wasn't there now; it was just him and Vallarya. And he couldn't fight it any longer.

He cried into her embrace as she rubbed her hand through his hair. It was the first time since they met that he had ever broken down. He was always collected. Nothing ever seemed to bother him to this point. But even he could no longer keep his emotions bottled up. Vallarya was unsure of what to do other than hold him, her fingers flowing through his dark brown hair.

Tears began to pool in her eyes, sliding down her cheeks, off her chin, and down onto his head. She tried to be strong and hide them from him. Thinking about McKenzie, the mother she never had, brought nothing but sadness. Her fingers began to tremble ever so slightly, catching Kenjo's attention. He pulled back from her and looked straight into her eyes. Her soul laid bare, she weakly smiled.

"Val," said Kenjo as his tears finally stopped.

"Yeah?" she replied, drying her eyes with the back of her hand.

"Thank you. We're going to live for them, Val. We're going to become the heroes we wanted to be. We'll surpass the tale of Crimson and the Age of Heroes. We—"

"And when Samil finds us again?" she interjected, pulling his head out from the clouds.

"Samil or the world, I don't care. We will stand against them," he said, taking both of her hands in his. "No matter who it is, we will beat them. We will live our lives the way we want to. Here, we will be free to do that."

Some of Vallarya's hair fell down and covered her left eye. Kenjo moved his right hand, gently swiping against her cheek as he placed it back behind her ear. She was blushing now. Her body moved on its own, nuzzling against the hand while it was there.

"Promise me," she said, her eyes closed, her cheek still pressed against his hand. "Promise me you won't jump into every situation to get us in trouble. I don't want to take another voyage across the world."

"I will try my best, but—"

He was silenced by a finger against his mouth. "Just promise."

"I-I promise."

Vallarya put a hand on his that was still against her cheek. She didn't want him to let go. The warmth and the quiet moment between them she wanted to last forever. Kenjo felt his heart beating faster, warmth growing in his cheeks. Vallarya moved his hand away slowly. She wrapped her arms around him in a hug, kissed him on the cheek, and ran out of the room before he could react.

Kenjo sat there at a loss as the door shut. He touched his hand to where she had kissed him. "Idiot," he mumbled to himself as he crawled under the blankets and shut his eyes, ready to face the nightmare that haunted him night after night. But this time, it was different.

He was still surrounded by darkness, but this time he was sitting down at a small wooden table, illuminated only by the small orange flame of the lamp above it. Across from him was someone he had never seen before dressed in strange golden robes embroidered with black silk. From what he could see all along the robes, the black silk had formed what looked like runes. But in the poor lighting, it was hard to make out what any of them said.

His head was concealed beneath a hood; the only part of his face visible was his mouth. He began to speak to him, but it was all inaudible. Kenjo tried to speak back but found his own voice not working. Waving his arms to get his attention, the man stopped speaking. The man stood up and walked away, his golden robes fading into the darkness.

Kenjo jumped up to chase after him. His legs felt heavy, another step, and the familiar tentacles from his past dreams appeared. They yanked at his feet and pulled him once again into the unending darkness where his father awaited him once more. Face-to-face, he stared into the lifeless eyes of the one he couldn't save.

His mother flashed before him next; there was still light in her eyes. Kenjo's hand instinctively reached out. Right before he touched her, the light faded, her head slouched down, and the tendrils dragged her away. Kenjo looked down at his hands to find them in his black-plated armor. The golden cracks appeared next, followed by the blood of his victims. He began to shake as he fell to his knees. His scream echoed across the void, eventually silenced by a tendril that wrapped around his throat and began to suffocate him.

Kenjo grasped at it, trying to pull it away. There was no give in it; every time he tugged at it, it only seemed to get tighter. He tugged once more and caught a gasp of air. Before he could get any more, a tendril grabbed each of his hands and held them down as the one around his neck tightened once more.

"You need to move past this," said a voice, the first sound he ever heard in that dream. In his fading vision, the man in the golden robes appeared once more. As he spoke again, Kenjo realized it was the same voice that spoke to him during the execution in Manfo.

"If you become hung up on everything you do, on everyone you kill, it will end up devouring you like it is now. These tendrils are the physical manifestation of your fear, of your failure, and your worries. Every negative thing you feel toward what you've done, they will leave you hollow."

There was silence. Kenjo could no longer keep his eyes open; his consciousness was fading as he spoke again.

"You need to understand that some need to die before they hurt another. That some can only be saved by the act of a merciful death. You need to understand you wield a power that is meant to guide the world. You cannot become hollow due to your own doubt. After all, this path you walk leads to Nothingness."

10

9th of Japhim; Mortal Year 523

Jasmine

asmine was standing in front of the alchemist's shop again. This time, the sun was shining down on her, and she wasn't here with the intention of fighting. She was here as an apprentice alchemist with a few questions. Also, because she felt bad when she found the coins she had given to him as payment stuffed in that box among the other supplies.

This time, she was in more casual attire consisting of a black shirt, brown cloth pants, and short leather boots. Her hair was up in a ponytail again. Part of her hoped he forgot about her. But as soon as she stepped inside, that hope was quickly dashed.

"Ah, hello, missy!" said the old shopkeeper as he placed a glass jar onto one of his shelves. She noticed the box next to him and figured he was stocking.

Right, she thought. *His assistant was arrested.* "Hello again. I wanted to say thank you for bringing me those items. I heard you almost got arrested for it."

"That wasn't a problem at all. Anything for a fellow alchemist."

He was no longer wearing the white sash he wore that night. Nor was he acting in any strange way. The old man was just being himself.

"I wanted to ask you something. That sash you wore that night... What does it mean?"

The old man finished stocking and moved back to the counter. He pulled up a white sash from behind the counter and placed it there for her to see. "You mean this thing?"

"Yeah."

"It's how the rebels notified one another who was an ally, even if they never met before. Sure, it stands out. But keep low without drawing attention, and it can just be a fashion statement. Anytime someone asks about it, they make up random things. Nothing ever ends up being concrete. And for the record, I was never 'with them.' Most of us shop owners throughout the city have a connection to them."

Jasmine's face lit up at the thought of it.

"Don't worry, it's not like that. Well, for the most part, I'm sure there are some who support the growing rebels. But I myself am not one of them. I was threatened. They used my supplies without my say and held their meetings in that room that was once my spare workshop for my more dangerous experiments."

"I see... Why did you help me, then?"

"You were bloody, and I assumed you were dying. I reported it to the guards, and soon enough, some orange-haired lass came over and talked my ear off. Girl had sooooo many questions."

Jasmine giggled; that was definitely Forsythia. She reached for a bag on her side and counted out twenty gold coins. Pushing them toward him, she wandered over to the books.

"I gave you it back for sparing my life," he said, not making a move for it.

"And I owe you money for what I had in that box. Plus, I feel a bit bad for hitting you that night. And tying you up..."

The old man laughed as he slid the coins into a drawer behind the counter. Pulling out a book, he grabbed a pen and began checking the stock of the supplies behind him. Jasmine combed through the books, but when she couldn't find what she wanted, she took the easy way out.

"Hey, do you have a book on sense augmentation or enhancement?" she asked, looking them over again.

"Try the seventh in the S section," he replied without a second thought. And sure enough, he called out the book she wanted: *Sensory Alchemy for Beginners.* She cursed at herself for overlooking such an easy to see book. Next to it were two other books, one for advanced and the other for master.

"Does this stuff actually work?"

"In the right amount, it can. You can overdo it and comatose *or* you could possibly enhance your senses so much you can't handle it. Those are just two possible outcomes." The old man began to laugh at the thought and recited a story of a previous student who almost went completely deaf when a glass shattered after he enhanced his hearing.

"Good to know. How much for it?"

"Five gold."

"I like that better than last time," she said with a smile as she placed five gold coins on the counter. "One more thing before I go. Do you know anything about a man who wears black robes with a single white sleeve?"

The old man's face stiffened. "He's a mystery. Other than the fact he goes by Sleeve, I hardly know much else. Personally, I have not had to deal with him… I would say try the blacksmiths, more so Ian. He may have some more info on him. I know he worked alongside them at some point recently."

"Ian the blacksmith. All right, I'll swing by sometime. Thank you."

Jasmine left the shop and headed back to Forsythia's room to grab the rest of her stuff. She would be coming back tomorrow and wanted to make sure she was long gone before she got there. When Jasmine got to the room, she grabbed her box of alchemy supplies and headed right back out the door. Taking one more good look at the room, she was still baffled by the difference in lodging between Sovereign and Royal Fingers.

One day, I'll stand with her, she thought to herself as she walked down the castle hallways. Walking out the castle gates, she headed left to the barracks of the Fingers. Once inside, she climbed the two flights of stairs and made it to her room at the back of the third floor. Compared to Forsythia's, it was nothing; only enough room for her bed, a dresser, and a small table.

Setting her box on the table, she emptied it of its contents before stuffing it in a corner. She stacked the books on top of each other and organized her containers from small to large. Grabbing the *Alchemist's First* book, she moved to her bed and took a seat. Shifting her pillow to support her back, she cracked the book open and continued where she left off.

*****

A few hours passed, and a knock came to her door. Closing the book, she hopped up and opened it to reveal a guard.

"Cardinal requests to speak with you," he said. "He's in his office and expects you there before sundown."

"Did he happen to tell you what he wanted to speak about?" she asked.

"No, ma'am."

"All right, thank you."

The guard nodded and took his leave. Jasmine wanted to continue reading but decided it was best just to deal with Cardinal now than later. Locking her room, she headed out the barracks and back to the main castle. Taking a right at the entrance, she quickly ran up the steps and moved down the long hall that led to his office.

Cardinal was the treasurer of the entire nation of Samil and the current head of the merchant's guild that dealt across the entire world. He had wealth to rival kings and could sell anything to anyone, even if it put them into debt. There was no denying he would take advantage of it and gladly punish anyone who didn't pay their debts to him. His silver tongue had harmed more lives than he had harmed with his sword.

He sat behind stacks of gold, silver, and copper coins. A large book sat before him, and he was diligently looking it over, checking numbers from left to right. Cardinal had dark tan skin and long pointed ears. His brown hair reached down to his shoulders. The red cloak he wore was his defining trait, a bright scarlet red that you could easily spot against anything in this city, let alone the world. It shone with an indescribable brilliance when the sunlight hit it.

Cardinal didn't look up from his work as Jasmine entered his office. Instead, he remained focused, counting to himself as his eyes darted across the pages. She stood there, silent, waiting for him to acknowledge her. Minutes passed by, and he still hadn't looked up.

"You wanted to see me, sir?" said Jasmine as she took a seat in one of the chairs opposite his desk.

"One..." he said to himself. "Two... Three hundred. That's absurd. You could easily have sold this down south for double that. What were they thinking?"

"Sir!"

Cardinal nearly jumped from his chair, the pen in his hand flying from his hand and hitting the ceiling. "Oh, Jasmine. I didn't expect you to get here so early." As the pen fell, he snatched it out of the air. "Usually, my best investment likes to wait until the last minute to show up for me."

"Well, tod—" She stopped as she watched him go back to looking at his book. She coughed to get his attention.

With a sigh, he sat down his pen and leaned back in his chair.

With a smile, she continued, "Well, today your messenger arrived before I got started on anything. So I figured I would get it out of the way now."

"I should feel honored. Wait, no, scratch that. I am honored to be put so far up your busy schedule, young Jasmine."

The sarcasm in his words struck a chord in her. Her eye began to twitch as he laughed.

"What did you need, sir?"

"Forsythia told me everything you told her as well as giving me quite possibly the biggest scolding of my life since I was a child."

Jasmine busted out laughing at the thought as he continued.

"Now then, this character who almost killed you, do you know anything about him that you didn't mention to her?"

Jasmine's laughter faded away as her thoughts drifted to the man with the white sleeve. "Sadly, no. Beyond the fact that his magic seems to eat away at light and your senses, I have nothing right now. According to a contact I have, there is someone who may give me more information. But I am here instead of there right now."

"Hmm... Well, that's unfortunate and fortunate at the same time," said Cardinal as he started tapping his fingers on his desk. He was clearly thinking of something, and Jasmine waited patiently. "I'm going to talk to the king about these white sashes. Probably have them all run out of hiding and taken in. I want you to follow up with your 'contacts' and see if you can find out anything more about him."

"As you wish, sir. Any other assignments you need me to look into?"

"Nope... Actually, this will be your last one from me."

"What?" she asked, confusion filling her face. "What do you mean your last one?"

"Forsythia talked to me about more than just the event that transpired," he responded as he picked up his pen again. His eyes remained looking at her this time. "I already approve of it. You two have been friends for a while now. And even though you are my favorite investment and rapidly becoming my favorite little bird, I don't see a reason to keep you two away from each other."

"Y-You really mean it?" she asked, standing up. She looked like a small child eyeing gifts on her birthday. Her eyes gave off a sparkle that made him a little uneasy as her hands slammed on the desk.

"Y-yeah... Yeah, I sure do. Just stop looking like that at me."

She stopped instantly and went back to her neutral face trying to fight her excitement.

"But you bring down this man first. Then we can worry about the transfer."

"Yes, sir!" she practically shouted as she stood up and headed for the door.

"And Jasmine. Please be careful."

Jasmine shut the door behind her and headed back to her room in the barracks. She didn't acknowledge his last words because deep down, he didn't really care about her like that. He was worried about the money and time he had invested into her. About the chewing out he would get by Forsythia if something were to happen. That was the real Cardinal. He only cared about himself and the monetary value of something. Whether that something be an object or a person, they all were made of coins to him.

That's not to say he was completely heartless. Generally speaking, so long as you were actually worth something, he cared. He handpicked the members of his group, invested some money and time into trainers. Show no promise, and he tossed you to the streets. Show him promise, though, like Jasmine did, and he would begin to see you a little bit more as a person. He also donated a hefty sum to orphanages across Samil, though it was hard to tell if he saw the children there as children or walking coins with the chance to earn him more.

But honestly, Jasmine didn't care how he viewed her. Their king trusted him, and he stood among the Sovereign Fingers. That was more than enough for her. They were the heroes of the nation she aspired to be like and the closest thing to the real deal since the Age of Heroes and the time of Crimson. Continuing down the halls, she noticed the sun beginning to set and decided she would visit the blacksmith early tomorrow.

Once she was in her room, she cracked open her alchemy book and began to experiment into the night. It was one of the worst nights she ever had. The book suggested that hearing be the first thing she attempt to enhance. Her first experiment into sense augmentation concluded in a purple liquid that fizzed up the vial. Unfortunately for her, every experiment in here required her to drink the concoctions she made. Hesitantly, she moved the vial close to her mouth. The smell filled her nostrils, and she vomited.

The vial dropped to the ground and shattered as she rushed to find a bucket. Unable to contain her vomit, most ended up on the floor with very little actually landing in the bucket. She was sitting on the floor, breathing heavily. The bucket sat between her legs, ready and waiting in case more was to come. Someone knocked on the door and asked if she was okay, in which she gave a simple, "Yep! Everything is A-OK!"

When she was sure no more would come up, she got up and left her room to get some cleaning supplies. With how the barracks were set up, at the end of each hallway was a cleaning supply closet for personal use whenever they needed it for spills or, in her case, vomit. Unlike those who lived in the castle itself, like Forsythia, there were no personal maids for the regular Royal Fingers.

Instead, a servant would come and restock that closet. At the beginning of each month, they would change out the bedding. But other than that, they did nothing else. They did have their own chefs, however, that cooked in a kitchen on the bottom floor. They were better servants than the others and happily cooked them up food. And should they not want what they were serving, they happily would whip them up whatever they desired.

It honestly wasn't bad living. For most of the Fingers, Jasmine included, this single room and the accommodations of the barracks were rather similar if not better than her previous living arrangements. Jasmine lived in a small house with her family out in the country. She grew up a farmer, hearing stories of heroes due to her parents. Her grandparents fought during that time, and it made it all the more real to her. However, as days went on, she started to think she would never even visit the capital.

That was until the day Forsythia—Ariya back then—made her way through her village. At that time, she was just a Royal Finger five years her senior. She stayed in the village for a few nights, and in that time, she and Jasmine began to develop a bond that turned into the sisterly friendship it was today. Jasmine, with help from Forsythia on the final day she stayed there, convinced her parents to let her come with her to the capital.

From then on, Jasmine trained with her, and eventually, it led to her recruitment into the guard. Quickly, Jasmine rose in the ranks to become a Royal Finger and ended up in Cardinal's division. Though they were separated from each other during work, their friendship never ceased. Had it not been for that chance meeting, she wouldn't be where she was today, more or less, still stuck on a farm out in the country, only imagining heroes instead of striving to become one.

She finished cleaning up her room and put the mop, bucket, and broom back in the closet. But she wasn't ready to stop for the night. Instead, she picked up her book from her bed, moved to her desk, and started again, this time slower and rereading each step multiple times. This time, it came out with no fizz. Bringing it close to her, she wafted the contents toward her and braced herself for vomit. However, this time, there was no gut-wrenching smell. She was fine and was ready to move on to the next part: drinking it.

Hesitantly, she placed the glass against her lips. Her hand was shaking; seconds turned to minutes, and the liquid had not moved any closer to her mouth.

"All right, Jasmine," she said to herself, moving the bottle away and staring it down as if it were a hated enemy. "You can do this. This is nothing. You've been stabbed by your own leg. Come on!"

She chugged it.

It ended up tasting just like an ordinary glass of water, and not a single drop remained when she was done. Placing it back on the desk, she clasped her ears as the noise resonated. She screamed in pain, only to hear it echo in her ears over and over as shell fell to the ground. Rolling back and forth, trying to block out the noise, she started to realize she could hear everything. From the guards talking among themselves outside to the other Fingers talking in their own rooms, she could hear things as simple as a chair sliding and the few eating in the dining area at this time of night. Getting up, she tried to move to her bed. Every movement of her body could be heard, all to the rhythm of her heartbeat.

Grabbing her pillow, she folded it over her head to try and block out the noise as she lay there. It lasted for six hours. She wanted to scream but knew it would only lead to prolonged agony. Even her thoughts as she tried to figure out a way to stop it were too loud. Her solution was just to lay there as still as she could. The only noises being made were from those in the barracks. Her breathing and her heartbeat were as quiet as she could make them.

When the effects finally wore off, she was in tears. She couldn't get to sleep, so she grabbed her book and took it back to her bed. The potion had the intended effect, just way too much of it. She looked back over the recipe to try and find her error. Before trying to sleep again, she decided to get everything ready for another trial run tomorrow.

Figuring she added too much of something, she carefully measured out everything. Grinding up less of the herbs, she placed them into a vial, keeping the liquid separated until morning. She wished she could have one of her spiders sample it and be her test dummy. But sadly, stuff like this would have no effect on their magical bodies. Plus, it wasn't like they could speak and give her the exact feedback she needed. *I could try Forsythia,* she thought as she jumped on her bed. *No, what am I thinking? I couldn't let her suffer like this. I can't let anyone suffer like this from my own failure.*

She gazed up at the ceiling for another thirty minutes before she was finally able to get to sleep. Her mind kept thinking about the white-sleeved man, about how he could be killing guards, soldiers, or other Royal Fingers at this very moment. Convincing herself it was something she could face tomorrow, her mind finally let her sleep, only for him to visit her in her dreams.

She was back in the backroom of the Alchemist's shop. It was empty from what she could tell as she walked around. Tables were kicked over, weapons and supplies meant for soldiers were scattered around, like a storm blew through. She was looking for something without knowing it, turning over the supplies until she finally found it: a white sash.

Picking it up, she felt a sharp pain in her stomach—the same sharp pain she felt back then when she was stabbed by her spider leg. Looking down toward the pain, she watched the leg slowly manifest, blood flowing along it and dripping onto the sash in her hands. The man's laughter could be heard all around her. She looked around in fear as her heart skipped. But he was nowhere to be found; she was very much alone…

Jasmine woke to the sound of rapid knocking against her room door. Her hair was a mess, covering her face and obstructing most of her vision. Slowly opening her eyes, she looked through the parts in it at the ceiling, her hand rubbing along the scar on her stomach to make sure the leg wasn't still there. Ignoring the knocking, she rolled onto her side and shut her eyes.

Another repeated knock came to the door, making her start to shake from anger.

"It's way too early to be knocking on someone's door!" yelled Jasmine as she sat up. The knocking stopped for a moment before continuing again, this time faster than before. Getting out of bed, she grabbed her Bo Staff, extended it, and moved to the door, ready to hit whoever was on the other side, whether it be a guard or her own king.

Unlocking the door, she cracked it just enough to see who it was. Spiky orange hair and similarly colored eyes looked back at her. Jasmine glanced up to the ceiling as if asking someone, "Why?" She opened the door to let Forsythia in.

Forsythia was in her combat attire this time, save for the mask she wore into battle. Unlike Jasmine who preferred fighting in a one-piece battle dress, Forsythia preferred to wear a skirt, the dark orange folds of which reached halfway down her thigh where it exposed the light tan skin of her legs. Metal boots reached up to her knees. The plates, which protected her knee caps, were shaped into little suns.

Each scale of the scale-mail she wore on her upper body was outlined in glowing orange. Occasionally, the glow rippled like a wave across the surface of the scales, giving off the appearance of the sun's surface. Minus it's blinding magnificence, of course, Forsythia didn't need her appearance to catch anyone's attention. The way she moved in battle was enough to captivate anyone.

Her gauntlets were slightly different. Orange scales covered her hands, but that was it. Regular plate covered from the wrist upward, shaped to make her forearms look far larger than they were, the back of which was hollowed out in the shape of a rectangle. Most of her magical energy coalesced in her arms, and these hollow points in her arms were meant to pool it.

Jasmine noticed the curve of her harp against her back, a body of beautiful gold strung with snow-white string. On the top of it, resting where it curved in, was a small little sun that mimicked the one's on her knees. It had been a while since she heard her play it, but she could never forget the music she made with it.

Many believed it was what a choir of true angels would have sounded like singing to the Father back in the Age of Gods. She was the gold standard in which any aspiring musician followed. Forsythia, however, never let that get to her head, and she always laughed it off if anyone ever mentioned it.

"Hiya, sis!" she said, smiling as she closed the door, watching as Jasmine walked back over and fell face-first on her bed. Her blonde hair spreading out in a wide arc. "Hey! Hey! No, no, no sleeping." Forsythia was poking her. When she didn't budge, she took both hands and rolled her onto her back. "It's time to get up."

"No," Jasmine replied, attempting to roll on to her side again. "It's too early."

"It's going on nine. You're usually up at seven."

"It was a long night. Now go away, Mom," said Jasmine weakly throwing a pillow at her. "Come back later."

"I really hope that's not how you talked to your mom before you left home," Forsythia said as she placed the pillow down. She stood up and began to rummage around her room, looking for a brush. Finding it atop her desk among the alchemy supplies, she took a moment to look over everything she had.

With a smile she returned to the bed and helped her friend up so she was seated on the bedside. Jasmine was far too tired to fight it, her head moving ever so slightly with each brush. To be honest, though, she enjoyed it, even though she winced every time the brush pulled at her knots. It brought back memories from when they were younger, when Forsythia was determined to make a country girl's hair presentable for kingdom. Forsythia hardly had to worry about it. The longest part of her short-bobbed hair was her bangs, but even they took little to no effort to get ready in the morning.

It took her almost twenty minutes to finish. When she finally stopped brushing, Jasmine turned to look at her.

"So," she said as Forsythia placed the brush back on the desk, "what are you here for?"

"I have a gift for you," she replied. "Well, not actually on me right this second, but it's a gift waiting for you at the training field."

"Uh…why?"

"Oh, stop asking questions and come on!" Forsythia was motioning at her to go as she went for the door. "You can sleep later."

Jasmine took a few long blinks before finally answering her, "Ugh, fine, lead the way."

The castle training field was empty at the morning hour that they arrived. Beautiful emerald green grass was surrounded by the stone arches and walls of the main keep. Higher up the walls, windows allowed passersby to glance out and see those training below them.

Standard issue weapons of basic craftsmanship lined racks against the walls. Next to each rack was an identical set of wooden weapons. Weights were added to each one to allow people to spar with the "safe" weapons but still grow accustomed to the weight of the real deal.

At the far end for those more interested in ranged weaponry, targets were lined up with ropes creating lanes for each one. Three different types of bows and a quiver full of arrows rested at each lane where the archer would stand. For those who didn't like the bow and who fancied to throw something instead, spears and hatchets filled up racks next to the large standing quivers.

Jasmine and Forsythia stood in front of a table with a large ornate wooden case. It was hinged in gold clips, lined with gold, and small gems formed the crest of Samil's smiths: The top half of a skull resting atop an anvil, a hammer striking against the top of it, causing the skull to crack in the middle. It was extravagant and completely unnecessary in most people's eyes. But to the smiths who prized and cherished every last thing they created, it was one of the most important pieces.

Not to mention whoever was behind this particular order had a case made of a very special wood. The ivory wood of a Lifa tree, native to the northern tips of the continent, a type of wood that was incredibly difficult to shape without splintering and breaking the wood itself, leading it to become a lost profession and sending the prices for something made from it far higher than they used to be.

Forsythia undid each latch on the case and opened it for her, revealing the contents to her. Her eyes shone with childish wonder, the contents of the case gleaming at her in the morning sun.

"T-this is for me?" asked Jasmine, picking up the dress and holding it out in front of her. Its design was a perfect copy of her original one that got damaged in the fight with Sleeve. However, it was lined with scales, each one gleaming in the rising sun. As she turned it around, she noticed how well the craftsman kept the web pattern. It seamlessly flowed from cloth to scale.

"Oh, stop looking it over and put it on, sis," Forsythia said as she crossed her arms, her foot tapping impatiently on the ground.

"Sorry," said Jasmine. She grabbed the boots and gloves that were in the case. Leaving Forsythia alone, she moved to a changing room that was inside the castle adjacent to the training field.

She slipped out of her clothes and proceeded to try it on. It fit perfectly. She began to wonder when Forsythia had gotten her measurements but shook her head quickly to rid herself of the thoughts. Putting on the boots and gloves, next she found herself taken aback by the weight. Even though metal was woven into it, it felt far lighter than her original dress ever did.

As she moved around in the room to get a feel for it, she began to realize what it was, and her jaw dropped. Slamming the door open, she sprinted back to the field; it felt as light as if she was wearing nothing at all. Forsythia was standing exactly where she left her, a large smile on her face.

"Good, looks like you can move quite well in it," she said, looking her over. "Looks like it fits all of you just right too."

"Forsythia!" she yelled, stopping in front of her.

"Something the matter?" she asked, looking her over. "Does it not fit right somewhere? I can have them reshape it."

"No, no, it feels fantastic. The problem is this is a battle dress made of sky metal! Even my boots and gauntlets!"

"Oh...you noticed?" Forsythia's was feigning shock.

"Not at first," said Jasmine. "But after moving in it, seeing how the metal moves with the cloth, it's the only metal in the known world to work like this with cloth. Why am I wearing this and not you?"

"I'm a skirt's girl, come on, you know that."

"Then a skirt of this?" asked Jasmine, unsatisfied with her response.

"Eh," she shrugged. "Eventually. Your dress cost me all the money from the last mission I was on. But when I get paid next, you can bet I am gonna spoil myself. After all, it's the only piece of my outfit not made of the stuff."

Jasmine began to tear up. She didn't know whether it was happiness or the fact Forsythia giving up the money for this. Maybe it was a mix of both. Forsythia just smiled at her as she grabbed a baton from the crate. An item Jasmine never noticed was in the crate when she first grabbed the armor.

"One more gift," said Forsythia as she handed the rod to her. "Now don't hate me."

Jasmine placed one hand on it. Forsythia pressed a button, and it extended like her old one into a full Bo Staff. Sliding her finger along another button, Jasmine watched as the tip of the wood parted. Metal folded out from in between the wood, forming into a large curved blade. It was now reminiscent of the naginata used commonly in the far north.

Lifa wood had formed the staff itself, its sturdy ivory wood showing off its beautiful engravings. Although the wood was frail when being worked with, there was no equal to it when it was finally shaped. The emblem of Samil was carved into the wood next to the button that activated the blade. Jasmine was captivated by the wood as she looked it up and down. The moment her eyes drifted back to the bladed tip, however, those feelings were instantly drained away.

"The finest engineers got this to work for me," said Forsythia as she let go of it, leaving Jasmine to hold the weapon alone. "The blacksmiths helped with the blade and the body. The mechanism to make the blade deploy took some time. I know how much you liked

166

your original. This was the closest they were able to come to replicating it. Since…well…you know."

Jasmine pictured herself dropping it, letting it hit the grass beneath her and never touching it again. But she put her other hand on it and held it tight, her eyes not moving from the blade. "Since my brother can't make them anymore, yeah, I know… I do love it, it's so beautiful. But Forsythia, you know I don't kill people. There's no need for me to have this blade on my weapon. I can't use this—"

"Just because you have a blade doesn't mean you have to use it," interjected Forsythia. "It's there in case there is no other option."

"There's always another option."

"That man you fought the other night, he would've been better off killed. He broke free and is out doing who knows what. You start sparing the wrong people, they'll start taking advantage of you. And any problems they would cause with a new chance at life would be avoided. You keep this kindness of yours…you may just end up dead from your own fault."

"But—"

Forsythia shook her head. "You surviving is far more important than holding onto that rule of yours not to kill anyone. If you die, then there won't be anyone to help the people you could've if you were alive. And I don't want to find out you died because your guts were cut from you by the very one you showed mercy to. You don't have to use it, but it is there just in case. I know you'll be smart with it."

"Fine," she said reluctantly and started to twirl it, getting a feel for the weight with the blade added to the end. "Thank you for all of this, sis… Really."

"You bet!" Forsythia responded as she placed a hand on her head and ruffled her hair. "Now we get to spar a little. Help you get a feel for the weapon and the armor in a fight. The armor is lighter, the weapon is a bit heavier. No better way than a quick friendly spar."

Forsythia stepped back and pulled her harp from her back, splitting it in half perfectly down the center. The curved body of the harp produced blades, the strings attaching to the rectangles that formed in her fore arms. The metal of the blades glowed with the same orange light that rippled across her armor.

Finding a spot a fair bit away in the middle of the field, she assumed her initial combat stance—a slight crouch, one hand in front of the other, her right leg back—waiting patiently for her opponent to take her place opposite of her.

Jasmine walked over and faced her. Giving her new weapon one more twirl, she listened to the blade slice through the air. The more she moved it, the lighter it felt. To the point, it was the same if not lighter than her original weapon. She held it parallel to her spine in one hand behind her, her left arm out in front of her.

A gentle breeze blew, causing the emerald grass to dance with it. Time felt like it held still, neither making a move toward each other, each one waiting for the other. The only movement between them was their breathing. With a deep breath, Jasmine stepped off, and Forsythia answered in kind. The distance between them closed in seconds.

The air filled with the sounds of their weapons colliding. Strike met with strike, neither one gaining ground on the other. Almost three months had passed since they last fought. A smile grew on their faces as they kept up with each other perfectly.

Jasmine began to incorporate her magic into her fighting. Spider legs sprouted from her back as silk wrapped around her forearms. Forcing Forsythia to block her weapon gave the legs an opening in which to strike.

Forsythia jumped back as the tips of the legs scratched the scales of her chest plate. Her eyes began to glow, miniature suns staring at Jasmine. A tune began to fill the air, the strings on her arms being plucked along by invisible fingers.

It started off slow, each note resounding in the field. Carried by the breeze, Jasmine felt herself begin to lose balance. Trying to recover, once she gained her footing, it was too late. Forsythia was already on her. The music was ramping up speed, and Forsythia moved perfectly along with it, a punch landing with each beat. Jasmine tried to keep up, but her body was moving far slower than her mind was thinking.

Forsythia easily slipped through her weapon and spider legs. Inside her reach, Jasmine was defenseless. Her defeat played out in a crescendo of music. A moment later, Jasmine was on the ground, looking skyward. Her naginata a few feet away flung from her hands during the assault.

"Didn't expect you to use magic, sis," said Forsythia as she fused her harp back together. She stood it up in the ground and laid down next to her. "But you didn't expect mine either."

"Not in the slightest," responded Jasmine, disappointed with how easily Forsythia had beaten her. "Thought I could catch you off guard. But you caught me off guard, even more playing music without even plucking the strings yourself."

"A lot happened in three months. Had you not told me what happened the other night, I never would have expected you to have six of those creepy spider legs."

"Hey!" Jasmine's face was beginning to turn red. "They aren't creepy."

She began to laugh. "Let's be honest, Jasmine, they are pretty creepy. I still think your starlight should've manifested as something other than...spiders."

"I like them," she said, touching the tips of her fingers together as she looked down away from her. "If you don't mind me asking, what was your mission these past couple days?"

"Something rather boring honestly. Mostly guard duty, another of these white sash rebel groups sprung out in the eastern town of Lifollow. We already had some in custody. King was worried they may try and rescue them. So I was sent out there to watch over soldiers and the two Fingers stationed there."

"Was there any problem?" asked Jasmine, turning to look at her. From this close, she noticed the new scar on her cheek that ran up past her eye, ashamed of herself for not seeing it earlier. Two lines, which she presumed were made by a blade, narrowly avoided her eye.

"Nothing that some restorative magic couldn't fix. Though, I'll always have this little scar here to remind me of my failure." Her head turned toward Jasmine, and she saw the worry on her face.

"Hey, now, it's okay. They were sneaky bastards dressed up as civilians. They snuck up on us. It won't be happening again."

"Uh-huh," Jasmine said, clearly unsatisfied with her answer. A moment of silence passed between them again as they looked back up at the sky, the gentle breeze moving their hair.

"So I have some bad news, sis," said Forsythia, breaking the silence. She placed a hand on hers.

"What is it?"

"The king's sending me west."

Jasmine sat up instantly. "To Zell? B-B-But we're on the verge of wa—"

"And that's exactly why I'm going. Pitch and Daniel have already departed. I'll be going as backup. Hopefully, it doesn't come to war… But Victor believes in the stubbornness of Zell's kings. So in an effort to end it as soon as it starts, he wants some of us there, ready to go."

Jasmine's heart sunk. "But…why? Why you?"

"Oh, are you that worried about me?" she laughed as she sat up, messing with Jasmine's hair like she was a child. "You have your own thing, your own life to worry about. Sleeve and the White Sash—that's your problem on the home front. And I expect it to be dealt with before I get back."

Those words instantly snapped away Jasmine's worry. "I'll have it taken care of before you even make landfall."

"Now that's what I like to hear," Forsythia said as she got up. Offering her a hand to help her to her feet, Jasmine took it and smiled. "And when I get back. You'll be working with me. Don't forget."

"You better come back, Aliya." Jasmine's eyes drifted to the grass, unable to keep looking at her. Her eyes began to water, her body started to shake. Then she felt arms wrap around her, squeezing her tightly.

"I promise I'll come back, Jasmine," she said, her head now resting on her shoulder. "Just be waiting when I do."

"I will be."

Jasmine closed the case and took it with her as the two walked back to the castle entrance. There waiting with his arms crossed, back against the wall and one foot against it, was a man Jasmine respected almost as much as the king himself—the Sovereign Finger known as Jet. Jasmine had no idea what his real name was. Honestly, she was quite sure no one knew what his actual name was. Forsythia asked him numerous times. Each time, he promptly responded: "Beat me in a duel." In which she eagerly challenged him unaware of just how talented he was. After ten losses she gave up and just began to hope one day he'd tell her.

Jasmine tried to convince her to keep trying over a year ago. But she refused, saying that his power was inhuman and farm beyond the normal limits of a Kryzen. Following that conversation Jasmine tried to fight him herself. Forsythia however, refused to let her. Telling her that only two people in all of Samil had ever beat him in a fight. Those being King Victor and Cerulean, the first of the Sovereign Fingers.

But even after his defeat, he challenged them again and won. Jasmine nor anyone who watched him fight could forget the smile he always had. He loved the rush of combat, but it was strange, for in victory, he always frowned. Yet those two defeats, his smile shone brighter than ever before. Besides finding out his name, that was the reason that pulled at Jasmine to fight him. She wanted to understand why it was he never smiled in victory.

A small grin crossed his face as he noticed them approaching. He halfheartedly waved at them.

"Sorry, but I'm going to have to break you two up," a deep voice carried his words to their ears. He looked to Jasmine and then to Forsythia. His left eye was covered with an eyepatch, his right a faintly glowing ruby red. Spiky brown hair reached down to his shoulders, bangs covering the top half of his eye patch. "Victor wants to meet with the Sovereign Fingers still here before anyone else departs."

"Why?" asked Forsythia as she looked to Jasmine, longing to spend more time with her.

"I don't really know. It's something to do with Zell. A new tactic maybe? Something I don't know nor do I really care. I'm not going over there anyway as it stands. He'll fill you in."

Forsythia was shocked by his words. "He's not sending you to Zell?"

"Nope, I'm going up north to Ivofir."

"Oh, I see…you're upset, aren't you? That's why you don't care. You're going to miss all the fun."

Jet's facial expression said it plainly how he was not amused by her comment. "Did you want to fight me again today? Because it sure sounds like you are, and I am down to fight before we see the king."

"Nope, no, no," Forsythia replied, waving her hands in front of her. "That is A-OK. Jasmine, I'll see you when I get back. Be careful."

"You too," said Jasmine. "And Jet, be careful in Ivofir."

Jet just turned and walked away. Forsythia hugged Jasmine before backpedaling after him, waving the whole time until they could no longer see each other. Wiping a tear from her eye, Jasmine walked away. She had business to take care of before Forsythia made landfall.

11

10ᵗʰ of Japhim; Mortal Year 523

Jasmine

O nce again, she found herself in the Crafting District. This time, near the northern end bordering the Merchant District. Tuesday was a quiet day for most shops in the district. Very little traffic would pass through, most just placing orders and then leaving. Had it been a weekend, it would have been a different story with everyone picking up their orders and comparing them with other shoppers.

As she walked down the cobblestone street, she started to whip up a lie to tell him with the hopes to convince him as easily as she did the alchemist. Nearing the shop, the sounds of the forge could be heard out on the street, hammers striking metal time and time again. The smiths were hard at work in their workshop out of public view. Above the wooden door that led inside the main shop was a crooked sign in the shape of an anvil. On it was written "Landon's Smithy" in faded letters.

Jasmine took a deep breath and then opened the door. Stepping inside she took note of everything in the room. Two other customers were in the shop, one to her left, and one to the right. Weapons of all designs lined the wall from tiny daggers to massive war hammers—

the talent of the smiths was on display. In the middle of the shop, opposite the entrance, was a counter in which, who she assumed was, the shopkeeper stood. Behind him, the wall was lined with bows, and much to her surprise, a few rifle designs, which felt odd to her, for rifles were strictly being made by the castle smiths only.

The shopkeeper was a middle-aged man with bleach blonde hair, a well-kept beard, and sideswept bangs. His hands were covered in black and dirt. He looked up from a paper on the counter in front of him as he heard the door close.

"Welcome to Landon's Smithy," he said cheerfully. "You here to place an order today? Maybe purchase something already made?"

Jasmine took her baton from her back and hit the button, allowing it to extend and change into a naginata in front of him. Placing it on the counter, she smiled. "I was actually hoping for an appraisal."

His eyes went wide as he looked over the weapon. "Where did you get such a remarkable weapon? The quality of this is similar to that of the castle smiths. And it's such a pure sky metal. To see it like this is incredible!"

Jasmine leaned closer so that the other two customers wouldn't be able to hear her. "I had to kill a Finger for it."

Jasmine didn't believe it was possible for his eyes to get any wider than they had. But by some feat, they managed to, and she began to worry they would pop out of his head in front of her.

"A Finger, you say? I don't know whether to be impressed or to report you to the nearest guard."

"Well hopefully the former, because I'm just traveling through and don't want to go through that hassle."

He picked up the weapon and got a feel for its weight. Stepping back to give himself room, he swung it a few times. Placing it back on the counter, he looked at her. "Ten thousand gold would be the lowest price, and even then, you could probably get anyone to go higher on it."

Jasmine's jaw almost reached the floor. *Forsythia! What the hell is wrong with you?* "Do you happen to know anyone who might buy it?"

"Take it to the merchants... For the best luck and price, try to talk to one of the higher up ones in the guild. When it comes to goods like this, they give you your payment, though I would admit to have something like that hanging around here would be something."

Jasmine hit the button, and the weapon shrank. Placing the baton back on her back, she glanced around and noticed the other two customers had left.

"Well, thank you," she said as she moved to the door. Strands of silk starlight formed around her arms. Webbing the door closed, she turned back to him. "I do have another question for you."

"And what's th—" He cut himself off as he noticed her arms. "What's going on with you there?"

He was pointing at her arms. She looked to where he pointed and shrugged. "Doesn't matter. I want to know about Sleeve."

"Who?"

"Sleeve, the bastard in black with one white sleeve. Him and the White Sash. I want to know what you know."

"Listen, girl, I know nothing of a 'Sleeve' or a 'White Sash.'"

His tone hadn't changed. His face never changed expression. He wore the same look he gave her before she said anything to him. Deciding that he easily could be lying, Jasmine place one hand on the counter and created a small spider.

The shopkeeper jumped back in fear. "What in god's name is that?"

"Just a friend," replied Jasmine, placing a hand on top of it as if it were a cat or dog. "I'll give you one more chance before this friend of mine gets to you. Sleeve and the White Sash. What do you know about them?"

"I don't know a damn thing! And if someone like you going around threatening someone with a spider is asking about them, I'm sure it isn't anything I want to be a part of!"

A side door swung open, and another man walked in. He was looking down the whole time at a weapon in his hands.

"Hey, Tate," he said, drawing closer to the counter. "The boss wants this hung up. He just finished it and thinks it would be a great display of our wo—"

He stopped speaking as he finally looked up within arm's reach of Jasmine, looking at the exchange going on between them and the spider. The man was beginning to find himself unable to speak anymore.

He knew something.

Jasmine took her hand off the spider, and it leapt at Tate, covering his face. He stumbled back into the wall as he tried to claw at it. Jasmine shot a string of silk at the man's weapon and yanked it free while she shot another at one of his feet, sticking it to the ground.

Trying to pull his leg free, he started to yell. Silk found its home on his mouth and silenced him. Realizing his leg wasn't going to come free, he gave up and focused on the girl standing in front of him. Her yellow eyes giving off an eerie glow.

"Good," she said, taking a quick look over at the shopkeeper who had just finished being wrapped in a cocoon. The spider crawled back to her and climbed onto her shoulder. "Look, I have a question for you. All you have to do is give me an answer, and I'll let you go. And I will go my own way, and we don't have to see one another again. How does that sound?"

He nodded. Jasmine pulled away the silk and took a step back. "All I want to know is what you know about Sleeve."

Fear would have been the word to describe his face when he saw Jasmine. But when he mentioned Sleeve, sheer horror filled his face. His skin went pale, and he started to shake. "N-No one wants to know about Sleeve. No, no, no."

"Are you okay?" Jasmine asked, crouching down and placing her hands on his shoulders. "If it's too hard to speak about him, what about where to find him? Can you tell me that?"

"You… You don't want to find him. Not unless you want to die. Whether you be friend or foe, to seek Sleeve is to sign your life over to death."

Jasmine took her hands off his shoulders and looked toward the side door he came out of. "Is your boss back there?" she asked, realizing he wasn't going to give her anything at this point. He nodded slowly as she looked back to him. She knocked him out and then cocooned him.

Moving to the door, she was able to hear the sound of hammers hitting against metal. Even had the man called for help, she was quite confident the sound of the smiths working would've drowned it out. Pushing the door open slowly, she peeked inside and was amazed by the sight.

Ten large forges sat arranged in a rectangle around the room. In the center was an eleventh that dwarfed all the others to the point it seemed out of place with the gold trim and gems that lined it. Along the main body were intricate designs similar to that of Jasmine's weapon.

Jasmine grew her spider legs and leapt up to the ceiling before anyone noticed her. As she crawled along she studied the forges. Each one had a singular smith and everything they could have asked for to manage their craft. Each forge seemed focused on a particular weapon. The one she was currently above had molds for axes. Others had ones for swords, spears, and so on.

Chimneys extended from each forge and out through the ceiling. The flames of each forge burned brightly. She was getting hotter as she neared a forge. Making her way to the center, she started to wonder how they were able to stay in this heat and work all day. Now above the center one, she looked down and watched another smith approach the one below her.

"Hey, boss," he said, "how many spears did they need again?"

"His direct words were as many as we have ore for," the smith below her replied as he scratched his gray beard. "With the war coming, our troops need all they can get."

A long sigh came from the other man as he turned and made his way back to his forge.

"Hey, don't worry, we'll be well compensated for it. Plus, think about it, it's not every day we get to work for the military. Shows our worth as smiths. Meaning we can compete with the best in the world!"

The room shook with a triumphant yell from all the smiths. It had drowned out the sound of the hammers for that moment. It wasn't much. To Jasmine, it wasn't that rallying at all, but it had done something for the smiths. They were working even faster than before.

Wrapping a silk strand around her leg and holding onto it with one hand, she descended upside down stopping when her head was at the same level as his.

"Hey," she said.

The smith jumped in place, his hammer striking bare anvil as he missed the blade.

"Woah, woah, calm down. Just keep working. All I want to do is talk.

"Most people just ask for me at the front," he replied as he went back to work.

"You're Landon, right?"

"Aye, that's me. This is my shop. What can I do for you, little spider?"

"How did you know?" she asked caught off guard.

"Old boy Mark, the alchemist, told me about you. Though I expected you yesterday. Or even earlier this morning. When you didn't show today, I decided to start working on orders. And alas, here you are, dangling from the ceiling."

"Then you should know why I am here."

"Sleeve," he mumbled as his hammer struck against the blade one more time. He cooled it off in the water next to him. Placing both the hammer and the blade back on the anvil, he dusted off his hands. "Follow me, girl. I would rather not talk about it around them."

Jasmine hopped down as the silk dissipated. Her spider legs disappeared, and she gladly followed him. Now that she was on ground level, she felt rather small. Landon looked more like a Zellian than a Samilian. He was a man of very large build who stood a couple heads taller than she did. She shook her head so she could focus more on what was important instead of that.

She followed him out of the forge room and through another door in the back. Inside was a desk with stack after stack of papers. A bookshelf to the left of it filled to the brim in books on blacksmithing. Landon took a seat in the worn leather chair behind it and started to rummage through a desk drawer.

Jasmine found herself drawn to the bookshelf by her curiosity. She giggled at the names of some of them and how they compared to the books from the alchemy shop. The exact same names, but anything to do with alchemy was replaced with blacksmithing.

"Here it is," said Landon, making her look toward him to see what he had. He placed a white sash similar to all the others she saw the other night. Jasmine shot daggers at him. "When you have a blade to your throat and no other option. And you value your life. You start to do what they say. But since that incident a couple days ago, you Fingers and guards have been hunting white sashes down like crazy."

"You don't support it?" she asked as she moved to the desk and looked down at the sash.

"The world is cruel, that much is true. And while I would love to support their ideas...they're going about it the wrong way. There's too much blood for my taste."

"For a maker of weapons, that seems almost uncharacteristic."

"Maybe, but I'm just a maker and a dealer. What one does with the final product is not my problem. But this isn't really about me, is it? You want Sleeve."

"How is it you're able to say his name so calmly. I mentioned it to someone out front, and I swear I've never seen a person go that pale before in my life."

Landon tapped his fingers on the desk. "It really is difficult to do."

"I don't understand."

"Sleeve isn't normal... I don't know what it is. Maybe it's because you're a Kryzen. You don't feel it. But even having a conversation with him makes your spine tingle, goosebumps form, and he makes you want to drink just to calm you down. I can say his name fine, but have me talk to him for any manner of time, and I want to hop straight out of my skin."

"Anything else you can tell me?"

"Just a possibility of where to find him."

Jasmine's hands slammed on to the desk, and she stared directly into his eyes. "Where?"

"It's only a possibility, so if it comes back with nothing, don't bite my head off. To the north in Montlimar, a meeting will be happening two weeks from yesterday. Invitations went out to everyone connected. My guess is more of the higher ups will be present."

"Why haven't you brought this to the guard?"

"Because if you do, don't you think they would scatter? This may be a rebellion of fools, but they are not foolish. Take my sash. It's all you need to get through. If you don't find Sleeve, maybe you can find something else worth your time."

Jasmine hesitantly took the sash from the table and folded it up as small as she could, holding it under her arm against her side. "Thank you, Landon."

"Thank Mark when you see him again. Had he not said anything…well, this day may have been different for both of us."

Jasmine gave him a half-hearted smile before walking out the door. Making her way back through the forge room and into the main store, she undid the cocoons of the two unconscious men and waited for them to wake. When they were both up, she undid the silk on the door and disappeared out into the sunlight.

She decided to return to the barracks, pack up some belongings for travel, and head out for Montlimar by dusk. Jasmine packed the current alchemy book she was reading in her bag amongst her supplies. When she was ready, she headed to the military stables on the western end of the castle. Showing her necklace, the stable master showed her to a horse without question, and she took off.

At the northern gate, leading out of the city, a guard stopped her. A small red bird was perched on his shoulder. It hopped from his shoulder and onto hers. *Oh, Cardinal, this really needs to stop,* she thought to herself as the bird got comfortable. The bird was an eye of sorts for Cardinal, something any member of his group was to leave the city with if they ever had too. And the guards knew exactly who to look for to make sure they got one.

The guards opened the gate, and the horse broke into a full gallop, heading toward Montlimar.

12

After spending over a month in Zell, Kenjo and Vallarya began to find they enjoyed the weather there a bit more than back home. Even though it was summertime, their armor felt comfortable. Not even a bead of sweat dotted their brow. Back home, they would have been drenched. The sun's rays cast down on them through an empty sky.

The group of six had been traveling for the past four hours, having departed early in the morning for Blaebus. Elijah's parents had agreed to let him go with them, having the two hands promise them one more time to look after him. Mary stayed behind, deciding it was best for her to be with her family in his absence, especially after everything that had happened to them.

On the road, they ran across two traveling merchants who offered them some brand-new sleeping rolls. Vallarya refused to pass up the opportunity. Kaldana and Luna agreed with her as well, making up a story of how their backs were starting to hurt and go stiff from the previous travel. Kenjo and Arlo reluctantly agreed too.

A few hours later, they ran into a family traveling by wagon. Arlo decided to talk to the wagon driver who turned out to be the father of the family. They had the same destination in mind. The family took yearly trips to Zell at the same time. After traveling together for a bit, Arlo decided to call the group to a halt and offered the family lunch.

Kenjo and the others wanted to keep going, but the growl of their stomachs pushed that thought well out of their minds. Vallarya, Kaldana, and the mother of the family worked to get a meal prepared while the others sat around the campsite, talking, save for Luna who found herself a rock a little way from camp to sit on and keep watch.

"So why do you do this yearly trip?" asked Arlo before taking a drink from his waterskin.

"Besides seeing all of the kings together?" replied the Father as he looked over at his three children, two boys and one girl running around and playing with one another, all of them spitting images of their parents. "Why would anyone care to make such a long trip to see none other than the Colors of Summer?"

"Ah, yes, that's something quite spectacular. I remember my first time seeing it. It was incredible. I couldn't pull my eyes away."

"Yeah, I swear it puts everyone under a spell," he laughed, and Arlo laughed along with him. "The kids love it, so while they're still young and at home, thought we would make it a tradition."

"I'm sorry, what exactly is the Colors of Summer?" asked Kenjo, curious as he listened to them.

"Oh, you don't know?" asked the father as he looked him over. "Oh, I see most of you aren't from Zell form the looks of it. Hmm, well, not many know about it outside the nation. But for those of us here, it's one of the greatest times of the year, celebrated with more oomph than that of a new year."

The Colors of Summer marked the end of the Coup of Santiago. Way back when Zell was still a young nation, shortly after the six kingdoms had agreed on uniting into one true nation. A man named Santiago was fed up with the way things were going to be. He felt that under one king, the kingdoms would begin to lose what made them who they were, and none of the current kings deserved their throne.

It all started with the spreading of lies and misinformation. Within a few short months, he had acquired a massive following and laid the seeds for his plans, putting groups in each kingdom while he himself worked out of the capital. It was the bloodiest event in Zell's history, rivaling that of the Blood Rain during the Age of Heroes. More than half of each kingdom was set on fire; direct supporters of the current ruling parties were executed without a second thought.

Within two short years, the surrounding kingdoms had surrendered, leaving only the capital itself. The current Lord King backed into a corner, his royal knights all that stood between him and Santiago's forces. Victory was in reach for Santiago, yet favor was not with him that final day.

An unnamed adventurer carrying seven different colored swords had traveled into the capital, unfazed by the carnage and destruction around him. He singlehandedly cut down Santiago and his forces after they dragged him into the fight. Then he just disappeared, not a word, not a clue to where he may have headed. He was just gone. The only sign that he ever existed was the bodies of his victims strewn out along the concrete.

No longer with a head, the coup fell apart. Across the nation, weapons were thrown down without hesitation, no one wanting to assume Santiago's spot after word of what happened got around. Within a year, the kingdoms had been recaptured. But unrest amongst its citizens and all of those involved was still there. At the Meeting of Kings, the Lord King planned for something special. And on the final day, seven massive birds known as Atma flew over the capital, each one a different color after the hero's blades: red, yellow, blue, green, orange, and purple—all led by one as white as snow. They flew around each one, tasked with recreating the sigil of a kingdom. Trails of flame behind their tails, allowing them to recreate them in the sky. When the six had been made, they came together to recreate the sigil of Zell.

The flaming sigils burned away the unrest that still stirred in people's hearts. The faith in their kings reignited by the fading flames. And since the coup, Zell had never seen days as dark as those ever again.

"That's just the gist of it, though," said the Father as he noticed the food was done and moved to help the ladies with it. "No matter who you ask, though, they will all say that it was the darkest days in all of Zell's history. And we survived the Blood Rain."

"Yeah," said Arlo as he grabbed his own bowl. "The academy in the capital should have all the books on it if you want the finer details."

"Yeah, me and Vallarya will probably take a look into that." Kenjo got his bowl, and the three of them took another seat.

Luna stopped by just to grab a bowl of food, returning to her rock without a word. Kaldana took a seat next to Elijah as Vallarya found a spot next to Kenjo. She glanced at him and then quickly tore herself away as she felt herself begin to blush. Kenjo looked the food over quickly before he chowed down.

Soft chicken pieces sat amongst various vegetables and a piece of bread. They would've used plates for it, but all they had originally taken were bowls. They sat and chatted for another hour or so about nothing in particular before they decided it was time to go their separate ways.

Kenjo and the others took off first in a full gallop to help them make up lost time, not stopping again until well after dark. They got off the main road and walked through the forest for a little while before they found a small clearing that was good enough for them to set up camp. Kenjo took first watch as the others set up their sleeping rolls around the fire and tried to get as comfortable as they could.

Finding a fallen log, Kenjo took a seat, standing his sword up against it as he dug the tip of it into the dirt. He pulled his cloak tighter around himself as a cold breeze blew through, causing him to shiver. The sky had been clear during the day, but now clouds blanketed out the stars. Moonlight tried to sneak in through the occasional gap.

A cracking twig and the crunch of leaves from behind him made him turn around. He saw Vallarya walking toward him. Turning back in the direction of the road, he felt his heart skip a little. She took a seat next to him and joined him in looking toward the road.

"Um..." said Vallarya, fidgeting on the log to try and get comfortable.

"I don't think I've heard you start a conversation with 'Um' in a long time," said Kenjo. "Usually, you know exactly what you want to say."

"It's not that I don't know what to say," she replied, turning to look at him. "I just don't know if I should."

"Huh?" asked Kenjo as he turned to her. Her red eye glowed brightly in the night.

"About last night…"

"Yeah?"

Her hand found its way to his on the log. She opened her mouth to speak, but nothing would come out. Squeezing his hand, she hoped it would give her the ability to speak. Only silence came out. She looked away from him, then back to him and away again. He put his arm around her and pulled her close.

"Kenjo," she muttered, "can we stay like this for a while?"

"Yeah," he replied. *Absolutely* was what he thought, but he refused to show it.

They sat together until the end of his watch when Arlo touched him on the shoulder to switch out. The two moved back to the camp and lay next to each other, quickly finding themselves taken by sleep's embrace.

*****

Kenjo woke to the sound of chirping birds and a rising sun. The rest of the group was asleep still, save for Kaldana who was keeping watch from the log. Kenjo moved slowly in an effort not to wake Vallarya. Getting to his feet, he stretched before placing his sword on his back. He started to hear whistling, just a little quieter than the birds chirp, but not in tune enough to blend in.

He looked around and found it was coming from Kaldana who was now standing on top of the log. Her flames juggled between her hands as she walked to one end, then turned around and walked to the other end. She repeated this about five more times before she noticed Kenjo was looking at her. Hopping down, the whistling stopped, and she sat with her back to him.

Kenjo laughed as he took his sleeping roll and placed it back on his horse. They would leave as soon as the rest of them were up, eating a small ration of bread on the way, which he personally thought was the best bread he ever had. The bread he had back in Samil came nowhere close in both taste and texture, soft and fluffy bread with a sweet aftertaste to leave you satisfied. Not to mention one piece could tide you over on the same level as a full meal, according to Elijah's mother.

Within the hour, the others were up and storing their belongings on their horses. Then they made their way back to the road with Kenjo and Arlo in the lead. It would take them another two weeks to reach the capital. Blaebus was about three days away if they kept a good pace. The weather was in their favor again today. No clouds in sight as the sun slowly drifted along.

By noon, the group had broken free of the forest. A plain of green grass stretched out before them on either side of the road. Out in the plain that stretched, on their left, grazed a herd of cow-like creatures. A long horn extended from the right sides of their foreheads, wrapping back about halfway down their bodies, large tails with bushy tips resting peacefully on their back ends. They were moving further inland away from the road and civilization.

"They're called karmos," said Arlo as he saw the fascination on the faces of his Samilian companions. "As long as you don't hurt anyone in the herd, they're some of the friendliest creatures. It's believed that their horns are all connected in some weird way. If any of them get hurt, all the others know."

"There's nothing like this back home," said Vallarya as she continued to watch them until they became specks in the distance. "Well, we have a similar beast called rantals. But their horns don't do anything special like those. Do you guys hunt them often?"

"There was a time for it," said Arlo as he looked toward the fading herd. "Back some forty years before I was born, they almost went extinct, making the kingdoms all agree on outlawing both the hunting and selling of them. Their number has increased over the years, but they're still an endangered breed."

"Meat tastes similar to that of a mamo," said Elijah joining into the conversation.

Arlo scowled at him.

"Hey, we didn't hunt it. A dying one was separated from its herd, wandered close to town. There was no way for it to be saved nor were there any other karmos in sight! Anyways, mamo and karmos are very close in taste. Right seasonings, you probably wouldn't be able to tell."

Arlo sighed as he turned his focus back front. Kaldana giggled at the exchange between them.

Another hour of travel, and they found the grassy fields replaced with farms. They lined the road all the way down as far as they could see. Mamo were moving as a herd inside large fenced-off areas, feeding on the grass beneath them.

In between every four fields was a large farmhouse. Barns and chicken coops were easy to pick out. Some of the farms, however, were solely focused on crops. Not an animal in sight, each field filled to the brim in growing vegetables. The main road diverged at a set point, cutting a dirt path through the plain and in front of the farms, allowing the farmers and their wagons easy access to the road.

As their horses trotted along, a wagon drawn by two beautiful brown horses pulled onto the road behind them, heading toward Gitving. Elijah waved as they passed by, and the farmer smiled as he waved back. When it was finally dusk, they were still surrounded by farms. Elijah informed them that it was the main purpose of Blaebus. The fields around here enjoyed some of the best soil in the west. And the crops produced from it were easy to distinguish from those grown anywhere else.

During harvest season, the farmers had enough crops to last through winter, the only time of year that led to the soil being unable to grow anything. Outside of the few cold months, however, the soil never went bad. It never failed them, nor could it ever be overused. The soil was perfect here, and any who were willing to devote their life to the craft had a very lucrative business opportunity.

With no end in sight for the farms, the group began to worry about where they were going to sleep for the night. None of them wanted to trespass yet. They knew there wasn't much point in them traveling on into the night. Eventually, they found a road that split from the main one that didn't lead to another farm. Following it down a little ways, they pulled off onto the plain and set up camp.

Arlo went to work, preparing a fire. Kaldana and Elijah fed the horses. Luna, being her same quiet self, found a bush closer to the road and took a seat in front of it, taking first watch over the group. Kenjo and Vallarya took care of dinner that night, first gathering up everyone's sleeping rolls and laying them out around Arlo's fire before cooking.

Elijah dropped one of the apples he was treating the horses to. Before it touched the ground, Kaldana grabbed it and handed it back to him.

"Careful now," she said. "You don't want them angry at us."

"Do you really believe they're going to get angry from a fallen apple?" Elijah asked as he held it out for the horse to eat, his other hand stroking its mane.

"I would like to believe they might. They can be pretty smart creatures sometimes, even if they can't voice their thoughts."

Kaldana finished feeding her horses and started to walk back to camp when she tripped. Elijah caught her before she hit the ground.

"Careful now."

Kaldana laughed as he took his arms off her. "Thank you, Elijah."

They returned to the fire and waited patiently for Kenjo and Vallarya to finish cooking. When they were done, they greedily accepted their bowls and dug in. Kenjo noticed Luna had not come back for hers. Taking his with him, he grabbed another bowl for her and headed out to the bush.

Luna was kneeling. Had it not been for her hair, she would have been nearly impossible to make out in the night. Her bow was at the ready, an arrow already knocked. All she had to do was pull and release for a target to meet the end of its life. Kenjo rustled the bush as he passed by. She snapped around, drawing the bow back, arrow aimed right between his eyes.

"Is that three times now?" he asked, looking at her past the bow. "I thought you weren't going to point that at me anymore."

"Sorry," she replied, slowly releasing the tension of the bow as she lowered it. Turning back to the road, her head moved back and forth, checking each side. When she realized Kenjo wasn't leaving, she began to grow annoyed. "Can I help you?"

"You can eat this. If you want to, that is, I won't force you. Just thought you may be hungry."

The aroma wafting from the bowl was enough to make her drop her guard. Luna stored the arrow back in her quiver and rested her bow against the bush, happily taking the bowl from Kenjo as he took a seat beside her. Her eyes passed over him, still focused on the road as she ate.

"Luna, may I ask you something?" asked Kenjo as he swallowed a bite.

"If you must," she replied scooping up another bite.

"You're a Detheo, aren't you?"

The spoon slipped from her hand, landing in the bowl with a clank and splash of the broth. She looked at him and just stared. Luna was at a loss.

"Yeah, that's all I needed to confirm it," said Kenjo, taking another bite of his food. "You can't hide that reaction from me."

"How do you know of the Detheo?" she asked, now refusing to look at him in an effort to hide her expression.

"My mother mentioned it before. Your attire and weapon fit the description she gave me a long time ago. Though I never thought I would speak to one, sure as hell not have one traveling with me."

"Who was your mother?"

"Someone who knew some of Samil's greatest secrets. Luna, why haven't you gone back to Samil? I know you mentioned they would probably kill you, but as a Detheo, wouldn't you have the ability to escape that punishment?"

She started to shake. "You should just read my memories. It would be easier on both of us."

"Why would I do that now?"

"It would be easier than me telling you. If you want to know, just do it."

Luna turned back around, grabbing one of his wrists. She raised the hand up to her forehead. All he had to do was channel the magic, and her life would be a part of his memory.

There was no doubt that Kenjo was curious. He wanted to delve into her mind, see the life of the Detheo through their eyes. But before the magic could go, he saw tendrils of black wrap around his forearm, slowly inching their way to her.

"Hurry up. This is awkward."

"I can't do it, Luna," he said, yanking his arm away.

"Why? Why can't you? You have the Hands, don't you?"

"Yes…but there's something else. I don't want it to attack you."

Luna cocked her head to one side, confused. Kenjo stood up and walked away without another word, taking her bowl with him as he made his way back to the fire.

"What do you mean something else?" It came out in a whisper as he left. He was too far away to hear.

Luna just watched in silence around the bush as he joined the others sitting around the fire. She looked down at her hands and found them shaking involuntarily. *Why am I afraid?* she thought to herself as she grabbed her weapon. With bow in hand, her hands grew still again as she resumed watch.

Kenjo placed the bowls to one side as he laid down on his roll. Rolling onto his side, he closed his eyes. Waiting for him in his dreams was the man in gold and black. Once again, his voice wasn't audible, and once more, the tendrils wrapped themselves around Kenjo, suffocating him through the night until the crack of dawn.

*****

In the morning, they made their way back to the main road and continued their journey. The sky was cloudy. Each cloud looked as if it was ready to rain down on them at any moment. The wind began to pick up, and the horses were starting to get antsy as they galloped along the dirt road.

A few minutes later, the rain began to fall, slow at first, just a light shower that didn't bother them. An hour later, it was a downpour. Refusing to stop the group pushed on, the horses slowing down from a gallop to a weak trot, making their way through the muddy ground beneath them.

"I don't think this is going to stop anytime soon," said Kaldana as she moved closer to the front with Kenjo and Arlo. "We might want to reconsider stopping."

"Why's that?" asked Arlo as he spit rainwater from his mouth. "Oh, that's right, you don't like thunder and lightning, do you? I bet that will be coming soon."

"This isn't about th—" Kaldana's words ended in a screech of terror as thunder boomed across the sky. She refused to speak anymore, knowing it would only humor Arlo more as he grinned through the rain.

"We need to stop," said Luna, coming up from the rear.

"Holy shit, she can speak again?" asked Arlo, baffled by the fact she spoke. "She's right, though, this mud is dragging the horses down. Eh, Kenjo! See anywhere that can give us some shelter?"

"I only see farms," yelled Kenjo as more thunder filled the air. "We mise as well try a barn. There shouldn't be a Siv in all of this, right?"

"Nay. This is just a normal summer storm. Come on, let's try that house over there." Arlo pointed at the next farmhouse down the road.

Following Arlo's lead, the group made their way to the next farm house down the road. The house itself was smaller than most of the others; however, the barn that was positioned behind it dwarfed many of the others they passed. Vallarya hopped off her horse as the group came to a halt in front. Pulling her cloak tighter, she ran through the rain to the front door. Protected by the rain from the awning above her, she waited patiently.

An older woman opened the door, and Vallarya smiled softly as her body shivered.

"I'm sorry to bother you, miss," she said, looking back toward the group, "but we were wondering if there was a way we could stay here for the night? We're just trying to get out of this rain."

The old woman looked over Vallarya's shoulder at the others and then looked back to her "You can stay in the barn. There should be plenty of room for all of you."

"Thank you so very much!" said Vallarya with a bow.

The barn reeked with the smell of horses and pigs. But it was dry and had a roof. That was enough for them as they waited out the storm. Throwing their cloaks over wooden gates of empty pens to dry, the group huddled atop hay. Vallarya shivered again as the moments passed. An arm wrapped around her, she felt herself pulled in to Kenjo's embrace. She didn't fight it, just smiled and silently enjoyed it as warmth came back to her body.

A few hours later, the rain had stopped. Grabbing their damp cloaks, the group headed out again. Vallarya thanked the old woman once more before they began their journey atop the muddy road. The horses were forced to move slower. Combined with the rain, it added another day to their travel time.

When they finally did arrive at Blaebus, it was another beautiful summer day. The town was surrounded by stone walls with large wooden doors marking each entrance. Guards stood at the ready, two stood outside the gates. Another two positioned atop each gate on the walls. It only took Arlo a quick moment to get them inside. A small flash of their trophies, and the guards seemed to be worshipping him like he was some kind of legend.

Blaebus was exactly like Elijah had said, a hub for all things farming. Many offered their harvests, various stalls lining streets from corner to corner. As they passed through, they overheard people discussing their farming techniques and other things they had picked up for the best harvests possible on the plains. A few merchants browsed the stalls, their guild badges glinting in the afternoon light.

The quality of the fruits and vegetables were impeccable. Elijah hopped off his horse and purchased an apple for each of them. Giving the first to Kaldana, he eagerly awaited her to try it. Kaldana looked at the red fruit in her hands for a moment before baring her fangs and taking a bite.

"Ooooh, that's delicious!" she exclaimed as she took another bite.

Elijah became entranced by her excitement, accidentally bumping into Kenjo's horse. Kenjo looked back at him, then to Kaldana, and back again.

"Can I try one?" he asked, reaching out a hand.

"Yeah," Elijah replied, placing one in his out reached hand. "These are the best ones you'll find out here. Least that's what Mary has always told me."

Kenjo took a bite. It was the perfect amount of sweetness. He found it difficult to put down until all that was left was its core. Elijah passed the other apples out, and they were all in agreement, save for Luna who took the apple he gave her and pocketed it instead.

The group made their way through the busy streets, their goal being the northern gates so they could continue their journey. Although Vallarya, Kaldana, and Elijah all wanted to stay in the town for the night, they reluctantly let Kenjo and Arlo convince them that they needed to carry on in order to make up for the time they lost.

In the center of town, however, they were brought to a complete halt. A large group of people was forming a circle in the middle of town. Inside the circle were four individuals: Two knights, halberds in one hand at attention. In their other hand, a large chain connected to the shackles of a prisoner kneeling between them; the fourth, a woman, calling out to the people.

Judging by her attire, Kenjo figured she was a captain of the guard. Her uniform was similar to the silver chain mails that adorned the rest of the guards they had passed. However, hers was more decorated, and she sported a tabard with the emblem of Zell situated in the center of it.

"This man has committed a crime in your dear city!" she said. "He stole from you, claiming that it was his, committed murder for it. And now he sits before you, waiting for your judgment. How do you answer?"

"Oh, he's gonna die," said Arlo. "Move out of the way, you animals!"

The crowd looked to him, confused at first, holding their ground so they could watch the events unfold. But as Arlo drew closer to them, the horses determined to knock them down, they picked up the pace as he shouted at them again. "Come on, move! We've seen enough executions as it is! You aren't missing much."

The Angel-born prisoner was breathing heavily. Blood splashed onto the ground beneath him as he coughed. What must have once been his clothes were little more than torn rags hanging onto his body by threads. His once white wings, covered in blood, blackened by dirt and dust, were pinned to the ground underneath the guard's feet.

"Stealing that big of a crime here?" asked Kenjo as they continued along. He couldn't pull himself away. It was Manfo and Caprae all over again.

"Yeah," replied Arlo, "it's a grave sin in Zell. Wait, why are you focused on the stealing of all things? He murdered someone!"

"I didn't do it!" yelled the prisoner. "It was that bastard, Lukas! He stole all of those things. He was the one that killed that merchant!"

The people began calling for his death, spitting in his direction, careful to avoid the guards holding him. Kenjo looked back to Vallarya. She began to shake her head. His words sounded so sincere; he was afraid for his life.

"Kenjo," she said as he pulled his feet out of the stirrups and crouched on the saddle of his horse. "Don't you dare!"

Kenjo was already picturing it in his mind, stepping right into the captain's shadow and diffusing the situation. He had the Hands. He could read that man's memories and find out the truth. But as he stared, he began to feel his conviction waver. Glancing at his hands, he could see the tendrils wrapping around his arms, another around his neck and holding him firm.

"Kenjo, what are you doing?" asked Kaldana, finding just enough room for her to pull her horse up to his side. "Can you not see it well enough?"

Arlo turned around and realized what Kenjo was doing in an instant. The tavern scene where they met played out in his head. He remembered Kenjo catching his blade before he hit the guard over the head.

"Why haven't you stopped it yet?" asked Arlo, pulling his horse to a halt. Kenjo turned to face him. "You had that same look in your eyes when we first met. You remember catching my sword? If this doesn't sit well with you like that time did, why haven't you moved?"

Kenjo looked down at his hands, defeated. "That time was different. You didn't aim to kill the guards, just the men who were attacking you. He, however, could possibly be a criminal."

"Is that possibility the reason you're crouching on your horse?"

"His plea was too sincere..."

Arlo hopped down from his horse. He handed the reins to Elijah and began to wander through the crowd, calling back to him, "Let's make this quick!"

Arlo pushed his way through the crowd as it became a thicker mass of people toward the front. He found himself shoving them out of the way to get by. Once he was clear of the masses, he walked into the circle, catching the eyes of the guards and their captain. She drew her broadsword and pointed it at him.

"What exactly are you doing, young man?" she asked, the guards behind her shifting their weight, ready to attack him if needed.

"I have reason to believe that your claims are false!" Arlo said loudly for the entire crowd to hear. "That the man you have beaten bloody and shackled is innocent!"

Murmurs could be heard from the crowd around them. Kenjo watched the movements of the guards. While the captain remained steadfast in her stance, the two behind her wavered slightly. *Did they not fully believe it either?* Kenjo asked himself as he hopped down. Making his way to the front of the group, he saw the Angel-born had his head raised, looking to Arlo with hopeful eyes.

"Do you have something to back this belief?" she asked.

Arlo just shook his head and shrugged. "No, not really. But one of my traveling companions does. And he has the Hands of the Children." The crowd grew completely silent at that remark, the captain's face a mix of bewilderment and fear. "So if it's all the same to you. I would like the very one blessed by the gods to pass his judgment here and now, instead of letting our savage nature come loose on an innocent man."

Kenjo hesitantly walked forward, blackened stained glass gauntlets covering his hands. The Angel-born looked up at him, a shining ray of hope in his darkening world. Tears slid down his dirt-caked face, revealing the tan skin underneath. The woman hesitated, looked to her fellow guards and then back to the approaching Kenjo. The crowd remained silent, eagerly awaiting the response.

Luna's hand fingered her bow, another reaching for an arrow in her quiver. Kaldana mirrored Kenjo from earlier, crouching on her horse, the amethyst flame crackling in their lanterns. Vallarya could only sigh. Her forearms were gone again. Kenjo had roped them into another problem that wasn't theirs.

"What kingdom do you hail from, Hand?" she asked, slowly lowering her sword. Her body remained tense, ready to raise the sword and attack should his response be unsatisfactory.

"I hail from Samil," replied Kenjo, eyes watching the three guards for any movements. They gripped their weapons tighter; he was losing favor with them. "But I pledge no allegiance to any kingdom. I am a Hand for the people."

The woman chuckled a little. "What an honorable young man. Then prove to me that you are one. Or are those gauntlets all that you can manifest?"

Vallarya disappeared from her horse as the blackened armor formed around Kenjo's body. When they were fully embraced, he took a step forward, raising his hands in a sign of peace.

"You look like a knight out of a nightmare!" she said, looking him over. "But there is no doubt, that is the armor of the Hands." The captain sheathed her blade and stepped aside, motioning for him to come forward and take responsibility. "Just note, if he is innocent, he becomes your problem. You will take care of him from here."

"Can they drop the chains?" said Kenjo, stopping in front of the prisoner. "And step off his wings. He deserves that, at least."

The captain motioned at the two guards. With a nod, they dropped the chains and made some space between them and the prisoner, taking position on their captain's side they watched as Kenjo reached out his hand and placed it gently on the Angel-born's forehead. Then tendrils reached out of his gauntlets, seen only by him. They began to circle around the hopeful eyes looking up at him.

"Kenjo," said Vallarya, snapping him back into focus. "Is this really safe? Or is he going to end up another on the list we didn't want to kill?"

"There's one thing going for us," said Kenjo. "If the voice doesn't like what it sees, and he isn't innocent, then we'll just be saving the guards the trouble. As it is now, he's a dead man. Look at his eyes, Val. We're his hope."

"I hope it likes what it sees."

"Me too," Kenjo said as he took a deep breath.

His eyes began to glow, the tendrils around his hand disappearing, revealing cracks of golden light underneath, a warmth emanating from his gauntlet, filling the man's head with comfort. Kenjo and Vallarya were standing in front of the tapestry of his life. They walked their way down the road the prisoner, Ricardo Amengual, had carved out for himself.

*****

Lukas in turn was his friend. Or he was. He had done exactly what he said. He set him up, stealing from a merchant who was staying at one of Blaebus's inns. Ricardo and Lukas were gambling along with other patrons, one of which was a rather wealthy traveling merchant, showing off his gem-inlaid rings with pride.

Ricardo had folded early in the hand. The cards in play and the hand he was given turned out to be worthless. Lukas was the last one standing, going all-in against the merchant who had been winning the table since the night began. Towers of gold coins spread out in front of him, a mound of coins in between them. Ricardo watched as Lukas placed an amulet into the pile, the only way of making the merchant call him.

It was a beautiful amulet. Even in the lamplight of the inn, it shone with a brilliance that caught everyone's eyes. A large ruby sat in the middle of a golden oval. Four legs like strands of metal reached up and held it in place at its corners. The outer edge of the ring was inlaid with smaller rubies, each one catching the light as Lukas held it above the pile.

The merchant's eyes went wide. It was clear that in all his time, he had not seen an amulet as beautiful as the one before him now. He wanted it, and with a greedy smile, he accepted pushing all of his winnings in without a second thought. Lukas laid down his hand, four of a kind. Ricardo was patting his back. He was confident in his friend's victory.

Then the merchant played his hand: A royal flush. As Lukas stared at the cards before him, he felt his heart beginning to sink. The merchant smiled and began to bag up his winnings. He took extra care with the amulet, wrapping it in cloth before placing it in a separate small red bag. Lukas just sat there as Ricardo looked over the cards, believing he had cheated.

"Come on, Lukas," said Ricardo as he found nothing wrong with the deck. "Let's just go back to the room for now."

"I," he said, still focused on the table where his amulet once was. "I... I can't have lost that."

"You shouldn't have wagered it in the first place."

"How could I not? It was all I had left worth anything to him. Plus, I was confident I could win."

"There's always a chance of losing," said Ricardo as he lifted him up to his feet. The two walked up the stairs and retired to their room.

Lukas was silent the rest of the night. Ricardo tried to speak to him but was only met with silence and a defeated gaze. He wished he could get it back for him but knew there wasn't much he could do at that point.

Lukas had obtained it from his father before he died to some unknown disease, a family heirloom passed down from parent to the firstborn of their children. Usually, it occurred whenever the child had their first kid. But Lukas was the exception as his father went ill and became bedridden. When he knew he wasn't going to make it, he handed it over to him to keep the tradition going.

Lukas was never exactly sure when the tradition had started in his family. Even his father did not have an exact idea how many generations had passed. Yet, the gold nor the rubies had lost any of their appeal over the passage of time. And now it was in the hands of a greedy merchant who only saw it as a monetary value instead of something more.

Ricardo drifted off to sleep, knowing they had to head back north in the morning. The two of them were knights of Burrium, visiting Blaebus on the request of one of their commanding officers. A few hours later, he was woken by his door being kicked open. He sat up instantly, eyeing the four guards that walked into the room, weapons drawn. His heart began to beat faster. One stepped forward with shackles.

"What's this about?" he asked as the guards drew closer.

"The murder you committed," said the guard, pulling the shackle's chain tight. "Now either come with us quietly or we can put you down right here and save us all the trouble."

"I have no idea what you're talking about!" Ricardo looked down for a moment and saw blood on the floor. Following the trail, he noticed it led to his lance. Fresh blood covered the tip, and he realized Lukas was nowhere to be found.

"Where's Lukas?" he asked as he began to reach for the lance.

One guard hit him over the head and dragged him to the floor. The one with shackles pinned him down and began to bind his arms.

"Search the room for the amulet he stole. This man is no knight."

Ricardo was confused as they grabbed his hair and yanked him upright, his eyes darting around the room. *Where's Lukas? Where the hell is he?* he thought to himself as they walked him out of the room.

"Is this Lukas fellow your accomplice?" asked the guard, shoving him to the stairs. "Where is he hiding?"

"Accomplice in what?" Ricardo asked before he tumbled down the stairs, hitting his head with a hard thump. "I didn't do... anything."

His words meant nothing to the guard as another one grabbed one of his arms, and the two began to drag him out of the inn, across the gravel road, and into the jail at the eastern end of town. Lukas was still nowhere in sight, and with nothing but evidence stacked against him, Ricardo found himself beaten over and over again for a crime he slept through.

For three days, they beat him, asking him to confess. Ricardo remained adamant in his defense the first two days, saying over and over again that he didn't kill anyone, that he didn't even bet the amulet. Each time he replied, he met the fist of a guard. They were taking turns on the second day, alternating who struck him from sunrise to sunset.

On the third day, as he realized that Lukas had truly abandoned him, Ricardo could barely feel the hits against his body. The pain of losing a friend he had for so long was nothing compared to the iron fists that smashed into his ribs and face time and time again. Then they arrived at the present, dragged by the three who stood around him now, to the center of town. Hopeful eyes cast upward past a warm hand.

"He didn't do it," said Kenjo as Vallarya split from him. "It's as he said. His friend Lukas did it after losing his amulet in a bet. If you want justice for the merchant murdered in your little town, then find Lukas and treat him the same way you did Ricardo here. Remove the shackles and give him his belongings. And then we leave."

The captain was blinking rapidly. "Get the shackles off of him. One of you go grab the belongings of his that we still have. This Hand has spoken."

The crowd began to disperse. Some were clearly disappointed that no one had died today. But others were equally fascinated seeing a Hand in person, talking among themselves as they walked, a few of the kids imitating Kenjo with their friends. As the guard who went to fetch his belongings, Kenjo reached out a hand to help Ricardo up.

"T-Thank you," he said weakly.

"Don't mention it," replied Kenjo. "For now, at least you're stuck with us. Let's have you meet the others."

"If anything hurts severely, let me know," said Vallarya. "I only know a handful of healing magic, but it should be enough to mend you properly. I'm Vallarya, by the way."

"I'm Ricardo. No, you know that already. Thank you for saving me."

"*Save* is a loose word," said Arlo. "You may have been better off just dying here, you know?"

"What?"

"Sorry, poor joke," he said. "You're our problem now, though, so you've got some work to do. Come on."

Arlo led Ricardo toward the horses and their waiting companions that were easily visible now that the crowds had dispersed. Vallarya followed them, asking Ricardo where his pain could be felt, taking note of it mentally to treat him later.

"Hey, Hand," said the captain, stopping Kenjo in his tracks. "Although your Samilian, I do not doubt the words of a Hand. Should you find this Lukas fellow before we do, pass a letter around, would you? Whether he's dead or alive, let us know, just to have some closure on this murder."

"Will do," said Kenjo. He saw the others of his party waiting for him, motioning for him to hurry along. Vallarya, however, was glaring at him. He could tell he was going to hear it from her tonight.

"There's room next to the head in the wagon," said Arlo.

Ricardo looked at him a mix of curiosity and fear crossing his face. "Oh... Er, it's a trophy, don't worry. Plenty of room, though, and it doesn't smell."

Ricardo said nothing as he hopped in and took a seat. Kenjo hopped back on his horse and made his way to the front next to Arlo. Then they continued their journey, making their way out of Blaebus as quickly as they could, the eyes of guard and townsfolk alike following them, each one staring daggers at them. Something felt off, but no one stopped them as they passed through the northern gate.

They were on the home stretch, and the capital of Zell, Rastoram, was only days away. Soon Kenjo and Vallarya would be where they needed to be, a place that would give them the fresh start the west promised. Soon the two of them could focus on their dreams while a man in gold and black tapped his fingers atop a table, a single dim lantern hanging above his head.

13

4ᵗʰ of Cresozis; Mortal Year 523

Kenjo

By nightfall, they had put some distance between them and Blaebus. Finding a spot off the road, they set up camp on the grassy plain. After setting up camp, they sat around the campfire, enjoying one another's company for dinner—shish kebabs of meat and veggies prepared by Kaldana. Luna sat away from the group and took watch. Vallarya got up and walked over to her. Kaldana, not wanting to be the only girl at the fire, decided to go after her.

"So Ricardo," said Arlo after the girls left. He bit off the last piece of his meat before continuing. "What's your plan? You thinking of going after Lukas?"

"I…" He was slow to reply. He had only taken a few bites of his food. His eyes focused on the flames in front of him. "I don't know."

"Well, as you can probably tell, we're headed to the capital," said Arlo, taking a drink of water. "I have no objections to you tagging along till then. I don't think the others do either. Do you Kenjo? Elijah?"

"No," replied Kenjo.

Elijah just shook his head with a mouth full of food.

"But it's up to you, Ricardo. You don't owe us anything. And they just demanded you leave town with us. So you're free to leave us when you want to or tag along till then."

"Then... I'll stay at least until we hit the capital," said Ricardo, taking another small bite of his food. "May I ask you something?"

"Me?" asked Kenjo as he noticed Ricardo looking at him instead of the flames.

"Yeah."

"Shoot."

"Why is a Samilian helping me?"

The air around the camp came to a still. Elijah could hear himself swallowing as he finished off his food and waited for him to reply. He slowly placed his sticks on the ground and reached for his water, his eyes not moving from them.

"Is it so wrong for a person to help another? No matter their features," asked Kenjo, staring back at him.

"When the world is on the brink of war between two of the greatest powers, is it wrong for one to be suspicious? The girls are all Samilian too. Arlo and this boy here are the only ones native to Zell. Call it my knight's intuition, but a group of Samilians this large moving around seems odd, no?"

"Name's Elijah," said the young boy, not wanting to stay quiet any longer. A glare from Ricardo made him second-guess saying anything else. Keeping his mouth shut, he went back to listening silently.

Kenjo looked down at his hands as he clasped them together. Taking a breath, he looked back up at Ricardo. He went on to tell him everything he could about what led up to this day, sparing the details of his parents' death, instead saying they just ended up separated, hoping to meet them in the capital. Then tension in Ricardo's body began to ease as he spoke. And he finished his food at a quicker pace as Kenjo told his story.

"So you're a prince?" asked Ricardo, looking at Arlo when he finished.

"Out of all that...that's what you want to focus on?" asked Arlo, seemingly annoyed by the question.

"Like I said previously. This whole thing reeks of odd. You could easily be viewed as a prisoner."

Arlo burst out into laughter. "Me a prisoner? No, no, the only prisoner here is you, and it was this very group of Samilians that set you free. It was his idea to free you. He just got cold feet, so I initiated it."

Ricardo sighed, taking a drink of water he stood up. "I'm going back to the wagon. Thank you for this wonderful story."

"I could feel the sarcasm coming out of his voice," said Elijah as he watched Ricardo pull himself into the wagon. "I don't understand why he doesn't like you guys. You saved his life."

Kenjo just laid back on his sleeping roll. Placing his hands behind his head, he gazed up at the starry night sky without another word. Moments later, he was off to sleep. Elijah looked to Arlo who only shrugged before moving to his own roll.

Vallarya and Kaldana took a seat on either side of Luna, the three of them eating their food in relative silence, eyes following a small rodent that was looking for something to eat on the road. Its yellow fur made it stick out against the dirt path.

"All right, that's it, Luna," said Kaldana, breaking the awkward silence between them. "Why the hell don't you sit and talk with us?"

Vallarya spit part of her food out at the words. Clearing her throat, she went back to taking another bite as if nothing happened.

"Someone has to take watch," replied Luna as she tossed aside her empty wood skewer.

"I would buy that if there was, you know, like two of us. But what do we have? One, two, three…" Kaldana was using her fingers to count off everyone in the group.

"Six of us," said Vallarya. "Seven if you want to include Ricardo. But I wouldn't."

"Exactly! Six of us. Six! Luna, you need to stop this. Someone else is easily capable of taking watch. Even Elijah, and he doesn't fight!" Kaldana was standing up at this point, waving her hands with every word.

"I just like to be alone," responded Luna, paying little mind to the theatrics of her wolf-eared companion.

"The world's too big to be going about it alone like that," said Vallarya as she looked at her.

Luna turned slowly to face her warm smile.

"You need at least one other person. It makes life that much more worth being a part of, no matter who you are."

"Yeah, I mean, just look at her and Kenjo!" said Kaldana as she began to laugh. Vallarya's face began to turn red, and she looked away so neither of them could see. Luna let out a small chuckle. Vallarya and Kaldana slowly looked to one another, then to Luna who now sat stone-faced, following the squirrel once more.

"Anyways, Luna," said Vallarya, still in disbelief that she laughed, "you don't have to tell us every last thing, but we've traveled for a while now, and I hardly know a thing about you. I really want to know about you, especially how you keep your hair that silky looking."

"What do you plan to do at the capital?" asked Luna, avoiding her comment.

"Hmm, well, Kenjo and I will probably join one of the academies there. It's what we were doing back home before we ended up here."

"He doesn't seem like the type."

"What do you mean?" asked Vallarya, taken back by her comment.

"He doesn't seem like someone to sit still in a lecture hall. I, of course, don't know him as well as you do. But from what I've seen, that doesn't seem like a good fit."

"Well, after the academy, he… We wanted to become heroes."

"Like from back in the Age of Heroes? Like Crimson and all the others?" asked Kaldana, her eyes wide and brimming with excitement.

"Yeah," replied Vallarya with a laugh.

"That sounds a bit more fitting," said Luna. "Although I think with a coming war, all of it will be put on hold."

"As long as we don't have to be a part of it, I am okay with a hold."

Luna didn't say anything to that. She knew Samil was determined to pull the whole world into war. Civilian and soldier alike would have to grab a weapon. But she didn't want to tell her that. She didn't want to crush Vallarya's dream for a peaceful life at the capital. However, she did want to ask Vallarya about what Kenjo said the other night about there being something else. Though the question never came as she found herself starting to shake again and focused on hiding it from her companions. She didn't know what it was, but the unease moving through her didn't bode well, especially not for a Detheo.

Vallarya stood up and stretched. "Well, I think that's the most I've ever heard you say at once, Luna. I'm going back to the fire to check on the boys. Kaldana, don't let her stay out here too long."

"Will do," she replied as Vallarya walked away.

Kaldana and Luna sat there in silence for the new couple of hours. The squirrel had left some time ago, leaving the two of them with nothing to watch but an empty road. Kaldana opened the lanterns and let the two flames out to dance along her arms. A moment later, she felt something fall against her shoulder. Looking to it, she found Luna's head resting on it.

"You can go back to the campfire," said Kaldana, tapping her awake. "I'll take over, sleepyhead."

Luna didn't argue. She was red with embarrassment at the thought of falling asleep like that.

"Hey, Luna," said Kaldana before she got away.

"Hmm?" she replied, stopping in her tracks.

"What will you do when we get there?"

"What does it matter?" she growled.

"Matters as much as it did when you asked Vallarya."

"T-That's...fair. I... I'll go wherever they go. After all, there isn't much life for me outside of this little group."

"Even if it leads into a lecture hall?" asked Kaldana, turning to her with a look of confusion. "Of all people in our group, I think you would be the most out of place in that kind of situation. Hell, I don't even know if I could do it."

Luna shot her a glance that let her know how unamusing her words were to her. "They won't end up in a lecture hall."

"What makes you say that?"

"Just a feeling. Goodnight, Kaldana," the tone of her voice making it clear she was done talking.

"Oh, um, goodnight, Luna."

Kaldana went back to playing with her flames. "Going wherever he goes, huh? What made you start to think like that?" As she asked herself this aloud, she began to realize she was in the same boat as her. It wasn't too long after she met Kenjo and Vallarya that Luna joined the group. But unlike Luna, she didn't make any oath.

She was there for another reason as selfish or silly as it may have seemed to someone else. Kaldana was there to see the heroes she saw back then, to see what they would become. She was fascinated by them.

"I hope it doesn't end in an academy," said Kaldana as she tossed her flames into the sky. "That wouldn't be right for them, would it? Not for the two who slew a creature of Nothingness like that beast of Crimson."

*****

When day broke, the group quickly broke camp and hit the road again. A few more days was all it would take, and Vallarya was finding it difficult to contain her excitement. She had seen pictures and read countless descriptions of Rastoram, but never did she imagine she would be going there in person one day.

By noon, they found themselves pulling off the main road to make room for a large battalion of soldiers passing through. Cavalry led the group, powerful warhorses decorated in thick armor. The plates formed in such a way to make them look more akin to monsters than steeds. They were perfect mounts for the knights that rode them

The knights were towering, covered from head to toe in gleaming plate, shields holding the sigil of Zell on one side, swords sheathed on the other, fearsome lances with a sharp points and a bodies covered in jagged edges resembling that of a saw blade held firmly in their right hands. No one's face could be seen, hidden beneath winged helmets, a single slit cut above their eyes to grant them vision.

Behind the cavalry, massive war wagons transporting troops were being pulled by a set of eight horses. There was no telling how many soldiers were stored inside the towering wooden wagon. Judging from the size of the vehicle, Kenjo figured there was roughly five hundred holed up inside of them. As the horses drawing the wagons passed by in front of them, it became apparent that they were not ordinary horses at all.

Two jagged bone horns stuck out of their heads, the helmets adorning their heads molded to fit around them. Glowing emerald eyes peered out from underneath, similar colored energy crackled around their bodies and hooves. As they stepped, they noticed the ground beneath them cracking, only to return to normal a second later as they lifted off.

"Uh, Arlo or Elijah, what the hell are those things?" asked Vallarya as she watched them.

"Quals," said Elijah. "They're more native near the jungle kingdom. Not only are they larger than a normal Zellian warhorse, they can manipulate magic to a minor degree, which makes them perfect for dragging those wagons. I can't remember how many, but it would take *a lot* of regular horses to accomplish that feat."

"Why does the cavalry not use them?"

"Well, that's just because this is the capital's army. The soldiers of Adristan ride nothing but quals. While they are fine with doing labor, they aren't particularly fond of riders. Even the riders of Adristan take quite a bit of time breaking them in."

Catapults and ballistae followed behind them, each one dragged by a single qual. There was no doubt in their mind it was possible for them to take down even the largest warships sent by Samil, let alone their capabilities against an army on land alone. Elijah shifted in his saddle, excited when he saw what was at the back of the battalion. Arlo was shifting in his saddle as well, but judging by his facial expression, Kenjo could tell he felt like something was wrong.

Bringing up the rear were five knights in golden armor, each one atop a qual, red capes flowing from their shoulders down onto their mounts. White fur lined their collars. The wings sticking out of there helmets looked as if they were on fire. On their backs rested their weapons: two of them with large claymores, one a staff, the fourth a rifle. The one in the middle had two longswords, one sheathed against each hip.

"Those are royal knights," said Arlo. "If they are being sent out, then something terrible has happened."

"Do you think they know about Gonall?"

"No... No, those bastards covered it up too well. The only ones who know the truth about Gonall are us right here. We didn't even tell a soul back in Caprae."

Once the detachment had passed, they continued. Arlo snapped at his horses constantly to increase their speed, the others struggling to keep up with the wagon that blazed ahead.

"We need to hurry," yelled Arlo as he led them down the winding road.

"Why are we going so fast?" asked Kaldana "The horses won't like this. Is seeing that battalion that big of a deal?"

"Very much so," replied Elijah, pulling up alongside her. "Like Arlo said, something tragic must have happened. It's the only thing that would warrant the sending royal knights anywhere."

"Tragic like what?"

"Either a member of a royal family has been killed or a kingdom has fallen. And if they don't know about Gonall..."

"Then another kingdom..."

*****

They wouldn't speak again until a while after nightfall when the horses were exhausted and on the verge of collapse. Arlo wanted to keep going, but his horses refused. They pulled off the main road to a spot in the plain with a circle of rocks, all of different sizes, but the way they were arranged made it seem as if someone had placed them there on purpose.

Kaldana and Elijah tended to the horses. Making small talk amongst themselves. Arlo was the only one not eating dinner as the others took a seat on a rock. He paced back and forth, unable to sit still.

"We'll be in the capital tomorrow," said Ricardo. "You should probably just sit and wait. You nearly killed the horses."

"How can I sit still after seeing them marching by?" he asked, flailing his hands with every word. "You shouldn't be able to sit there so calmly either!"

"I'm a knight, not a soldier. Just because the royals pass by doesn't mean I should lose my shit. We don't even know why they're moving."

"If a tragedy did happen, Ricardo, say a kingdom has fallen, then you know damn well all of Zell will be called upon. You knights will become soldiers in seconds."

"If I get drafted, so be it. The war, however, isn't exactly my priority at this moment. I need to find Lukas."

Arlo looked to Kenjo and Vallarya for support, but they just shrugged. They were in the same boat as Ricardo. The war wasn't their top priority, although they understood why Arlo would be freaking out over it, but not the knights. When he realized he was alone, he grabbed a plate of food and retired to a rock in silence.

"So why are you acting like this now?" asked Vallarya as she watched Arlo eat.

Arlo placed his plate down beside him and looked toward them. "Well…"

The royal knights were one of the most prestigious groups in all of Zell, comprised entirely of Kryzen from all six kingdoms they were a force akin to a storm. Kids selected from a young age to be trained under the most rigorous of the training regimens across the continent, thrown into harsh weather of varying temperatures from grueling heat to blizzards to storms and hurricanes, placed in the jungles of Adristan with no food and told to survive.

During these lessons or trips, as they were sometimes referred to by their teachers, unlike Hands who were trained how to use every weapon in the known world as well as the hand-to-hand combat style unique to them, the children who would become royal knights picked one weapon on their first trip. From that day forward, it would be the only weapon they would ever use and it would never leave their side.

Teachers taught them how to fight and adapt. To use their weapon regardless of situation, for those with close range to effectively fight those at a distance and vice versa. Each day, they would be taught by a teacher using a different weapon, allowing them to learn on the fly. When they were satisfied by the kids' progress, they would move onto the incorporation of their magic.

Taking away their weapons and forcing them to only use their abilities for days on end, coupled with the weather, this was one of the worst parts for the kids. As the magic drained away at them from the inside, the weather battered them physically on the outside. Those that could no longer stand were taken away from the course, never to stand amongst their brothers and sisters again, usually placed in the capital guard or another section of the army entirely.

Those that did pass and were satisfactory moved on to coupling weapon and magic together. During this time, there was no harsh weather thrown in. Just months and years of training from fighting beasts to teachers to each other. This was their life; this was their purpose. They were hardly given a life outside of training during these long years. Their friends were the ones they trained alongside, and that was it.

When the current group of knight candidates turned eighteen, the trial to become a true knight would begin. For three months, a current Royal Knight would take a recruit under their wing and teach them. Then they were given three more months to best a knight in a one-on-one duel. On average, current royal knights beat the new recruits senseless numerous times before any of them ever won. It was the tradition; it was a symbol of the belief that Zell was built on: Strength was everything. Anyone who could not show it did not deserve to stand at the top.

For those who passed, their names were shouted and praised by the Royal Knights for close to a week, welcoming them amongst their ranks. They were given a weapon and armor made of traecium, a metal akin to Samil's sky metal, forged by the greatest smiths across the land. Once they had those, they were sent to Adristan one more time to tame a qual. Although it is a difficult task, it was the easiest out of everything they had done since the start.

Quals are rather smart creatures, and after spending time like they had among the people of Adristan, they began to recognize who the royal knights were and welcomed them into their home. When a Royal Knight comes seeking a mount, they line up and wait for the knight to choose one he or she prefers. Once done, they return to Adristan's capital to have a saddle and wardress forged for the qual before returning to Rastoram a full-fledged knight.

The royal knights were the strongest blade in the nation and the answer to the Royal Fingers of Samil. If they were to be sent out, it was only under the Lord King's order. Their fights were usually quick, finished in the blink of an eye, leaving destruction and slaughter in the wake of their appearance.

"They were one of the only reasons we survived the Blood Rain," said Arlo. "Next to Crimson, of course. Anyways, the Lord King of Rastoram sent them somewhere. And seeing as they didn't want to talk to us, I wanted to hurry to the capital and figure it out. Not to mention the possibility that bastard on the throne of Burrium could betray Zell again."

Ricardo's ears perked up, and he looked over at Arlo with wide eyes. "What do you mean betray you again?"

"Did I skip out on that detail earlier?" asked Arlo, placing a hand on his chin as he thought back to their conversation from the other day. "Hmm, he's the reason Gonall fell. He's Samil's damn puppet."

Ricardo stood up, grabbing his lance against the rock he was sitting on. He leveled it at Arlo's eyes. Vallarya merged partially with Kenjo as they followed the two of them.

"You take those words back!" said Ricardo, anger clearly visible across his face. His breathing was getting heavier.

"Absolutely not. That puppet is the reason my kingdom is gone. From the military to the women and children. Every. Last. One. Cut down and buried in the very routes they should have escaped out of."

"I will not hear this anymore!" Ricardo lunged forward, his lance still aimed at his head. A wall of ash arose between them, and Arlo directed it sideways, throwing Ricardo off his feet and onto the ground. He clutched his side as he sat up, his body still recovering from the beating he received as a prisoner.

"What don't you believe?" asked Arlo, hopping to his feet. "Huh? Is it the fact he's a goddamned puppet? Or the fact that every last citizen of Gonall was butchered in one day, save for me? Cause if it's the latter, let me tell you, I left their lifeless bodies right where I found them! You can go back and see them for yourself!"

"It's the truth," said Luna, walking up to the circle. "I know you may not want to believe me, Ricardo. But Arlo is telling the truth. Burrium betrayed Gonall. There are strings attached to Burrium's king that run to the other side of the world."

"Why... Why would my king do this?" said Ricardo, weakly attempting to get up. Letting go of his lance, he reached for the rock closest to him and pulled himself up on it. "I refuse to believe it... My king couldn't possibly have anything to gain from this... I can't—"

"That I do not know," said Luna, taking a seat on her sleeping roll. "But I assure you, the king you made your oath to is gone."

"I...see. Arlo, I can't bring myself to fully believe it. But nonetheless, I am sorry for reacting the way I did just now."

"Don't worry about it," said Arlo, sitting back down, the ash following his command and refilling an empty vial. "I only hope that if I ever become a king that I can have knights who love me as much as you love yours."

There was no more conflict that night as the group sat quietly at the fire. Kenjo was the last to fall asleep, and when he finally did, he found himself in that dark room again. Across from him sat the same man, his face hidden in the dark, the single dim lantern hanging above them.

"I never thought I would talk to you when you're not being suffocated by your own doubt," he said. Kenjo could tell he was laughing from his body movements, but there was no sound that came from him.

"What are you?" asked Kenjo. "You've been with us since before we even arrived in Zell."

"What? Well, that's an unexpected question, I must say. For a man sits across from you and you deem to ask him what he is, like he isn't a person instead of who he is."

"You speak to me in my head. You appear only in my dreams. You aren't any sort of normal person."

He raised his hands in defeat. "You got me, I'm not. I'm not human nor elf nor giant nor any of the other races that walk along the world."

"Then?" Kenjo was growing annoyed, his index finger tapping rapidly on the table.

"Does it really matter?" he shrugged. "That's rhetorical. It doesn't, not in the least. However, what does matter is the fact this path you are on now leads only to Nothingness. Each step you take toward a fate you cannot escape."

The words were like ice, a chill running down his spine.

"You do understand, don't you? That your path leads you to the same fate as your parents?"

Ryan and McKenzie's faces flashed before his eyes, both being suffocated by the black tendrils that plagued him each night.

Kenjo sat up, breathing heavily, sweat beading along his forehead. He looked around and found himself back at the campsite. The others were still asleep. Kaldana sat by the horses, keeping watch along the road. He thought of waking Vallarya but decided against it at the last second, choosing to do it later when they were finally in the capital.

He lay back down on his side, pulling his sleeping roll tightly around him. He closed his eyes in an effort to get back to sleep, but the words of the man in his dream echoed in his mind. Kenjo dwelled on them for at least another hour, his mind filling more and more with dread.

As his mind descended into the rabbit hole of thought, he began to worry. Would they end up like his parents? Would they begin to attack those closest to them? Who would be there to stop them if they were to change like that? Kenjo sandwiched his face between his hands, slapping himself back to reality and out of the hole. *That's not going to happen,* he thought to himself.

He rolled over and inched his way toward Vallarya, reaching an arm out. He pulled her and her sleeping roll closer to him. Closing his eyes once more, sleep finally won over and took him into its embrace until morning.

14

17ᵗʰ of Japhim; Mortal Year 523

Jasmine

asmine woke to the sound of thunder, her ears quickly picking up the whistling wind and pouring rain. The dirt road she had been following along the cliff side of the Kama Mountains had turned to mud. When she tried to push the horse through it, it had gotten stuck at one point, and she was forced to pull it out, leading her to her current situation of being holed up in a cave to avoid the weather.

The cave was rather spacious, however, plenty of room for her to spread out and for her horse. Getting up, she moved to the front of the cave to take a look. She was unable to see the other side of the road through the downpour of water before her. Leaning her head out slightly, she looked left and right, the only thing visible to her about five feet from where she was. There was no end in sight. With a sigh, she returned to her sleeping roll, pulling her cloak tighter around her as she stoked the fire before lying down again.

It had been six days since she left Samil. For the past two days, she was traveling through the Kama Mountains that stood to the north. The winding road that cut through the mountains made the travel easy, but on her trips, she preferred the cliffside road, which in turn was one of the few unpaved and hardly maintained by the workers on a monthly basis. She regretted her choice as she shivered in the weak warmth of the flames.

"Would you like to leave a report?" asked a voice. A small chirping followed.

Rolling onto her side, Jasmine looked at the red bird that was standing atop her horse's saddle.

"No," she replied, "there's nothing to report."

The bird she had left the capital with was Cardinal's main way of keeping up with his subordinates in the field. Usually, they remained silent to the point you would forget about them. When you don't leave a report, though, they tend to get more vocal, becoming more and more of an annoyance until you finally feel pressured enough into doing one.

"Are you sure?"

"Y-yes, I am very sure," said Jasmine, rolling onto her back. "Now let me sleep. Cardinal can get a report after we arrive."

The bird fell silent at that remark, and Jasmine closed her eyes once again.

Another blast of thunder boomed, forcing her eyes open to stare at the cave ceiling above her. A loud sound filled the cave. Dismissing it as thunder, Jasmine closed her eyes again. The sound echoed again, sounding like a faint roar against the backdrop of the thunder. Turning her head toward the cave entrance, she squinted in an effort to see something. Lightning flashed outside, illuminating the hulking figure of a creature standing at the entrance. Its posture was hunched, but its head still almost hit the head of the cave as it ducked inside. The lightning shot across again, illuminating the large claws extending from its paw-like hands. It was eyeing her horse, licking its lips. It began to walk toward it. The horse was unaware that it was becoming prey.

Jasmine reached for her weapon. Hitting the button to deploy the blade, she hopped to her feet. Moving quickly, she rushed forward and stabbed her weapon into its side.

With a growl, it turned and grabbed her, lifting her off the ground. It threw her out of the cave with ease. She was soaked in seconds as she hit the mud. Stumbling to her feet, she narrowly avoided the claws lashing out at her. Inside her effective range, she found herself pushed back to the cliff's edge. At its next swing, she ducked under, circling around its left side.

Stabbing her weapon through its side, she sliced out it's back. Swinging wildly as it spun around, she ducked underneath once more. Spider legs sprouting from her back, she pierced them through the creature's left arm. When it attacked with its right, she severed it from its body. Jasmine jumped up, kicking the creature in the chest with both feet. She hit the mud on her back, her foe howling against the thunder as it fell off the cliff.

Spitting water from her mouth as she got back up, she made her way back into the shelter of the cave. Inside, the horse stood against the back wall, the bird unmoving from its saddle. It cocked its head as she became illuminated by the fire. Hitting the button on her weapon, it returned to its original baton. Jasmine curled up next to the fire, pulling her cloak around her as tight as she could. Despite it being soaked, it was still warmer than if she were to go without it due to its craft.

"Would you like to make a report?" asked the bird, flying down to the ground to look her in the eye.

"If you ask me one more time before we get there," said Jasmine as she swatted at it, "I will clip your wings and throw you off the cliff after that beast."

The bird said nothing as it flew out of reach of her hands. Perching back up on the saddle, it remained silent for the rest of the night. Jasmine tried to sleep but found herself constantly looking toward the cave, eyes wide and on alert in case of another surprise visitor. About an hour later, the thunder and lightning had stopped. The only sound was the pouring rain.

*****

By morning, the rain had stopped. With bags under her eyes, Jasmine slowly broke camp. Throwing her supplies back on her horse, she led it toward the warm sunlight. Before she continued to her destination, she moved to the cliffside. The beast's arm was still there, gray flesh revealed by the light. She found the limb surprisingly heavy as she pulled it free. The longer she looked at it, the more it looked like an experiment that had gone wrong.

The claws were made of bone, breaking through infected flesh above each knuckle. Red fur ran along the top of its forearm, running up the length of its arm up to the shoulder. Eyeing it closer, she found the flesh was stitched on rather than natural. Producing one spider leg, she reached it over her shoulder and sliced underneath the fur to reveal more infected mass beneath. Nearly vomiting, she tossed it off the cliff, no desire to look at it anymore as she returned to her horse.

The mud was far deeper than she thought. The horse had difficulty getting into a full gallop. Jasmine took a piece of bread from her bag and began to snack on it. The cardinal perched on her shoulder, trying to peck at the bread as it neared her mouth. At first, she passed it off as an annoyance, but when it repeated, she realized it wanted to share. Taking off a piece, she held it up. It chirped happily as it took it from her.

She looked off over the cliffside at the forest of Lema, that stretched east as far as she could see. The verdant green of the trees reached all the way to the coast. As beautiful as the forest was now, it had nothing on the springtime beauty. When the spirits of the forest were at their liveliest, the very trees lit up with life. From her soldier's knowledge, she knew it was full of untapped resources, but not for lack of trying.

In the past, Samil had tried to colonize a portion of it, planning on setting up a town and lumberyard directly in the middle of it. The spirits and the wildlife of Lema, however, tore down and destroyed anything they created. Trees that were cut down, land that was cleared, began to regrow in seconds, recovering fully as if they had never been touched by mortal hands.

As the death toll started to rise, the king of Samil back during that time called off any current and future attempts to colonize, having warning signs erected and guards positioned to turn people away. Eventually, though, whispers reached his ears, whispers of emeralds with no equal anywhere else in the world. His greed made him send out one last expedition, which he personally led.

When he went, the forest elves known as the Oshunsian, were the ones to greet him. It took some time, but he succeeded in making an alliance. Samil would have her military might against the Nothingness that, during those times, was running rampant. Elves, beasts, and spirits all falling to its corruption. For their aid, the elves traded them gems, as well as allowing them to harvest trees from the outer edge.

Jasmine hadn't been this close to the forest since she was seven years old, before she had any desire to be a soldier. As the horse trotted along, the memory of that day made her smile, the beautiful lights of the spirits that illuminated alongside the chorusing elves and the howling beasts. But most of all, it was the last day she spent with her brother.

On the seventeenth of Opacus, for her seventh birthday, he took her to a large hill that overlooked the southern side of the forest. He laid out a blanket and cooked her one of her favorite dinners. As the sun began to set, the spring festivities of the spirits began. She sat there, wide-eyed for over an hour, lost in the beauty and music until her brother pulled her away, giving her one more gift, the Bo Staff that she had used up until Forsythia had given her a new one.

Pulling herself away, she shook her head, trying to get the memories out her head. She had more to focus on right now instead of her missing brother. It was late afternoon when she made it out of the mountains. A pole with two small signs attached to it designated the roads, she took the right path heading toward Montlimar.

Thick knee-high grass lined each side of the road. A few trees scattered here and there, others cut down, leaving only the stumps behind. Traveling well into the night, she pulled off and set up camp next to one of the trees. After making a fire and eating, she rested her back against the tree and took out her book.

She read long into the night, learning everything she could for when she got back and could experiment again. Hopefully avoiding another night like before, writing ideas down and marking pages, she began fighting for her eyes to stay open. She closed the book and went to sleep.

The next morning, she pushed her horse into a full gallop. Jasmine had time to make up, and she planned to scout out the town. Not only that, she wanted to find Sleeve and deal with him before the meeting took place. Best case scenario, she could get him before he could fight back. Though the chances of that all lining up was rather low.

Around midday, she came to a river that ran from the east and cut north all the way to Montlimar. She took a moment to refill her water skin as well as let her horse drink. At sunset, she could see the stone walls of the village as little dots atop a hill far in the distance. With still a ways to go, she decided to make camp. That way, she could arrive during the daylight hours.

Washing the mud out of her clothes from the previous day and setting up a fire, she sat close to it as a cold breeze blew across. The grass and flames danced with the wind. Pulling her cloak tight, she sat with her knees against her chest and rocked herself. Jasmine began to wonder how Forsythia was doing as she gazed at the fire.

She wanted to talk to her, to have her here going after the White Sash together. The longer she thought about it, the memory of one of their first missions together popped into her mind. It would be the first time she met Queen Rose. About four years ago, they were chasing after an escaped Angel-born.

*****

The two had chased him far to the west of Samil into the Valley of Ikam. As far as Jasmine knew, it was the deepest place on land. It had been mined for the past few decades for its ores and minerals. And yet it showed no sign of running out, becoming one of the biggest slave labor camps in the world.

For a while, all that worked in the valley were professional miners and criminals forced into slavery to atone for their crimes. But once Victor rose to power, his hatred toward the Angel-born laid bare, slaves were no longer just criminals. Innocents in the hundreds were forced into the hard physical labor and the countless beatings for refusing to part with their wings.

As she walked around in the valley with Forsythia, looking for their escapee, she couldn't help but feel bad for them. Jasmine wanted to help them. So many were bleeding and bruised, wings hardly recognizable from the sheer abuse they suffered at the hands of the guards. But like all the others, all she could do was turn a blind eye and keep walking, reminding herself constantly to focus on what she was there to do.

They had no luck on the upper areas. The guards apparently hadn't noticed anyone sneak in. Most of them even laughed at the thought, asking them what Angel-born would be stupid enough to come here on their own free will. With massive sighs, Forsythia led her down ramps that ran along the valley sides to the deeper parts where caves had been dug.

Forsythia began to question the slaves, but none of them were talking. Jasmine did the same, and they just looked at her with empty eyes. One was a little livelier, swinging his pick axe with more spirit than any of the others.

"Excuse me," said Jasmine walking up to him. "Have you happened to see a man named Maurico? He has a black stripe down each of his wings."

The Angel-born swung his pick down once more. "Yeah, I have," he said, letting go of the pick. He turned to face her. He stood about two heads taller than her and was rather intimidating. His wings had grayed like his hair, feathers loosely hanging along their length. Looking closer at them, Jasmine could see holes throughout.

"Can you tell me where he ran to?"

There was no audible response, just a wad of spit that collided with her face. Jasmine wiped it away in disgust. In a moment, the man was face-first on the ground. Forsythia twisted one of his arms back as she placed once foot between his shoulder blades, slowly applying pressure as he began to yell.

"Apologize to her," said Forsythia as she twisted more.

"You two little girls can go to hell!" he exclaimed through gritting teeth before groaning in pain.

"Very well." Forsythia broke his arm in that instant. Lifting his head by his shaggy gray hair, she slammed it into the ground before stepping off him. "Come on, Jas, let's look over th—"

Jasmine was about to question her words when she followed her gaze and saw Maurico pushing slaves over as he ran deeper down the valley. The two sprinted after him, shouting for people to move out of the way, shoving anyone who didn't. He ran into a cave two floors below them. Once they were outside of the cave, they caught their breath, drew their weapons, and walked inside.

Torches lined each side of the cave, a few dozen slaves tending to the walls, the buckets at their feet almost filled to the brim with copper. They proceeded slowly, checking each Angel-born's wings for their target. Jasmine found him acting like a slave, pretending to mine the wall. She placed a hand on his shoulder as she leveled her Bo Staff against his neck. He spun around, his pick aimed at her side. She shifted her weapon to catch the attack in the nick of time.

The force behind the swing took her off her feet, and she hit the ground with a loud thud. Forsythia lunged at him before he could bring the pick down on her skull. She disarmed him and punched him against the wall. Distracted by the enemy in front of her, she had no idea of the slave coming up behind her.

Jasmine struck from the ground, thrusting her staff into his stomach and taking the air out of him. Forsythia turned around as his pick hit the ground and noticed the other slaves had quit working, their eyes solely focused on the two Royal Fingers. Another swift punch sent Maurico falling to the ground. Helping Jasmine up, the two began to fight their way back out of the cave.

It was a constant stream of screaming, battered bodies flailing their pickaxes in front of them. When one fell, the next climbed over him without regard. They were determined to strike them down as the two fought through the masses, Forsythia's eyes began to glow, the strings in her gauntlets humming with energy.

"Jasmine, protect me for a moment," she said, starting to pluck at the strings.

"Uh, okay," she said, spinning her staff, low tripping all of those around them. "But what are you doing? Oh."

Forsythia's music began to fill the cave. It was a gentle melody that made Jasmine feel extremely calm despite the situation she found herself in. Where she found a calming melody, the slaves felt their bodies began to slow. Reaction times delayed, allowing Jasmine a much easier time of fighting them, quickly disarming them before knocking them out cold.

When the music stopped, they stood, surrounded by unconscious bodies. Forsythia went back and grabbed Maurico. He was still out cold with blood dripping down his face. Making their way out of the cave, they found themselves greeted by chaos. The slaves were rebelling across the valley. Guards were finding themselves overwhelmed, pickaxes burying their way through their armor. Any weapons they dropped were scooped up by the slaves to continue their fight.

Their battle cries for freedom echoed throughout the walls, and Jasmine felt a feeling of fear stirring inside of her. Forsythia placed Maurico down and reformed her harp from her gauntlets.

"Jasmine… Forgive me," she said, moving to the edge of the ramp. From there, she was able to peer down and across the mine. "I know you hate killing, but what I am about to do is all that can ensure peace. Protect me again, please." Forsythia turned and faced her, a weak smile lining her lips. Her eyes were sad, on the verge of tears.

Jasmine nodded. Taking her place at her side, she readied herself for anyone who would try and come near. "Do what you need to," Jasmine said as she swept the legs out from one of the slaves, a swift blow to the head, knocking him unconscious. "I'm with you."

Forsythia brought up her harp and took a deep breath. Slowly, her fingers began to pluck at the strings. Single notes began to sound out, softly at first, a crescendo with every pluck. As it grew louder, so too did the speed of which she played. And the very sky began to dance to the music.

Clouds began to swirl in the sky directly above the mine, moving faster and faster with her music. The swirl tightened inwards on and on until it appeared as a massive ball above them. The battle cries of the slaves were beginning to die down as the sky darkened. Forsythia's harp was now echoing throughout the entire mine. Everyone could hear it, and their attention was now focused on her.

The slaves rushed them; Jasmine pushed herself to keep up with the onslaught, ducking and dodging what she could, blocking what she couldn't. It would have been easier to do, but she had to keep an eye on Forsythia. Not one could be allowed close enough to get her while she was exposed like this. Jasmine moved quick; lining the tip of her Bo Staff with starlight energy, she drew a circle around them. As another slave stepped at them, a spiderweb barrier pushed them back and onto the ground.

"Forsythia, you gotta finish that sometime soon," said Jasmine, heavy with worry. The two were surrounded. Their enemies struck the barrier. If they got knocked down, they came at it again. They were being consumed by their desire to be free. To them, the only thing between them and freedom was the two girls in front of them. If one dropped their weapon, another picked it up to continue the fight.

The cloud sphere above exploded outward, forming rings in the sky around a black sphere. Heat began to radiate from it, forcing the slaves to back away. Sweat began to bead on their brows. They started to collapse, one after another. Heavy panting could be heard all around them.

"Don't move any further from me," said Forsythia as she plucked the final string. Her song finally finished. The black sphere above the mine was like a mini sun, life eating heat washing out over their enemies.

Jasmine watched as their clothes began to catch fire. For some of the Angel-born, their wings were the first to catch flame. Screams began to ring out all around. Some gripped their faces; dragging their hands along, they found their flesh coming with it. Their bodies were beginning to melt. Jasmine tried to locate any of the guards, and when she finally found one, she saw they were unaffected by Forsythia's magic.

Eventually, the screams died down. Jasmine got rid of her barrier as Forsythia dissipated the abyssal sun with a simple *fin*. They looked to each other; Forsythia's right eye was practically on fire, black flame burning all around it. And then when she blinked, it was gone. The flames absorbed by her eye turned it pure black; another blink, and her eye was normal, orange and radiant like the sun.

"Are you okay?" asked Jasmine, rubbing her eyes after what she just saw.

"Yeah," she replied with a smile. "Don't worry, that's what happens to my eyes whenever I use that magic. I call it the Ballad of the Black Sun. Normally, my eyes would just shine brighter like you're used to, but…since I started dabbling in that altered magic, my eyes do that instead. Sorry to worry you. Come on, let's grab Maurico and get out of here."

Before they could react, someone sprinted past them and leapt. Jasmine caught a glimpse of white wings with a black stripe. But he didn't take off; no, he plummeted to the very bottom of the mine. They leaned over the edge and saw his body barely outlined by the light. It wasn't moving anytime soon.

"Well. There are so many other ways that could have gone better."

"Why did he do that?" asked Jasmine, falling to her knees, catching her breath. "He was given his life. He was spared."

Forsythia placed a hand on her shoulder. "He must really not have wanted to go back." Forsythia knew the truth, or at least her own. Had she witnessed this happen to her own people and been as weak as him, she probably would have done the same exact thing without a second thought. It was a far better an idea then living after seeing all that they went through. Though she was curious when he had woken up.

The ground began to shake, and the two of them stepped back quickly to make sure they didn't fall after him, regaining their footing as the ground went still again. The shaking occurred again, a loud growl rising from the pit of the valley.

Before they knew it, something was on them. It pinned Forsythia to the ground, her harp flung from her hands. Claws dug into her shoulders, and she let out a small scream of pain. It was a creature with six legs and a large spherical head. Gray skin covered its body, a long barbed tail extended from its back and curled up like a scorpion.

Sharp teeth hung over its bottom jaw in a massive overbite. It sniffed her as it reared its head back, ready to sink its teeth in her.

Jasmine hit it across the head, but it didn't move. Instead, its two large red eyes turned from Forsythia and looked up at her. Stepping back, Jasmine barely dodged its attack as the tail smashed into the ground where she just was. The creature got off Forsythia and charged at Jasmine. Its tail came spinning around the side, and Jasmine attempted to block it. Unable to hold her ground, she was slammed into the cliff wall.

Her arm was broken the moment she made impact. Sliding to the ground, she clutched at her broken arm as she looked at the beast. His face now directly in hers, she watched a third eye appear in between the others, the mouth of sharp teeth opening wide to reveal a long red tongue. Jasmine felt fear form in her chest, her heart racing faster than it ever had before. She wasn't ready for the end.

Then she was overcome by a smell of roses. It was comforting. It made her feel like she was back at home in her family's garden. The creature shut its mouth and backed away from her, eyes spinning in every direction, trying to figure out where the smell was coming from. Jasmine could tell the fear in its eyes as it looked around in panic.

A beam of gray energy shot down from a point above them, removing its tail at the base. Its owner jumped down and stood in between Jasmine and the creature. From where she was, all she could see was their black cape decorated in red roses. The caped figure drew a sword with a slender red blade and held it down at their side.

In an instant, they stepped off, thrusting repeatedly at the creature. Blow after blow landed, the creature unable to keep up with the speed of its new foe. In a few quick moments, the creature's four front legs had been severed, two of its eyes sliced out as it was forced to the edge of the cliff. The red blade pierced through the third eye, gray energy blasting out as they sent it plummeting to the ground below.

Streams of gray energy came rising out of the pit as the figure raised their left hand. It was covered by some special looking gauntlet, gems lining the length of the red plated armor. Once it was all absorbed, their savior sheathed their blade and walked over to Forsythia.

Forsythia was lifted off the ground. Seconds later, Jasmine felt a hand grabbing her, pulling her up off the ground. She wasn't inclined to move and accepted whatever fate was to follow. Moments later, she found herself out of the mine. Her arm was wrapped in bandages and in a sling. Forsythia's wounds had been cleaned and wrapped over.

During that time, Jasmine was able to get a good look at their savior. Black armor lined with red trim covered most of her body. The plates were interlaced with some type of thread that created roses along her armor, not nearly as flashy as Jasmine's web designs. But nonetheless, it was clear how much they liked roses. At their hip was their sword, hidden inside a white sheath. The style and appearance of the sheath made it clear they had been granted access to the forges of the nobility.

Their right arm wore no armor but instead was covered in red bandages from the tips of their fingers all the way up to their shoulder. Their left arm seemed to wear enough armor for both, however. Thickened plates ran down the length of her arm. Various sized gems, which to Jasmine looked like diamonds, lined the arm. On the palm of this gauntlet, a much larger diamond was embedded. The only skin that could be seen on their hero was around their right eye.

They wore a mask that covered the rest of their face, black like the rest. On the left side, the royal emblem of Samil was engraved in the same red. Hair was concealed beneath their cloak, only a few stray strands of black and red sticking out.

"Who exactly are you?" asked Jasmine as she watched them dig around in their horse's saddlebags.

"Just a passerby," responded a very feminine voice. She pulled two small boxes from the bags and walked over to them. "I saw the sky dance around and a rather peculiar sun appear. I came rushing over, and when I got there, it was gone. And I found you two facing that creature. Here, open and eat."

Jasmine took one of the boxes hesitantly. Opening it up, she smelled something equivalent to fresh warm bread. She emptied the contents into her hands and found it to be a small cube-shaped piece of bread. Turning, she found Forsythia had already eaten hers, and she decided not to ask any questions. Popping it into her mouth, she began to chew on the fluffy cube. It tasted wonderful to her, causing her to smile more and more with each chew. And when she swallowed, she began to feel oddly full as if she had just had a full meal.

"What exactly was that," Jasmine asked curiously, her eyes meeting their savior's. She noticed an enlarged pupil with a rose looking back at her.

"A new ration their working on," she replied. "Makes it a lot easier to keep soldiers and the like fed. Were there any other creatures in that mine?"

"Not that we are aware of. Before that creature, slaves were rebelling. Forsythia here put a stop to all that. But the one we were after quickly jumped from where you found us and fell to his death. Moments later, that thing appeared."

"Is this really what it's coming to? Why are these fools trying to beckon the Nothingness?"

Jasmine went wide-eyed as her words rolled out of her mouth, "The N-Nothingness? Excuse me, what do you mean?"

"That creature was of the Nothingness. I'm sure whoever you had chased gave his life in return for that…thing. It was ready to feast on you two. Have you never seen a creature of Nothingness before?"

"Not… Not in person." Jasmine felt embarrassed for not realizing it back when they fought.

"Which reminds me, your majesty," said Forsythia, finally breaking her silence. "Why are you here exactly? Not that I'm not grateful. Just a passing interest."

"Majesty?" asked Jasmine.

"Oh, you didn't know? Our hero is the queen herself."

Jasmine's heart dropped, and then it began to beat as fast as it did when that creature was about to eat her. She quickly went from sitting to her knees and began to bow down. "Forgive me, your majesty, I had no idea who were. I am so very sorry! Thank you for saving us!"

"Relax, there's no need to be sorry nor so formal out here like this. Forsythia, a little subtlety wouldn't hurt."

"I know," laughed Forsythia, clutching her sides. "But I couldn't pass up the chance to see this reaction. But really, Rose. Why were you so close?"

"Something felt off. Souls were drifting from the capital. I followed you guys slowly just to make sure when I noticed you two were walking in the same direction. I had turned around when nothing happened. And then when the clouds and your black sun appeared, I felt it necessary to turn back around. My guess is it was in him that whole time. And he just decided to give himself a final push to release it..."

15

The fire crackled loudly, pulling Jasmine out of her thoughts. She began to wonder if that creature she met on the cliff was something of the Nothingness as well. Its gray flesh was very similar, and the teeth had the same sharpness. Shaking her head, she figured it was impossible. Not this close to civilization. The Royal Fingers before her made sure of it.

Jasmine wished Rose was here to deal with Sleeve. She was sure in that hidden room of theirs where they fought, she would have made quick work of him. It probably would have given a little fun to her life. With all the political dealings she had to deal with, the coming war, she and Victor had hardly left the castle, let alone been seen in the public eye. She fell asleep, sitting up, taking off again in the morning.

When she finally arrived in Montlimar, she held up her neck-lace for the guard to let her in. He welcomed her with a bow, signaled someone above, and the large wooden gate began to open. Going in, she moved to the stable that was to the left and stored her horse before proceeding down the cobblestone street that led to the heart of the town.

Near the gate, houses lined either side of the road all the way up to the center of town. Most of the people here were hunters, and the fur that almost every single one of them wore was proof of it. Montlimar was surrounded by wildlife that seemed to have no end in sight. If they weren't hunting on the plains to the west, they ventured into the forest on the east and northern side.

Fishers were also in the village, but they were few and far in between. The river that led to the village broke off and emptied into a large lake to the south of the forest. For those who preferred it over the hunt, it provided a large quantity of different species. Montlimar was a huge supply center for Samil, and if the rebels were here, they could easily begin to hinder the capital.

Making her way to the tavern, she found it empty, except for three men playing cards at a corner table. A fair woman was dancing on the stage, a green silk dress covering her body. Sharing the stage with her was a dark-skinned woman in a similar style dress but white in color. She was providing her voice to her dance, a soft voice that resonated throughout the tavern. Jasmine was taken back; she figured talent like hers was only found in the capital.

Finding a stool at the bar, she took a seat and waited for the tavern keeper who was finishing up wiping a glass. He was a head shorter than her, balding with a bushy mustache. Placing down the glass, he put the towel on his shoulder, wiped his hands on his gray apron, and walked over to her.

"Care for a drink, missy?" he asked. "Or food perhaps? Kitchen is open, limited to just a few choices right now. But open nonetheless. The chicken is quite good, I must say."

"If you don't mind, just some water," replied Jasmine with a soft smile. He nodded and quickly got her a glass. "Do you normally have a show for this many people?"

He chuckled. "No, not at all. There's a big event going on here in a few nights, so those two wanted to get a little bit of practice in before it. And who am I to say no to such a beautiful sight?"

"Yeah, they complement each other very well," said Jasmine, taking note of his words. "They seem like a perfect duo."

"Mm-hmm, not the usual sight around here. Sure, we get traveling entertainers from time to time, but not of this caliber. I must say we also don't get people like you here often either. Are you by chance a Finger?"

Jasmine rubbed her collar, making sure her necklace was underneath her armor and out of view. "No, just a traveler on my way up north. Decided to stop by for a quick rest."

The tavern keeper looked away from her, and Jasmine followed his gaze. One of the men at the corner table was flagging him down. He filled up three glasses from one of the large barrels behind the bar, foam spilling over the sides as he walked over to them and came back with their previous glasses. During this exchange, Jasmine noticed a white sash hanging over the side of one of the men.

In two days, this would be the place then. She could finish what she started with Sleeve and bring him in as well as find out the faces of anyone else in charge. The little cardinal raised its head slowly out of her cloak's hood and eyed the table before ducking out of view. Jasmine finished up her water, thanked the tavern keeper, and left, deciding to get a room rented out at the inn.

The inn was situated on the opposite side of the town center. Lining the streets all around the center were various market stalls, most of which contained fur, meat, and other pieces of their hunt from scales and claws to teeth and horns. There were a few outside merchants set up, and they were crowded. Montlimar was a good place for any merchant. For not only could they get high quality goods from the hunts, especially furs coveted for their comfort in the north. But any foreign merchant sold out of stock in Montlimar in less than a week's time. Many of the citizens wanted the goods they brought, tired of spoils from the hunts.

Whether it be something as simple as dishes and clothes to the more extravagant gems and paintings, it was like a different world here, and Jasmine began to wonder if the village close to her parents' farm had a similar reaction to outside merchants. When she was younger, she had little care in the dealings of the town, only tagging along with her parents at their behest. She kept her head down at all times, preferring to stay on the farm with the animals.

She was also able to spend more time with her friends, Cecilia and Liam, who were the children of their neighbors. And that was always ten times better than going to the village to sell their harvest or frolic along the streets. Jasmine went inside the inn and rented a room, asking the innkeeper specifically for a room with a window overlooking the tavern. Sliding an extra few gold pieces in to sweeten the deal, she got exactly what she wanted.

Placing her bag down next to the bed, she took off her cloak and tossed it onto the chair next to a corner desk. Laying her weapon down atop the desk, she took a look out the window. From her vantage, she had a clear line of sight of the entrance. She could easily see the faces of anyone coming or going; it was perfect. The tiny cardinal chirped noisily from on top of the bed, and she turned to look at it, aggravation clear on her face.

"Oh, right," she replied, taking a seat next to it, her face going back to normal. "I guess I promised to make a report when we got here. Though you have been watching me the whole time." Jasmine cleared her throat. "Wings of red, may you push away the sands and reveal the way to the *Lofatalm*."

The cardinal's eyes turned from black to white, and its mouth opened wide. It stood still as if frozen in place. And Jasmine moved her face closer to it so she could speak directly at it.

"Everything is okay here, Cardinal," she began. "I just arrived in Montlimar today. I believe I already found where their meeting is going down two days from now. Then once I'm done with my business here, I'll head back, hopefully with some prisoners for the others to interrogate. Can you do me a favor, though, sir? On the way through the Kama Mountains, I encountered the strangest creature, gray flesh, with weird red fur that looked sewn on. It was humanoid-shaped, razor-sharp teeth, bones sticking out of its arms. Not to mention its claws were as sharp as swords. Of course, sir, only do it if you get a chance to pull away from your money. Thank you! *Conseala Lofatalm*."

The cardinal's mouth closed, its eyes returning to their normal color. It began chirping again as it hopped around the bed. Jasmine smiled and went back to the window, the cardinal flying over to her cloak and taking a rest. Its eyes shut as it began to send the message to Cardinal back in the capital.

A man with a white sash around his waist walked into the tavern. He almost looked like a native of Zell. The way he was built, he seemed more likely to grapple his hunts then actually use a weapon on them. Though that wasn't to say he didn't have a weapon, for against his back was affixed a large battle-ax with a head almost as wide as he was.

Jasmine had known it would probably come down to a fight that went beyond just Sleeve. But if there were more people that looked like him in there, she began to think how horribly this could go, especially if any of them turned out to be Kryzen or had some inkling of magical knowledge under their belt. Continuing to watch the door, she made mental notes on everyone who came in and out of the tavern throughout the day.

When she found her stomach growling at her for food, she decided to stop. She had counted closer to twenty people all wearing their white sashes. Though one only entered after another had left. In the twenty, thirteen of them had visible weapons. The other seven seemed unarmed, but she wouldn't have put it past any of them to have a weapon hidden underneath their clothing.

Proceeding downstairs, she talked to the innkeeper about a good place for food. She suggested a small place near the western side of town that had some of the most delicious meat you could get your hands on. Jasmine was about to argue that nothing beat what they had in the capital, but she decided she would test it first before voicing her opinion, promising to put her in her place if it wasn't as good as she was saying.

Jasmine wandered through the busy streets toward the western side, her eyes moving from side to side to try and find anyone else who bore a white sash. There were none. As she began to head down the street, she noticed two hunters bringing back their kill in a small horse-drawn cart—a massive boar with four tusks sticking out of its head.

As she got closer, she could pick out the wounds that covered one of them. His left arm had been pierced in the shoulder by one of the tusks. Blood had soaked through the white bandages, changing the color to a light red. He stumbled, and his partner caught him before he fell. Jasmine peered inside the cart for a better look at the boar.

The same gray flesh of the creature that had attacked her on the cliff side covered the animal, wounds along its side where the hunters' arrows had pierced through. Blood caked one of its tusks while another was chipped at the point. A red foam had formed around its mouth and puddled in the cart around its head.

"Are you two going to eat that?" she asked, curious of their intention bringing what appeared to her to be a sick animal back to town.

"This rotten beast?" replied the uninjured hunter. "Wasn't planning on it, but this is the first time I've seen an animal out here sick like this. We brought it back to have it examined."

Jasmine didn't ask anything else and continued on her way, the rest of the questions she wanted to ask lost at the growling of her stomach. With a little skip in her step, she made it to the restaurant that the innkeeper had mentioned. Ordering a small plate of food, she took a seat in one of the corner tables where her back could be against a wall. From there, she was able to keep a view of both the ordering counter and the entrance. A few minutes later, a waitress brought out her food and placed it before her. With a bow, she left to take care of another customer.

Taking a bite of the meat, Jasmine felt an instant rush of bliss. A smile crept across her face as she took another bite, then another. She couldn't stop herself, and in seconds, her plate was empty, and she sat there in satisfaction. It was without a doubt one of the most delicious things she had ever had in her nineteen years of life.

Placing a tip of a few gold coins on the table, she left the restaurant and made her way back to the inn. She was stopped by the innkeeper when she came in, asking how it was. With a smile, Jasmine apologized for what she said earlier. Nothing she had in the capital was as delicious and satisfying as the plate of food she had just finished. This small-town chef made the cooks of the nobility and military look like amateurs.

Jasmine made her way back into her room and perched up by the window again. Glancing down, she kept her eyes on the tavern entrance until nightfall. She repeated this process for the next few days, spying on the tavern in the morning, getting food at that same restaurant, and then returning to her window to spy again. By the night of the meeting, she had counted over sixty different people adorned in their white sashes walking to and from the tavern.

With how bold they were, she could only assume either word had not yet reached Montlimar in regards to the White Sash Rebels or that the guards here were practically in their pocket and paid to look the other way. Whatever the case, she was prepared to put an end to it tonight. She reached into her bag and grabbed her sash, making sure her cloak covered up most of her body so that Sleeve couldn't recognize her. Placing the sash over her shoulder, she walked out and headed to the tavern.

A line had been formed, and they were slowly funneling into the tavern. Once she had made it inside, she found the place completely packed, the complete opposite of the first day she stopped in to take a look. With all the tables full, she made her way to the counter, got some water, and took a spot against the back wall. Leaning against it, she looked out over the sea of white sashes between her and the stage.

On stage, the two performers were putting on a show. Their clothing seemed alive; the dancer's dress flowed like water with her movements. As her hands moved, light-blue water appeared in the air by magic, adding an extra flash to every move. The singer's dress hummed with lightning, sparking up here and there along her body, silently as she sung. At the very end, it burst forth from her body, washing over the crowd. A round of applause went out as the two curtsied and walked off the stage.

Six individuals took the stage after them, four men and two women. The sashes that crossed over their bodies were embroidered with some gold symbol that Jasmine had never seen before. A sword crossed over a singular wing. Jasmine figured they must have been the leaders of the entire thing. Her eyes moved back and forth between the stage and the crowd as she tried to find Sleeve.

"Welcome, my dear friends!" said one of the six on stage, walking forward to the edge. He was about a head shorter than the rest of them, but there was no denying the authority behind his voice. A well-trimmed mustache and brushed back hair covered his head; at his hip, a sword, his hands moving with every word that he spoke. "I am so glad to see all of you here tonight. I do hope the travel wasn't too bad and the accommodations were satisfactory. But onto important matters. As you should all be aware by now, the alchemist' shop we had in the capital has been discovered."

A rush of boos came from the crowd. People began to demand who the traitor was. Without a word, just the raise of his hand, and they all went silent.

"I hear you all. None of you need worry your pretty heads. The so-called ally that ousted us has already been dealt with. I'm sure the guard has already found his body over the past week and is looking into his murder. Though we all know they won't find anything. So I humbly ask all of you for a volunteer. Someone who is willing to reestablish themselves in the capital. To become the tip of our spear."

No one was moving, the roar of them talking amongst themselves filling the room as if each was discussing why the other should go up there. The talking only grew louder as no volunteer made their way to the stage.

"Now, now, my dear brothers and sisters," the man on stage began with a voice of understanding. His voice was making Jasmine uneasy. His words reminded him of Forsythia's music, as if it was laced with magic. "Remember why we are here. To put an end to this savagery, to put the throne of Samil back in proper hands. Not many of you here have been alive all thirty years that the monster known as Victor has sat upon that throne. But we all know it doesn't even take a week, let alone a day for you to see it. To see that he and the nobles spit nothing but lies about the state of our kingdom. The voices of truth silenced before blind eyes!"

His arms were raised high as he paced along the stage. His voice growing louder with each word. The crowd was eating it up. Jasmine was beginning to grow sick to her stomach. Suppressing her anger as much as she could, she forced herself to listen on as he continued.

"Angel-born hunted down in the streets, Kryzen taken from their families. The guard, the RFs, the military. They parade around like they own it all, enforcing the so-called justice that Victor demands. But we all know that is just bullshit! That our kingdom is oppressing its people and is reaching out to oppress the world! Our time to act is soon upon us. Now I ask again, which of you will become the tip of our spear? Who will guide us? Who will be the first to pierce the heart of a kingdom of lies?"

The only liar is you, thought Jasmine as she looked around, waiting for someone to step up. Eventually, someone did. He looked young, no older than Jasmine. His sash was wrapped around his waist and dangled off one side. On his back was a rifle, which made him more peculiar to her. There was no way he was a civilian. They never made it into their hands. *Maybe a mercenary? Or perhaps a true traitor?* she thought to herself. Either way, she had never seen anyone like him before.

His hair was rather odd; a dark purple with white highlights reached down to his shoulders. Purple hair was common among the northern elves or those from Ivofir. But he looked like a pure Samilian in every way, the blue eyes of his like sapphires gleaming in the light of the tavern.

"Ah, my young boy," said the leading man on stage as he joined him. The young man knelt down, an arm resting on one leg, his head pointing at his feet. "Rise, my brother, I am not one that you need to kneel too. For from this day forward, you are an equal among us who stand on this stage. What is your name so that all in here know who from this day forward is the tip of our righteous spear?"

"Nathanael Lundquist," he said as he rose.

The man placed his hand on his shoulder and turned him to face the crowd.

Why does that family name sound so familiar? thought Jasmine as she listened to the thunderous applause and cheers that followed. And that was when her heart sank as she saw a man stand up in a pitch-black robe, a single sleeve of white. She moved around slowly to not draw attention as she got a look at his face.

Shaggy brown hair with an equally shaggy beard. On his right hip was the same black curved blade that he had when they fought in the underground hideout. This night was going well for her. She knew who was going to be in Samil. And she found the one person she came here for. Now it was just time for her to get him alone and finish it.

The man on stage presented Nathanael with a brand-new sash, one embroidered just like his, taking away his previous one. He waited for Nathanael to put it on. Just like the others, the golden wing and sword shone in the light. He was one of them now, a head on a rebellious beast that threatened the very kingdom she swore to protect.

Jasmine moved back to her spot on the back wall, her eyes only moving from Sleeve if she felt someone was looking at her. The seven on stage dispersed. The leading man took Nathanael around, introducing him to various people among the crowd while the other five began to talk among smaller groups in the tavern. Each of them had their own people, it seemed. It was worrying for Jasmine to think about how far they really were spread throughout the nation. They even found a way to wiggle inside the capital. When she finally returned, she knew she would have to pay Nathanael a visit before he got situated.

Sleeve spoke with him for a moment as well as the leader. After a small exchange, he headed for the exit. Jasmine watched him leave, waiting for some time to pass before she headed out after him. Luckily, someone else was going out with her to help hide any suspicion. Stepping outside, she looked left and right, finding him walking down the street to the eastern side of town. Trailing behind him, she kept her distance. She thought of using her silk, but she didn't want to risk him sensing her magic. He made his way up a small hill near the eastern wall. At the top was a lone house.

The grass came up to his knees. The fence was hardly a fence at this point, just a few scattered posts and a gate hanging on one hinge, one end digging into the gravel as he pulled it open. House windows were broken in multiple places; even a corner of the front door was missing. He placed his hand on the doorknob as he heard the crunch of gravel beneath a different pair of boots. Jasmine came to a halt behind him.

"So the little spider is alive and well," he said, pulling his hand off the knob and returning it to his side. He remained facing the door. "Did you learn what you wanted to in that little meeting?"

She quickly cleared the shock from her face. *Had he known that whole time?* "A good deal but not enough. I figured I would just get it out of you instead."

"Oh, is that so? Do you not remember the last time we fought, little spider? I'll give you the chance to reconsider. Leave this all behind, and return to your precious capital. Stay, however, and I assure you, you won't see it again."

Her heart was beating faster. It was hard for her to tell if it was fear or something else. Sleeve had yet to turn away from the door. And yet the way he talked made her almost want to believe he had already won. Drawing her weapon, she entered into a low stance.

"You know I can't do that," she said. "You're going back with me."

"And here I thought you were a smarter RF than the others..."

She dashed across the gravel that separated them. Her weapon plunged into the door as Sleeve leaned out of the way. He still had yet to turn around, dodging it as if he had eyes in the back of his head. His elbow came back and connected with her nose, making her stagger back. With a spin and a kick, he sent her into the grass.

Sleeve walked over, raised his foot high, and brought the heel crashing down. Rolling out of the way, Jasmine hopped to her feet as the ground indented from the impact of his heel. His head turned to her; a grin crossed his face as he lunged at her, forcing her onto the defensive.

Even though he fought unarmed, each of his strikes felt like a war hammer striking against her. When she blocked, she felt her arms shake underneath the force. Had it not been for the sky metal dampening the impact, she was quite certain her ribs would already have been broken. On top of that, when they separated, he was light on his feet, hopping from one foot to the other; his style had changed entirely from their first fight.

Jasmine threw off her cloak as she sprouted spider legs from her back. Her eyes darted between his feet, trying to figure out which would lead. Sleeve lunged, right foot forward, ducking; the hit went past her ear. She attempted to sweep his legs, swinging low. He raised a foot up and pinned the naginata to the ground. He pulled his arm back to strike her head when the six legs struck forward, forcing him to jump back before being impaled.

Wasting no time, Jasmine ran forward, keeping the momentum of her attack. Thrust after thrust, forcing Sleeve back toward the house. Mixing it up, she did a wide horizontal sweep at stomach level, catching his clothing and drawing blood as he attempted to avoid it. Sleeve touched his stomach and looked at the blood in the moonlight. Anger filled his face, and Jasmine found herself stopping her attack. Making some distance between them, she assumed a defensive stance, her blade pointed toward the ground, watching him closely.

Darkness burst forth from him and enveloped the hill. Jasmine summoned three starlight spiderlings before she found herself lost in the all-consuming darkness. Her sight went first, then her hearing. She could no longer smell the grass nor feel the gentle breeze of the wind against her face. The ground beneath her feet had no feeling. All she could tell was that she was still holding her weapon, squeezing with whitened knuckles as she looked around.

The darkness had changed, just like his fighting style. Even though her spiderlings were on her body, she could not feel them. Her spider legs sat motionless, the connection between her and the magic all but severed. She wished she had mastered her alchemy before coming here. Her heart was beating faster, sweat beading against her brow as she slowly crept through the pitch black.

One quick jab into her side, she swung wide. Nothing. Another two jabs to her other side, another swing. Nothing. He had trapped her again. Again, he held every advantage. He made sure she was still allowed to feel pain, assaulting her stomach, sides, and head, taking the wind out of her. She felt her senses come back as her back hit the ground. The darkness disappeared around them.

"Did you really think it would've changed?" Sleeve asked, placing a foot down on her stomach, grinding in the spot where he stabbed her in the previous fight. "Did you really think pursuing the White Sash was a good idea?"

Jasmine gave no reply, her face in pain. Her spider legs and spiderlings wouldn't respond to her. They just sat there like inanimate objects.

"Nothing?" he asked. Letting out a sigh, Sleeve knelt. "Goodbye, little spider." Bringing his arm back, he prepared to beat her. But the hit never came. Sleeve staggered back, swiping at something in his face. It was small and red, flapping wings as it darted in and out of his attacks, pecking at his face all the while. It was the little cardinal that had silently been with her the whole time.

He was then taken off his feet and sent flying through the house wall. Jasmine sat up in shock, baffled by the strength of the bird. There was no bird anymore, just a man wearing a cloak of one of the most beautiful shades of red she had ever seen.

"Jasmine," he said as he drew his sword, a scimitar with a jeweled hilt, a blade that shifted between gold and silver. "I assume you are either not fully recovered or something else distracted you. You fought this man once before. This should have been easy for you."

"Cardinal, I—" Jasmine didn't know how to respond, still baffled that he was standing before her.

"No need to explain. His magic isn't natural. I even had a harder time than usual sensing my bird. If you can still fight, help me. Otherwise, make some distance between you and here."

"I can fight," Jasmine responded, getting up to her feet and taking a place beside him. Sleeve still had yet to appear from the house. A blast of dark magic came flying from inside, forcing the two of them to hop out of the way.

Another two blasts followed before Sleeve stepped out of the house. Dark magic was swirling around his left arm while in his other hand, he held the sword with the black blade. He eyed up the two of them before rushing forward at Cardinal. Their blades clashed, their feet moving quickly as their dance began. Jasmine circled around; from her view, it was like watching Cardinal fight a copy of himself.

From their footwork to the attack patterns and parrying that followed each swing, they knew exactly how the other would strike. When she was in range, she thrusted forward and connected with Sleeve's left shoulder. He let out a howl as Cardinal capitalized on it. A swift slash severed his left hand from its arm. Darkness erupted forth, taking both of them off their feet as Sleeve made room for himself.

However, Jasmine still had her senses this time around, though unable to see anything really in front of her. She could see the starlight strands of her silk and that of her spiderlings that skittered about the darkness, trying to find him. She could still hear and feel the ground beneath her. Directing the spiders toward the last spot she remembered him being, she prepared herself for whatever might come.

Cardinal was still fighting Sleeve, the sound of their swords ringing in the darkness. Jasmine struggled to find them. The sound echoed in the darkness in every direction. Cardinal leaned back low, Sleeve's blade slashing over where his neck once was. Swinging back from his low angle, he gave him another wound above where Jasmine had hit his stomach earlier. A blast of sand magic erupted from his hand and pushed him back.

The darkness began to be sucked away into a tornado of sand that swirled all around Cardinal. Jasmine stared in awe at the red-cloaked man she could barely see. Sleeve was kneeling before him, clutching his stomach. He looked up at him and watched the tornado dissipate.

"You're an interesting one," said Cardinal. "You're trained in the way of the sand elves from the south. And yet you look nothing of the part. That on top of this odd dark magic you have. Tell me, are you truly a Kryzen?"

"Ah, dear Cardinal," he said, getting to his feet. "If I told you I was one of the first, what would you say to that?"

"What do you mea—"

Sleeve cut him off before he was prepared, the black blade carving a large wound in his side. Cardinal's blade shone gold; an axe of sand materialized in the air behind Sleeve. It came down over his shoulder, removing his right arm entirely from his body. Cardinal struck him in the head with enough force to render him unconscious. Stepping back, he clutched his side.

"Cardinal!" yelled Jasmine as she sprinted toward him, her weapon returning to its baton shape as she placed it on her back. She looked at his wound, expecting blood to be flowing out and pooling on the ground. Instead, sand was falling out of him, beginning to pile up on the ground as if Sleeve had just broken an hourglass, its contents now spilling out over the ground.

"What... What the hell?" she asked, unable to believe it. "Is this just a dummy made of sand?"

"I wish it was," he replied. "Sadly, I can't do that with my magic. At least not at this kind of distance. I guess outside of the Sovereign Fingers, no one really knows this. Keep it a secret, Jasmine. After all, I did just save your life."

"Can you at least explain?"

"When we're back in the capital, sure. You have a right to know it. Can you get him back to the capital?"

"Yeah...wait." She looked down at the unconscious Sleeve still bleeding from his wounds. "Can't you just teleport him with you? It looks like he's going to die from blood loss."

"No, me switching places with my little birds is meant for one person and one person alone. And I assume with your silk, you can keep him from bleeding out and cocooned the entire trip back. I know others of the rebellion are here... But right now, you should take him and leave."

"Will you be okay?"

"Yeah, I'll be back in the care of the medics back in the capital," he said with a laugh and a short-lived smile as he winced in pain. "Hurry back now, no unnecessary delay."

And just like that, he was gone in a swirl of sand, replaced by a little red cardinal that flew onto her shoulder. Jasmine palmed herself in the forehead for forgetting to ask if he knew anything about Nathanael. With a sigh, she conjured some more spider lings and directed them to cocoon up Sleeve tight enough to stop the bleeding but not so much to kill him.

Hauling the cocoon back down the hill over her shoulder with the help of her additional legs, she remained out of sight. Creeping through the back alleys of the town, she made her way to the stable. Throwing him on the back, she tied him down to the horse with additional silk, placing one spiderling on his cocoon for the journey. Were he to stir, it would bite through the cocoon and into his flesh, rendering him unconscious again.

Jasmine headed back to the capital with the worst enemy she had ever fought strapped to her horse, questions about Cardinal burning in her mind. And yet, for as curious as she was about him, she also respected him more than before. Tonight showed how much he really did care, even if she was just a walking stack of gold coins to him. She always thought those birds were just a way of communication, but now she knew he always watched over those who worked for him. With a smile she rode through the night, unaware of the eyes that watched her...

16

23rd of Cresozis; Mortal Year 523

Kenjo

The capital of Zell, Rastoram, was the largest city the two of them had ever been in. It dwarfed their small home town of Saussion and was what they expected the capital of Samil to have been like in size. Large walls of white surrounded the capital, reaching up toward the clouds. Guards patrolled between the large pointed lookout towers that topped various points along the wall.

The guards themselves didn't shy away from the royal knights they had seen on the way in. Their large statures concealed beneath plates of gleaming steel. Chain mail could be seen sticking out from various parts where the plates were gapped for ease of movement. Shields bearing the sigil of Zell were fastened around their backs. Swords sat sheathed on one hip, a quiver full of red-feathered arrows on the other. A long bow that was at two heads taller than them held in their hands. Faces hidden beneath helmets forged in the shape of a bear head.

Near the massive steel doors that opened into the city sat two stables, one on each side of the street, one designed for hunters, the other meant for civilians and travelers. With the head of Maximus and the Siv, Arlo was able to get free use of the stables for all of them. On top of that, the workers helped them walk the two trophies into town up toward the capital.

The city was then divided into rings, each ring divided by water that flowed throughout the city thanks to the Lantar River that reached all the way from the western coast to where Rastoram was. On the outer ring were mostly various training fields and guards' barracks. On the next ring were the shops and the taverns of the capital. The third ring was where all of the capital housing was for anyone who did not live in the kingdom itself. The central ring held the castle, the white marble-walled heart of the capital.

Its highest towers reached up as high as the walls surrounding the entire city. A beautiful garden full of various flowers lined either side of the stone path leading to the front gate. The royal guard, as motionless as statues, lined each side, great swords in their hands, tips pointed at the ground. Capes flowed down from their shoulders, gently moving with the wind. Their helmets, while still resembling that of a bear head, had an almost angelic aesthetic to them, complete with wings on the sides and a halo sticking up from behind their heads.

Kenjo and Vallarya had wanted to explore it all. But instead, they found themselves sitting awkwardly at a large black table. Arlo was next to Kenjo. Across from them sat the Hands of Zell—a woman known as Araceli Marsallas and her Other, a man called Pacore Crispian. And at the head of the table was the Lord King of Zell himself, Nikyn Vergilius.

"Prince Arlo," said Nikyn as he rubbed his trimmed and graying beard. "Explain yourself to us again here. Not your trophies, as impressive as they are, but this so-called belief that one of the six kings of this nation has betrayed us and kept up a charade, implying that Gonall is still there this whole time."

"As you wish, your majesty," said Arlo as he pushed his chair back. Standing up, he began to walk around the table. Kenjo couldn't help but notice his shaking companion and figured the walking was helping him calm down. "The King of Burrium—forgive me, his name escapes me—is in Samil's back pocket. They assaulted the front, siege towers and all. My father ordered the civilians to be evacuated out the escape tunnels. But what just happened to be waiting for them? Butchers!"

Arlo raised his arms high as he said it as if hoping to incite some response from those before him. Araceli leaned back in her seat with her arms crossed. Nikyn sat stone-faced, his eyes staring straight down the table as Arlo spoke. Silence followed. Vallarya raised a hand to her mouth and coughed, snapping Arlo out of his trance to continue.

"Why would this be so surprising, you may ask? The only ones who know of these escape routes outside of Gonall are the kings and their most trusted generals. Following the battle, Samil retreated, heading back down south to the coast where we know they have taken over the port city of Adana. Bandits led by Maximus, who we killed, were than stationed in the ruins to make it seem as if they had truly been the ones to conquer it. But the outside world would not need to see that far inland, for they had already replaced the civilians along the roads, making it look as if nothing happened. Anyone going inside that they wouldn't want to see...well, they ended up on the other end of a sword or shackled by them."

"And these letters bearing your family's seal?" asked Pacore as he tossed a bundle of scrolls onto the table. Arlo walked over and grabbed one; the seal was indeed his family's. Even the handwriting matched his father's perfectly. "Each one explains how everything was okay, save for your mother falling ill and that he would not be able to make it to this year's festival."

"My mother was never ill," mumbled Arlo as the scroll began to crumple in his hand as anger began to build in him.

"What was that?"

"My mother was never ill! My mother is buried in a tunnel beneath bloodstained ruins next to all the others slaughtered because of that bastard who has the audacity to call himself a king of Zell! And my father has served long enough for you three to know that my mother would not have let him miss this year's festival, no matter how ill she became!"

Arlo slammed his hands on the table, his heart pounding, his face flushed as he stared at the other scrolls all filled with lies, all forged by someone else's hand.

"Our companion, Luna," said Arlo when he finally regained his composure, "she knows the truth. She's the one who told us. Let's bring her in here!"

"The Samilian assassin?" asked Araceli, baffled by his words. "She's the one you trust? How do you know she didn't tell you a lie so that this very thing could happen? So that our unity could be brought into question with war on the horizon?"

"I—" Arlo was at a loss. He took his seat next to Kenjo, unsure of what to do next as he thought about her words.

"Do you have anything to add to his accusation before I go get her?" asked Araceli, waving a hand at Kenjo and Vallarya. "Anything at all?"

"It's the truth," said Vallarya, locking eyes with her. "When we read Maximus's memories, although a great deal of them were gone, the most recent ones weren't. Conversations with his subordinates, personal thoughts on the matter. He exposed it. He was there as a pawn so that Samil could move on. They struck Gonall, left, set up a hold in the port city of Adana. There's no reason to doubt they may strike somewhere else again and leave as well as if they are trying to skirt around all-out war, searching for the Blades of the Mother."

Araceli chuckled as she listened to her with unmoving eyes. Vallarya's tone was direct and knowledgeable; not a single ounce of fear could be felt. Lord King Nikyn shifted in his chair, leaning back. He looked to Vallarya with curiosity.

"Do you come from a noble background, Miss Vallarya?" he asked.

"No, your majesty," she replied, hardly able to hide how flustered she was being spoken to by a king directly. "I grew up in a small village owned by the Seers of the Children. My parents, as far as I know, weren't nobility."

"Hmm... You speak very well for one who isn't. Most younglings like you only have that sort of voice around here if your family comes from nobility or is involved in the political scene. If you plan on staying here, I must recommend you visiting the academy."

Vallarya could not hide the large smile that filled her face. She fell back in her chair, unable to say anything. Her heart was pumping faster as she squeezed Kenjo's hand under the table, trying to tell him just how excited she was.

"Well, then, who are you two?"

Kenjo cleared his throat to speak as he noticed Vallarya still unable to. "We're just—"

"The son of Crimson and his Other," said Pacore bluntly.

Kenjo felt his heart leap out of his chest and beat before him on the table. Vallarya's smile faded as quickly as it appeared, gazing stone-faced back at the man who had apparently knew the truth. Arlo screamed a whispered, "Whaaaaaaaaaat?" as the words hit him.

"What...what do you mean the son of Crimson?" said Kenjo. "That is ridiculous assumption, probably even beyond Arlo—"

"There's no need to lie here, boy. And you know just how futile it is before a Hand—" Pacore paused as he noticed the confused look filling Kenjo's face. He looked to Vallarya and she wore the same expression. "Wait, you two really didn't know, did you?"

"No... Sorry. Your majesty," said Kenjo, looking to Nikyn who seemed unaffected by the newest revelation. "I am Kenjo Alexander, son of Ryan and McKenzie Alexander. This is Vallarya Aberdanth, my other."

Arlo's jaw seemed ready to become unhinged at a moment's notice. With how wide his mouth was, a simple tap would jar it loose.

The tense look in Nikyn's face relaxed at his words. His eyes grew a little, lighting up with some unseen hope.

"Are they here?" he asked, placing his arms on the table. "Is Crimson here?"

"No." His hands began to shake as the thought back to the day outside of his parents' lifeless body before him, their blood on his hands, their body almost unrecognizable in the form it had taken—a creature straight out of a nightmare, a kill justified by the unknown voice inside his head.

"I'm sure they came with you," said Araceli. "So where are they?"

"They're dead."

Silence followed. Kenjo's words had sucked out the very noise from the room. Now it was Araceli and Pacore whose jaws reached for the floor. The newfound light in Nikyn's eyes faded away, and his face returned to its initial intensity. Arlo sat back as he noticed him shaking in his chair.

"Bullshit," said Araceli. "Bullshit! There's no way they could be dead! I thought you would realize how dumb it would be to lie to us. But now I see you haven't learned."

"I'm tellin—"

Araceli leaped across the table. Pacore's arms disappeared as they fused. A crackling blue armor formed around hers as she took both Kenjo and the chair down to the ground. Vallarya was preparing to fuse with Kenjo, but he looked at her and shook his head. Araceli placed her hands on his head and began to channel her magic. She met no resistance as he allowed her into the tapestry of his memories.

From the countless sparring matches with his parents to the days the two of them spent at the academy near their village; to the sleepless nights of them watching over that village and surrounding ones, keeping villagers safe from bandits and thugs, the moment that led to their alleyway encounter with Arthur. She was beginning to find herself impressed. And seeing Ryan and McKenzie again began to warm her heart through the anger welling inside of her after what he had said.

Araceli was slowly beginning to realize how much Kenjo longed to be a hero. The execution in the city streets of that port city and the awkward encounter with Lucios, how his young heart pounded in his chest as fast as it did when he ran from the guard. The fear she saw on McKenzie's eyes was so genuine it hurt her to see her like that. But Araceli pressed on, trying to find the truth in his lies; instead, she just stumbled into more sadness as she learned of their curse.

Then she saw Kenjo looking out the ship window as smoke crawled its way into the sky. Pillars of purple flame shooting up past the walls, then coming crashing down at some unseen location. Kenjo and Vallarya found no trace of Ryan or McKenzie on the ship and began to sprint in the direction of the fire. They arrived to see them there, towering over a dead and bloodily beaten Lucios. She could feel his fear as he slowly reached out his hand for his parents, only to be on the receiving end of an assault.

Reluctance filled them at first until they were able to steel themselves enough to see it through. But Araceli could tell it was something else. There was something else helping them along. And then she felt her hand break through Crimson's chest like Kenjo's did, filling her with the same sadness that he felt that day—the same regret and fear soon washed away by that same presence so they could escape before the guard came.

Kenjo felt a drop of water hit his cheek. He looked up and found another one fall from Araceli's face. She was crying; seconds later, she was shaking. Her grip on his head slowly eased as she leaned back. Pacore rushed to her side, his arms returning as he helped her to her feet, and started to walk her back to her chair. She shrugged off his hands and headed for the door.

"I'm going to get that Samilian girl," she said, wiping away another set of tears.

Kenjo picked up his chair and took a seat, Vallarya and Arlo checking to make sure he was okay as Pacore crossed his arms, staring at the two of them.

Nikyn sat, unmoving, as if nothing had happened in the past few minutes.

"I am sorry for doubting you," said Pacore. "You spoke nothing but the truth. And yet we still assaulted you, read your memories. Albeit, you were far more willing than I expected. It truly does hurt to know they are no longer with us."

Kenjo had no reply, his eyes focused on him as he spoke. Anything he had wanted to say prior had already been yanked from his mind by Araceli. Minutes later, Araceli came in, dragging Luna by her wrist. She practically threw her into the room. Luna stumbled as she tried to maintain her balance. It was one of the few times she had ever been without her mask or hood, and she practically felt naked.

Araceli placed a hand on her head, and Luna didn't fight back. She understood what was happening. Araceli, however, couldn't reach into her memories. She instead found herself standing in a pure white room alongside Pacore. All along the sides of the room, black pillars reached up into the ceiling. Black cobblestone began to form before them in a path, beckoning them onward. The two traveled down what felt like an endless hallway until they arrived in a large circular room.

The pillars on each side circled around the room. In the center lay a large cat-like creature, curled up as it slept, one large tail with a frayed tip wrapped around its gray body. It had four eyes and large ears with folded tips. Emerald green spots dotted its side from the neck down to its hind legs. Before the two could get any closer, they felt themselves yanked from her mind. Araceli found herself back in the room, her wrist now gripped by a black gauntlet.

Kenjo was staring at her. Luna had been screaming in agony the whole time, breathing heavily her back against a chair, hand clutching at her heart.

"If you plan on continuing this, you'll have to deal with me first," he said. "I willingly let you into my memories. But whatever you're doing to my companion is something I cannot sit by and watch. Give this up or get your weapon ready."

Araceli opened her mouth to reply, but it wasn't her words that came next but loud clapping that filled the room. The two turned and saw Nikyn, grinning like a fool from the head of the table.

"This is true Zell politics at its finest," he said heartily. "But this fight isn't meant to be between you two. So please, my loyal friend and my dear guests, take a seat. Let us continue our talk. I have a meeting with the surrounding lords soon. So I would like to get this taken care of before then."

Kenjo was hesitant to let go, Araceli glaring at him all the while as if she was preparing to strike him the moment he let go.

"*Now!*"

Nikyn's voice carried a weight behind it that rivaled Maximus's yells. Kenjo let go quickly and helped Luna to a seat next to Vallarya as he sat down back in his. Araceli practically jumped back to her seat as if trying to look as if she had been there the whole time to avoid punishment.

"There we go," said Nikyn, his voice returning to its original tone. "Arlo, how do you plan on accusing King Tiberius? Even with what we have discussed, even with two Hands that could potentially oust him before the public. War on the horizon, the Colors of Summer flying by week's end. What would make the people listen to any of it? What would make the kings listen to any of it?"

Arlo let out a small chuckle. Looking Nikyn straight in the eyes, he spoke without an ounce of hesitation. "Simple. The true language of our nation. Combat."

17

23ʳᵈ of Cresozis; Mortal Year 523

Kenjo

Kenjo, Vallarya, and Luna met up with Kaldana and Elijah in the second ring. The two of them were gorging themselves on sweets and smiling at one another all the while. Arlo had stayed behind in the castle to continue talking with Nikyn about his plans. Ricardo, as Elijah soon told them, was wandering around in search of information on Lukas.

Two days from now would be the Meeting of Kings. It was going to be a big day, not just for them but for all of Zell. Between the final decision on whether to answer the call to war or hand over their Blades of the Mother and the callout of a fellow king for betrayal, it was a day that would shake the world.

As they walked around the second ring, making small talk with one another, Vallarya came up with an idea. She wanted to visit the academy where Kenjo and herself would soon be studying now that they finally reached their goal. With nothing else to really do as they waited for Arlo, there was no argument from the others. They asked a guard for directions who pointed with his finger toward a lone bell tower that stood out on the third ring. Making their way there, Vallarya found herself in awe as she stopped in front of the academy.

The stone walls shone with a magnificence that rivaled the castle. Stained-glass windows lined each wall along the top. A stone path lined with statues of cavalrymen led up to large ornate oak doors. A symbol of Zell engraved onto each with a golden hue. Gardeners tended to beautiful white and yellow flowers that filled the gap between each statue. The bell tower they had seen from a distance was situated on the left side of the building, stretching past the various points of the rooftop. The bell began to ring; shortly after, the doors opened wide, and students began to pour out.

Most were wearing what appeared to be the school uniform—white bottoms with a black top. Some girls wore skirts with leggings underneath. Others wore pants or shorts similar to that of the boys. In the back of the group leaving were students brandishing weapons and wearing armor, sweat beading their foreheads after an exhausting day of training. Red faces were easy to spot among them. To Vallarya, this was an academy of her dreams, one that put their old one to shame.

While Vallarya was smitten with it, Kenjo, on the other hand, felt off. There was no way he would soon forget the sight. He thought it was incredible. But something was pulling on him to leave, something telling him that he should be somewhere else instead of right here. Vallarya turned and smiled at him, and those thoughts melted away. She then led the group inside.

Inside, the entrance was surprisingly small compared to how the school looked on the outside. Golden lamps lined the walls at even intervals to spread the light around. Opposite of them stood a large double door; to their right were chairs scattered around some tables, and to their left sat two women behind a counter, each one looking up at them, curious.

"Excuse me," said one them. "You five don't look like students. Is there something that you need help with?"

"Actually, we were hoping to know more about this place," replied Vallarya as she grabbed Kenjo's arm and pulled him to her. "The two of us were also hoping to enroll here."

A smile formed on her face. "For aspiring students, these doors are always open. Though I must admit not many Samilians enroll here. Usually, they stay away from the capital academy. But nonetheless, if studying here is what you seek, you are most welcome to join. Now then…"

She stood up and turned around, running her finger along the spines of books that sat on a table behind her. "Your family names?"

"Aberdanth and Alexander."

"Ah, two As. That makes this a little easier then," she replied, pulling a large book from the table. For a Zellian, it seemed average in her arms. But if it had been a Samilian women in her position, they doubted she would have been able to carry it. Placing it on the counter in front of them, she looked at the others who were standing silently behind them. "What about the rest of you? Interested in joining as well?"

The others shook their heads. "Just here for them and the sights," said Kaldana.

The woman shrugged as she opened the book to two blank pages. Pulling a red-feathered quill from behind the desk, she handed it to Vallarya. "Along the top, write your name. Boy, you'll be writing on this page," she said, pointing at the next one. "Beneath that, your blessed day, and beneath that, what exactly it is you want to learn at this academy. Whether it be basic knowledge, combat training, particular specializations or fields, or something else entirely."

Vallarya quickly wrote her name along the top but stopped when thinking of what she meant by blessed day. The woman behind the counter noticed her stopping, and it clicked in her head like a light going on.

"Oh, forgive me," she said. "Blessed day is your day of birth. You just call them birthdays in the east, right?"

"Yeah," said Vallarya. "Thank you."

Knowing this, she quickly wrote hers down and finished writing what was requested of her before handing the quill to Kenjo who stared at his page hesitantly. He wrote his name and his birthday, but as he prepared to write next, he found himself unsure of what to put. His eyes glanced over at Vallarya's page and saw she had chosen politics.

Of course she chose that, thought Kenjo as he looked back to his page. She had always wanted to be on the council since she was younger. Even though almost all of the seats were reserved for nobility, she was determined to have a seat among them. Although she had no qualms with fighting alongside him as his Other, she believed in a world built upon peace and debate. Kenjo copied her, writing politics down for his goal here as well. Handing the quill back to the woman, he pushed the book toward her.

Flipping it around, she looked it over. "Politics for both of you? Interesting, you don't look like a politician at all, boy. You fit the part, though, Miss Aberdanth. Anyways, this will be a most interesting class for you. Zell politics are a little bit different than those of Samil or Ivofir for that matter. And I promise you will learn a great deal from the professors here. They are all quite gifted. That is enough for me, however. Kundra, would you mind showing them the academy grounds?"

The other woman behind the desk stood up slowly. Stepping around the desk, she beckoned them to follow her and led them through the large double doors. The hallway was lined with similar golden torches and windows. It opened up into a large room, which she explained was the main hub of the academy. To their right, left, and opposite wall were doors leading further into the building. On the opposite wall, on either side of the door, large staircases reached up and wrapped around the walls, leading up to the second and third floors.

All along the walls were paintings of knights throughout Zell's long history. Beneath each one, a small stone was carved with their names. They began with the right door. It led to the actual lecture halls where most of the actual teaching was done. In each hall sat about twenty to thirty desks all facing the blackboard and desk of the teacher at the head of the classroom. Near the end of this hallway were the larger auditoriums, which Kundra stated held special classes for a much larger audience, closer to one hundred to two hundred people, or a particular event decided upon by the headmaster.

They proceeded back to the hub and went through the left side doors. This one split into two paths, one leading to a courtyard filled with beautiful green grass and various benches scattered around for students to sit. In the center stood a large fountain, the sun shining down upon the blue water that ran through it. Standing in the center of the fountain were statues of four royal knights. The water ran through their arms and down their swords, which pointed down to the pooling water at their feet. It was a place for relaxation and a quick breather for most students that wanted a small taste of the outside before returning to their studies.

The second path led down to the training fields. Some fields were built like arenas for proper combat, others seemed attuned for endurance training. An archery range was at the far end along with a field that looked like it was meant for some type of survival training. Vallarya thought maybe it was for anyone aspiring to be hunters in Zell. After they were satisfied, Kundra led them back and through the middle door between the stairs.

This led to the mess hall. Table after table filled the center all the way to the far wall. On one side was the kitchen. Empty as it was now, it wasn't hard for them to picture the chefs running back and forth through it, preparing the days' meals for all the students who came here. On the other wall, a smaller kitchen but meant for desserts. Fruits were piled on one table separated in baskets, allowing the students to grab anything they wanted. Sunlight came in through the windows; anything that the light couldn't reach was filled by a lamp to illuminate all of the mess hall.

Finally, they headed upstairs. On the second floor was where all of the magical studies took place. A room for each type of magic. Kryzen and normal folk were not separated, though the teachers typically required more of Kryzen in this particular field. They had no intention of separating the students so they wouldn't feel isolated.

"Not many Kryzen are actually enrolled here," said Kundra as she guided them down the magic hallway. "For the most part, they are taken in by royalty for military or other endeavors."

Just like Samil, thought Kenjo as they continued following her.

"However, they're given a choice should they not be RKs. They can stay with their new home or they can come here and learn. And honestly, most can't pass up the chance to continue living in royalty nor can many resist their call to battle that fills most Kryzen. But the odd exception or two shows up, and I would personally say they come out better for it. Anyways, carrying on."

Or maybe... Kryzen really do have freedom here. A place for anyone aspiring for greatness.

The third floor was set up with the dorms for any students who wanted to live on campus. Though right now, it was completely deserted. With the Colors of Summer and the Meeting of Kings, most students spent time with their families. Today was the last day of classes for the week until after the festivities. The rooms were spacious, even with four beds laid about, one in each corner of a room. There was still plenty of room in between for the residents to move about.

Once they were done, Kundra led them back to the main entrance where her friend greeted them with a smile.

"So what did you guys think?" she asked, standing up. "Was Kundra a good tour guide?"

"It's amazing!" said Vallarya, unable to contain the excitement in her voice. "And yes, she was."

"That's good to hear. Well, then, after the Colors of Summer, return here. We'll have your uniforms and get you situated with your classes. Should the uniforms not fit on the first go, don't worry, we will get them measured to fit you comfortably. Until then, you all have a good time during the festival."

"Thank you!"

*****

The group left the academy and headed back toward the center ring in hopes of meeting up with Arlo again. He was walking toward them from the castle, chatting with a man wearing a full suit of green plate armor but no helmet; two swords were sheathed on each of his hips. It immediately became clear as they got closer that he wasn't a Zellian.

Although he wore the armor of Zell's knights dyed green, his ears were long and pointed, a ruby earing hanging from the tip of his right ear. Long blonde hair was tied up in a ponytail, and long bangs

261

came down and covered his left eye. He stood a head taller than Arlo, and the two of them seemed like old friends with the way they were talking. When Arlo noticed the group approaching him, he raised his hand up in greeting and ran over to them, the knight close behind.

"There you guys are!" shouted Arlo with a smile. He was far happier now than he was when they had left him. "Allow me to introduce you to Leaf."

The man next to him bowed a much different bow than they were used to from Samil. Hands together in front of him, he bowed as if he were in prayer. Kenjo and Vallarya noticed it almost immediately that he was an elf from the northern reaches of Samil. As he raised his head, his emerald eye had an uneasy calm about it.

"Pleasure to make your acquaintance," he said, offering his hand out to Kenjo for a shake.

"Kenjo," he replied, grasping his hand. His grip was far firmer than he expected. "This is Vallarya, Luna, Kaldana, and Elijah."

"Pleasure to meet you all as well."

"Leaf here is an old friend of mine. We met back during my training as he was traveling through Zell with his family. Gonall was one of their stops due to his mother being extremely interested in ash-weaving. My mother happened to teach his and introduced us, blah, blah, blah. It's been what, three or four years since we last saw one another?"

"Indeed it has. My father found his work here in the capital. Mother still weaves just like yours taught her. I must admit it will be quite painful to tell her the truth of this all."

"The Colors of Summer are about to fly overhead. There's no better time than now. Anyways, you guys follow me. King Nikyn has given us access to the estate reserved for my family."

Arlo led them out to the third ring and around to the eastern side of the castle. There stood a house meant for royalty surrounded by stone walls that fenced in the yard, A cast-iron gate locked in the center. Beyond it, a cobblestone path led to a small fountain and then to the house itself. Emerald grass filled the yard, rose bushes lining the stone walls on the inside. Arlo unlocked the gate with a key he produced from his pocket. Pushing the gate open, he stood there, motionless.

Kenjo looked around as the others moved forward and took in the sight. The beautiful house sat nestled against the back wall. The front door was engraved with the crest of Gonall. As the others began to move inside, Kenjo turned to see Arlo still had not moved. His hands were shaking. His gaze cast downward at his feet.

Placing his hand on his shoulder, he gave him a little shake. "You all right, Arlo?"

"I-I don't know," he said, slowly raising his head up to meet his gaze. "I'm here, exactly where I need to be in the capital to get that bastard. Nikyn and Araceli are onboard with it all. I met up with Leaf. Hell, even without that, the Colors of Summer are about to fly, the most beautiful sight in the world! But I... I can't move. W-when I look at this house, I see them. I see the days we spent here over the years. They all just look at me with lifeless and disappointed eyes. Like I have failed and that they are just waiting for me to join them in the after. And I can barely keep my composure. My legs don't want to take another step. This insufferable shaking won't stop no matter how hard I try!"

Arlo flapped his arms to try and quell the shaking. They stopped momentarily. Soon as they returned to his side, he found them shaking again with a will of their own.

"It's painful, I know," said Kenjo, taking a step forward. "I see my parents in every choice I make. But you believe in what you're doing, don't you? You can't give up on something like that. Not when you still have life flowing within you. Arlo, we're here. After Maximus, after that Siv. We are standing right here in the heart of the nation. What you want is right around the corner, something that very well may save the entire nation from the same fate as Gonall. The people of Zell need you more than they realize, and we're all here with you. Er, at least I am. And if you think your family really wants you in the after, tell them to wait. You still have things you need to take care of here."

The shaking stopped. His hands were finally back under his control. He looked back at the house where the others had disappeared inside. The ghosts he had hallucinated were still there, but they gently smiled at him, reaching their hands out to welcome him inside. Their lifeless eyes illuminated with a newfound feeling.

"Thanks, Kenjo," he said, taking his first step forward, followed by another and another. "When this is done...what will you do?"

"I-I will..." Kenjo stopped mid-reply. He had no clue. A voice was whispering to him, telling him to say something else than what he was about to. He pushed the voice to the back of his mind as he walked after him. "I plan on studying at the academy with Val. That's actually where we were when you were finishing your discussion. We're enrolled and begin after the festival."

Arlo looked at him in disbelief. He wasn't buying it. "You know, for the one who killed Crimson, that doesn't seem at all like your kind of place. Speaking of which, you have a lot to tell me."

"When you no longer have to worry about Tiberius, I'll tell you."

"That's fine."

*****

An hour after dinner, Kenjo found himself on the balcony of the third floor looking out over the city before him. From the estate's position, he was above the rest of buildings in the city, save for the castle and the academy. The sight was calming. Torches of patrolling guards were like little stars walking along the walls. The now luminescent water that flowed between the rings of the city bathed the stone walls in a beautiful blue.

Tapping his fingers on the rail, he found himself getting bored. He felt slightly naked after all the time spent traveling. His sword lay in his room behind him against a wall, its weight no longer on his back. His cloak and armor were thrown on the floor. It felt like an eternity since he had been in normal clothes. Turning to go back inside, he found the door open and Vallarya stepping through. She was smiling, holding a cup of tea in her hand, steam rising gently from the green liquid.

"There you are," she said, closing the door and joining him at the rail. "Wow, this city is even more beautiful at night. I wonder if the capital of Samil was anything like this."

"Mmm, I'm guessing if it was, it was in a time before Victor."

"That would make a lot more sense." She took a sip and jerked back, holding her tongue out in the air. It was still too hot.

"Did you need something, Val?"

"Not really. Figured you were someplace alone and that you would need company. You always do tend to wander away from people. And I know it's been rather difficult to do so these past few weeks."

"I... I do not wander away from people," he replied, his cheeks beginning to turn red.

"Please. Kenjo, sometimes you avoid them like a plague when you don't actually need to be involved with them, which I still find odd because you handle yourself with them rather well."

She tried to drink her tea again, testing it with the tip of her tongue first. Satisfied with the temperature, she took a sip. It was a sweet green tea. It reminded her of the kind back home. Holding the cup in both hands before her, she looked out over the city, her eyes glowing.

"Hey, Kenjo, are you sure you want to join the academy?" she asked. Her voice was weak, like she didn't want to ask what she just did.

"What do you mean," he replied. His heart started to beat a little faster. *Did she see me hesitate earlier?* His words came out unsure. "You know that's the reason why we're here. To finish our studies in a place that doesn't enslave Kryzen like back home."

"One could argue that the royal knights are enslavement. But then again, it is apparently all voluntary. Anyways, you don't need to lie. Your words, your tone, it's always like that when you do. Slightly higher, slightly shaky. It was the same way with your father."

Vallarya took another sip of her tea. Her eyes drifted down to the liquid as she lowered it from her lips. "So tell me, Kenjo, what is it? What's on your mind?"

He gripped the rail tightly with his hands. He wasn't angry; he was just lost. Kenjo tried to think of a way for it to come out without it sounding horrible. The longer he gripped that rail, the more he realized it wasn't going anywhere, and the floodgates began to open. "I don't really want to join the academy anymore, Val. After everything that's happened, it just doesn't feel like the place to be. Say we go to the academy and we learn all we want to. We become heroes on the side. It doesn't change the fact that across the sea, on the other side of the world, sits a king who wants to make the world suffer."

"Kenjo, that is a problem beyond us."

"Is it?" he asked. His voice had hardened in seconds. It was stern, and his eyes pierced into hers as she looked up from her tea. "Vallarya, that problem has been with us since the beginning since before we were even an Anchor and an Other. Samil forced us out of our first home. The army cut down our neighbors, our friends, and your parents. You have a sister out there we haven't seen in how many years? Vallarya, this is our problem, and right now, all around us are the people who oppose it."

Vallarya shook her head. "You aren't serious right now, are you? You don't want to join Zell's military, do you? You don't really want to be a part of the war?"

"I—"

"Just tell me you're joking right now!" she demanded.

He looked at her with apologetic eyes. She knew his answer before it left his mouth. "I'm not. I mean it, Val."

"We're not soldiers! Yes, you're a Kryzen. Yes, we have the Hands of the Children. But *we are not soldiers!* We are just two people living in a world going to shit. We have a chance to live, to carry on with our lives. Lest I remind you, a life your parents died for!"

She began to jab a finger into his chest. Her cup of tea left on the rail so she could vent all her anger. Rage had filled her eyes, something he had never seen before.

"Val, listen to me."

"No, I don't want to hear your stupid excuse for why this idea entered your mind in the first place!"

Vallarya grabbed her tea and walked to the other end of the balcony, keeping her back to him. She sipped it in an attempt to calm down, the full moon above casting its light down on the quiet world. But to any outsiders, it was as if the moon itself was focused on that little balcony in the capital as if it knew something no other outsider did.

"Vallarya, listen to me," said Kenjo, starting to move closer to her.

"Don't take another step. I can only handle your stupidity calmly from a distance. Any closer, and I may hit you before you get a chance to speak."

"That... That doesn't really sound like a politician."

She turned around and glared at him.

He sighed. "Look, Vallarya, it's not great, I know. The idea, the very thought of it, is damn near absurd. But I believe in it. Whether we like it or not, our lives will be dictated by the future. We ran from Samil. Should they win the coming war...there is no doubt in my mind that they will hunt us down again, root us out from wherever it is we decide to hide. We... We don't get the option to have a peaceful life. I promise you, I wish there was another way that we could just focus on our studies, be heroes in our spare time, and just live a peaceful life."

"Do you want to be like them?" she began, the anger quickly rising in her voice. "After hearing who they actually were? Is that it, Kenjo? You just want to be Crimson so badly, don't you? And after hearing that your parents were actually him, you want it even more!"

"You know that ever since we were bound to the Hands that I wanted to surpass the legend of Crimson."

"And do you really believe this war is how you'll do it? Is this the way you make history?"

"No, that's not it..."

"We aren't... We aren't soldiers. This war isn't meant for us." Vallarya looked out to the city below in an effort to calm down once more.

"Are you so focused on what we aren't that you of all people doubt what we could be?" asked Kenjo bluntly.

His words made her turn around to face him, her mouth agape, but no words came out. She was at a loss. And for the first time in their many years together, he had bested her in a verbal argument.

"I take that as a yes." He walked toward her and placed his hands on her shoulders. Looking her in the eyes, he continued, "I would rather fight alongside those who stand against them now in this moment than stand against them alone in the future."

She shook free of him and headed for the door. "I'm done talking about this tonight. I'll be with Kaldana. Goodnight, Kenjo."

He reached his hand out for her as she opened the door, falling back to his side as it shut, a loud thud echoing across the balcony. Kenjo turned around to gaze out at the city once more.

"*Oh, so you do feel it too?*" said a voice.

Kenjo looked around, but there was no owner. The door was still closed, and he was very much alone on that balcony.

"*You can keep looking, but you'll never find me. Least not in this plane. How great it is to know we're growing closer. You have the same feeling as me that something is wrong, that you can't just sit there and do nothing.*" The voice laughed as it continued talking. Kenjo remembered it—the man in gold and black. "*You have a cruel fate, don't you? The one you love just wants a peaceful life behind a desk and mountains of books. But you feel the call to something more, something that stretches out across the world. You put on a strong face for her just now. But I know you're scared, still afraid that you'll fail everyone again and again. Remember, boy, no matter what you do, your path leads to Nothingness.*"

"Tell me your name. Tell me what you want from me!" he screamed at the heavens.

There was no reply. He was only met with silence.

18

1ˢᵗ of Cresozis; Mortal Year 523

Jasmine

*J*asmine sat in Cardinal's chair, looking over his books and filtering through stacks of paper. Since his injury, he'd been in the medical ward for over two weeks. He decided to have Jasmine help him with his work. And the longer she poured over the papers before her, the more she became impressed by how he kept up with everything.

It was going on four, and she decided it was time to visit him. Extinguishing the lamplights, she locked the door and headed out. Making her way through the hallways, she found her way to the medical ward. Had Cardinal shown any sign of proper recovery, he would be resting in his own room. But much to Jasmine's worry, Cardinal did not exactly have a normal body or recovery process.

His cloak was thrown over one of the chairs in the room. He lay on it at an incline, flipping his fingers through a book. Bedding was gathered at his ankles, bandages wrapped around his abdomen. As Jasmine entered the room, he bent the corner of a page and closed the book. With a smile, he turned to her.

"Welcome back," he said, greeting her. "How's it look?"

"Well, you still look like crap, honestly," she said, noticing the bags under his eyes as she got closer. "How much have you slept?"

"Not near enough. Very hard to do when your body is, er, leaking. But what about the logs, merchant guild, Samil's treasury? How does it all look?"

"From what I could tell, everything looked fine. Improving, if anything. With war more and more likely, trade all around is starting to rise. Rebels will probably start to hit the trade routes soon, though or at least look for something to weaken us with. So I do feel we should speak with the king and his council in regards to it."

"Yeah? Hmm, I guess with Sleeve in our custody, it would make them want to do something a little more desperate and direct. I'll talk to our Sovereign soon then. Hopefully, I'll be in walking shape for that. It would be rather embarrassing to have him come down here."

"Can you really not heal yourself?" asked Jasmine as he adjusted himself on the bed, wincing all the while.

"I told you before I can make weapons. Hell, I can do a lot of things with sand. My magic also makes it materialize out of thin air, but I truly cannot heal myself. And sadly, there isn't a sand weaver in the entire capital. I really need for us to invest in some."

"Is there one coming?"

"Yeah, called upon them a little over a week ago. They should be here soon. It will be nice to see a fellow sand elf. Do you mind continuing my work in the meantime?"

"As long as you don't mind answering my questions when I have them."

"Not at all," he laughed.

"Why is your body like this?"

Cardinal's smile faded as he heard her question. Looking at her, he could tell how serious she was, and she wasn't planning on letting it go without an answer. He glanced out the window, down at his hands, and back at her. Running his hand through his hair, it stopped at the back of his head.

"Short answer, I was a foolish child, always wandering around in places I shouldn't have been. One night, I snuck out, explored one of the many great temples that stand in the desert down south. I missed my footing on a jump and fell down and down into darkness. When I woke, I was surrounded by spirits of the sand. My body already changed. It was the only way I could live. And they made that choice for me. My heart no longer beats. Where blood should course and fall, sand does instead. A trade-off of that being my body is damn near indestructible, at least to conventional weapons and arms. Magic, on the other hand, still has quite the effect."

Jasmine's eyes were downcast, focused on her hands as she listened to him speak. "I'm sorry to hear about that. Truly." Her eyes went wide. "You mean you encountered one of the great spirits? And Sleeve's blade was enchanted?"

"Not exactly enchantment, A type of magic I had not expected. I have smiths and other experts looking into it for some more information. Jasmine, if you haven't pieced it together already, Sleeve is a very peculiar person for the rebels. Not only does he know the sword dancing of the south, he carries a blade that can wound me. Even his magic has no record in any log, at least from what my contacts have reported to me."

"What magic is it?"

"They'll be bringing the research to my office later. You can read it there. I need some sleep. Oh, before you go, have you talked to Sleeve since he became our prisoner?"

"I plan on questioning him before he's taken to the executioner's block," Jasmine said, standing up as Cardinal's words bounced back and forth in her head. "Find out all I can. When I do, I'll come back. Sleep well."

"Don't forget to do my paperwork!" he yelled as she disappeared out the door.

Jasmine headed back to Cardinal's office. On the way, she stopped by the mess hall for a quick bite she could take with her. Filling up a plate, she carried it with a smile on her face, munching on bread as she walked. Taking a seat at the desk, she pushed a ledger aside and dug in. A knock came to the door as shortly after she finished.

"Come in," she said quickly, hiding the plate on the floor and opening the ledger.

A slender woman walked in, carrying a bundle of scrolls. "Oh, excuse me, I thought this was Cardinal's office."

She bowed and turned around to walk out. "It is!" yelled Jasmine, stopping her in her tracks. "Sorry, I'm filling in for him while he's recovering... Did he not mention anything?" Jasmine's face filled with disappointment.

"Oh! I offer my apologies again. These are the reports from everyone he reached out too in regard to Sleeve and other various things. He said they were important, so if you're filling in, I recommend reading them or taking them to him."

She placed the bundles on the desk in front of her. Quickly moving to the door, she bowed to Jasmine and left without another word. Jasmine blinked a few times, amazed by how quickly she moved. Looking at the stack, she reached for the first one, breaking open the seal. She began to read it. It was from the smiths looking into the blade.

> Dear Cardinal,
>
> We have looked over the blade over a hundred times, passed it along to sorcerers and alchemists. And every one of us here in the smithy have looked it over. We've all come to the same conclusion. This is no enchanted blade like thought at first glance. It also does not gain that magical glow of black energy that you report it having in our hands. We brought it near the one known as Sleeve, and the blade began to blacken almost instantly. It seems to have a deep connection to him. We can only imagine what it is when his hand grasps the blade.
>
> On another note, the sorcerer that accompanied us believed the magic that surrounded the blade to be something we lost long ago. Something ancient, something wrong. Yet he refused to acknowledge it as truth. He believed it to belong to the Nothingness. And I know, I

know it shouldn't be said. No one in their right mind wants to hear that. But dearest Cardinal, we cannot put it out of the realm of possibility. Especially with the magic that you mentioned…

The scroll ended there. Jasmine reread a few times, baffled by what she read. Reaching for another scroll, she found the second part and continued reading:

The sorcerer left to talk with his fellows. Though, let's be honest, magic can only help us so far here. You came to us first, after all. Back to the more important blade itself. A mystery. But I decided to speak with a wielder of a Blade of the Mother. It was an idea of one of my assistants. We all know how the Blades grow when wielded by one person for so long. They kind of awaken and form a bond with their wielder. Well, we tested it out. We tried to break it with everything imaginable. What Sleeve has is the 41st Blade of the Mother.

Jasmine dropped the scroll and sat back in her chair, rolling the words over and over again in her head. She didn't know how it was possible in every record she knew of. Only forty such blades ever existed. And they were all accounted for within the kingdoms, save for one. But even that had a record. She let out a long sigh. She still had more scrolls to pore through. Pushing the thoughts back to her mind, she grabbed another one. Leaning back, she held it up to the ceiling and began to read.

I must say tis quite odd for one such as yourself to reach out to a northern city. Especially one that deals with us hunters. Alas, it is nice to be thought of by a Sovereign Finger. In regards to the boar you inquired about. It is almost as odd as you reaching out to us. The gray flesh is, well, as you guessed, not normal. It's rotting and diseased. A constant state of decay, but at the same time, it's just as alive as the rest of its flesh. I cut it apart myself. The insides were not the what they should have been. A black slime flowed along with the blood. Each organ was drenched in it. When I tried to separate it, I found the organ I cut away chewed up where the slime had touched it. A comrade of mine recommended that I bring it to the church. He was getting a bad feeling from it. I did. And you would not believe it, the black liquid and the gray flesh combusted in holy fire. The Father did not take kindly to it being within his house. The rest of the boar was untouched and disposed of. Cardinal, I'm not studious nor do I care much about the goings of the world. But I know Nothingness when I see it. It is the only thing that reacts like that in a holy site. If there is any more, I assure you we will keep in touch.

Jasmine was standing hunched over the desk, both palms on either side of the scroll. Her body was shaking. Sweat began to bead her brow as she looked at the final lines again.

"How? How is this possible?" she said. Her right arm became uncontrollable. She felt fear gripping at her. "The Nothingness should be gone! Not infecting wildlife. Not being used by someone…no, no, no, no."

Jasmine grabbed all of the scrolls up and sprinted out of the room. She could barely catch her breath as she avoided all the people that she could. The unfortunate ones who got in her way she barreled through with a simple sorry. She didn't have anything else on her mind but this. Cardinal had to know. He had to know everything that was contained in the scrolls. Anything she left unopened they could open together.

She tripped through the medical ward and crashed through the door. Jasmine stopped in the door frame. Cardinal looked at her, anger clear on his face. A nurse was tending to one of his wraps. Sand had erupted forth and piled on the ground.

"I'm so sorry," said the nurse, quickly finishing up the bandage before cleaning up the sand.

"Don't be," he replied. "It was my assistant's fault for scaring you. Just add it to the rest for when the weaver finally gets here."

Jasmine closed the door and waited outside for the nurse to finish, back against the wall, one foot holding her up as the other rested on the wall. She felt bad for causing a problem, yet she wasn't planning on apologizing. What she knew now was far too important. A few minutes later, the nurse came out, bowed to her, and wandered off to another part of the medical ward.

"Oh, you're still here," said Cardinal, putting forth no effort to hide his annoyance.

"Sure am," she replied, taking a seat in the open chair. "You have to look at this or listen to me say it. I don't care which, but you need to know. This goes beyond your merchant business."

Cardinal opted to read the scrolls himself. Jasmine handed them to him in order, watching his face go from annoyance to shock and awe in a matter of moments, eyes slowly widening as he moved across the scroll. When he was done, he just turned his head and looked out his window up at the moon its light now breaking free of the clouds.

Jasmine waited patiently at first, rolling the scrolls back up and tying them. As silence filled the room, it became replaced with her tapping foot. Cardinal had still not said anything when her other foot joined in, alternating taps between them.

"Um," she said, reaching a hand out to poke him. "Cardinal?"

"Can you do me a favor?"

"Yes, sir."

"Don't be formal," he said, unamused, his gaze not moving from the window. "See my cloak there? Can you grab it for me? Hurts to move."

"Certainly," she said, standing up and moving to the other chair, holding it up in between them. "Did you want me to cover you with it or help you get it on?"

"No, no. I want you to put it on instead, my little bird."

"Oh, okay. Just sit up a little. I can help you—" She stopped. His words repeated in her head. "What did you say?"

"I said I wanted you to put it on. Don't tell me the most attentive and well-invested bird that I have is falling deaf on me now."

Jasmine looked at the red cloak in her hands. It looked brand-new; the previous rips and tears in the fabric were gone. Stains that had once dotted the surface had been removed. Slowly, she threw it over her shoulders. Clasping it in front, it coiled up around her neck, ready to be lifted to mask the lower half of her face. The hood was a tad large on her, but with her hair up the way it was, she wasn't inclined to pull it up anyway. It felt heavier on her than it did in her hands.

"How does it feel?" he asked, his head slowly turning. A mocking smile crossed his face, followed by a suppressed laugh.

"Weird," she said. "Um, why exactly did you want me to put this on? I feel silly."

"Because, Jasmine, should I not make it, I want there to be someone to fill my shoes. A successor, if you will."

"W-Wait, but a weaver is coming!" She was at his bedside now, yelling in his face. "So you don't need to think of anything as absurd as that!"

"That they are. And they will weave and weave, and hopefully, I'll go back to normal, no longer leaking sand, my body back to 100 percent." His smile was gone. "However, should worse come to worst, I want to be prepared."

"But!" Her eyes were beginning to tear at the thought of losing him. It was her fault...

"Samil will need someone to fill my shoes. In this past week, you have picked up far more than I expected of you, like you have a natural talent for this type of work. Before I pass on, I plan to teach you as much as I can. About being a merchant. About being in my seat. Note that this does not make you a Sovereign Finger. That is up to King Victor only. And before you ask, I choose my successor. No one else. Not even Victor will elect another for me."

"Cardinal." She stepped back from him. Looking down at her feet, she was at a loss.

He reached his hand out and placed it on her shoulder. "Look here, my bird. Stop looking so down. You aren't the reason for me ending up like this. It's my fault for fighting him so casually. You need to hold your head high. Death is just a part of life. It happens when we least expect it sometimes. You know it, I know it, everyone knows it. No need to waste your time and tears on me because of it. The spirits of the sand aren't calling me just yet."

"And if I say no?"

"Then you would be turning your back not only on me, your leader, but on your nation that includes your family and your dearest Forsythia."

She glared at him. "That's cold, even for you."

"Not as cold as my body will be soon." He looked at her and noticed she was prepared to strike him. "Poor joke, forgive me. But for one who has already survived death—twice, I may add—you kind of look at it differently when you know it's coming. Anyway, I looked over the scrolls. This truly is out of the range of my merchants. Hell, way above it, Finger and Sovereign grade. You need to talk to Sleeve when you're ready, any last bit you can get out of him. As for Nathanael. Mention Lundquist at the merchant's guild. They'll direct you to his father."

She had almost forgotten about him. She completely forgot she had mentioned it to Cardinal. Nodding slowly, she placed a hand on the hand still resting on her shoulder. It was cold. *Was that how cold he always was? Or was this new?*

"Go get some rest. Question Sleeve tomorrow. Once he's dealt with, you can worry about Nathanael. By the way, the cloak fits you more than you think. Keep it. Tomorrow, we can start your training."

Jasmine headed to the door. Looking over her shoulder at him, she said, "Goodnight."

"Sleep well."

*****

When Jasmine returned to her room, she found herself unable to sleep. She was growing accustomed to how the cloak felt. It no longer felt as heavy as it did before. Moving to her desk, she opened up one of her alchemy books, realizing she wanted a break from it all. Picking up where she left off, she pulled out the recipes she had worked on during her trip and started brewing. The end result was a light-blue liquid. With a gulp, she drank it down.

It was fine. Everything was normal. She began to tap on her desk. As the noise grew louder to her, she tapped softer and softer until she could hear herself rest her hand on the desk. Pushing back her chair, she reached for her ears in pain, the screeching of wood on wood echoing throughout her ears. *Come on, focus,* she thought to herself, *Focus on one thing.* Holding her hands in front of her, she stared at them, scooting the chair back some more until she was able to block it out entirely.

The night continued this way for hours until she finally passed out on her bed, making various noises louder and louder while focusing on different things. Before she had passed out, she had attempted thirty different tests. Hearing through walls at the conversations going on all around her, Jasmine had no difficulty hearing the footsteps of anyone walking through the barracks. And had she focused in one direction, she managed to hear it from her room to the opposite end of the barracks.

She woke up, her hair a mess, and her body sprawled out over the bed. The cloak still around her body was the perfect blanket. Slowly moving through her routine, she bathed and got ready for the day. Donning her armor and weapon, she fastened the cloak around her and headed out toward Cardinal's office. Unlocking the door, she lit a few lamps and took a seat. The newest report from the merchant's guild had come in. Breaking the seal, she quickly began to read it.

Cardinal, we have a problem. Those white sashes, rebels, whoever the hell they are, they are causing a massive problem in the north. I wouldn't personally reach out to you about this, the others were highly against it. However, with only one trade route, two if we're lucky during these final days of summer, I see no reason not to ask for your assistance. They are holding down the roads, going through everything aimed for the capital. Goods have been destroyed. Weapons, armor, and coin have been seized. No goods from the north will be coming anytime soon until it is dealt with. I do apologize again for this inconvenience.

With respect,
Your humble merchant, Reinhold.

"I wonder which one of those people on the stage the other night is in charge of that?" Jasmine said, putting the scroll to the side and opening the ledger from the guild. She ran her fingers and eyes along the information, stopping about a quarter down the page, realizing the rest was just red. "The hell is this?"

She looked it over and over again. Flipping through the pages, all of them the same story. The white sashes had moved far faster than she imagined. Even the hunters in the town of Montlimar had already been hit. It wasn't going to hit the capital's supply anytime soon; however, if it kept up, prices would begin to rise. Jasmine found her way to the shipping logs and realized it was the exact same story. The north of the continent was being cut off. "I... I don't understand. How have they seized all of this? How are they on the sea and the land this fast, cutting it all out? How did they slip through the navy? They couldn't possibly have infiltrated the military..."

Jasmine headed out with the ledger and Reinhold's scroll. She passed into the medical ward and saw a woman walking out of Cardinal's room. She was wearing a brown dress, her hair was in a bob, revealing her long ears. Brushing hair out of her face, she passed Jasmine with a smile.

Knocking on the door, she waited for Cardinal to acknowledge it before going inside.

"Hey, Cardinal, who was that?" she asked, taking a seat. He was looking at her the whole time, a smile growing as she got closer. "What is it?"

"I... Nothing," he replied with a shrug. "As for that woman, she was the sand weaver I called for. That wound was eating away at me, like the darkness of Sleeve eats away at our magic. The little she accomplished today drained her of all of her magic. She may not have showed it, but she will probably need help making it to her room. Don't worry, I already have an aide on standby."

"How...are you that prepared?"

"Hmm, I dunno. Instinct? Maybe another magic of mine besides sand."

"Yeah, that's borderline inhuman."

"Well, I mean... I can't disagree completely. What do you have in your hand?" he said, pointing at the ledger and scroll.

Jasmine passed him the scroll. "Read it. It's from some guy named Reinhold."

"Reinhold! That old sum bitch is still kicking?"

Jasmine could only blink as she watched him. The way he nearly leapt from the bed, taking the scroll from her, made her worry he would hurt himself. But if he was in pain, he showed no signs of it. He read through it with a gleeful smile. Even after he was finished with the troubling news, his smile had not faded.

"Were you...close friends?"

"What? Oh, heavens no. This sum bitch owes me money."

"Huh?" Jasmine was lost. *Had he really read the rest of it.*

"I'll send the other birds to look into it. Oh, I cannot wait to get my money. The interest, Jasmine. *The interest!*"

"Sir...about the trade routes."

"O-Oh, yes, of course," he cleared his throat, the smile fading from his face as he rolled up the scroll. "As I said, I'll have some other birds look into it. You're not the only one under my wing, you know.

And your problem is right here in the capital, locked in a jail cell. I'm guessing there's a lot of red in that book there."

"Where the north is concerned, more red than black."

"Marvelous," he sighed. Scratching his head, he closed his eyes to think. "I really wish one of the other Sovereigns were here." He looked over and noticed worry on Jasmine's face. "Oh, don't think there's a problem. I always have plans. I'll reach out to the navy, see what we can do. Don't want to bother the big man just yet. Even though I probably should."

"You mean the king?"

"The Sovereign. Please. But yes, him."

Both of them then twiddled their thumbs in silence. Cardinal had become lost, deep in thought. Jasmine sat patiently, waiting for him to give her at least the general idea of his plan. When she realized he wasn't planning on saying anything, she got up and left. She knew someone who might talk. And like Cardinal said, he was her problem, sitting in a jail cell.

19

25ᵗʰ of Cresozis; Mortal Year 523

Arlo

Arlo felt out of place in the circular meeting room. Across from him sat the kings of Zell, including Nikyn who sat at the head of the circle. Separating them was a massive marble table, a completely detailed map of the nation sitting on top. Every road, mountain, forest, body of water— you name it—was recreated and labeled there. Each chair had a banner draping over the back, sporting the emblem of their respective kingdoms. Arlo had stared at the emblem of Gonall a long time before taking his seat. The thought of his father sitting in this very chair at this time every year made his heart skip, his body uneasy. It was only when Nikyn spoke did he find a sense of calm.

"I now declare the Meeting of Kings officially begun," he said, his voice calling all of them to attention. "This one, I fear, holds far more weight than any of the others we have had together. Samil has given us its ultimatum. The last remaining Blades of the Mother that we hold or war. Whoever wants to begin may."

"I'll start us off then," said the king directly opposite of Arlo. He was the king of Liniacum, the Star Kingdom. The man was a head shorter than everyone else. His face was concealed beneath strands of

282

various gems, each one made into the shape of a star. Each time he spoke, the gems jingled along their white chains. Curly blonde hair reached down to his shoulders. Arlo wondered how he even saw past the chains in front of his eyes. "I do believe we should not hand them over. Battle has been the way of our people for centuries. If they want to give us that option, I say we accept."

"I say nay," said another king, his hand slapping the table. It was the king of Nepte, the Desert Kingdom of the south. Unlike the others, his hair was a mess. He wasn't wearing his traditional kingly attire. Instead, he wore tattered robes and looked more like a beggar than anything close to royalty. His beard had wine stains from the previous night. The alcohol on his breath carried across the table as he spoke. Yet, all gave him the time to speak. "You only want us to wage war because your kingdom has one of the two blades our entire nation has left. It is sheer greed you would rather spill blood over. Nothing better than those Samilian bastards in the east."

"My dear friend, Aulus. I assure you, you misunderstand my intentions. Yes, my kingdom holds a blade. But it is not the reason I choose for us to answer the beating drums of war."

Aulus pulled a jug from the depths of his robe sleeve and took a swig. "Tell us then, great Mettius of stars. Why?"

"Because for us to bend the knee to an eastern tyrant not only is shame to the highest degree. There is no way to know he won't just declare war after they have hold of them all. Look at what that crazy man on their throne has done. He rips wings off his citizens, forces Kryzen into the military! Let's not argue the fact we know their will is gone. He sees them as tools of war, not people. It's a just cause written by the stars themselves. We can be liberat—"

"There's that bullshit," interrupted Aulus, his free hand pointing a long finger at Mettius as he took another swig. "Stars this, stars that. Those gods are silent, Mettius. You need to stop listening to their whispers."

"Even without whispers from stars, I am sure Mettius would feel the same," voiced another king. Arlo recognized him instantly. It was Caelius, the king of Adristan. His long brown hair stretched down past his back, vines with small red flowers weaved into it. As far as men were concerned, he had an inhuman beauty about him. Sapphire eyes seemed to capture the light and radiated out a comforting glow. "The forest talks about it too. Though they normally care little for the dealings of us mortals, the spirits are afraid of something. And whenever myself or another asks them about their fear, they all give us the same reply—Samil."

Aulus erupted into laughter, chugged the rest of his jug, and slid it back into his sleeve to wherever it was hidden before. "Of course they're afraid of Samil! The forest will be in trouble if there's war! Think of all the fires, the destruction carved through fallen trees!"

"They aren't afraid of the war, Aulus. They would gladly sacrifice their home if it got rid of their fear." Caelius' eyes turned serious. The calming light of his eyes now radiated an intense anger toward his fellow king.

"Calm it down there, Caelius," spoke another who had yet to speak. He was wearing full armor. A shaggy beard covered the lower half of his face; bags formed under his eyes. And as he continued, Arlo felt anger surging through his breast. His hands were shaking, forming into fists in his lap. "There is no way there is something in Samil that the forest spirits fear, dear Fairy King."

"Are you insulting me, Tiberius?" The angry gaze shifted to him.

"Oh no, no, I am not. This is a meeting of friendship. We do not insult here. But I agree with Aulus. It's all bullshit. You listen to trees and woodland creatures. Mettius over here sits alone, gazing up at stars, having full-blown conversations. And you're saying they each think it's right for us to risk our lives, the lives of our people in a war that will span the known world? I think not. This is not their world to decide. The gods had their time, and they failed. The rest of time is on us."

Of course, a traitorous coward like you would say that! You don't want to fight because you are already cozied up next to King Victor in his bedchamber! Arlo stopped thinking as he noticed everyone else was staring at him. His face began to turn red out of the embarrassment. Those thoughts had been said out loud.

"What did you say?" asked Tiberius. His gaze became murderous. But the other kings were too focused on Arlo to notice it.

Damn! thought Arlo. He glanced around the room, and even Nikyn wasn't planning on offering help. With a deep breath, Arlo stood up. "I said you're a traitorous coward!" His anger had boiled over, his palms slammed against the table, and Arlo locked eyes with him, shutting the other kings out entirely. At this table was just the two of them.

"Those are some heavy words, boy. Why are you even here? Where is your father?"

"W-Where is my father? He's in the after because of you! Along with everyone else who lived in the castle of Gonall!"

"You dare accuse me of treason at the meeting of kings? I should cut your tongue out here and now for those words!"

"I bet you would love every second of it because you know I speak the truth!"

"This has escalated quickly," said Aulus. "And I didn't bring another jug. Anyone else got some wine or beer on them?"

"Silence, Aulus!" said Nikyn whom Aulus offered no rebuttal. Instead, he sat there, quietly watching the two yell before him.

"What did they offer you? Land? Money? What the hell did they offer you that you would offer up a fellow kingdom in exchange?"

The air in the room had shifted. Eyes turned to face Tiberius. Sweat began to bead on his brow. Beneath the table, his foot was tapping nervously. "I have not betrayed anyone. I took an oath the day I donned my crown. An oath to my people and to the people of every kingdom in the nation. I will not stand for this. You are no king, young prince. You have no right to accuse me of anything, let alone sit in the chair meant for someone far more worthy than you."

Arlo chuckled. "I know I'm not worthy of this chair, and I wish the reason I was here was different. I really do. I wish my father could be here, talking with you all. Yet, sadly, I am the only one who can speak for Gonall now. Because you robbed him of that. You robbed my people of their futures. And now you sit here, lying to not only me but to the other kings of Zell. The only one unworthy of their chair is you!" Arlo raised a finger, pointing it straight at Tiberius.

"Lord Nikyn, with this outburst and these false accusations from a prince of all things, I declare this meeting officially over."

285

Tiberius pushed his chair back and stood up. The other kings stood up as well in unison.

Arlo looked at them in desperation. They seemed to believe his words at the start, but now they were all in unison with Tiberius. Save for Nikyn who remained seated, his eyes looking to Arlo, silently asking, "What will you do now?"

"I invoke the Right of Gavinus," said Arlo.

Every king froze, their heads turning as if on swivels to face the prince. The only sound that filled that room were the heartbeats of its occupants.

"You dare call that name?" asked Tiberius as he returned to the table.

"I win, you confess every last thing. You win, all of Gonall is yours. Every last bit of land, every resource, all of it. The ash lands were already fading weeks ago. By now, I am sure they are much more suited for your people."

"You think I want your land?"

"I think you'll accept and take what you get."

"I agree with the boy." Arlo turned and found Mettius had spoken. "The Right of Gavinus. Think about it. You wanted to cut out his tongue, didn't you? What better place than in the arena before the people of the capital?"

Tiberius began to shake with anger as the kings one by one raised their hands and nodded in agreement. To say no now would strip him of his crown, of his lands, and his authority. His eyes made their way back to Arlo. "Very well, Prince of Ash! I will fulfill the right with you. On the day the Colors of Summer fly, they will fly over a nation with one less kingdom." He left without another word.

"I must say, King of Ash, that was quite impressive," said the one king who had not said a word that entire time. He was clapping and chuckling. His name was Sergio, the king of Sipontum, the kingdom of gems, and his robes were lined with them, each one shining brilliantly. But they paled in comparison to the ruby that adorned the front of his crown. "The Right of Gavinus, my word."

"I am no king," said Arlo, his eyes finding their way to his feet.

"Trust me, if anyone has the nads down there to invoke the Right of Gavinus, they are worthy of being called a king in my eyes. You just need your crown."

"Pray forgive me," said Mettius as he was getting up to leave. "What was your name again, young prince? I know we've met a few times over the years, but I do not recall it."

"Arlo, son of Marcus and Nemaria, Prince of Ash."

Mettius eyes went wide like he was afraid.

"Are you all right?" asked Arlo with concern.

"Y-yes, of course. Lord Nikyn, is there anything else you need from us before we depart?"

Soon after the meeting was adjourned, Nikyn took tally of all who were in favor of the war and all who wanted to hand the blades over. Five of them were for it with Nikyn and Arlo included. Aulus and Tiberius were the two against it. Yet even with the odds, they were in a stalemate. It was long established that only one vote could be against the idea for the idea to pass.

Arlo was the last of them to leave, once again finding himself staring at the back of his kingdom's chair. He kept thinking that something was going to light up or pop out at him, some type of sign that would burst forth from the emblem. Nothing did. With a deep breath, he headed back toward the estate, trying to put distance between him and this place. It was then that he realized he much preferred the company of his companions he had met only a short time ago over that of the kings he had grown up listening to.

*****

"All right, keep your arms up and close. You want to protect your face and core. Keep your feet firmly spread apart, hold your ground."

Elijah's body followed Kenjo's instructions. Forming fists with his hands, he felt a sharp pain surge up his arm as Kenjo slapped his wrists.

"Keep your thumbs outside of your hands, floating between your index and middle fingers, unless you would rather break them!"

"Did you really have to do that?" asked Elijah as he did what he was told.

"Do I really have to teach you anything?"

"Tch... Whatever..."

"That's what I thought," said Kenjo, stepping in front of him. He raised his hands, palms toward him. "Now then, hit my hands."

For the next few minutes, Elijah swung at him, soft thuds sounding out as his fists connected with the extra padded leather that covered Kenjo's hands. Whenever he broke form or threw a punch improperly, Kenjo slapped his arms and corrected him. Once he was satisfied, he began to move his hands around, making Elijah follow the moving target.

At first, it almost led to Kenjo getting hit in his jaw as Elijah did not expect it. But after a few misses, he picked it up and was making contact again. Once he had passed the next step, Kenjo began to move his feet. He was faster than him, and Elijah was finding it hard just to keep up with him, let alone swing at his hands.

Moments later, he was bent over, hands on his legs, sweat dripping down his brow. "I'm done."

"Nah, I think you got at least another hour in you," said Kenjo, patting his back.

"You're insane!"

"I assure you I am quite sane. Here, drink."

Kenjo handed him the waterskin that was draped over his side. He was reluctant at first to the idea of training Elijah. It reminded him of his father too much and how he did not want to resemble him any more than he already did. But Vallarya convinced him. Albeit, loosely convinced him; she had not talked to him since the previous night's conversation. So when she showed up after turning Elijah down, it only took a few words for her to bring him around.

And as he looked at him, he found himself actually enjoying teaching him, even if the reason was because he thought of them as heroes, which they were quick to deny. They weren't even close yet in their eyes, but to Elijah, ever since the meeting in the inn, that is exactly what they were. Kaldana hadn't helped that matter over the past two days either after hearing the truth about Crimson.

She and Elijah decided to spin ridiculous stories about how they would come to their rescue, Kenjo and Vallarya always arriving in time to save them or some other helpless soul. Vallarya was quick to remind Elijah that Kaldana was more than capable of being a hero on her own, making him begin to spin a tale about her and stopping her storytelling days.

Elijah chugged all the water and handed it back to him, wiping the excess on his mouth with his sleeve. "Thanks."

"You ready?"

"Nope."

"Good." Kenjo ducked low and swept his legs out from under him. He hit the ground with a solid thud as Kenjo took a few steps back, raising his hands and waiting.

"That right there was unnecessary," groaned Elijah, standing up and dusting himself off. Assuming his stance, they continued their training.

Two hours later, he gave up falling to the ground. He gazed up at the sky. Purple and orange streaked across the fading blue as the sun set. He had not landed a single hit since Kenjo began to use his legs. In fact, Kenjo had hit him more times to correct him than Elijah had landed all day.

"You all right?" asked Kenjo, kneeling down beside him.

"Yeah. Just catching my breath. Thanks for training me."

"No problem. Well, I'm going to head inside. Arlo should be here soon, and it's our turn to cook dinner. When you are ready, come help me in the kitchen."

Kenjo disappeared inside. Vallarya glanced over the couch as he entered. When she saw it was him, she immediately turned back to a game of dice she was playing with Kaldana. With a sigh, he walked toward the kitchen and noticed Luna sitting on the windowsill, one arm on her knee, the other on her bow.

"I've said it before plenty, you don't have to be on watch all the time," said Kenjo as he passed by. "Especially here. You can relax, Luna."

"After what happened in that meeting room, I can't agree with you," she replied.

Kenjo peeked his head around the corner. "Please, relax. I won't let that happen to you again, I promise." He was gone again, replaced with the sound of chopping as his knife hit against the cutting board. "Luna, can you come here?" he called out.

Shifting uneasily, she hopped down from the sill, leaving her bow behind. She walked into the kitchen. He was still chopping away, not even giving her a glance as she leaned against the opposite counter.

"Do you need help with something?" she asked. "I thought it was only you and Elijah cooking dinner today?"

"It is," he replied, tossing vegetables off the cutting board and into a pan. "This isn't about dinner. Why were you in pain back when she was reading your memories?"

Luna crossed her arms. "Read my memories, and you'll know."

"If it involves hurting you," began Kenjo as he lit the fire in the stove, "then I want nothing to do with it."

"Then you'll never know," she said, walking over to him. She took his free hand and placed it against her forehead. "Just make it quick."

Hesitating, Kenjo began to fear the tendrils and the voice once more. Then he remembered that Araceli didn't kill her, even though she knew exactly who she was. With a light sigh, the magic began to flow, and he found his conscious teleported away. He was standing in a marble hall, Luna at his side.

"What the hell is this?" he asked, looking around, worried.

"The marble hall," Luna shrugged. "I've only been here with Detheo, not with anyone outside of their ranks."

Noticing a room in the distance, Kenjo began to walk forward, Luna sheepishly following behind him. Once they were standing in the room, they found themselves staring at a large sleeping creature.

"What is that thing?" asked Kenjo, taking cautious steps forward. He was fascinated by it. After all the memories he had read, none had transported him to a place like this nor did any not give him any insight into the person whom he was reading.

"That... That is our protector," she replied with a gulp. "He's the real reason I was in pain. He is the Detheo's answer to the Hands of the Children. He begins to hurt us if our memories begin to be forced to the surface by outside means, killing us before you can learn anything useful."

"I devour your consciousness as well," a voice growled.

Kenjo hopped back as one of its eyes flickered open, the horizontal pupil scanning the room before fixating on him. Luna walked forward, reaching a hand out to the creature, resting it against the side of its face as its head turned. "But it would seem unnecessary to send you back into the normal world an empty shell. Unlike those other two who escaped, she let you in here. Pray tell me, why is it that she did such a thing?"

Kenjo looked to Luna for an answer. She looked back at him, then back to the beast.

"Do you really need to ask him a question that you know the answer to?" she asked, petting his face.

The creature looked Kenjo over before resting its head on top of its right front leg. "I don't see the necklace, so I can only assume by his silence that you haven't told him."

"Told me what?" asked Kenjo.

Both turned in unison to look at him.

Luna stood up, reaching for something around her neck. She walked toward him. She pulled at a tiny star-shaped emblem hanging from a black chain. With a quick tug, the northern point of the five points comprising the star came loose. A separate chain appearing from it dangled over the side of her hand as she handed it out to him.

"Take it," she said before it slid down into his awaiting palms.

"I don't..." said Kenjo, looking it over. "What is this?"

"The northern point of my star. It is my family tradition to give it to the one we owe are lives too. The one that we would follow into the gates of hell and back."

"L-Luna, I don't think I am someone worthy of this," said Kenjo, thinking back on his parents and Maximus.

"You spared me once, you saved me in the throne room. Even Rygas here woke up in your presence. Please take it."

He looked to her again, wanting to voice his displeasure. Instead, he formed a gentle smile. Fastening the necklace around his neck, he found Rygas looking at him as if he were looking through him. Kenjo was beginning to feel naked. The beast was bearing into the very depths of his soul. Rygas blinked before curling his head back around his body to sleep once more.

The marble room disappeared, and the two found themselves back in the kitchen of the estate. Luna walked toward the doorway, longing to return to the window.

"Why would you give this to someone you barely know?" asked Kenjo, looking down at the necklace, Luna came to a halt with one hand resting on the door frame.

"I told you, it was my family tradition. I owe you my life. It's how we mark it."

"And what if it wasn't me? What if it was someone else who would use or abuse you for their own personal means?"

"Then so be it. I wouldn't fight it. My life would be there to be spent as they see fit. No different from a slave to a kingdom."

"That isn't a way to live," sighed Kenjo as he thumbed the necklace point. "So long as you owe me your life, I want you to live it how you want to. Not at my beck and call, not by my demands. Just as you want to."

"That seems almost contradictory," said Luna, hiding the redness that began to form on her face.

"I still didn't see your memories, you know," remarked Kenjo as the pot of water on the stove began to boil. "Just Rygas."

Luna turned to him. "Yeah, it would seem Rygas saw something that he didn't want near them... Maybe that thing you yourself were afraid of. I guess I'll have to tell you them myself."

"Some other time then," said Kenjo as Elijah came barreling past Luna. It seemed no time had passed since he delved into that alternate world.

Luna nodded without another word and walked out as Elijah washed his hands to assist Kenjo. Apologizing relentlessly for being late, he had not wanted to move after the training session.

"Oh, Luna!" yelled Kenjo. "If you're in that window sill again, you aren't eating tonight!"

Vallarya and Kaldana looked up from their game of dice. Luna had one leg up, about to retake her spot when his words cut across the living room. With a sigh, she slowly lowered it back down. Turning, she found the two girls looking at her. Vallarya waved her over, and she reluctantly obliged.

A few minutes later, Elijah came out of the kitchen, carrying plates to set the table, briefly returning to the kitchen and popping back up with silverware. As he finished getting everyone set up, Kenjo began to bring out the food, the smell of his cooking filling the room with a mouth-watering aroma.

"S-should we wait for him?" asked Kaldana, eyeing her food hungrily. She licked her lips; her tails were wagging uncontrollably.

"Arlo was supposed to be back by now, wasn't he?" asked Vallarya, looking at his empty plate and chair.

"Yeah, he said it wasn't going to last past sundown," replied Kenjo "I'm sure he will be he—"

The door opened, and Arlo walked in, slamming the door behind him. He sniffed the air and noticed the food. Without a word, he dished himself up and took a seat in the empty chair. He began to eat, eyes making contact with no one.

"So...we can eat, yeah?" asked Kaldana.

"Yeah," said Kenjo, disappointment clear in his voice. "Dig in."

It wasn't till after they were done eating and a loud burp followed by a pat on his stomach did Arlo even look at his companions. Kenjo and Elijah began to clean up the table as the girls went back to their dice game.

"I've got to say, that was delicious," said Arlo. "Kenjo, you are not a bad chef. But Vallarya has you beat."

"I'm gonna ignore that comment," said Kenjo as he disappeared into the kitchen, reappearing to grab the larger plates where the food had sat. "How did the meeting go?"

"Great! I challenged Tiberius to a Right of Gavinus."

A loud crash of a falling plate followed, putting everyone on alert. Elijah apologized as Kenjo went to grab a broom.

"W-w-what did you say?" asked Elijah.

"I challenged him to a Right of Gavinus. Only option I had. He accepted, and that will be the big event before the Colors of Summer fly overhead. No parades this year, not now. I am going to make that bastard confess before the kings before everyone, and that will put any possible parade to shame."

"Excuse me," said Kaldana, poking her head up from the couch. "What's this Right of Gavinus?"

"It got its name from the second Lord King of Zell some three hundred years ago," said Elijah as he grabbed another plate. "At the time, one of the other kings was upset that he was picked over him. He challenged him to combat for his spot, which was kinda wrong because the Lord King is viewed almost like a divine position. While the other kings were against the challenge, Gavinus accepted, beating him but ultimately sparing his life. He then proposed a new law that was named after him once he passed. It can be invoked by any king at any time."

"What if they say no?"

"They can't or they automatically give up their crown, status, and everything. You see, the invoker puts everything on the line while requesting less of their opponent who has no choice but to accept, which begs the question, Arlo. What did you offer him?"

"Oh, just Gonall. Like I told him, the ash lands are gone. It's even more suitable for other folk to settle in than it ever was. In turn, if I win, I get his confession. Where is Leaf, by the way?"

Another plate slipped from Elijah's hand. Kenjo dove and caught it just in time. Standing up, he looked at Arlo. "He wanted us to give you his regard. His father requested his assistance with some work-related things. Apparently, they are headed back to Ivofir."

"That's a shame. I was really hoping he would get to watch me fight. Speaking of which, I need you to train with me. He uses a great sword like you do, so it should be a good warm-up."

"All right."

"Wait, wait, wait. Am I the only one who cares that he offered up Gonall?" asked Elijah, looking around, but the girls were focused on their game, and Kenjo was back in the kitchen.

"Elijah, are you worried I will lose?"

"N-no…but—"

"I feel like you don't believe in me." Arlo flashed him saddened eyes.

"Well—"

"Ouch," said Arlo, standing up, clutching his heart in fake agony.

"Look at the bright side, Elijah, if he loses, we don't have to hear his voice anymore," said Kaldana. "Victory is mine!" she screamed as the dice stopped moving. It was a perfect roll.

A knocking came to the door, and Arlo answered it. "I'll be damned. I thought I was done with the traitor kingdom today."

Ricardo was standing in the doorway in a full suit of armor with the Burrium insignias. No longer a prisoner, he appeared before them a proper knight, wings folded against his back, sticking out of his armor through large slits. His lance was positioned between them, held there by a strap that wrapped around his front.

Biting his lip to fight the anger he felt at the remark, he looked at him. "Good to see you too. May I come in?"

"Certainly!" Arlo stood aside, motioning him in with his arm and closing the door behind him.

"What is wrong with him?"

"I think something's getting to his head," said Kaldana as she won again. "He's been acting strange since he got back. Talking about the Right of Gavinus. But Elijah is keeping him entertained."

Ricardo took a seat at a chair near the fireplace and looked out at the group. Kenjo walked into the room, drying his hands on a towel.

"Oh, hello, Ricardo," he said, stopping at the couch behind Vallarya. "Any luck with Lukas?"

"Sort of. It turns out he's already gone, headed north. Possibly to Burrium. I was about to set off when I heard that some fool had invoked Gavinus's name and my king was involved. One thing led to another, and here I am to talk with the prince."

"What is it?" asked Arlo. His voice had changed tone. He was serious now, his head pulled from the clouds. His voice mimicked how it was in the meeting, a voice meant for a prince.

Ricardo stood up and drew his lance. Pointing the tip down, he knelt before them in the center of the living room. "I want to first apologize for what I did on the road. After you all so kindly saved me, who to you was a stranger at the time. And to offer this, should your claims be true, I swear my lance and my life to all of you. Wherever you shall go, I will go with you, even if that means I must turn my lance against my very own kingdom. There is no doubt in my mind their eyes would have been clouded like mine."

"Oh, I never thought I would see the day when someone would pledge themselves to me," said Kaldana, taken aback by his statement. He glared at her. "No. Honestly, besides a future husband, I never thought this would happen. I'm not exactly worthy of having knights."

"Regardless, I am pledging nothing here today."

"You should. It would save you time from doing it later." Arlo walked toward him and offered out his hand.

Ricardo stood up, placed his lance on his back, and shook his hand. "Bold words. We shall see if you can follow through."

20

19th of Japhim; Mortal Year 523

Jasmine

asmine sat on a stool in the prison hallway, arms crossed, foot tapping against the floor, waiting for a response. The tapping of her foot increasing in speed as the seconds passed, filling the quiet hall with a steadily increasing rhythm. Facing her through iron bars was Sleeve, a large smile across his face and lifeless eyes gazing out at her. She almost felt sorry for him. His prisoner's rags were torn with dried blood peeking out from holes in them. His face was bruised entirely on the left side along with his arm.

"Answer me, Sleeve," she said again as her foot came to a rest.

"I am quite all right, little spider," he replied, taking a seat, crossing his legs. His eyes never moved from her.

"Do you really want this beating to continue?"

"No. However, it just adds on to how terrible this nation is behind closed doors. Did you know because you two took my fingers, they've been taking it out on my toes?" He raised up a foot to her, pressing it against the iron bars. More dried blood ran from where toes used to be to his heel. As she looked at it, she realized his two smallest toes were missing. "You already have me lined up for the executioner's block. What is the point of even keeping me alive? Just to dish out more cruelty? To treat me like how you treat Angel-born?"

Jasmine opened her mouth to reply. Her words were stuck in her throat. Sleeve began to chuckle as he pulled his leg back. He looked at the stump of his left arm and then back to her. "It's the will of our king to have prisoners punished, even if going to the block, to have them receive equal pain for all that they have caused others before their head is removed from their shoulders. Otherwise, death is way too nice of a punishment on its own. As for the Angel-born, that too is the will of the king, a reminder of Nothingness to be removed."

"Oh my, the king and all of you would probably be dead before you could inflict pain equivalent to what I have caused." He leaned back in laughter, falling onto the floor. Sitting back up, he wiped fake tears from his eyes. "Are you just a mouthpiece of your king and his will? I thought I sensed more from you, little spider. Unlike the others, your eyes spark with a light that makes me disgusted, a light of your own will. Oh! Speaking of wills that aren't their own, how's Cardinal doing?"

Her face flushed with anger, and she kicked at the bars. The clang filled the silent hallway, echoing all the way to the door. Sleeve's smile widened, practically reaching from ear to ear.

"That good, huh? I'm sure I would be dead already had I succeeded in killing that bird."

"I am going to ask again," said Jasmine. The look on her face made it clear she was done entertaining him. "Where are the leaders of the White Sash? How did they secure both sea and land trade routes at the same time, even those owned by the army and guard?"

Sleeve shrugged. "I wish I had an answer for you. But alas, what they do is out of my knowledge. I'm just a sword."

"Lies!" Jasmine stood up and grabbed onto the bars. Pushing her face through the gap, she stared him down. "Tell me the truth, Sleeve!"

"Oh my, such anger. I didn't think you so capable of it." Sleeve raised his arm up in fear as he scooted away. "Alas, I have nothing for you."

Jasmine screamed internally, her head falling down in defeat. She grabbed the stool and headed for the door.

"Give Cardinal my regards!" yelled Sleeve before she slammed the door shut.

She told the guard to torture him extra today and relay anything he said to her should he decide to finally speak. The execution was tomorrow, and once he died, they would be back at square one.

Moments later, Jasmine found herself in the castle training yard, practicing her strikes on one of the many dummies lined up by the wall. Her blade was not deployed yet, instead focusing on nonlethal strikes, targeting every spot she remembered from her training days. At times, some of the others in the field would stop and watch her. She had a grace about her that captivated onlookers when she fought. They were entranced by her movements, as precise as a dancer's, on an internal beat all her own that led to the downfall of the dummy that was her unfortunate partner. The crimson cloak she wore only drew more attention.

As the minutes turned to hours, she was approached by a few of the other soldiers, each asking to be her sparring partner. She happily obliged. With none of them being Kryzen, she decided not to use her magic, and with a satisfied smile, beat everyone who challenged her. The sun was beginning to get low in the sky when she was finally done taking out all of the anger she had built up toward Sleeve. Three dummies were entirely destroyed and in need of repair while about ten soldiers limped away bruised and battered. Her apologies did not stop until they were out of sight.

Jasmine stood in front of one more dummy. Hitting the button, the staff widened slightly, the blade deployed, the sky steel gleaming in the dimming light. She swung it a few times, stopping it just before hitting the dummy. Once she was used to the added length, she jumped back and lunged forward, stabbing straight through the chest. It pierced through the thick hay like a knife through butter. Pulling it free, she spun around and aimed higher, removing the head in one quick motion.

A few quick thrusts where the vital points would be in a normal person, she let out a sigh as she pressed the button again. *Why am I even training with the blade deployed?* The blade folded back into the staff. Another button press, and it shrunk into a baton. Fastening it to her back, she grabbed the dummy head and placed it back on top. It tilted slightly to her before slowly toppling off. Grabbing the dummy and the head, she headed toward the equipment tables, dropping them off at the repair counter as she left the training field.

Before retiring to her chambers, she decided to visit Cardinal one more time to see if he had come up with some sort of plan. She hoped he would be more talkative then Sleeve. As she walked through the medical ward, she noticed the sand weaver that was mending Cardinal was helping out with some of the children. She looked almost motherly, and the children who were by her smiled happily as she spoke. All of them were taken to her. It was probably the first time in their lives that they'd seen an elf in person.

"Excuse me," said Jasmine, approaching her with a smile, "do you have a second to talk?"

The woman looked up at the smiling young woman. An equally gentle one formed on her face. "Yes, of course. Be good, children, I'll be back soon, okay?"

A resounding, "Yes, ma'am!" filled the room as she stood up and followed Jasmine down the ward.

"I think the children are out of earshot now," said the elf looking back. "How can I help you, Miss…"

"Jasmine," she replied, standing opposite her in the hallway. "And you are?"

"Qamara."

"Nice to meet you. I was just wondering if you could tell me how sand weaving works."

Qamara shifted, taken aback by the question. "That's an odd request from someone in the capital."

"Is it a problem?"

She waved her hands in front of her and shook her head. "Oh no, no. Just usually, you northern folk don't care for it. You are more focused on the primal magic than the spiritual and elder. So to hear someone actually ask is just…it's crazy, really."

"After what Sleeve did to Cardinal," said Jasmine, her hands were forming into fists, shaking as she spoke. Her eyes fell to the floor for a moment. "If it is possible to learn it, I want to so I can help him in the future should something like this happen again." She looked back up and at Qamara. Her eyes were wide, looking toward her but not at her as if they were seeing through her, through the wall, and so on to some distant target. "Qamara?"

Her head shook again, and she smiled at her. "Oh, yes, sorry. That is a very sweet gesture. He must mean a lot to you."

Jasmine began to blush. "Hardly, but if he's willing to put his life on the line for me, I might as well pick something extra to help him."

She giggled, covering her mouth with a hand. "Well, I can teach you the basics. But without the sand spirits, I can't promise you will be able to do much."

"The spirits?"

"Yes," she said, waving her arms around, forming a glyph in the air between. Three small lines of sand swirled along her arms, collecting together in her palms as she brought her hands together. They formed into a small squirrel-like creature. A curved horn stuck out of its forehead and arched back over its head to its neck. Dark-red fur covered its body; its chest had a small glass-like sphere in it filled up with sand. Its tail was comprised entirely of sand.

Jasmine was amazed by it. Not a single piece of sand fell from the tail as if it were held in place by some invisible container. "This is my spirit, Ede."

"She's adorable!" exclaimed Jasmine, barely able to contain herself she reached out to pet her. Ede accepted it gratefully, nuzzling her head against her palm. "Oh, who's a cute spirit?"

"Ede has been with me since I was a youngling. For us sand weavers, they act as a sort of catalyst to allow us to form sand out of thin air should none be around for us to use. For Kryzen, they do offer the same thing, but it's a bit harder to find a compatible spirit that can mix sand with their magic."

"Do you think it would be possible with starlight?" asked Jasmine, discouraged as she pulled her hand away from Ede.

"I am sure there's a spirit out there that could if you sought it out," said Qamara as Ede climbed up her arm and perched on her shoulder. "But the basics here with spirit magic are they assist you with their own strength and help guide your body through the motions. They are a catalyst in which you can increase your own natural mana flow as well as become more attuned with it. But most importantly, they are the best of friends."

Ede made a happy noise when she finished speaking and nuzzled against her neck. Qamara smiled as her hair fur tickled her.

"I guess when I have free time, I might need to make a trip down south," said Jasmine. "See if I can't find me a spirit that will accept me."

"If you do, any weaver there would be more than willing to help. And should we bump into each other again after that, I myself would gladly teach you."

"It's a deal! Thanks for the chat, Qamara. I'll let you get back to what you were doing."

"Anytime," she said with a bow before walking back to the children's area. They all cheered at her return.

Jasmine walked to Cardinal's room. She knocked once before walking in. Inside, he was asleep, wrapped up in his blankets, his head barely sticking out. With a quick shrug, Jasmine decided to let him be, figuring the weaving from today had taken more out of him than she realized. She decided to return to her room in the barracks. She wanted to make the potion last a bit longer than it did the previous night.

*****

The next morning, Jasmine struggled to get up. As the sun rose higher and more light reached into her room, she scooted further to the side of her bed, avoiding the sun's bright hands for as long as she could. One more scoot, and she plummeted to the ground, hitting the wood with a solid thud. She sat up and wiped the sleep from her eyes.

She had gotten no sleep last night. Instead of increasing just the duration of her potion, she had managed to also increase the sensitivity to the point she couldn't focus through it. Throughout the night, she got a couple of fleeting moments of rest, only to be awoken by the sound of a guards' footsteps as they patrolled.

Tossing her blankets back onto the bed, she got ready for the day. Seeing as tonight was to be Sleeve's execution, she decided it was best to wear her armor and be presentable before the audience that would no doubt gather to see it. Putting on her cloak, she pulled her hair out from it and brushed it. wincing in pain as she pulled at the knots as she looked on in the mirror. Bags were beginning to form under her eyes, and she almost screamed. Putting her hair up into a ponytail, she rested it over her right collar and headed out.

First thing was the logs and reports from the merchants. The merchant guild itself was fine when it came to goods for the common folk. No problems to report from them. The rebels seemed to have no interest in them directly. But anything meant for the army or a noble was targeted. The list of missing and stolen goods had almost doubled in a single day. The guild merchants were incredibly efficient, and the fact the rebels had already cut down the imports to the capital was worrying. *There's no doubt they had a connection to the guild through Oliver and the Lundquist family, but do they have more?*

There were no reports from any of the northern villages this time around. And although it wasn't yet time for their weekly check in, it wasn't hard for Jasmine to assume that the White Sash had silenced them. Not to mention understand exactly how the checkups went. As she flipped through the ledger, she found herself wishing more and more she could talk to the other birds of Cardinal's. But they were hardly ever in the capital anymore.

Jasmine signed off on the day's ledger and closed it. She was getting up to leave when she heard a tapping at the window. Looking over, she noticed it was one of the tiny cardinals that accompanied you whenever you left the city on Cardinal's order. It tapped faster, and Jasmine rushed over to open the window for it. It flew in, flying in circles above the desk before landing on top of the closed ledger.

The bird froze in place. Its mouth opened wide, and words poured forth: "Cardinal, this is Angeline. The White Sash that you had mentioned has taken over the town of Levappes. That was one or two a night ago. Then today. they sprung up like weeds and over-powered the guards. I—" There was an audible knocking that could be heard through the bird. Jasmine tensed up. She thought of closing the bird's mouth to stop it from saying anymore. A crash followed, and Angeline's voice came back "They found me! Fly, little bird, fly." Clashing steel, screams of pain, and then nothing. The bird had stopped listening to escape.

What the hell is going on? "Oh, who am I kidding, I need to get to Cardinal!"

Jasmine sprinted out the room, the bird perched on her shoulder, talons hooked onto the metal plate of her armor. She was moving faster than she had the previous day after reports. Her heart was racing. It felt like any second, it would burst forth from her chest. She stumbled through the medical ward and barreled through Cardinal's room door. Inside, Cardinal was sitting up in his bed, looking at her with worry.

"Damn, Jasmine, what's the matter?" he asked. "You nearly gave me a heart attack like the nurse the other day!"

"A report..." She tried to catch her breath in between words. "A report from... Angeline. It's bad!"

He whistled a sharp whistle, and the bird on her shoulder flew to his lap. Jasmine shut the door. It was off one of its hinges now. The bird repeated its message to Cardinal. He tensed up, anger clearly visible on his face, followed by a sorrow that did not sit well with him. Jasmine took a seat and waited for her orders.

Instead, Cardinal threw off the blankets and stood up. He nearly crumpled to the floor. His hand grasped for the nightstand to hold himself up.

"Cardinal!" Jasmine was on her feet and at his side, hands ready to grab him.

"It's okay," he said. "Sands just taking its time moving through my legs. Got to get a quick warm up in."

"You're meant to stay in bed. Where are you going?"

"To talk with the queen. If I am lucky, talk to the Sovereign as well. I've put this off far too long, believing it not to be as urgent as it was. But if Fingers are continuing to die, if my birds are at an

THE HANDS OF THE CHILDREN

even greater risk, then I will request for another Sovereign Finger to be involved. Even with a war going on, this fight at home is just as important."

"I can go talk to them. You don't have to push yourself!" Her face was full of worry, her hands still supporting him as he hobbled to the door.

"No, they will hear it from me. After that, I can rest. Jasmine, have you got anything from Sleeve?"

"No, he wasn't cooperative last time."

"Then while I am doing this, try one more time. He dies tonight."

"Are you sure?"

"Yes!" he yelled as he opened the door. He used the wall for support and hobbled down the medical ward. Jasmine reached a hand out toward him. Silk formed along her arms, and she prepared to loose it toward him. As he got further, her arms fell back to her side, the magic disappearing. Turning to leave the other way, she made her way back to the prison.

Sleeve was lying down on a bedroll, a small cushion on the stone floor. His head turned toward her approaching footsteps. The same smile filled his face when he noticed who it was. He took a seat at the bars. The right side of his face now mirrored the left. Blood had stained his ragged clothing. "You come to give me a goodbye before tonight?"

"I have one question," she said, arms crossed. "What is the purpose of the White Sash in Levappes?"

His smile faltered. Gritting his teeth, he turned his head toward the ceiling of his cell. When his head tilted back down to look at her, he wore a curious smile. "Levappes? Hmm. What would they want in Levappes? Why don't you tell me?"

"I'm tired of this game, Sleeve!" She rattled his cage. One of the bars groaned under her strength.

"Why would anyone want that city so close to the Frozen Wasteland? Resources... Wait..." He looked at her. There was a sense of astonishment on her face followed by confusion. "Don't tell me you don't know about it. Aren't you an RF?"

Jasmine let go of the bars and stepped back. She wanted to stop listening, but she couldn't pull herself away. "What are you talking about?"

"There's two things in the north, one I am sure you know of. And that is the northern elven city of Yokobetsu." Jasmine nodded as he continued. "The other is the resource that came out of the incident that created the Frozen Wasteland in the first place. Solidified mana, but not the pure kind, like what flows through your body. No, no, something else, something impure. And when the desperate get involved, there is no amount of gold in the world that wouldn't be spent."

"What do you mean by impure?"

"Oh, you know," he said with a sly smile.

The words came to her lips in a skipped heartbeat. Fear gripped at her chest again.

Sleeve said it for her. "The very thing that was thought to be eradicated during the Age of Heroes." He let out a laugh as he went back to his sleeping roll, head turned over his shoulder It came out in a sinister whisper. "Nothingness."

"I hope you enjoy wherever it is you end up, Sleeve," said Jasmine as she left, hiding her fear from him.

As the door shut, Sleeve chuckled again. Lying down, he looked up at the stone ceiling. "Oh, little spider... We still have a long road ahead of us."

*****

Jasmine found herself back in the mess hall of her barracks. Save for a handful of fellow Fingers, it was relatively empty. She was enjoying a late dinner, flipping through one of the castle library's books on alchemy. It was the only thing that would clear her mind. She tried training again, taking her fear and using it to lash against the dummies. But no matter how many she destroyed, she kept seeing them infected like the boar or the wolf-man that attacked her in the forest.

The moon had replaced the sun in the sky, and it was only two more hours until Sleeve's execution. Finishing off her meal, she closed the book and took it with her. She walked through the hallways of the second floor of the castle. Her thoughts were on Arya. She wanted to talk to her about everything. She wanted to know how the voyage was going. *Who am I kidding? I want her here because I am afraid. She wouldn't be afraid of the Nothingness, let alone just the mention of it.*

Jasmine missed her warm smile as radiant as the sun, even at night like this. She really was blessed by it. Looking out one of the windows, she noticed the crowd had begun to gather before the executioner's platform. Slowly, people trickled in, nobles and common folk alike. Executions were held at night to keep them out of sight of the children. After the parents had put them to bed, they would sneak off to watch it. That is not to say some children would not sneak out and follow after their parents. But guards on duty would hold the kids back or keep them distracted.

She decided to go to the medical ward. *He will probably want to watch it.* With a quick step, she moved to his room and knocked. The door slowly opened from the knock alone. Inside, Qamara was standing at his bedside. The moonlight gently shone down on his still body. Cardinal was leaning back against the head of the bed, head drooped down over his shoulder. One arm was on his lap, the other dangling off the side of the bed, sand falling from his fingertips onto the floor, forming a pile as his hand began to crumble.

The alchemy book fell from Jasmine's hand and hit the floor with a thud. Qamara turned to look at her. Ede was perched on her right shoulder. But her form had changed. Her fur was gray. The horn that was smooth against her head was now bent forward over her nose. Sharp fangs reached down from her upper mouth. Ede screeched at Jasmine.

Jasmine's focus was no longer on Cardinal, though, it was stolen by white cloth. Qamara's right sleeve was as white as snow. Rage welled inside of her, her body moving before her mind did, tackling into Qamara before she could use her magic. The two crashed through the window and plummeted to the ground below.

21

30th *of Cresozis; Mortal Year 523*

Kenjo

"After I win tomorrow, I'll owe you something."

"You won't owe me anything."

"No, I do. The only reason I even made it back here was because I ran into you and Vallarya."

"After the fight with Maximus, I would say we're even. Honestly, me and Val will be settling here for a while anyways, spending all our time at the academy. There—"

"Why would you say honestly and then lie? You don't seem like a liar, Kenjo."

"I'm not—"

"You are. Listen. Tell yourself as much as you want. We both know you won't be in that academy. If you do end up there, I give you a month. Whatever you do, I'll support you with it."

"Arlo… We can worry about what you owe after you win."

"Oh, now you're starting to sound like Ricardo."

The conversation from last night replayed in his mind. He still believed he didn't deserve a favor from a prince, of all people. But even this morning, Arlo was very adamant about it. Kenjo was sitting next to Vallarya. She had reluctantly accepted it. But with how crowded the stands were, there wasn't much room for argument after the others had sat down with them. Kaldana, Elijah, and Luna were on the other side of Kenjo. Even Ricardo had decided to sit with them, much to their surprise. Though Vallarya figured it was just so he could gloat in their face if Arlo lost.

All around them, cheers could be heard. Citizens of all shades had come and filled out the arena stands. Stone bench after stone bench was filled. There was room to do little more than clap. To stand up would lead to your seat instantly being taken by the pushing crowds. Vallarya wandered how long the arena had been standing. A lot of the stone had begun to erode. The stone that walled in the arena pit below had chips and chunks missing from constant fights. Blood from countless battles had stained the walls. Some had even reached up to the stands. She was baffled that they had never cleaned it up.

The dirt floor of the arena had, on the other hand, seemed well-maintained. It didn't even look touched, almost giving off the illusion that the arena had never actually seen combat before, the blood and stone erosion created by the artist instead of the violence.

Behind them and to their left, in the upper reaches of the arena, sat the king's seats, seven chairs beneath a red canopy, two of which were empty. The other kings sat down in their respective chairs, Nikyn in the center. He had a certain aura about him that the other kings didn't. Araceli and Pacore stood behind him at his sides, the shadow cast by the red canopy above them hiding their faces, but their unique armor made them easy to distinguish.

Nikyn rose from his seat and held up a hand. Guards appeared on the arena walls, seemingly from thin air, each one a different member of a kingdom who had traveled here with their king. In their hands was a banner of their respective kingdom. As Nikyn's hand lowered, they raised their banners high and then brought them down in unison. A loud thud echoed across the arena. Again, they raised and brought them down. The roar of the crowds began to die as the rhythmic thudding continued until, at last, complete silence fell.

"Open the gates!" shouted Nikyn, his voice booming to the far end. He took his seat as the two gates began to open. The crowd remained silent until Tiberius came forth into the light of the sun, and the roar that followed was almost deafening.

His hand was raised as he walked onto the dirt, great sword of blackened iron slung over his shoulder. He waved at the crowd, taking in all of their adoration. It was clear they all knew who he was, even beneath the heavy plates and helmet that covered his body. Kenjo and the others were the only ones not cheering. People around them bumped them a little, trying to get them to join them, but they refused to budge.

In the gaps between his iron plates, you could pick out the chain mail that he wore underneath for extra protection. His helmet was shaped like the head of a lion, eyes peering out of holes made in the metal between its gaping maw. Taking his sword, he plunged it into the ground, hands resting on the guard. He stood, waiting for his challenger. And when he stepped forward from his gate, the crowd went silent.

Arlo's friends, however, were all but silent, cheering as loud as they could, even though the whole arena looked at them like there was something wrong with them. Arlo walked forward, his gaze focused solely on his opponent. Anger had filled him since he woke up that morning. Or maybe it had never left since he heard his voice in the meeting. His fists were clenched tight at his side. To him, there was no one else there. It was only him and the traitor.

He wore his family's armor that he took from the ruins, freshly polished steel gleaming in the sunlight. A blue cape stuck out from his neck. On its back, Gonall's crest. Arlo's head was hidden beneath a winged helmet, his sword at his side, vials of ash lining his belt. He stopped a little out of sword's reach. Drawing his blade, he pointed it at Tiberius's heart as he awaited the beginning of the duel.

"It truly is a shame that the only survivor of Gonall survived just to die here," growled Tiberius.

"He hasn't started it yet."

Tiberius looked up to Nikyn, their gaze meeting briefly. "You can walk away with your life, young prince, instead of throwing it away on this empty accusation."

"If I do that," said Arlo, clenching his free hand in a tighter fist at his side, "then that would make me the same as you. A coward who betrayed his people. And I swear to those who lost their lives that day and those who have yet to hear the truth that I will make you confess before I remove your head from your shoulders!"

Tiberius's gaze turned back to Arlo as Nikyn clapped, the standard bearers atop the arena walls raising them once more. "On this day, I bury the last son of Gonall!"

Tiberius pulled his sword from the dirt and took it in both hands. Spreading his feet apart, he planted himself firmly. Arlo popped two corks from his vials, letting them fall to the ground. A single thud rang out. Arlo ran at him, consumed by his fury and resolve. Tiberius swung.

Arlo felt his arms buckle under the strength of the blow as he blocked. His feet left the ground. In seconds, he was smashed against the wall near the gate he entered. A line of dirt and dust kicked up between him and Tiberius from the force of his flight. The crowd's jaws dropped in awe. Tiberius rested his sword on his shoulder and began to walk toward him. Beneath his helmet, he was smiling. Arlo was no longer moving.

"That mortal isn't normal," said a voice in Kenjo's head. He looked all around, hoping for once it wasn't who he thought it was. "If your friend isn't dead already, he will be by the time he gets there. I can save him. Hand me control, just like you did in those times you were afraid."

With those words, Kenjo realized his hands were shaking. The memories of his parents and Maximus played over again in his mind. Had he really given him control?

"Will you kill someone against my will again?" asked Kenjo as he looked to his friend.

Arlo fell from the hole, hitting on his stomach. He tried to struggle to his feet, falling back to the dirt the moment his arms extended.

"If it leads to the preservation of life, without a second thought. Do you really believe you're in a position to ask, child?"

"No—"

"Then why?" interrupted the voice. "Why hesitate? Why question when within your own hands, you have the power to save him? Are you that afraid? Is it because every time you have tried to bring shadow into the light, it has been met with failure?"

Kenjo looked down at his hands, then tendrils had once again manifested. As they shook, he began to feel them wrap tighter, just like in his nightmare. He began to feel them slither up his body and wrap around his neck. He looked to Arlo again as the voice's words echoed in his head once more.

"I hope you can go on living with the fact you didn't even try," it said to him. "To think you even had a name for yourselves. Shadow the coward won't even be remembered—"

Tiberius was almost upon him; the crowd was beginning to cheer. They knew what would happen when he got there.

"Vallarya!" yelled Kenjo, standing up as he tried to shake away the tendrils. Turning away from the arena ground to look up at the king's seats, he found Araceli looking at him. *Has she been watching us this whole time?*

"What is it?" asked Vallarya, still in awe at what was going on before her.

"We need to embrace."

"Excuse me?" His words pulled her away from the fight, confusion clear on her face as she looked up at him. "Is there an enemy?"

"Tiberius."

"Wait, Kenjo!" She was shaking her head. "This isn't our fight! Arlo said we can't interfere."

"It's not Arlo's either!" he yelled back at her. His hands were on her shoulders now. Her face filled with shock. He was out of time. From how close they were, she could peer into the very depths of his eyes and see something moving inside.

"I don't know what you see," she said as the shock began to fade away, quickly being replaced with determination. Placing a hand on one of his, she nodded. "I'm with you."

*****

"Yo, Pacore," said Araceli, watching Vallarya begin to disappear. "Tell me something. When we read Kenjo's memories, what did you see?"

"A cruel hand given to an unknowing boy and his Other," he replied. Following her gaze, his eyes widened when he saw Kenjo standing in his embraced armor. The helmet was the last thing to form. He was pulling up his hood as the plates concealed his face. "A boy who has the eyes of his father and the heart of his mother. A second Crimson. What did you see when you gazed upon the tapestry of a foolish boy?"

"I would say the same as you, but..." Her voice trailed off as Kenjo disappeared, reappearing in the arena right between Tiberius and Arlo, standing atop Tiberius's shadow. "Just now, I saw Crimson looking at me in the stands. That same damn look those two had on them that you could never get out of your head. A fierce gaze that you never wanted to be on the wrong end of. But they have their own name, don't they? Shadow...fitting." She chuckled a little.

There was no time for Tiberius to react as an armored hand grasped his face. Shadow energy erupted forth, forcing something out of the back of his head. Kenjo pulled his hand away, and Tiberius fell to his knees, dropping his sword as he grasped at his steaming face. The right side of his helmet had been eradicated by the energy; the flesh beneath it was seared. Tiberius was screaming in agony as the something that had been expunged from his body collected in a pile of goop in the center of the arena.

"You held me back," said the voice. Kenjo expected anger, but instead, it sounded like he was more surprised than anything. "Am I bleeding over that much?"

"We aren't killing him," said Kenjo as he moved to help Arlo to his feet. "He is meant for Arlo."

"Then I hope you all are prepared to pay the price for this foolishness."

"What?"

"Kenjo," said Arlo as he pushed his hands away when he was back on his feet. "Vallarya, what the hell are you two doing here? This is my fight and my fight alone!" Arlo had yet to notice the pile of goop that was steadily growing bigger. "All this will be for nothing!"

"Your fight is with Tiberius," said Kenjo as he drew his sword. The white blade gleamed as if it were absorbing the sunlight itself. "Our fight is with that!"

The goop was bubbling now. Limbs began to take shape, starting as sharp bones. They reached out and planted themselves in the ground. A body soon took shape, the legs widening as it grew larger. The ends of the sharp bones split open, bending and forming into large claws. Muscle and sinew spread out from the remaining goop, wrapping itself around the ever-growing skeleton. When it finally stopped growing, it stood just slightly below the king's seats.

A head similar to that of a feline, a mane of blood red hair formed around it. Three eyes spun round and round into place as if they were being screwed in by some unseen hand. Eventually, they stopped moving, concealed beneath gray lids. Blinking open, burning red pupils stared down at the ones who had forced him out. Its mouth opened, a gaping maw that ran from one ear to the other, three rows of teeth visible for all to see as gray flesh formed around the exposed muscle.

The last bit of goop was on his rear end, expanding outwards into a long tail that split halfway up into two barbed tip ends. Spikes of black bone formed between its legs and from the base of its skull to the tips of its tail.

"What the hell is that, Kenjo?" asked Arlo, taking a step back. Tiberius had stopped screaming, slowly moving away as he got to his feet.

"I…really don't know," replied Kenjo, gripping his sword tighter.

Arlo looked toward the king's seats. The crowd had begun to panic, sprinting and knocking people down in the stands as they tried to escape. Yet, the kings did not move, let alone flinch. Their eyes were focused solely on the two the duel was between as if this creature standing before everyone was not actually there.

"Can you deal with it?" asked Arlo as he looked at Tiberius who was steadily increasing the distance between them. "This rite isn't over." He pointed toward the kings.

"He's insane," said Vallarya. "You're both insane. You wanted to interrupt their fight for this?"

"Go, Arlo," said Kenjo, focusing on the creature. "We will handle it."

*****

Kaldana was prepared to leap into the arena after them, but a firm hand from Luna stopped her. She pointed out the guards of Burrium who had dropped their banners and were now trying to make it into the arena. Her flames burned happily as she opened the lantern's gates.

"Elijah," said Kaldana as Luna took off, an arrow already nocked. "You need to get out of here. We will meet again after, okay?"

"What are you planning on doing?" he asked.

"They're going to need our help to make sure there's no interruptions." Kaldana smiled at him and stood up. "Now go."

Elijah did as he was told, and Kaldana took off after Luna. Ricardo sat there in awe. He didn't know what to think, what to feel. A creature that now towered over them all had just been expunged from the man he swore to protect. Dread was beginning to fill him, and while the others scattered about, he remained firmly planted like a statue.

Luna loosed an arrow. It struck a knight's shoulder, forcing him to drop his blade as well as catching the attention of the other knights. She readied another, aiming this time for their legs. The arrow found its home in a knight's thigh. She fired again before they were on her, wounding another. Using her bow to block, she tried to create some distance, but the stands and the crowds were making it difficult for her to maneuver.

Two blades came down as she raised her bow to block. She pushed back with all her might, throwing them off balance. Drawing another arrow, she aimed, loosing it right before Kaldana arrived in the fray. She started with the one in front. The narrow stands were perfect for her. The purple flames engulfed her fists. Catching one sword, she yanked it free, disarming him and melting the blade in the process.

Kaldana struck his sides, flames melting through the armor. They cooled down as her fist made contact with his actual body. Preventing the flames from setting him ablaze, she continued down the stands, disarming each guard before beating them into submission. Luna loosed arrow after arrow to support her and stop them from surrounding her. There were far more guards than they expected.

Seven unconscious knights later, Kaldana knocked out another, his body falling into the stands below. They were ready to join Kenjo and Vallarya in the arena when more guards came rushing forward from the fleeing crowds.

"How many did he bring?" asked Kaldana as she stepped back, finding her back pressed up against Luna's. "I don't remember seeing this many. This isn't even his castle!"

"Worry about it after," said Luna "This would be so much easier to kill them."

"Kenjo, Vallarya, nor Arlo would appreciate that."

"And I don't appreciate these ridiculous acts he does!"

A blade swung by Kaldana's face. She retaliated with a quick gout of flame, followed by a barrage of punches that sent the knight tumbling back into the others on her side. Jumping forward, she slammed the ground. Flames rushed forth from her impact, forcing them all to leap out of the way. Those unfortunate enough to remain found their armor melted, dropping to the ground in pain. Other knights tried to pat out the flames consuming them.

An arrow whizzed past Luna, striking Kaldana in the arm. Throwing off her next punch, she missed, finding the butt of the guard's sword colliding with her nose. Staggering back, she lost balance and fell. The last knight before her pulled back, readying a killing thrust.

*****

"Lord Nikyn," said Pacore as he stood in front of them. "And my other kings, is the very sight of the sworn enemy of life not a reason to call off this rite? To reconvene at another time? You surely all know what that is, even if you have never seen it in person."

"The Hand has its attention," replied Sergio. "Arlo is on his feet again, clashing with Tiberius. Tell me, Pacore, why would we call this off when it seems the real duel is just about to begin?"

"Because the Nothingness itself has manifested before us!" yelled Pacore as he began to move his hands with his words. "I have respect for all of you beyond that of any other mortal in the living world. But this is no longer a duel, not with that…thing! We need the royal knights! We need to bring—"

"And that is why you will never be a king of Zell Pacore," said Aulus, interrupting him, his eyes glancing at him for but a fleeting moment. "You still hold fast to the beliefs, the nonsense of the Samilian known as Crimson. He may have done great things for this world, without a doubt. But the Nothingness is but a remnant of the past. Those two dueling, that is the future. And Zell's rules acknowledge the future defined by this duel, not by that creature nor by the actions of one foolish enough to interrupt the rite of Gavinus."

"N-Nikyn…" Pacore looked to him, but he only shook his head. He felt a hand clasp his. Looking down, he found it was Araceli's.

She leaned in and whispered into his ear. "There's no point in talking to them, my love, no matter the pain that follows. Shall we join the son of Crimson?"

Pacore only nodded.

Down on the arena floor, Kenjo stepped toward the creature, slowly walking from one side to the other, trying to find an opening or a weak spot on its body. The creature's sheer size rivaled that of some of the biggest dragons in record, its tail, when extended up, reaching past the walls of the arena. All three of its eyes followed after him, each one lagging slightly behind the other.

"So the sin still breathes in this world," it growled, all three rows of sharpened teeth rippling like waves as it spoke. "In the name of the Sovereign, I shall cleanse the world of your taint!"

There was a clap of thunder as storm clouds gathered over one side of the coliseum. Lightning struck the arena grounds, drawing the attention of the creature and Kenjo alike.

*****

Araceli stood tall in barbaric fur-lined blue-plate armor. Her stomach and thighs were exposed, hulking boots rising up over her knees. Lightning crackled along the fur and along the tips of the large two-handed mace that was resting over her shoulder. Plates formed along the right side of her neck. Reaching up, it covered the right side of her face like a mask. A small slit carved out for her to see from. The top formed into a half crown with a half circle of spikes that wrapped around the side of her head. On the exposed side of her face, along the surface of her eye, lightning danced around, bouncing between lids like it was trapped in a cage.

"Another," said the creature, its eyes looking one after the other to her. "Sin. Diluted. A husk. A pale imitation of something far greater. Nonetheless, sin echoes from within. You must both die."

The creature lunged at Araceli with powerful hind legs, the ground beneath its feet cracking from the force alone. She jumped aside, the creature barreling past and colliding with a stone wall. Preparing to attack her exposed flank, Pacore pulled her back in time as its tail whipped around. Arching back, it stabbed down where she was but a moment ago, shaking the ground as it broke through the earth. Pulling free, it prepared to strike again, Araceli jumping again and again as it struck after her, leaving a trail of holes and cracked dirt.

She made her way to Kenjo as the creature pulled itself free from the wall, turning to face them. "The ground itself is cracking under his weight alone, just like a qual. I recommend avoiding anything you can."

"Alright," said Kenjo as the beast lunged again. Front claws spread wide, it practically dove at them, attempting to sweep them together in one motion. Both leapt up over them, bringing their weapons down on top of the legs. The weapons bounced off, repelled by hardened flesh. The tail whipped around overhead, slapping them like flies out of the air. They tumbled across the ground to opposite ends.

Kenjo pushed himself off the ground, clutching his side where the tail had struck. He felt the leather beneath his hand. "Val, are you okay?" he asked worriedly.

"Sort of," she groaned. Her breathing was labored inside his soul. "Move your hand, and try not to get hit again."

He listened to her, moving his hand so the plates could regrow. Looking toward where Araceli had been hit, he saw they were already on their feet, charging at the creature again. Taking a deep breath, he pushed off in a full sprint in an effort to catch it off guard and strike its back end while it was focused on her. He slid to a halt as the tail arched back and lashed out at him. Piercing into the dirt, the barbed tip erupted from underground a second later. Stumbling from the shaking earth, Vallarya grew an extra leg and pushed him out of the way before the barbs impaled them.

The tail pulled free, splitting into two all the way down to the base. Kenjo deflected one into the ground with his sword as the other followed up. His feet pushed off the ground in the nick of time. While he was airborne, however, the other tail had already come back around, hitting against his side and slamming him into the dirt. The twin tails reared back and began alternating their strikes against him, pounding against him like he was a drum. All the while, the creature's front legs kept Araceli and Pacore at bay.

Kenjo could hardly see the light in-between the kicked-up dirt and striking tails. The dirt beneath him was cracking. They were being beaten further and further into the ground. Vallarya was barely keeping up, regenerating broken armor as fast as she could. The barbs had broken through, and Kenjo let out a yell in pain as it pierced into his stomach. Soon he felt himself scooped up by one tail and flung to the far side. Hitting the ground, he slid the rest of the way into the wall, leaving a dent in the stone.

Getting to his hands and knees, he coughed up blood. The armor surrounding his upper body was completely broken in the front, blood dripping out of the wound where the barb had pierced through. The lower part of his helmet was gone. Kenjo reached for his sword and pulled it toward him. Weakly looking up, he saw Araceli still fighting the creature.

Thunder boomed in the clouds overhead, lightning surging down from the heavens at her call with each swing. And yet the creature remained unfazed, pushing her back with each attack until she was up against the wall. The split tail reached over its body and stabbed into the wall on either side of her, blocking off her escape. It bared its teeth and let out a low growl.

"If you're going to hinder my control," growled the voice in his head, "or outright refuse it, at least fight back. Stop this pathetic shaking. Your weakness is not something that your parents died for. Or maybe it is. Maybe in their final moments, they knew you wouldn't last long and passed on in sadness and anger, knowing that they left a failure like you behind—"

"Shut it!" yelled Kenjo, getting to his feet.

"His parents would never have thought that," said Vallarya. His broken armor was beginning to regenerate.

"Oh, you can hear me too, girl? Then tell him to prove it and cast out this fear! This is your real enemy! The enemy of all who wield the Hands of the Children! Nay, of the entire mortal world! What happened to that bravery, that bravado you had in everything else you have done up until this point from strangers to ones you care about? I felt that fire inside of you in that meeting room. Had it continued, you would've fought Araceli. You would have even fought that Lord King if it got to that point for your friend, that Luna."

"Shut—" Kenjo cut himself off. As much as he wanted to fight back, to keep yelling at him to shut up, the truth in his words had already dug in. His hands were still shaking. It was suffocating his heart and throat. The sword was slipping from his hands as he noticed exactly why he was afraid. The aura that the creature gave off was so similar to his parents in their final moment. That creature they had become gave off this same feeling, the terror and fear of hopelessness.

"How many more must die," said the voice, "before you two really become Shadow?"

Kenjo stopped shaking. He felt Vallarya's hands on his. They were warm and gentle. Wiping away the fear grasping at him, tendrils that had begun to form began to fade away. Relief rushed through his body as he felt the air rush back into his lungs. They stepped off into the shadow. Grabbing Araceli, they leapt back out underneath the far end of the storm cloud. The creature turned around in anger, chewing through the stone that filled its gaping maw, tails slamming down in anger. It destroyed the stands behind it before charging at them.

"Block it," said the voice.

"Excuse me?" they both said at once.

"Get some distance between you and Araceli before he gets here. Grasp the power you refuse to grasp. Spread your legs. Dig in. Point the tip of your sword at a slight angle to the ground, right arm over your body to hold it, left arm braced against the side. If you continue to fight with this sword, you will learn how to use it as a shield too. Girl, mimic his movements. Copy his limbs to properly support him."

Shadow limbs reached out, stacking up with his arms and legs. The creature was upon them. Araceli was trying to rush to their side, but Pacore held her back, instructing her to watch. There was a shift in the air. Time came to a still. The creature's large claw crashed against it, but they did not budge under its strength.

*****

"Why are you running, you bastard!" yelled Arlo as he commanded the remaining ash he had on him to trip Tiberius. It was like the fights were occurring in their own separate worlds, neither interfering with the other. "You're not escaping this!" Arlo swung down. Tiberius rolled out of the way and hopped to his feet. "Where'd all that drive to cut out my tongue go?"

Tiberius swung his sword horizontally. Arlo leapt back, coating his blade in swirling ash. He lunged forward. Swing after swing, their swords met. Tiberius no longer had the inhuman strength he did before, allowing Arlo to meet him blow for blow with the help of his magic.

"Tell me what they offered you!" said Arlo as they disengaged, loosing a blast of ash it collided with Tiberius, pushing him back.

"I had no meeting with them!" he barked, plunging his blade into the earth it began to shake. "What happened to your weakling of a kingdom was your own fault! The result of a weak king unworthy of his throne and an even weaker people!"

The ground below Arlo shook. Looking down, he found himself being lifted into the air on a broken piece of the earth. Raising his fist, Tiberius opened his hand, palm facing the floating prince. The earthen platform beneath him crumbled, and he fell to the ground, landing on his back. The rocks rained down from above, pummeling his body.

Pushing the pile of rocks off himself, Arlo rolled to his feet. Tossing his dented helmet aside, his hair was a mess; sweat was dripping down his face. With a quick breath, he guided his ash in a line in front of him, blocking another volley of rocks. Tiberius swung through. Arlo leaned back. His blade cut through his breast plate and into the skin below.

Tiberius laughed as he brought his blade back to his side, taking note of the fresh blood coating the tip. Arlo had one hand on his chest, squeezing his sword grip tighter to take his mind off of it as best he could.

"It was land, wasn't it?" asked Arlo. "They promised you all of Zell."

Tiberius's face shifted at his words; he readied his sword.

"Nikyn was right. You wouldn't give it a second thought. No matter who it was you betrayed, if it was land, if it was wealth and power, you would offer them up on a silver plat—"

Arlo sidestepped as his sword came crashing down. As the dirt kicked up, Arlo thrust, his glass blade catching Tiberius in his sword hand. The sword hit the ground with a thud. Arlo took the moment to tackle him. Pinning his arms to the ground with ash, he began to pummel him, anger and rage consuming him with each punch.

"All of my people died, you bastard!" he yelled, another jab to the exposed right side. Blood burst from his nose.

Tiberius laughed as he swung again.

"You piece of shit! Can you really laugh at this, you bastard!"

Blood now coated his gauntlets. The right side of Tiberius's head was bruised and nearly unrecognizable. Even so Arlo continued, at that point, he didn't want him to confess anymore. His laughter threw that idea out the window; he just wanted him dead.

*****

"Now lift! Throw it off balance!"

They pushed with all their might, lifting the creature's right front leg into the air. Shadow energy traveled the length of the blade before bursting forth, giving it the final push needed to completely lift up its right side.

"Quickly, slice right where it connects to the body."

The great sword changed in his hands. The blade separated into four pieces, growing in length as a golden light formed between each piece holding them together.

"What the hell is this?" asked Kenjo as he looked at the changed sword.

"Don't gawk. Cut!"

Leaping up, they swung exactly where they were instructed, severing the leg in one motion. Purple blood spewed forth as a blood curdling screech rang out from the beast.

"Lightning hands! Hit it in the wound before it recovers!" The voice took over Kenjo's body for a moment, using him as a mouthpiece.

Araceli's face held visible displeasure as she listened to Kenjo. Lightning surged faster between the spikes on the head of the mace as it coalesced into a ball. Thunder boomed as the mace made contact with the open wound, causing the creature to screech again. Electricity pulsed from the impact site and into the creature's body. Struggling to stay standing, it hit the ground with a heavy thud.

Its attention shifted to the sunlit side of the arena where Arlo was still pounding away on Tiberius. The creature pushed up with its three legs with desperate strength, charging at them with reckless abandon, earthquakes shaking the arena with every step.

"Arlo, move!" yelled Kenjo as loud as he could.

Arlo looked up, eyes widened. Weaving his ash, he pushed it against the ground, using the force from the blast to propel him out of the way. The creature scooped up Tiberius in its remaining front claw. It stood up on to its hind legs before sitting, warm blood running down Tiberius's face and onto its gray flesh. It began to weep as it rocked back and forth.

"Oh, my dear Tiberius," it said between sobs. "You can't die here… No, no… The Sovereign still requires much of us… The sin still breathes…"

Tiberius's mouth opened to speak. The creature turned into mist and flew into the opening, violently flowing into his mouth and disappearing entirely from sight.

Tiberius hit the ground and began to spasm. Pieces of armor began to melt away, revealing gray skin underneath. Bones could be seen moving throughout his body. It looked painful as if they were about to break free of the confines of the flesh.

Then he went still. He sat up and let out a long sigh. Spitting blood from his mouth, he slowly got to his feet and turned around. He was now covered in something else entirely, a new set of armor that brought a sense of terror and confusion. Armor made of gray stained glass.

"Pacore," said Araceli as her head shook for a moment. "W-Why the hell is he wearing armor like ours?"

*****

Ricardo intercepted the blade with his lance before it reached Kaldana. He pushed it away and then kicked the knight in the stomach, sending him to the ground. The rest stopped attacking at the sight of him. Luna helped Kaldana up, her eyes darting between each knight around them. Ricardo lifted his lance, leveling the tip at the knight in front of him.

"Throw down your weapons!" he said, his voice bitter, refusing to look any of them in the eye. "All of you!"

"Are you betraying us Ricardo?" asked one of them. "After all that has been done for you?"

"I'm not betraying any of you! All I am doing is stopping you from fighting for a lie! That is not the same king you took an oath to protect!"

"He is our king—" He was silenced before he could finish, the tip of a lance sticking through his neck.

"Anyone else want to continue spitting lies to me? Anyone else want to continue fighting for a false crown?" Pulling his lance free, he looked at all of them, the tip of the lance following his gaze. One knight threw down his sword, and the rest followed in a chorus of steel and stone. "Good. No one else has to die for this."

"We need to help them," said Kaldana as she jumped. Luna grabbed her hand and pulled her back to the stands. "Why did you grab me? Let me go, Luna, they need us!"

"No," she said, holding her down as she struggled. "We can't be a part of that."

"Why?" Kaldana demanded. She looked to Ricardo ordering the knights out of the stands, then back to Luna, noticing the hand on her bow trembling. "Luna…" She took her hand and guided her out of the arena. Luna didn't fight it. Kaldana headed out and made her way through the crowds, finding Elijah waiting for them near the water.

"Hey, you two!" he shouted, waving his hands in the air. They moved over to him. Kaldana's smile made him start to turn red. "Are the others still in there?"

"Yeah," said Kaldana, nodding. "Watch after her for me. I'm going back to help." Luna grasped her wrist. Kaldana struggled against it. "Let me go, Luna! They need help! The monster may be gone, but I feel it too. It's only gotten worse!" Her arm pulled free, and she weaved back through the crowd and past the gates of the arena.

Arlo was walking toward her, one hand clutching his chest, the other holding onto his sword. He stumbled. Before he hit the ground, Kaldana caught him. Holding him up, she looked past him and saw the fight that was tearing apart the arena. Both the floor and the stands were becoming unrecognizable in the destruction.

"We're leaving, Kaldana," said Arlo weakly. "The rite is over. That fight is now for those who hold the Hands of the Children."

"I didn't just yell at Luna to be stopped by you of all people," she said bluntly.

Lightning surged past them into the wall. Pieces of stone shot back from where it struck, and Tiberius rode another piece back into the fray. Kenjo stepped into the shadow. Bringing his sword up, he broke through the rock, causing Tiberius to tumble out of the air and into Araceli's mace.

"And I know you aren't stubborn enough to be a part of that!" Arlo said, pulling her face away with his hand. He pointed at the exit. "That way! We go that way now!"

Kaldana only nodded. The earth began to shake; the storm clouds above were growing larger, casting a long shadow over the arena and the five pairs of eyes that still watched silently underneath a red canopy.

"Whatever your name is," said Kenjo as he deflected Tiberius's next swing. From an angle, he loosed a blast of energy that sent Tiberius flying back. The singed front plates of his armor regrew as Araceli leapt after him. Her mace hit the ground as she missed, lightning surging forth after her enemy. "Why does he have the armor of the Children?"

He was met with silence.

"Answer me."

"I… I don't have one," it replied.

Kenjo could feel Vallarya's worry as they stepped off. With the whole arena covered in the shadow of the clouds, they had more mobility than before. He was behind Tiberius, now swinging his sword to deliver a fatal blow. A gray claw reached out his back and grabbed the blade. Its gray skin was beginning to burn from just holding the blade, but it didn't let go.

With him held there, Tiberius turned around. His fist came up, striking into Kenjo's gut, breaking through the plates and into his ribs, just above where the barb had wounded him. He groaned in pain. Vallarya felt her consciousness slipping from the attack. As the plates came back together, Araceli jumped to their rescue, forcing Tiberius away.

"Are you okay?" she asked.

"No," he said, clutching his side. The ash that was holding his wound closed was still doing its job. *Thanks for this, Arlo.* He stood up tall, taking his sword in both hands again. "Val—"

"I can barely see," she said. "I feel so tired."

They prepared to charge him again. The ground shook. A wall of stone rose behind Kenjo. The ground underneath Araceli lifted up, tossing her onto her back. Tiberius was on him before he knew what happened. As their great swords clashed, Tiberius won out. Kenjo's front now exposed, Tiberius struck home, sending him crashing through the stone wall with a rock-lined gauntlet.

Tiberius shook his hand, rocks falling back down to the earth. He turned his focus to Araceli. Lightning and earth collided all around them in a violent storm as they danced, the clashing metal of their weapons barely audible over their magic. Araceli dove out of the way as Tiberius collapsed the stands behind her. With new stone at his command, he raised them into the air. The pieces spun around into long spears.

The volley rained down on her. She pointed her mace to the ground, the tips piercing into the dirt. A sphere of lightning formed around her, disintegrating the spears as they hit. It radiated outward from her, taking all of them out. Tiberius was on her before she could pull her mace from the ground. Forcing her away, he swung wildly at her. It took everything for the two of them to dodge. Pacore produced limbs to help throw her out of harm's way.

She hit the ground after a jump, and a spear of earth pierced through her foot. Screaming in pain, she fell to a knee as another reached up, aimed for her heart. Pacore manifested a limb, only able to push it away enough that it struck her shoulder.

"Pathetic," said Tiberius. His voice was distorted. It sounded like both he and the creature were talking at the same time. "Just like the ones who created your hollow husks."

"I'm hollow?" asked Araceli, looking up at him, gritting her teeth in pain. "Do you not see the size of the creature that went inside of you? But what does it matter? You had plenty of room in your traitorous heart. Didn't you, Tiberius? The prince of ash was right. You are a blight on this nation."

Kenjo rolled over and pushed himself back to his feet. His stained-glass armor was gone. He moved to the wall Tiberius had sent him through. Looking through the hole, he could see him and Araceli. *I have to do something.* "Vallarya, are you still with me?"

"I don't... I don't want to," she said. It had come out like a trembling whisper. "I want to run. All I see is their faces. Kenjo, please make it stop! Make it stop!" She was yelling directly at his soul, her words resounding throughout him.

"She's afraid," said the voice. "She was the one protecting you from the sheer terror of the Nothingness."

"What? What are you talking about?" asked Kenjo, confusion and worry flooding his mind.

"Do you not even know how an Anchor and Other work? Did you really miss that much training?"

"Our training was cut short when they butchered our village."

What to do, what to do? He practically has eyes in the back of his head. He hasn't slowed down at all, unless he is just pushing through the pain racking his body. Even still, without being embraced, I can't take another hit.

"They are going to die, and then you will," said the voice, cutting through his thoughts.

Kenjo listened to his words. For a fleeting moment, the scene before him reminded him of his parents. He felt the voice's presence, but it wasn't taking over this time. The storm clouds above began to disappear as Araceli and Pacore were losing strength, the shadows he could jump to no longer available. He began to run, his legs weakly pushing off the ground with each movement.

Tiberius readied his sword to strike, lining up for a clean beheading. "I thank you for jumping into this fight. Dealing with you here will make it a lot easier to deal with Nikyn. Goodbye, sins of Zell."

Araceli spat in his face as a bolt of lightning struck behind her.

"So weak you can't even control it. That looked like it might have at least stunned me for a moment."

Tiberius pulled his blade back slightly before swinging. The blade never made it to her neck as he grunted in agony. The great sword fell from his hand and hit the ground with a loud thump. Looking down, he saw a sword tip now covered in purple blood as more came through his chest. He saw the golden light that held it to the rest of the blade. The blood began to disintegrate in golden light, a gray hand reaching out from his chest, burning as it grasped the blade.

"The only sin," said Kenjo, the voice having taken over his vocals once more, "left in this world is that of you and your ilk... *Talakami*." His last word came out mentally to Kenjo. The gray glass armor that surrounded Tiberius and the purple blood dripping from the wound shattered into tiny pieces of golden light. He screamed louder than ever as pain ravaged his body.

As the screaming continued, it began to sound more and more like him until at last he collapsed in silence, the creature's voice no longer a part of his. He looked completely human again, save for the gray flesh that covered most of his exposed body.

Kenjo helped Araceli out from the spikes, the golden light in his eye fading and returning to normal. His sword did likewise. The light faded first before the four pieces reconnected and it returned to normal size. He smiled at them before he fell backward, exhausted. Vallarya manifested to catch him. Resting his head on her lap, she lowered his face mask and brushed his hair out of his eyes. The warm sunlight caressed his skin.

Pacore detached from Araceli, their blue armor fading away as he did. He immediately went to work on bandaging her up with bandages he produced from his pockets. "Look at these wounds, Araceli. Here, raise your arm so I can wrap it right. There we go. It will take some time for this to recover, not to menti—"

Araceli silenced him with a kiss. "You're adorable when you act this way," she laughed. "It's not like you at any other time."

"You know I hate seeing you hurt."

"Yeah, but with the way you act every time, it kind of makes me want to get hurt more. *Ow!*"

Pacore yanked the bandage tight as he finished it off. "It's been two hundred years, and you still think that's adorable."

"I also think you're still as handsome as you were when we first became bound. Maybe even more."

Pacore sighed as he took off her boot and went to work on bandaging her foot. "To think we would be saved by their son. Makes me almost think they never really died. I guess the gods are still smiling on us."

"If they were… I don't think Tiberius would have had the armor of the Children."

"Even so, look at them. The Cathedral could shine again. With a new guiding hand, shall we take them there?"

"When we are recovered. Without a second thought."

Arlo and the others came back into the arena, save for Ricardo who was still watching over the knights of Burrium. They began to make their way over to their exhausted friends, pausing as a loud screech filled the sky. Above them, six Atmas of different colors flew across the sky, flames flowing behind their wings in beautiful streams circling around the arena. They began to weave the symbols of each nation in the air.

"They're beautiful," said Vallarya as she looked up at them.

"Val," Kenjo said. He wasn't paying attention to the birds. His mind was still on Tiberius and the creature. "This is our fight."

She didn't look away, her head following the birds as they continued their flight.

"Val—"

She pressed a finger against his lips. "Just watch the Atmas." Her finger was trembling, his eyes widening as tears slid down her cheek. One landed on his face, and after a moment of silence passed between them, she spoke again. "I-I know it is, Kenjo, but I can't stop trembling. Can we just enjoy this moment? Can we just watch the Colors of Summer?"

Kenjo nodded, and she pulled her finger away. He reached up and wiped the tears from her cheek before turning to enjoy the show.

The Atmas were beginning to form the combined emblem of Zell. Vallarya ran her fingers through his hair and smiled at him. Arlo, Kaldana, Elijah, and Luna arrived. Taking a seat next to them, they all looked up and watched the multicolored emblem float majestically in the air.

*****

Nikyn stood at the edge underneath the canopy. The other kings had already left. They had their fill of fighting. Instead, they sought out their families to enjoy the Colors of Summer flying high above. The Atmas would continue to repeat their routine for two more hours, moving to different spots around the city so that everyone could see them up close.

Hearing footsteps from behind him, he turned and found King Aulus walking back toward him. He was pulling a beautiful jug from the depths of his sleeve. "I thought you went to find your family?" asked Nikyn as Aulus stood beside him, his gaze cast upward at the Atmas.

"That I did," he replied. Pulling the cork out from the top of the jug, he sniffed it twice before pressing it against his lips. But instead of drinking it like Nikyn thought, he pulled it away. "And I found them, watched with the kids. But here I am, needing to talk to you, my Lord King."

"What is it?"

"The knights that came here with Tiberius talked. It's only wise of us to assume Burrium is lost entirely, like Gonall. Unlike Gonall, however, like the prince said and the royal knights that we sent down that way have confirmed, Burrium is not destroyed." He spat before continuing, "It is possible that we could recover it. The knights, however, they are ready to meet the executioner's blade for the treason they have committed."

"Following the orders of the king you swore an oath to is no treason, Aulus."

Aulus shrugged. "Then what would you rather do with them? There's no way to tell if a creature won't burst out of one of them at any given moment just like Tiberius. Better for us to introduce their neck to the blade. Anyways, that's not the most important part of why I'm here. I've changed my mind."

"What do you mean?" asked Nikyn. Aulus answered by letting the jug go from his hand. It crashed, sending ceramic and red wine everywhere. Nikyn moved his feet to avoid the pooling liquid. "That looked expensive."

"That it was," chuckled Aulus. He placed an arm around him. "But I want to make sure you understand how serious I am when I say this."

Nikyn looked at him with aged and curious eyes. He wasn't much of a fan of Aulus. But he was a good ruler who led his people with such authority you could almost forgive him for being drunk at every important meeting. "Out with it, Aulus."

"Samil has crossed a line right underneath our noses, something that cannot be forgiven. I hear them, Nikyn. Their rhythm rings in my ears. My heart yearns to beat with them, joining in chorus." Aulus looked at him, hand outstretched to shake his. Nikyn took his hand with a smile. "And I want Samil to hear them too. From the northern tips of Zell to the southern ends. Let us sound the drums of war."

22

19ᵗʰ of Japhim; Mortal Year 523

Jasmine

The wind rushing past her face snapped her back to reality. Spider legs sprouted from her back and dug into the stone wall, slicing through it like a knife through butter until bringing them to a jarring halt. The ground stared up at her, awaiting its gift of a new body, and Jasmine was ready to give Qamara to it. Every fiber of her being said to let go, to open her hands and arms.

Ede climbed from Qamara's shoulder to her hand, leaping at Jasmine. She was intercepted by a small starlight spider. The collision sent the two downwards, mimicking their master's fall. A silk strand attached to Jasmine's boot, holding the spider up as it held Ede.

"Why?" Jasmine screamed at Qamara. *Please just give me a reason. Any reason at all not to let you go.* Her kind smile from the other day flashed through her thoughts. Where did that kind and gentle woman go? A genuine bond between her and Ede, a mother-like figure before those children. *You can't tell me it was all a lie, that you wore a mask this whole time.*

Qamara's irises turned black, the color no longer visible. A dull and lifeless abyss looked up at Jasmine. "I am but a humble servant," she said. A single tear formed in her eye before being taken away by gravity. "He asks, and I obey. For he holds the truth. The truth that all must recognize."

Jasmine's grip loosened. Qamara slipped. Her spider came back up, carrying Ede in a cocoon of starlight. Jasmine pulled her legs free and dove after her. *Why would I even think about killing someone? It isn't right. No matter what they did, it's not my place to carry that judgment.* Silk formed along her forearms, and she sent it out. Catching her, she yanked her back up. The silk strands split out from where they hit, quickly enveloping her in a cocoon by the time she was back in Jasmine's hands.

Creating a spiderling, it bit through the silk and injected its venom into her, rendering her unconscious and easier to manage. Crawling back up, Jasmine tossed her through the window back into Cardinal's room. Pulling herself up, she found a nurse looking back and forth between her and the cocoon. Eyes wide in fear, her hands covered her mouth, trying to fight a scream.

"Get a message to the nobility," said Jasmine as she stuck silk to Qamara's feet and began to drag her out of the room. "Let them know Cardinal is dead. His killer is being dragged to the prison right now."

"Y-y-y-yes, ma'am!" replied the nurse, her whole body shaking.

Jasmine made no eye contact with anyone as she made her way to the prison. Her eyes were planted straight ahead at all times. Those who looked at her during this felt the urge to give her a wide berth, stepping as far out of the way as possible, flattening themselves against the wall. Rage still burned in her eyes, and no one wanted to be next.

She dragged her down the steps and out of the castle onto the bumpy cobblestone that led to the prison. Jasmine chuckled a little at the thought. *No, stop it, this isn't something to laugh at.* Stopping at the prison door, she let go of the silk, knocked three times, and then waited.

There was no answer. She knocked again. *Where is the guard? I want to go watch Sleeve die.* No answer. Knocking once more, she crossed her arms, foot tapping impatiently as she waited. She twisted the knob, and the door opened. Grabbing Qamara, she walked inside. The entrance was empty. The guard who should have been on duty behind the desk was missing. *Odd, even with an execution, they would have at least put a rookie on duty or something.*

She cupped her hands around her mouth. "Hello?" she called out. Again, only silence answered her. With a sigh, she dragged Qamara down the back hallway and slid her into the first cell. Locking the door, she turned to leave. A noise filled the hallway, like that of a raindrop hitting a puddle. Jasmine froze as it happened again, trying to figure out where it was coming from. *Drip, splash.* It was coming from further down the hall toward where Sleeve had been held.

Slowly stepping, she checked each cell on the way down. They were all still empty. *Drip. Splash. Drip. Splash.* The further in she went, the more she began to hear. There were at least six falling close to the same time. Her heart began to beat faster as she arrived at Sleeve's cell. The dripping was now at its loudest. *Was there a leak? No, that can't be it... It didn't rain today either.*

It was dark inside, preventing her from getting a good look from the hall. Summoning a spider, she let it crawl between the bars as she pushed open the door. The door fell off its hinges and hit the ground with a large splash, sending the liquid out in all directions. Looking down at her feet, her eyes widened. Blood was covering her boots. Inside the cell, the spider crawled around over the door, blood covering everything but it's eyes.

Drip. Splash. Jasmine ordered the spider up as she made another. The two crawled quickly onto the ceiling. At first, they were crawling over the smooth surface, but then there was something they were crawling over, like a bump. Jasmine grabbed the torch off the wall and moved inside. Standing on the door, she looked up. One hand shot to her mouth as she noticed the bodies of four guards impaled to the ceiling by their own swords.

Looking all around the cell, one of her biggest fears came to her: Sleeve was missing. Growing her spider legs, she climbed up to the ceiling and took down all the guards. Laying them down in the hallway, she sprinted out back toward the executioner's platform. *Please be there, please be there, head or no head, just be there!*

Shoving her way through the crowd, she made it to the front. The guards were standing at the side. The executioner was next to the block, awaiting his prisoner. Jasmine frantically looked around the crowd. *Please, please, bring him up, someone, anyone! Just bring him up there!* No guards were moving. Sleeve had escaped, and he was roaming about the city.

She found the captain of the executioner's guard and pulled him aside.

"Listen to me," she said, the desperation clear as day in her voice. "The prisoner has escaped. I don't know how. I just came from the jail. Four guards are dead, and he is nowhere to be found."

"Are you certa—" he said, cut off by her putting her hands on his shoulders.

"Absolutely. Call the rest of the guard! Call them all! Search every house you can. Lock the gates. Whatever you can do, do it! He cannot escape!"

"Right away!" He saluted her and called the others to attention. They began first by breaking up the crowd, looking them all over before sending them on their way.

Jasmine ran back toward the barracks and to her room, alerting every Finger and guard she came across on the way. Grabbing the one finished potion on her desk, she chugged it down without a second thought. This would be a trial by fire. *Not this time. This time, you are staying right here.* Running back outside, she made her way through the streets and back toward the prison.

Guards were searching high and low, but there was no sign of him. Jasmine was finding it hard to believe he didn't have another accomplice in the city. He had no hands, was missing an arm, and the thought of him fighting four guards like that left her baffled. Moving out of the prison ward, she decided to check the housing district next.

The guards in the area only shrugged when she questioned them. They had begun combing over every house, knocking on doors, busting down some if they had to. Jasmine walked to the far end and searched the houses there. But like the others, she came up empty-handed. All trace of him had vanished, like Sleeve was never really there to begin with. *Think, think, damn it, where would he go?* Her thoughts were interrupted as she picked up a scream.

Jasmine began to focus on it. Another scream filled the air, and she began to hear the sounds of fighting, someone crashing through a wall, steel on steel, followed by a chorus of screams that was soon silenced. Her feet were already moving as she made her way toward the edge of the district, stopping in front of the building where the screams were coming from. It was the orphanage.

The first to arrive on the scene were dead in the yard. One had been tossed out the second floor, a large hole in the wall where he had been smashed through. She checked each one for any signs of life. There was none. Their hearts still, she drew her weapon. Sprouting her legs, she climbed up the wall quietly. Peeking up and over the hole, she scanned the room. There was nothing from what she could tell at first glance. Summoning a spiderling, she let it go into the room and start crawling around as she pulled herself inside.

Sticking to the ceiling, she watched for the spider to alert her; save for destroyed and overturned furniture, the room was empty. She listened intently, only hearing her heartbeat and her breathing. It was quiet. Another scream rang out. A few steps like two people running. She dropped down and made her way to the stairs. The running stopped. Something hit the ground. The first floor was pitch-black, the moonlight barely piercing through the windows.

The wooden steps creaked underneath her steps. Her heart was beating faster. She was finding it harder to breathe. She stepped on something soft. Easing up, she looked down. Without any light, she couldn't see it. She stepped slightly larger. Her foot touched something soft again, and she pulled away. The lamps around the room instantly came to life. Jasmine let go of her weapon at the sight, both hands on her mouth trying to fight back the vomit that was trying to break free.

There were countless butchered bodies lying on the floor. The soft thing she had stepped on was the back of a child's body. A large gash through them, the wound was the same as Cardinal's, eating away slowly at the surrounding tissue. Grabbing her weapon, she waded through the bloodstained floor and dead bodies of those who once called the orphanage home.

"You know, I would've expected a soldier to have more of a tolerance for this kind of thing," said an all too familiar voice. Jasmine turned and looked at him. Sleeve was walking out of a back room, licking his blackened blade. His arm and hands had regrown, but instead of the normal tan flesh, it was a sickly gray.

"How could you do this?" asked Jasmine, readying her weapon, her eyes following every movement that he made as he stopped slightly out of her reach.

"When one is desperate to survive, you find it pretty easy to do a lot of things. Don't worry, the children didn't suffer. I made sure it was quick for them. The adults, their caretakers, on the other hand, they suffered quite a bit. Now then, little spider, I give you the option to let me go, and you can go on living. I mean, you don't want his life to be in vain after he died protecti—"

Sleeve dodged out of the way as Jasmine's naginata thrust toward him. She pulled it back and thrust again. He sidestepped and leapt at her. Jumping back, Jasmine spun her weapon, forcing him backward before the blade cut into his chest.

"Have you gotten quicker?" he asked as their fight continued.

Jasmine kept trying to keep him as far from her as she could. Using the full length of the weapon to her advantage, she stopped any of his advances while forcing him off balance at the same time. "Do you know how painful his death was?"

Rage blinded her in that moment. Her swing was uncontrolled. Sleeve slipped through her guard. An assault of kicks found their way to her abdomen. She staggered back, the spider legs reaching forward to block his sword. Jasmine aimed at his feet in a wide sweep. He jumped on top, slamming the weapon against the ground. Sleeve stepped forward and kicked her in the jaw, sending her flying back.

Jasmine crashed into a dresser. She rolled out of the way as her weapon came flying toward her, piercing through the dresser. Yanking it free, silk formed along her forearms. Sleeve ran at her again. A spin and a parry sent his sword arm up. Silk shooting forth at his feet, she yanked him down onto his back. Swinging at neck level, the blade came down. Before it could make contact with Sleeve's neck, she withdrew the blade, the staff instead smacking into his jaw.

A blast of gray energy surged forth from his hand, knocking her off her feet. Another blast sent her flying through the wall to her right and into another room. Darkness spread out from Sleeve, devouring everything in sight. Jasmine found her hearing was still unaffected. He was walking around, at first moving away from her, then toward her.

"Unbelievable," he said. He sounded directly above her. "You still don't have the strength to kill me? What are you trying to be? Huh, little spider? What are you trying to be by sparing me? You know this is why he died, right? Why all of the guards are dead? Why all of those in this building are dead? Because you haven't had the strength to do it! You could have killed me so long ago! But yet, here I am once again all because of your weakness."

His words struck a nerve. Jasmine's weapon fell from her hands, quickly falling to her knees after it. She couldn't stop them from repeating in her head. Each time they did, they felt more and more like the truth, a truth that had been eating away at her, sapping away her very will. Cardinal, the guards, the children—their agonized faces all flashed through her head, the potion's effect only amplifying his laughter that followed.

"What a sad kingdom to make someone like you a Royal Finger... Goodbye, little spider."

Sleeve leapt down the hole from above her, blade pointed down to deliver the final blow...an attack that would never make it as his feet landed on something hard coming toward him, a force in the darkness pushing back against him, the hole he leapt down passing by him once again.

He felt his back pressed against the ceiling, the wood beginning to creak beneath the force. The cold night air was there to meet him. The orphanage began to break apart, no longer able to contain the ever-growing presence. Wood splintered, and bricks flew as his feet slipped from their hold. Quickly shifting his legs, he placed one on each side of the gaping maw trying to consume him.

In the moonlit capital of Samil now stood a massive spider, the color of its body mimicking that of the stars that dotted the sky above, white venom dripping from its large fangs onto the destruction beneath it. Beady red eyes looked at Sleeve, an angry hiss filling the air as its meal continued to elude it.

Sleeve twisted his sword, stabbing it into its head. He used it for leverage to flip up onto the top of it as the legs all came down on the ground below. He found Jasmine up there. She was on her knees, palms against the spider's back.

"What a nifty trick this is," chuckled Sleeve as he stepped toward her. She wasn't moving. "You were this close to avenging everyone." He imitated it with his fingers, a needle thin gap between his thumb and index finger.

Sleeve was now standing in front of her. She looked up at him. Leveling his blade against her temple, he let out a small laugh.

"I thought I hated your eyes before," he said, "but the feeling of hatred I had pales in comparison to that in me now. How they've changed for the worse. I'll carve them out before I kill you—"

Sleeve was interrupted by his own scream of agony as he leapt back, falling to a knee as he landed, blood pouring down from the wound onto the starlight body beneath him. He glanced toward his foe, an extended spider leg slowly pulling back to Jasmine's side. Sleeve began to try and mend the hole in his leg, flesh beginning to be replaced with the same sickly gray that covered his arms.

Jasmine was up now. With a quick thrust, she struck out. He narrowly dodged the fatal blow, instead only losing his left ear.

"You just need to go away," she murmured. "If you go away, the voices will stop. All of this regret will stop!"

Jasmine was in tears at the end of her words. She lashed out at him again, forcing him on the defensive as they danced a top the starlight spider, forcing him back to the head, striking at his feet. His next dodge caused him to fall. Gazing up at her, he was smiling. The blade pointed down between his eyes, a small laugh as the cold sky steel rested against his skin.

Jasmine pulled back and struck, replacing Sleeve's smile with a frown. The blade of her weapon was cold against the top of his ear, right above where it had sliced through his hair. It began to shake, making it clear to him it was no longer a threat in her hands.

"Even after all of this, you remain determined not to kill?" he asked.

Jasmine squeezed her weapon until her knuckles were pale underneath her armor, but it refused to move anymore.

"Then you deserve to die, and so did everyone else that I killed. To think they believe in such weak protectors such as yourself."

Black energy blasted out of his hand, striking into her chest and putting her on her back. She felt herself begin to tumble off the side of the spider as his foot connected with her side. Spider legs erupted from her back, wrapping around in front of her to dampen the impact, each one shattering like glass on impact with the cobblestone.

The giant spider remained still as Sleeve leapt down, his sword digging into a leg as he fell to slow his descent. Jasmine struggled to push herself off her stomach. Once on her back, she struggled just to keep her eyes open. She could make out another person standing over her next to Sleeve. It was Qamara.

"We need to go," she said to him as she tugged on his arm. "Kimor has our exit at the northern gate. We've wasted enough time with this stunt of yours."

"The only time wasted is the time I deem wasted. Now then—"

A plopping noise rang out as an object hit the ground beside Jasmine's head. Something splattered on her face. She listened as it rolled on the ground, coming to a halt at Sleeve's feet.

"Oh, look, it's Kimor," said Sleeve as he picked up the head at his feet. "Guess he doesn't have our exit. Qamara, you should get us another one now. I'll make this quick." Sleeve looked around; the woman who was previously tugging on his arm no longer next to him. "Qamara?"

Blood dripped down from above him. Looking up, he found a pair of legs dangling in midair, the rest of the owner's body gone from sight. Something brushed up against him. Before he could react, a force sent him across the street and into the side of a building. Coughing up blood, he felt pain wrack his entire body. He was certain that everything below his head was broken.

"Spit that out, Vikis," said a woman's voice.

Sleeve looked to who the voice belonged to. She was cradling Jasmine's head in her lap. Adorned in red armor, a black cape embroidered with roses. Three quarters of her face covered by a mask. Qamara's body or that which remained fell from the sky. Her waist looked like it had been chewed, her attacker still having yet to reveal itself.

"I didn't think," said Sleeve, coughing up blood again, "that the royalty actually got off their asses. A revolt brewing all across the land, and nothing but dogs are sent after us."

"And who are you exactly?" asked Rose as she laid Jasmine's head down. She had lost consciousness.

Rose began to walk toward him, drawing her rapier. "Are you anything more than a dog yourself? A dog of rebels determined only to ruin lives?"

"I prefer to be called the reckoning than a dog. The reckoning that your dear husband called forth. You pushed your people, suffocated them. You had wings clipped, replaced with metal, and lie to everyone saying it was for the better. Others are conscripted against their will. And let us not forget any who would dare speak out." Sleeve paused for a moment, spitting blood that had welled in his mouth, bloody teeth now smiling at her. "You silence for eternity. There is no life to ruin which isn't already in this kingdom."

Rose stabbed him repeatedly in both of his arms. Satisfied with her handiwork that they could no longer be moved, she knelt down beside him.

"You are no reckoning. You are naught but waste in the shape of flesh."

Sleeve laughed through blood and pain, the palm of her gauntleted hand resting against his forehead.

"Perhaps you're right... This body is failing me. The girl put up even more of a fight than I expected. But I assure you, your majesty. This mistake won't be made again. Tell her something for me... Tell her when I see her again, I will remove her cursed eyes from her head with my bare han—"

White lines of energy enveloped his face before it was sucked into a gem in her gauntlet. Sleeve squirmed silently, his voice was being sucked away along with his soul. The energy faded away as Rose stood up, eyeing the newly filled gem.

The soul felt wrong. It wasn't full of spite and hate like the one she had just killed. It only knew fear and sadness, like a lost child looking for their parents. Glancing at the slumped body, she found it, smiling. The soul she had absorbed was not her enemy's

*****

Jasmine woke in the warm embrace of soft blankets. Greeted by the morning sun, she sat up quickly and looked around the room. She was back in her room. It felt like a weight was resting on her legs. Looking down, she found what appeared to be a cat curled up on her.

Messy red fur lined its body, streaks of blue and black running from the base of its head to the start of its two tails. A small purr escaped its mouth as her leg shifted. Eyelids fluttering open to reveal silver almond-shaped eyes.

It blinked a few times before standing up to stretch with a long yawn. Turning around, it hopped off the bed, landing on the wooden floor without a sound. Jasmine watched it walk over to her desk. It hopped up into the lap of a woman sitting in her chair, curling up once again in her lap. It was Queen Rose.

"Your majesty!" exclaimed Jasmine as her heartbeat began to accelerate. She began to run her fingers through her hair, trying to make the mess look more presentable.

"You're awake," she replied with a smile. Her voice was almost motherly, her hand gently petting the cat-like creature in her lap. "I was beginning to worry when you didn't respond when Vikis here jumped in your lap."

Jasmine was starting to throw off her blankets in an effort to get out of bed. Rose quickly moved to her bedside.

"No need for that, young Jasmine," she said, grabbing the blankets with her free hand, her other hand occupied by Vikis as he watched Jasmine. His silver almonds looking at her soul instead of her. "Please relax."

Rose took a seat on the bed as Jasmine laid back down. She had no desire to argue with her queen.

"You've been through a lot," she began again. "Even as a Kryzen, it'll take a bit to fully heal. Not to mention once you're ready to go, you have a lot of work lined up."

"Huh?" she asked confused. "Have I been out that long?"

"No, worry not, the giant spider that destroyed an orphanage only appeared last night. But Cardinal left me with everything he wanted you to do."

Jasmine was red with embarrassment as she thought about the spider she had created. It made all of her other creations look like nothing. And she was still finding it hard to believe that she actually had made it in the first place.

"Are you that embarrassed by it?" asked Rose, covering her mouth slightly as she let out a small laugh. "Don't be. Vikis here grows even larger than that, and he's destroyed far more than one building in his lifetime. Never forget it's your power, Jasmine. There is nothing to be ashamed of. Not to mention I won't suffer for you to be embarrassed when I train you."

"I understand your majesty. I'll work on it..." Jasmine's eyes widened as she realized what she said at the end. "What do you mean by when you train me?"

"When you're not with the merchants, when you're not filling Cardinal's old role, I will be teaching you how to control your magic. As I said, Vikis grows too. It would seem we have similarities, no matter how small they may seem, so I have decided to take it upon myself to teach you. And of course, I would rather not have to order another building to be rebuilt."

"B-b-but your majesty, you are the queen! You have much more pressing duties, and not to mention the rebellion!"

Rose's gentle smile faded away as she looked out the window, the sunlight kissing her cheeks.

"There is," she said calmly. "And I need you at the strongest you can be. You have the most experience with them so far. I will make time for you, no matter what. Just as I will make time to destroy any of those who threaten the livelihood of our great kingdom." Rose stood up, Vikis leaping from her arms and landing on the ground next to her. "Now then, I must go. I was supposed to be with my husband a long time ago. But alas, I wanted to be here when you woke."

Rose headed for the door, Vikis at her heel.

"Wait, your majesty!" yelled Jasmine as she remembered something important. "Is Sleeve, the one I was fighting—is he dead?"

Rose stopped in her tracks. With a half-hearted smile, she looked to her. "I killed him myself. He won't be bothering you anymore."

With that, she left the room, leaving Jasmine alone. It felt like a weight had been lifted off her chest. The enemy that had plagued her for the past couple of weeks had finally been dealt with. And while part of her hated herself for being unable to finish him on her own, she felt nothing but appreciation for what Queen Rose had done for her.

Jasmine looked out the window with a smile, over the roofs of the buildings below the barracks, gazing ever so passionately at the kingdom she swore to protect. Her eyes burned with a new sense of life. A right eye of gold, a left eye of red.

ABOUT THE AUTHOR

*J*ose has been engrossed in fantasy worlds since he was eight. Engrossed in their stories of heroism and adventure, no matter the scale. Writing a bit here and there over the years, he finally settled on his first finished book. The first of many, he plans to give back in payment to thousands of stories he escaped into.

CPSIA information can be obtained
at www.ICGtesting.com
Printed in the USA
LVHW011044060521
686680LV00006B/104